# DEEPER
## THAN THE
# DEAD

**Center Point
Large Print**

Also by Tami Hoag
and available from Center Point Large Print:

*Sarah's Sin*
*Magic*

**This Large Print Book carries the
Seal of Approval of N.A.V.H.**

# DEEPER
## THAN THE
# DEAD

# TAMI HOAG

CENTER POINT PUBLISHING
THORNDIKE, MAINE

This Center Point Large Print edition
is published in the year 2010 by arrangement with
Dutton, a member of Penguin Group (USA) Inc.

The text of this Large Print edition is unabridged.
In other aspects, this book may vary
from the original edition.
Printed in the United States of America
on permanent paper.
Set in 16-point Times New Roman type.

ISBN: 978-1-60285-660-8


Library of Congress Cataloging-in-Publication Data

Hoag, Tami.
  Deeper than the dead / Tami Hoag. -- Large print ed.
    p. cm.
  Originally published: New York : Dutton, 2009.
  ISBN 978-1-60285-660-8 (library binding : alk. paper)
  1. United States. Federal Bureau of Investigation--Officials and employees--Fiction.
    2. Women scientists--Fiction. 3. Serial murder investigation--Fiction.
    4. Fathers and sons--Fiction. 5. Large type books. I. Title.
  PS3558.O333D44 2010
  813'.54--dc22
2009038302

For Gryphon.
My first effort without you, old friend.
I hope it measures up.

# ACKNOWLEDGMENTS

My first heartfelt thanks go to Jane Thomas, whose generosity to the cause of the United States Equestrian Team Foundation won her a place in this book. I hope you enjoy your character as much as I enjoyed creating her.

And to a true character and dear friend: Happy birthday, Franny-lein! *Ich liebe dich*.

# AUTHOR'S NOTE

Do you remember 1985?

In 1985, I was working at the Bath Boutique in Rochester, Minnesota, selling designer toilet seats and ceramic rabbit toothbrush holders. I was two years away from selling my first book (*The Trouble with J. J.*), and three years away from its publication.

In 1985, Ronald Reagan was in the first year of his second term as president of the United States. Real women wore shoulder pads, permed their hair, and lusted after Tom Selleck and Don Johnson. Cell phones were the size of bricks and had to be carried around in a case with a handle. The Go-Go's disbanded, Madonna was the hot new thing, and Bruce Springsteen was *Born in the U.S.A.*

As I began to develop the idea for *Deeper Than the Dead*, I knew the book would be set in the past. I thought this would be fun. Maybe I would dredge up some nostalgia for leg warmers and heavy metal hair bands (as in Van Halen and Mötley Crüe). It wasn't until I got into the book that I realized something very inconvenient about 1985: In terms of forensic science and technology, it was the freaking Stone Age.

Imagine a sheriff's department without computers on every detective's desk. I can actually remember seeing law enforcement agency wish lists in the late eighties longing for such exotic items as fax machines and photocopiers.

Imagine no DNA technology. The first case adjudicated in the United States in which DNA evidence was presented was in 1987, and the science was considered controversial still for years after that. That's hard to grasp today, in the days of the *CSI* effect, when juries expect DNA evidence and are often reluctant to convict without it.

In 1985, fingerprint examples were still matched by the human eye.

Now, I am by no means gifted in the technological sense. If it had been left up to me to harness electricity, we would all still be reading by oil lamps. I have no clue how my computer works. I still haven't figured out how all those tiny little people get inside my television.

And yet, compared with the 1985 Tami, I am a technology junkie. I am never without my iPhone or iPod. "Have laptop, will travel" is my motto. My DVR records every rerun of *House*. I even occasionally tweet on Twitter.

So, used to all this modern convenience, I found it a major inconvenience when I couldn't have my detectives jump on the information superhighway to gather information. And no cell phones for instant contact? How did we live?

In fact, criminal profiling—so commonly used today and so familiar to law enforcement and civilians alike—was still something of a fledgling science in the mid-eighties. That was what we think of now as the golden age of the FBI's Behavioral Sciences Unit. Those were the days of the Nine: nine legends in the making (Conrad Hassel, Larry Monroe, Roger Depue, Howard Teten, Pat Mullany, Roy Hazelwood, Dick Ault, Robert Ressler, and John Douglas) who came together in three or four different groups over that time span to bring profiling and the BSU to the forefront of law enforcement.

In 1985, the unit was housed at the FBI Academy in Quantico, Virginia, in offices sixty feet belowground—ten times deeper than the dead—in what agents referred to as the National Cellar for the Analysis of Violent Crime.

Setting *Deeper Than the Dead* in 1985 gave me the opportunity to write about those days and to insinuate a character into that mythical circle of the Nine. It also gave me a chance to walk down memory lane and remember the days of *Dallas* and *Dynasty*, Michael Jackson's *Thriller*, and Members Only jackets.

We were all happenin' in the eighties, and if anyone would have suggested then that we were living in an age of innocence, we would have thought them crazy. So much has happened in the decades since. Not all for the better, to be sure. Still, I'll definitely take the advances made in forensic sciences, and I'll definitely take my cell phone.

# 1

## My Hero

*My hero is my dad. He is a great person. He works hard, is nice to everyone, and tries to help people.*

His victim would have screamed if she could have. He had seen to it she could not open her mouth. There would have been terror in her eyes. He had made certain she could not open them. He had rendered her blind and mute, making her the perfect woman. Beautiful. Seen and not heard. Obedient. He had immobilized her so she could not fight him.

*Sometimes he helps me with my homework because he is good at math and science. Sometimes we play catch in the backyard, which is really fun and cool. But he is very busy. He works very hard.*

Her uncontrollable trembling and the sweat that ran down the sides of her face showed her terror. He had locked her inside the prison of her own body and mind, and there would be no escape.

The cords stood out in her neck as she strained

against the bindings. Sweat and blood ran in thin rivulets down the slopes of her small, round breasts.

*My dad tells me no matter what I should always be polite and respect people. I should treat other people the way I would like to be treated.*

She had to respect him now. She had no choice. The power was all his. In this game, he always won. He had stripped away all of her pretense, the mask of beauty, to reveal the plain raw truth: that she was nothing and he was God.

It was important for her to know that before he killed her.

*My dad is a very important man in the community.*

It was important that she had the time to reflect on that truth. Because of that, he wouldn't kill her just yet. Besides, he didn't have the time.

*My dad. My hero.*

It was nearly three o'clock. He had to go pick up his child from school.

# 2

*Five Days Later*
Tuesday, October 8, 1985

"You suck, Crane."

Tommy Crane sighed and stared straight ahead.

Dennis Farman leaned over from his desk, right across from Tommy's, his fat face screwed up into what he probably thought was a really tough look.

Tommy tried to tell himself it was just a stupid look. Asinine. That was his new word of the week. Asinine: marked by inexcusable failure to exercise intelligence or sound judgment. Definition number two: of, relating to, or resembling an ass.

That was Dennis, all the way around.

He tried not to think about the fact that Dennis Farman was bigger than he was, a whole year older than he was, and just plain mean.

"You suck donkey dicks," Farman said, laughing to himself like he thought he was brilliant or something.

Tommy sighed again and looked at the clock on the wall above the door. Two more minutes.

Wendy Morgan turned around in her seat and looked at him with frustration. "Say something, Tommy. Tell him he's a dork."

"'Say something, Tommy,'" Farman parroted,

15

making his voice really high, like a girl's. "Or let your girlfriend talk for you."

"He doesn't have a girlfriend," Cody Roache, Farman's scrawny toady, chimed in. "He's gay. He's gay and she's a lesbo."

Wendy rolled her eyes. "Shut up, Cockroach. You don't even know what that means."

"Yes, I do."

"Because you are."

Tommy watched the clock tick one minute closer to freedom. At the front of the room, Miss Navarre walked back to her desk from the door with a yellow note in her hand.

If someone had tortured him, held fire to his feet, or stuck bamboo shoots under his fingernails, he would have had to admit he was kind of in love with Miss Navarre. She was smart and kind, and really pretty with big brown eyes and dark hair tucked behind her ears.

"Twat," Cockroach said, just loud enough that the bad word shot like a poisoned dart straight to Miss Navarre's ear, and her attention snapped in their direction.

"Mr. Roache," she said in that tone of voice that cut like a knife. "Would you like to come to the front of the room now and explain to the rest of the class exactly why you will be staying in the room for recess and lunch hour tomorrow?"

Roache wore his most stupid expression behind his too-big glasses. "Uh, no."

Miss Navarre arched an eyebrow. She could say a lot with that eyebrow. She was sweet and kind, but she was no pushover.

Cody Roache swallowed hard and tried again. "Um . . . no, ma'am?"

The bell rang loudly, and everyone started to bolt from their seats. Miss Navarre held up one finger and they all froze like they were in suspended animation.

"Mr. Roache," she said. It was never a good thing when she called someone Mr. or Miss. "I'll see you first thing tomorrow morning at my desk."

"Yes, ma'am."

She turned her attention to Dennis Farman, holding up the note in her hand. "Dennis, your father called to say he won't be able to pick you up today, and you should walk home."

The second Miss Navarre dropped her hand, the entire fifth-grade class bolted for the door like a herd of wild horses.

"Why don't you stand up to him, Tommy?" Wendy demanded as they walked away from Oak Knoll Elementary School and toward the park.

Tommy hiked his backpack up on one shoulder. " 'Cause he could pound me into a pile of broken bones."

"He's all talk."

"That's easy for you to say. He hit me once in dodgeball and I didn't breathe for like a week."

"You have to stand up for yourself," Wendy

insisted, blue eyes flashing. She had long, wavy blonde hair like a mermaid's, which she was always wearing in the styles of rock stars Tommy had never heard of. "Otherwise, what kind of man are you?"

"I'm not a man. I'm a kid, and I want to stay that way for a while."

"What if he went after me?" she asked. "What if he tried to hit me or kidnap me?"

Tommy frowned. "That's different. That's you. Sure, I'd try to save you. That's what a guy is supposed to do. It's called chivalry. Like in the Knights of the Round Table or *Star Wars*."

Wendy flashed a smile and wound one blonde braid into a shape like a cinnamon roll pressed against her ear. "Does that make me Princess Leia?" she said, batting her eyelashes.

Tommy rolled his eyes. They turned off the sidewalk and onto a trail that cut through Oakwoods Park.

Oakwoods was a big park with part of it clipped and cleared and set up with picnic pavilions and a bandstand and playground. The rest of it was more wild, like a forest with simple trails cut through it.

A lot of kids wouldn't cut through the park because there were stories about it being haunted and homeless weirdos living in it, and someone claimed they once saw Bigfoot. But it was the shortest way home, and he and Wendy had been going this way since they were in the third grade. Nothing bad had ever happened.

"And you're Luke Skywalker," Wendy said.

Tommy didn't want to be Luke Skywalker. Han Solo had all the fun, blasting around the galaxy with Chewbacca, breaking the rules and doing whatever they liked.

Tommy had never broken a rule in his life. His day-to-day existence was orderly and scheduled. Up at seven, breakfast at seven fifteen, to school by eight. School let out at three ten. He had to be home by three forty-five. Sometimes he walked. Sometimes one of his or Wendy's parents picked them up, depending. When he got home he would have a snack and tell his mother everything that happened that day. From four until six fifteen he could go out and play—unless he had a piano lesson—but he had to be cleaned up and at the dinner table at six thirty sharp.

It would have been a lot more fun to be Han Solo.

Wendy had moved on to other topics, chattering about her latest favorite singer, Madonna, who Tommy had never heard of because his mother insisted they only listen to public radio. She wanted him to grow up to be a concert pianist and/or a brain surgeon. Tommy wanted to grow up to be a baseball player, but he didn't tell his mother that. That was between him and his dad.

Suddenly, behind them, came a blood-curdling war cry and what sounded like wild animals crashing through the woods.

"CRANE SUCKS!!!!"

19

"RUN!!" Tommy yelled.

Dennis Farman and Cody Roache came leaping over a fallen log, their faces red from shouting.

Tommy grabbed Wendy's wrist and took off, dragging her along behind him. He was faster than Dennis. He'd outrun him before. Wendy was fast for a girl, but not as fast as he was.

Farman and Roache were catching up to them, their eyes bugging out of their heads like a gargoyle's. Their mouths were wide-open. They were still yelling, but Tommy could only hear the pounding of his heart and the crashing sound they made as they bounded through the woods.

"This way!" he yelled, veering off the trail.

Wendy looked back, yelling, "FART-MAN!!"

"JUMP!!" Tommy shouted.

They went over the edge of an embankment and flew through the air. Farman and Roache came flying after them. They landed like so many stones, hitting the ground and tumbling.

All the colors of the forest whirled past Tommy's eyes like a kaleidoscope as he rolled, until he finally came to a stop on a soft mound of dirt.

He lay still for a moment, holding his breath, waiting for Dennis Farman to jump on him. But he could hear Dennis moaning loudly somewhere behind him.

Slowly Tommy pushed himself up on his hands and knees. The ground he was on had been turned over recently. It smelled like earth and wet leaves, and something else he couldn't name. It was soft and damp and crumbly like someone had dug it up with a shovel. Like someone had buried something . . . or somebody.

His heart jumped into the back of his throat as he raised his head . . . and came face-to-face with death.

# 3

At first, all Tommy could see was that the woman was pretty. She looked peaceful, like in *The Lady of the Lake*. Her skin was pale and kind of blue. Her eyes were closed.

Then slowly other things came into focus: blood that had drizzled down her chin and dried, a slash mark across one cheek, ants marching into and out of her nostrils.

Tommy's stomach flipped over.

"Holy shit!" Dennis exclaimed as he came to stand beside the grave.

Cody Roache, dirt on his face, glasses askew, screamed like a girl, bolted, and ran back the way they had come.

Wendy was as white as a sheet as she stared at the dead woman, but, as always, she had her wits about her. She turned to Dennis and said, "You have to go call your dad."

Dennis wasn't listening to her. He got down on

21

his hands and knees for a closer look. "Is she really dead?"

"Don't touch her!" Tommy snapped as Dennis reached out a grubby finger to poke at the woman's face.

He had only ever seen one dead person in his whole life—his grandmother on his father's side —and she was in a coffin. But he knew it just wasn't right to touch this woman. It was disrespectful or something.

"What if she's just asleep?" Dennis said. "What if she was buried alive and she's in a coma?"

He tried to push up one of the woman's eyelids, but it wouldn't budge. He couldn't seem to take his eyes off the woman's face.

To Tommy it looked as if something had been digging at the grave. One of the woman's hands was out of the dirt, as if she had been trying to reach out for help. The hand was mangled, like maybe some animal had chewed on her fingers, tearing flesh and exposing bones.

He had fallen right on top of a dead woman. His head swam. He felt like someone had just poured cold water over him.

As Dennis reached out to touch the woman again, a dog stepped out of some bushes on the other side of the body and growled deep in its throat.

None of them moved then. The dog was mean-looking, white with a big black spot around one beady eye and over the small ear. The dog moved forward. The kids moved backward.

"He's protecting her," Tommy said.

"Maybe he killed her," Dennis said. "Maybe he killed her and buried her like a bone, and now he's back to eat the body."

He said it as if he hoped that was the case, and he couldn't wait to watch the next gruesome scene.

Then as suddenly as it had appeared, the dog stepped back into the bushes and was gone.

In the next second, a man in a sheriff's deputy's uniform appeared at the top of the bank the kids had tumbled over. He looked like a giant looking down at them, his hair buzzed flat on top, his eyes hidden by mirrored sunglasses. He was Dennis Farman's father.

Tommy stood well back from the deputies who had come with yellow crime-scene tape to mark off the area around the shallow grave. He should have been home by now. His mother was going to be really mad. He had a piano lesson at five. But he couldn't seem to make himself leave, and he thought maybe he wasn't supposed to.

The light was fading in the thick woods. Somewhere out there was a mad dog, and maybe even a murderer. He didn't want to walk home anymore.

The adults on the other side of the tape weren't paying any attention to him or Wendy. Dennis hung around just outside the tape, trying to get a better look as the deputies did their jobs.

Cody Roache had run all the way back to the street and nearly got himself run over by Dennis's father in his squad car. Tommy had heard the deputies telling each other. Mr. Farman had come straight to the scene, but Cody had not come back.

"I wonder who she is," Wendy said quietly. She sat on the stump of a tree that had been cut down over the summer. "I wonder how she died."

"Somebody killed her," Tommy said.

"I think I want to go home now," Wendy said. "Don't you?"

Tommy didn't answer her. He felt like he was inside of a bubble, and if he tried to move the bubble would burst and all sorts of feelings would wash over him and drown him.

People had come into the park to see what was going on. They stood up on the bank—teenagers, a mailman, one of the janitors from school.

As he watched them, Miss Navarre appeared at the edge of the group. She spotted him and Wendy right away and made her way down to them.

"Are you guys all right?" she asked.

"Tommy fell on a dead person!" Wendy said.

Tommy said nothing. He had started to shake all over. Inside his head all he could see was the dead woman's face—the blood, the gash in her cheek, the ants crawling on her.

"A deputy came into the school and said something had happened," Miss Navarre said, looking over at the place where the dead lady was. She turned back then and touched Tommy's forehead and brushed some dead leaves out of his hair. "You're really pale, Tommy. You should sit down."

Dutifully he sat down on the stump beside Wendy. Miss Navarre looked as pale as either of them, but there was no more room on the stump.

"Tell me what happened," she said.

The tale spilled out of Wendy like rushing water. When she came to the part where Tommy fell on the grave, Miss Navarre closed her eyes and said, "Oh my God."

She bent down to Tommy's level and looked him straight in the eyes. "Are you all right?"

Tommy gave the smallest nod. "I'm okay."

His voice sounded like it came from far away.

"Wait here," she said. "I'm going to ask the deputies if I can take you home."

She walked over to the yellow tape stretched between the trees and tried to get the attention of Dennis Farman's dad, who seemed to be the big shot on the scene.

The two exchanged words. Miss Navarre gestured toward Dennis. Farman's father shook his head. They were arguing. Tommy could tell by the way they were standing—Miss Navarre with her hands on her hips, Mr. Farman puffing himself up and leaning over her. Then Miss Navarre raised a hand and ended the discussion.

She was angry when she came back, although she did her best to hide it. Tommy could feel it all around her like frozen air.

"Come on," she said, reaching out her hands to them. "I'm taking you home."

At ten Tommy generally considered himself too old to hold hands with an adult. He couldn't remember the last time his mother had held his hand. Kindergarten, maybe. But he didn't feel so grown-up now, and he took Miss Navarre's soft, smooth hand and held on tight as she led them away from the terrible scene and out of the woods.

But the scene came with Tommy, stuck in his head; he felt sick at the idea that it might never go away.

# 4

Anne Navarre felt herself shaking inside as she walked away from Frank Farman and the crime scene her students had stumbled upon—shaking from the shock of what she had just seen, shaking with anger at Frank Farman. He was too busy to deal with her. He would take care of his own kid in his own time—as if he thought letting his son watch the exhumation of a corpse would be good for him. Asshole.

She had already encountered Farman at a parent-teacher conference. He was the kind of man who only heard the sound of his own voice and would likely have gone to his grave swearing the sun rose in the west rather than agree with a woman.

Just like her father.

For the moment she couldn't examine the deeper cause of the trembling: seeing a murder victim—a woman killed and discarded like a broken doll —and knowing her students had seen it too.

She led Wendy and Tommy out of the park and back to the school, where she sat them down in the office and used a phone to call their parents.

Anne told Wendy's mother as little as possible, just that there had been an incident in the park and that she was bringing Wendy home.

The Cranes' phone was answered by a machine. She left the same message with as little detail as possible.

The children were quiet as Anne drove. She didn't know what to say to them. That everything would be all right? Their lives had just been changed. That was the truth. They would be seeing a dead woman's face in their dreams for years to come.

Anne scrambled through her memory for some kind of guidance. Her studies in child psychology seemed gone from her head now. She had never finished her graduate work, had never worked in a clinical setting. She had no frame of reference for this situation. Five years of teaching fifth grade hadn't prepared her for this.

Maybe she should have been asking them

questions, drawing them out, encouraging them to release their emotions. Maybe she was too busy holding on to her own.

Sara Morgan was waiting on the front step when Anne pulled into the driveway. Wendy's mother was a tall and athletic adult version of her daughter, with cornflower blue eyes and a thick mane of wavy blonde hair. She was in a blue T-shirt and faded denim overalls with the legs rolled up to reveal white socks with lace cuffs. There were tears in her eyes and uncertainty in her expression.

"Oh my God," she said as Anne and Wendy got out of the car. "My neighbor told me there was a murder in the park. He's eighty-five and he's in a wheelchair, and he listens to a police scanner," she rambled. "Was Wendy there? Did she see what happened? Wendy!"

Wendy trotted into her mother's arms as Sara Morgan dropped down on one knee.

"Are you all right, baby?" She scanned her daughter for any sign of damage.

"We were running, and then we fell down a hill, and then—and then—" Wendy gulped for air. "Tommy fell right on her! He fell right on a dead lady! It was so gross!"

"Oh my God!"

"And Dennis kept trying to touch her. He's so sick!"

Sara Morgan looked up at Anne. "Who was it? How did she—Was she shot or—or what?"

"I don't know," Anne said. "I'm sure they won't release any details for a while."

"And there was this dog," Wendy went on. "Like a wild dog. And he growled at us, and Dennis said maybe the dog killed the lady—"

"A dog?" her mother said. "What kind of a dog? Was it foaming at the mouth? Did you touch it?"

"No! It ran away."

"It could have had rabies! Are you sure you didn't touch it?"

"I didn't touch it!" Wendy insisted.

Sara Morgan raked a handful of blonde mane back from her face and looked at Anne. "What's going to happen? Will the police come?"

"I don't know," Anne said. "Dennis Farman's father is a deputy. He said I could take Wendy and Tommy home. Maybe the sheriff's office will call later. He didn't say."

"This is just awful. We moved here to get away from crime. And smog and traffic. I never think twice about letting Wendy walk home from school. Do you think the dog could have killed the woman?"

"That doesn't seem very likely," Anne said.

Sara Morgan turned to her daughter again. "If you touched that dog—"

"I didn't touch the dog!" Wendy insisted, irritated.

"Should I take her to see someone?" she asked Anne. "My husband's uncle's ex-wife's sister is a therapist in Beverly Hills."

29

"Whatever you think is best."

"I don't know what to think," she admitted. "There's no chapter for this in the parenting manual."

"No," Anne said. "It's not in the How to Be a Kid manual either."

"No. God, I've never seen a dead person myself. When I have to go to funerals, I won't look in the casket. The whole idea creeps me out."

"I should get Tommy home," Anne said. "I wasn't able to reach his mother by phone."

"I can call Peter at his office," Sara offered. "He's our dentist. He and my husband golf together."

"If you don't mind."

"Not at all. And thank you for bringing Wendy home."

Anne got back in her car and looked into the backseat where Tommy sat looking at his hands in his lap.

"Do you think your mom will be home by now, Tommy?"

He consulted his wristwatch. "Yes."

"She'll be worried about you."

"I'm supposed to have a piano lesson," he said looking worried. "Maybe we should go there instead."

"I think your piano teacher will forgive your absence when he hears what you've been through."

The boy said nothing.

"Do you want to talk about what happened?" Anne asked as they drove.

"No, thank you."

Why would he share his feelings with her? She had been his teacher all of two months. From what she had observed of Tommy, he was by nature reserved. He was very bright but did nothing to call attention to himself. If anything he seemed to do his best to be invisible.

Anne wondered why. She had met his parents. His father, the dentist, was charming and out-going. His mother was a little intense but had seemed nice enough at conference time. She was proud of her son's talents and academic abilities. She sold real estate and served on charity committees. The Cranes were the All-American Yuppie Family.

They lived four blocks from the Morgans in a beautiful two-story Spanish-style stucco house with lush landscaping and a big spreading oak tree in the side yard. As daylight faded, lights glowed invitingly in the front windows and along the sidewalk.

Through one window Anne could see Janet Crane in a fuchsia suit, pacing, speaking into a portable phone.

Tommy got out of the car and lingered by the door. Anne reached out her hand to him, and he took it. He hung on a little too tightly as they went up the sidewalk together.

The door flew open before they made it to the front steps. Janet Crane's eyes were a little too wide, the white showing all around the pupils.

"Where have you been?" she demanded, her fierce look on Tommy. "I have been out of my mind trying to find you! You knew you had a piano lesson—"

"Mrs. Crane—," Anne started.

"Don't you have any consideration for Mr. England's time? For *my* time?"

"Mrs. Crane," Anne said more firmly. "Didn't you get my message?"

Janet Crane looked at her as if she had only just appeared. "Message? What message? I haven't listened to the messages. I've been trying to find my son."

"Could we step inside, please?" Anne asked.

Tommy's mother took a deliberate breath and calmed herself. "Of course. I'm so sorry. Please come in, Miss Navarre."

Tommy still clung to Anne's hand as they went into the foyer. His eyes were on the Mexican tile floor. No warm hugs from Mom. No concern for his welfare. Concern for the piano teacher.

Anne leaned down beside him. "Tommy, why don't you go wash up while I talk to your mom?"

He went across the hall and disappeared into a powder room with wildly colored parrots splashed across the yellow wallpaper.

"I'm sorry," Janet Crane said. "I've been out of

my mind with worry. It isn't like Tommy to miss a piano lesson. He's always very punctual."

As Anne was sure his mother was, as well. Punctual, buttoned up in her fuchsia suit with the big shoulder pads and crisp peplum. Her dark hair was bobbed, puffed up, and spritzed hard. The word "brittle" came to mind. The parent-teacher conference persona had cracked a little under the stress . . . of her son missing a piano lesson.

Anne went through the story of the kids finding the body in the park, Tommy having actually fallen directly on the grave.

Janet Crane's eyes showed a lot of white again. "Oh my God!"

She turned abruptly and walked into a *Better Homes and Gardens* living room, the heels of her pink pumps click-clacking on the tile. She perched herself on the edge of a sofa cushion. Her eyes darted around the room as if looking for help.

"I think Tommy is a little in shock," Anne said. "He's hardly said anything since it happened."

"I-I-I don't know what to do," his mother announced. "Should I call a doctor?"

"He doesn't seem to be physically injured, but you may want to get him some counseling."

"Why didn't someone call me?" she asked, trying to work up some indignation. She seemed more comfortable with anger than with concern. "Why didn't Principal Garnett call? Why isn't he here?"

"Mr. Garnett was out today."

Tommy came to the doorway. His face and arms were clean, showing off the scrapes and scratches that had resulted from his tumble. He had wet and combed his brown hair as neatly as he could considering a couple of cowlicks. But his clothes were still dirty, and there was a tear in the knee of his jeans. Anne wondered if he would be allowed to sit on the furniture.

"Tommy!" his mother said, going to him. "I'm so sorry. I had no idea what happened."

Anne watched her touch her son hesitantly, as if she were afraid of catching something from him as she examined his wounds.

Through the front window Anne watched a sleek, dark Jaguar pull into the drive beside her little red Volkswagen. Peter Crane got out and walked toward the house.

He was a handsome man, medium height, lean, well-dressed in dark slacks, a shirt and tie. He called out cheerfully as he came in the front door.

Sara Morgan hadn't managed to catch him at the office, Anne thought.

Tommy turned abruptly away from his mother and went to his dad, hugging him around the waist. Peter Crane looked a little confused. His wife went into the foyer and told him what had happened.

Anne watched the shock cross his face.

"It was a terrible thing to see," she said, moving into the doorway.

"Miss Navarre brought Tommy home," Janet Crane said.

"You were there?" he asked.

"I went to the park as soon as I heard what had happened."

"Oh my God," he said.

"I'm going to go call Mr. England," his wife said. "To let him know why Tommy didn't make it to his lesson."

She walked away and disappeared into the interior of the home, heels clacking.

"Things like this don't happen here," he said.

Anne had been born and raised in Oak Knoll, a town of twenty thousand (twenty-three when the college kids were in residence). It was a civilized, upscale town nearly two hours removed from Los Angeles. Home to a prestigious private college, the population tended to consist of well-educated professional people, academics, artists. Crime here ran along the lines of small-time drug deals, petty theft, and vandalism, not murder, not women buried in the park.

"Do they know who the woman is? Do they know what happened to her?" he asked.

"I don't know," Anne said. "I don't know what to think."

He sighed and shook his head. "Well, thank you, Miss Navarre, for bringing Tommy home. We appreciate your dedication to the kids."

"If I can help in any way, please don't hesitate

to call," Anne said. "You have my number."

She leaned down to Tommy's level. "That goes for you, too, Tommy. You can call me anytime if you need to talk about what happened. Try to get some rest tonight."

Her mother's cure for everything: rest. Bad day at school? Get some rest. Dumped by a boyfriend? Get some rest. Dying of cancer? Get some rest.

In all her life Anne had to say rest had never solved anything. It was just something to say when there was nothing adequate to take its place, something to do when unconsciousness was the best option available.

As she backed out of the driveway and turned for home, she hoped Tommy would have better luck with the concept than she ever had.

# 5

"This is the third victim in two years."

"It's the second."

"In our jurisdiction. The second vic was in the next county, but it's the same perp. Same MO, same signature."

"Signature?" Frank Farman said. "Where's his signature? Maybe he left his address and phone number too."

Sheriff's Detective Tony Mendez clenched his jaw for a beat. Farman, chief deputy, was old-school and resented the hell out of him for being one of the new faces of law enforcement—young, college educated, a minority, eager to embrace all the new technology the future promised.

"Why don't we consult a crystal ball?" Farman suggested. "No need for any legwork at all."

"That's enough, Frank."

Cal Dixon, fifty-three, fit, silver-haired, uniform starched and pressed, had been county sheriff for three years. He had a long solid career with the LA County Sheriff's Department before he had moved north to the quieter setting of Oak Knoll. He had campaigned for the office on a promise of progressive change. Tony Mendez was an example of his promise in practice.

Mendez was thirty-six, smart, dedicated, and ambitious. He had jumped at the chance to attend the FBI's National Academy, an eleven-week course for senior and accomplished law enforcement personnel—not only from around the United States, but from around the world. Classes ranged from sex crimes to hostage negotiations to criminal psychology. Attendees went away not only with an advanced education, but with valuable contacts as well.

Dixon had seen sending Mendez as an investment that would pay off for his department in more ways than one. Mendez was happy to prove him right.

"MO is how he did it," Mendez said. "The signature is his own thing, something extra he does for his own reasons."

He pointed at the head of the dead woman as deputies and crime scene investigators worked around her, searching for anything that might resemble evidence. "Eyes glued shut. Mouth glued shut. See no evil, speak no evil. He didn't have to do that to kill her. That's what gets him off."

"That's all very interesting," Farman said. "But how does that help us catch the bad guy?"

He wasn't being sarcastic. Mendez knew there were still plenty of cops who doubted the usefulness of criminal profiling. Mendez had studied enough cases to feel differently.

They stood in Oakwoods Park. The sun was gone. There was a crisp chill in the October air. The area around the shallow grave was illuminated by bright portable work lamps. The stark light made the scene seem all the more surreal and macabre.

The body hadn't been buried there for long. Maybe a day at the most. If the corpse had been there for very long, it would have sustained more damage from animals and insects. If not for the gash on her cheek and the ants crawling on her face, the young woman would have looked like she was sleeping peacefully—undoubtedly a far cry from the reality of her death, Mendez thought.

He believed they would find she had been strangled, tortured, and sexually assaulted. Just like the two victims who had come before her.

He had worked the first homicide—Julie Paulson—eighteen months ago, still unsolved. The victim had been found at a campground five miles out of town, eyes and lips glued shut. There had been multiple ligature marks on her wrists and ankles, some older than others, indicating she had been held somewhere over a period of time.

Nine months later he had spoken with the detectives in the next county when their vic had been discovered. He had looked at the photographs of that corpse—a body that had suffered considerably from the elements before being found by hikers, just off a popular trail. The mouth had been more or less gone, along with one eye. The other eye had been glued shut. The hyoid bone in the neck been fractured, indicating strangulation.

"Neither of the others was buried," Dixon pointed out. "Let alone displayed like this one."

Their victim's head was entirely above ground, propped up on a stone the size of a loaf of bread. Staged for maximum shock value. This was something new: the body left in a very public park, off the beaten path, but definitely in a place where it would be found.

"It's risky," Mendez said. "Maybe he wants attention. I think we've got a serial killer on our hands."

Dixon took a step toward him, scowling. "I don't want to hear those words coming out of your mouth again outside my office."

"But this vic makes three. I can reach out to Quantico now."

"Yeah, that's what we need," Farman said. "Some Feeb strutting around like the cock of the walk. Who the hell cares if this creep wet his pants when he was ten? What good is that? They'll send some hotshot who just wants to be on the news to tell the world he's a genius and we're a bunch of stupid hicks."

Dixon glanced over his shoulder at the crowd still gathered on the other side of the crime scene tape. "Nobody says shit about this crime possibly being connected to any other. Nobody says anything about the eyes and mouth being glued shut. Nobody mentions the letters *F-B-I*."

Mendez felt the word "but" lodge in his throat like a chicken bone.

"I'm sending the body to LA County," Dixon announced, his stark blue eyes on the victim. "We need a coroner who isn't an undertaker by day."

"They've got bodies stacked on top of each other down there," Farman said.

"I can reach out to some people. We can get priority."

"Sheriff, if this guy has killed three, he'll kill four, five, six," Mendez said, keeping his voice down. "How many women did Bundy kill? He confessed to thirty. Some people think the number was closer to a hundred. Do we have to wait for some more women to die before—"

"Don't piss me off, Detective," Dixon warned. "The first thing we need to do is find out who this young woman was. She was somebody's daughter."

Mendez shut his mouth and reflected on that. Tonight some family was missing a daughter. If they even realized she was gone, they would still have hope she could be found. They would still have the dread of uncertainty. In a day or two or ten—when this corpse was finally identified and given a name—their hope would become despair. The uncertainty would be over, replaced by the stone-cold fact that someone had taken her life away from them, brutally and without mercy.

And that someone was still out there, very probably hunting for his next victim.

# 6

"Why are we watching this? You know I hate the news at ten o'clock. The only people who think the news should be on at ten live in Kansas and have to be in bed by ten thirty so they can get up at dawn and watch the corn grow."

Anne ignored her father's complaining, making her reply with the remote control by turning up the volume. The station was local, the field reporters fresh out of junior college, the news anchor a failed Betty Ford Clinic alum. The lead story was the body in the park.

The reporter's glasses were crooked, and his sport coat was too big for him, as if he had borrowed it from a larger relative. He stood near the Oakwoods Park sign, squinting against the glare of ill-positioned lights. Without a doubt, this would be the biggest story to date for a kid who usually covered town council and school board meetings.

"The corpse of a dead woman was discovered this afternoon by children playing in Oakwoods Park."

Anne's father, a retired English professor, cried out as if he had been wounded.

"Moron!" he shouted. "Could they have found the corpse of a living woman? Idiot!"

"Be quiet!" Anne snapped. "A murder trumps bad grammar."

"No one said anything about a murder."

"It was a murder."

"How do you know?"

"I just know." She hit the volume button again.

"The victim has not been identified. The cause of death is not known yet."

*"Not yet known."*

"I'm going to kill you," Anne said.

"Fine," her father said. "Then this jackass can report that my dead corpse has been found killed."

"We should all be so lucky that he have the opportunity," Anne muttered under her breath. She hit the volume button again as Sheriff Cal Dixon stepped up to speak with the reporter.

Dixon stated the basic facts. The victim was a woman who appeared to be in her late twenties or early thirties. No identification had been found with or near the body. He could not pinpoint how long she had been dead. An autopsy would be performed, and he would have more to say as to the cause of death when the results came back.

Yes, it appeared she had been murdered.

The sheriff stepped away to confer with Frank Farman and a handsome Hispanic man dressed in slacks and sport coat. A detective, Anne assumed.

The news coverage broke for a commercial and an ad for mattresses came on, the salesman screaming at the top of his lungs. If the telephone hadn't been on the end table directly beside her, Anne would never have heard it ringing. She picked up the receiver and cringed as a woman's voice shouted out of it.

"Your television is too loud! People are trying to sleep!"

Anne hit the mute button. "I'm terribly sorry, Mrs. Iver. My father is so hard of hearing, you know."

Her father glared at her even as he called across the room from his recliner. "Sorry, Judith! We were watching the news of that murder. You should keep your windows closed and locked. Would you like me to come over and check around your property for you?"

He would no more have gone out in the night dragging his oxygen tank along to see to the safety of Judith Iver than he would have flown to the

43

moon. Anne held the receiver out away from her.

"Thank you, Dick! You're so good to me!" Judith Iver shouted. "But I've got my nephew staying with me."

"All right," her father called out. "Good night, Judith!

"Her nephew," he said with disgust as Anne hung up the phone. "That rotten hoodlum. He'll slit her throat one night while she's dreaming about him amounting to something, the stupid cow."

The yin and yang of Dick Navarre: charming, handsome old gentleman on the outside; nasty old bastard on the inside. Professor Navarre and Mr. Hyde. And if Anne had described him that way to his casual acquaintances, they would have thought she was mentally disturbed.

She handed the remote to him as she got up.

"I'm going to bed," she said as she closed the living room window against the night chill and Mrs. Iver. "Did you take your pills?"

He didn't look at her. "I took them earlier."

"Oh, really? Even the ones that say 'take at bed-time'?"

"The human body doesn't know what time it is."

"Right. And, I forget, what medical school did you attend in your free time?"

"I don't need your sarcasm, young lady. I stay up to date on all the latest medical news."

Anne rolled her eyes as she left the room and went into the kitchen to get his last round of medication for the day. Pills for his heart, for his blood pressure, for edema, for arthritis, for his kidneys, for his arteries.

*I stay up to date on all the latest medical news.* What crap.

At seventy-nine, her father spent his days with his golf cronies, arguing about politics. If they had been discussing migrant farm workers, he would have claimed he was up to date on all the latest immigration laws.

Anne had never bought into his bullshit. Not when she was five, not when she was twenty-five. She had always seen him for exactly what he was—an egomaniacal, narcissistic ass—and he had always known it and hated her for it.

They didn't love each other. They didn't even like each other. And neither made any pretense otherwise, except in public—and then only grudgingly on Anne's part. Dick, the consummate actor, would have had everyone in town thinking she was the much-adored apple of his eye.

He had been the same way with her mother—putting her on a public pedestal, belittling her in private. But for reasons Anne had never fathomed, no matter how he had betrayed her, her mother had loved him until the day she died, five years and seven months ago.

Marilyn Navarre, forty-six, had succumbed to a short, brutal fight with pancreatic cancer, an irony that enraged Anne still. Her father's health had been failing for years, yet he had survived a heart attack, two open heart surgeries, and a stroke. He had been wounded in the Korean Conflict and walked away from a multiple-fatality car accident in 1979.

He suffered from congestive heart failure, and half a dozen other conditions that should have killed him, but he was simply too mean to die. His wife, a saint on earth nearly thirty years his junior, hadn't lived four months after her diagnosis.

Sometimes Anne cursed her mother for that. She did so now as she went upstairs to her bedroom.

*How could you do this to me? How could you leave me with him? I still need you.*

Her mother had always been her sounding board, her voice of reason, her best friend. She would have told Anne she was being selfish now, but like any abandoned child, Anne didn't care. Selfishness was the least she deserved.

At her dying mother's request, she had left grad school and moved back home to care for her father. Instead of earning her doctorate and going to work as a child psychologist, she had taken the job of teaching fifth grade in Oak Knoll Elementary.

And now three of her students had found a murder victim.

The thought hit her as she turned on the bedside lamp. *There should have been four.*

Wherever Dennis Farman went, Cody Roache was right behind him. Anne had forgotten about him in the chaos and confusion of what had happened. Guilt washed through her now. Poor Cody, always an afterthought. But he had been nowhere to be seen in the park. Maybe he had never been there. Maybe he had gotten a ride home from school.

The children should all have been in bed by now, asleep and dreaming. Would they close their eyes and see the face of the dead woman?

Anne went to her window and looked out at the night and the lights in the windows of other homes. What would she see if she could look in the window of the Farman home? Frank Farman would still be at the scene of the crime with the sheriff. Would his wife be listening to Dennis's excited account of what had happened?

Sharon Farman had struck Anne as being overworked and overwhelmed by life. She had a job, she had children, she had Frank Farman for a husband. Judging by Dennis's disruptive behavior at school, Anne guessed his mother did her best to ignore him in the hopes that he would simply grow up and go away.

She could easily picture Wendy Morgan and her mother, Sara, tucked together in bed with the bedside lights on. The Morgans appeared to have the kind of loving, well-adjusted family seen only on television. Wendy's mother taught art for the community education program. Her father, Steve, was an attorney who donated his free time to helping underprivileged families in the courts.

Anne's inner child envied Wendy her home life. Her own childhood had been lonely, standing on the outside of her parents' relationship, watching the dysfunction unfold.

As warm and loving as her mother had been with her, Anne had always known that her place in her mother's life was second to her father's. Even now. Even in death her mother had chosen the needs of her husband over the needs of her child. Her mother would have been horrified to realize it, but then, she never had, and Anne would never have pointed it out to her.

Anne had been a quiet child, a watcher. She had taken in everything that had gone on around her, processed it, and kept her conclusions to herself.

She recognized those same qualities in Tommy Crane. He tended to stand back a little from those around him, taking in their moods and actions, reacting accordingly. Of the children to find the body, he was the most sensitive and would be the one most affected by what he had seen. Yet he would be the least apt to talk about it.

If she could have seen inside the Crane home, would Tommy be watching and listening as his mother spent the evening on the phone arranging for him to see doctors and therapists? Would his father be the one listening to the story of Tommy's trauma, offering comfort and reassurance? Or would Tommy have gone off to bed on schedule, no trouble to anyone, left to deal with his bottled-up feelings by himself?

Anne's heart ached as she stared out at the night, watching the lights in the windows of other houses go out one by one. A long day was over, but for Tommy and Wendy and Dennis, an even longer ordeal had just begun.

# 7

Tommy sat alone at the top of the steps, listening. He was supposed to be in bed. He had taken a bath, like he did every other night of his life. He had put on his pajamas and brushed his teeth with his father supervising. His mother had given him his allergy medicine to help him sleep. He had pretended to take it.

He didn't want to sleep. If he went to sleep, he was pretty sure he would see the dead lady, and he was pretty sure that in his dream she would open her eyes and talk to him. Or maybe she would open her mouth and snakes would come out. Or worms. Or rats. He didn't know if he would ever want to sleep again.

But he didn't dare to go downstairs either. First of all, his mom would freak out because it was twenty-seven minutes past his bedtime. It wasn't a good thing to mess up the schedule. Second, because she was yelling—about him.

What was she supposed to do? What was she

supposed to say when someone asked her about what happened? People would think she should have picked him up from school. They would think she was a bad mother.

His dad told her to calm down, that she was being ridiculous.

Tommy cringed. Bad move on Dad's part. He should have known better. His mother's voice went really high. He couldn't see her from where he sat in the shadows on the stairs, but he knew the face she would be wearing. Her eyes would be bugging out and her face would be red, and there would be a big vein standing out on her forehead like a lightning bolt.

Tears filled Tommy's eyes and he pressed himself against the wall and wrapped his arms around himself and pretended his dad was holding him tight and telling him everything would be all right, and that he didn't have to be afraid. That was what he wanted to have happen. But it wouldn't.

Now his mother was going on about how they would have to take him to a psychiatrist, and how terrible that would be—for her.

"I'm sorry," Tommy whispered. "I'm sorry."

Sometimes he was a lot of trouble. He didn't mean to be. He hadn't meant to fall on a dead lady.

Very quietly, he stood up and went back to his room and crawled halfway under his bed to get his bear—which he was supposed to have given up by now. People would call him a sissy and worse if anybody knew he still slept with his bear. But tonight he didn't care.

Tonight, with his parents still fighting in the room beneath him, and visions of a dead lady stuck in his head, he was feeling very alone and very afraid.

Tonight was a night for a bear.

Wendy snuggled next to her mother, listening to her sing a song.

"Hush, little baby, don't you cry. Mama's gonna sing you a lullaby . . ."

It was a dorky song, but Wendy didn't say anything. Her mother had sung it to her all her life, whenever she was feeling sick or afraid of the dark. Even if she didn't like the stupid song, she liked the sound of her mother's voice. It made her feel safe and loved.

They were cuddled together in her bed, in her pretty yellow-and-white bedroom with all her stuffed animals and dolls looking on. The lamp-light was warm and soft. What had happened that day in the woods seemed long ago and far away, like a scary story she might have read once but had started to forget.

Of course, she hadn't forgotten. Not really. She just didn't want to think about it, that was all. Not now.

She wondered if Tommy was thinking about it.

"Will you stay with me tonight?" she asked, looking up at her mother. She had asked this question a million times already. She only wanted to hear the answer again.

"All night long, sweetie."

Wendy sighed. "I wish Daddy was here too."

Her mother didn't answer right away. "He's in Sacramento on business," she said at last.

"I know," Wendy said. They had already been over this a million times too. "But I still wish he was here."

"Me too, baby," her mother whispered, squeezing her tight. "Me too."

It was late when Dennis heard his father come in. His stupid sisters were asleep, but his mother was still up. She was sitting at the kitchen table, smoking cigarettes and watching TV. His dad would want supper now—even if it was practically the middle of the night—and she would heat it up and serve it to him because that was her job.

Dennis charged down the stairs, barreled into the kitchen, grabbed the back of a chair, and slid to a stop.

"Dad, Dad, what happened? Did you get to dig up the dead lady?"

"Dennis!" his mother snapped. "You're supposed to be in bed. Your father had a long night at work."

Dennis rolled his eyes. His mother was so stupid. His dad said so all the time.

"Yeah, they dug her up," his father said, pulling a beer out of the refrigerator and popping the top.

"Was she all rotten? Was she a skeleton? Was she all hacked up with an axe?"

"Dennis!" his mother said again, her voice a little higher and a little louder than the last time.

Dennis ignored her, keeping his eyes on his father. His uniform was rumpled, but not dirty. He should have been dirty if he had dug up the dead body himself. He probably supervised. He was too important to have to dig up a dead body himself—even if he probably wanted to.

Dennis would have helped if he had been allowed to stay. But his father had lost his temper at him for being in the way and had sent him home.

Dennis had been really angry about it, but then he got to ride home in a squad car with another deputy, and that had been pretty cool. His dad didn't let him get into his squad car. He didn't want Dennis to mess something up, was what he had said the first two thousand times Dennis had begged to play in the car. The two-thousand-first time Dennis had asked, his dad had lost his temper. Dennis hadn't asked again.

"No, she wasn't," his father said, popping a couple of Excedrin from a bottle on the counter. "We put her in the hearse and they took her to the funeral home."

Dennis's mother scurried back and forth from the refrigerator to the stove, banging pots and muttering under her breath as she hurried to heat up a pork chop. His father picked up the cigarette his mother had left burning in the ashtray on the table and took a drag on it. The television on the counter was showing a guy spray-painting his bald spot.

"Mendez wants to call in the FBI," his father said to no one in particular. "Prick."

His mother said nothing.

"Why don't you want the FBI, Dad?" Dennis asked.

"Because they're a bunch of pricks—just like Mendez."

"He's a spic prick," Dennis said, proud of his cleverness.

His father gave him a look. "Watch your mouth."

His mother wheeled on him. "Dennis, go to bed!"

She looked like her eyes were going to pop out of her head, like in a cartoon when one character had his hands around the throat of another character, choking him.

His dad turned on his mother then. "Cook the damn food! I'm hungry!"

"I *am*!"

He looked at her like he was just now seeing her for the first time since he had walked in the room. His face twisted with disgust. "You couldn't wear something better than that?"

Dennis's mother grabbed her old blue bathrobe together just below her throat. "It's the middle of the night. Was I supposed to put on a dress and makeup?"

"I've been at a murder scene all night. You think I want to come home and look at *this*?"

Dennis's mother reached up and shoved a big messy chunk of hair out of her face and behind her ear. "Well, I'm sorry I'm not up to your high standards!"

His father swore under his breath. "Have you been drinking?"

"No!" she exclaimed, looking shocked. "Absolutely not!"

She yanked the frying pan off the burner, dumped the pork chop on a plate, and all but flung it at the table. "There. There's your fucking dinner!"

His father's face turned purple.

His mother's face turned white.

Dennis turned and ran for the stairs. Halfway up, he stopped and sat down, grabbing the balusters and peering through them like he was behind bars. He couldn't see much of the kitchen, but he didn't need to. A chair scraped across the floor and thudded as it tipped over. A pan slammed against the top of the stove. A glass broke.

"Here's my fucking dinner?"

"I'm sorry, Frank. It's late. I'm tired."

"*You're* tired? I'm the one that's been working all night. I finally get home and all I want is a little dinner, and you can't manage that?"

His mother started to cry. "I'm sorry!"

There was a silence then that made Dennis more nervous than the yelling. He jumped a little when his father emerged from the kitchen, his expression dark, his hands on his hips. He turned and looked straight up at Dennis.

"What are you looking at?"

Dennis turned and ran up the stairs, stumbling twice, trying to go faster than his legs could possibly manage. He ran into his room and into his closet, pulling the door shut behind him and hiding himself under a pile of dirty clothes.

He lay there for a long time, trying not to breathe too loud, trying to hear over the pounding of his pulse in his ears, waiting for the door to fly open. But a minute went by and nothing happened. Then another minute . . . then another. . . until finally he fell asleep.

# 8

Wednesday, October 9, 1985

"I can't believe there was a murder and you didn't call me!"

"I had a few other things on my mind," Anne said.

They stood outside the door to the kindergarten room, on the patio near the sandbox where half a dozen of Franny's charges were busy with toy dump trucks and shovels and buckets.

Fran Goodsell, her best friend. Thirty-nine, cute as a button, irreverent as he could be. She should have called him, she thought now.

Franny had a way of turning situations upside down. He would have somehow found a way to distract her from the horror of what had happened. He would have said something outrageous, made a completely inappropriate remark, found a way to give her a lighter moment.

That would have beat the hell out of lying awake all night, seeing every detail when she closed her eyes: the mangled hand reaching out of the ground, quietly begging assistance to rise up from the shallow grave.

"Don't you watch the news?" she asked.

"Of course not," he said, offended by the very idea. "There's nothing good on the news." His eyes went wide as he was struck suddenly with a possibility. "Did they interview you? Oh my God. I hope you weren't still wearing that outfit you wore to school yesterday. You looked like a novice nun."

True to form.

Anne gave him a look. "No, I wasn't on the news, and thanks for the fashion advice, Mr. Blackwell."

"Well, honestly, how do you expect to attract a man, Sister Anne Marie? Image is everything." Fran's image: preppie with a twist. Today he wore khaki pants and Top-Siders, and an orange bandana at the throat of his blue buttondown oxford.

"I don't expect to attract a man at school. Who is there to attract? Arnie the janitor?"

"Mr. Garnett."

"I'm not interested in having an affair with our married principal."

"His wife is sleeping with her yoga instructor. He's as good as divorced, that's all's I'm saying," which he said with an extra-thick Long Island accent.

Franny was originally from Boston. Number fourteen of fifteen Goodsell children. Irish Catholic to the tenth power. "Eight girls, seven boys; two fags, one dyke; six married and divorced, six got it right the first time," was his standard description of the Goodsell siblings.

He had spent a number of years in New York City and the Hamptons, teaching brats of the rich and famous—his words, of course.

"You're horrible," Anne said without meaning it. "A woman was murdered. Three of my kids were there. *I* was there. It was terrible."

Franny put an arm around her shoulders and squeezed. "I know, honey. I'm sorry."

"And what now?" she asked. "Am I supposed to say something about it to my class, then just carry on with the day's lessons? They never prepared us for this in college.◆

"No," he said. "But they also never told me teaching kindergarten would make me sterile."

Anne managed to find a chuckle at Franny's

famous line. He professed on-the-job experience had driven him to drink and had brought him a better understanding of why some species eat their young.

In truth, he was an excellent, award-winning teacher, and his kids and their parents loved him.

Anne glanced at her watch. "I'd better go. My kids will be coming in."

"Come tell me if any of them get arrested."

"You'll be the first to know."


Principal Garnett and the good-looking detective (she assumed) from the news coverage were waiting for her outside her classroom.

"Miss Navarre." Garnett spoke first. He was a neat-and-tidy kind of guy—starched shirt, stylish tie tied just so. It had always been Anne's suspicion that he would be more likely to fall for Franny than herself, wife or no wife. "This is Detective Mendez from the sheriff's office."

The detective offered his hand politely. Square-jawed, stocky build, dark complexion, macho mustache. His expression was guarded in a way she would come to recognize as being common to his profession. His grip was firm, but not trying to prove anything.

"Miss Navarre, I'm sorry I didn't get a chance to speak to you yesterday. I wasn't informed until later that you had been there at the scene."

"Just to ask Frank Farman if I could take the children home to their parents."

"Detective Mendez has asked to use my office to interview the children who found the body," Garnett said. "He would like you to be there."

"I think they'll be more at ease with you there," Mendez said.

"I think they'll be more at ease if we aren't in the principal's office," Anne said. "Going to the principal's office is never a good thing for a fifth grader."

"This is serious business," Mendez said. "They should take it seriously."

"I'm not going to let you bully ten-year-old kids," Anne said, unconsciously standing up taller. "They're upset enough as it is."

Mendez looked a cross between perplexed and amused. "Don't worry, Miss Navarre. I left my rubber hose at the office."

Anne refused to be embarrassed. She turned to Garnett. "Could we use the conference room instead?

"It appears equally serious," she said to the detective. "But less intimidating."

"That's fine," Mendez said.

"I don't know that those kids are even coming to school today," Anne said. "I told their parents last night that if they needed to take some time—"

"The parents have all been contacted," Garnett said. "They're to bring their children here for the interviews. If they choose to take them home after that, that's up to them."

"What about the rest of my class?"

"I've called a substitute for the morning."

"What about a counselor? Someone who can help them cope with what happened. I'm sure they've all heard about it by now."

"I'm relying on you for that, Anne," Garnett said. "You have some training in child psychology."

"I know how to boil water. That doesn't make me a gourmet chef."

"You'll be fine."

Mendez looked pointedly at his watch. "The Morgan family should be here soon. I need to get set up."

Setting up consisted of Mendez making sure his cassette recorder was working and that he had his notebook and pen ready.

Nothing would come of this, he was sure. The woman was already dead and buried when the kids found her. Unless one of them saw the killer leaving the scene, there wasn't much they could tell him. But he would interview them, nevertheless, because that was the routine, and he prided himself on being thorough.

As he shuffled his stuff around, he glanced down the conference table at the teacher. Pretty and petite, she looked late twenties and very serious. She was uncomfortable, arms crossed defensively, pacing a little, frowning. Twice she reached up and tucked a strand of dark hair behind her ear.

"You have training in child psychology?" he asked.

She flinched ever so slightly at the sudden sound of his voice. "I took some courses in college. That's not even close to having a degree."

"But you know your kids. You can read them pretty well?"

"The school year just started. I've known them six weeks."

"I don't know them at all. Have you met the parents?"

"At conference time. An hour. One evening."

"So tell me about . . ." He consulted his notes. "Wendy Morgan. What's she like?"

That coaxed a little smile out of her—for Wendy, not for him. "Wendy is very self-assured. She has opinions and she won't hesitate to tell you what they are. She's the class feminist."

"She'll be an easy interview, then. Good. And the mom?"

"Sara. She seems like a very nice woman. Very caring of her daughter. She teaches community ed classes in art."

"And the father?"

"Nice guy. He's an attorney. Very busy. He does a lot of pro bono work in family court for the women's center. I think he even does some lobbying for women's issues in Sacramento."

She huffed a quick sigh. "What is it you want me to do here, Detective?"

"Reassure them. Make sure I don't break out the billy club."

Anne Navarre scowled at him, unimpressed with his sense of humor. Looking back on it, his fifth-grade teacher hadn't been impressed with him, either.

"When did you arrive on the scene?" he asked, hitting the Record button on the cassette player.

"The scene was already taped off," she said. "There were deputies everywhere. Are you taping this?"

"Just making sure the machine is working," he said, turning the thing off, rewinding, playing back the sound of Anne Navarre's voice. She sounded highly suspicious of him.

"And where were the kids then?"

"Tommy and Wendy were away from the scene. Dennis Farman was right there, trying to see what was going on. His father was there. You know him, I suppose. Frank Farman."

"Did any of the kids say they had seen anyone else in the woods?"

"No," she said. "They talked about a dog."

"I don't think a dog buried her there."

"That isn't funny."

"I didn't mean for it to be. I was being sarcastic."

"Nothing about this is funny," she snapped. "And you weren't being sarcastic, you were being facetious."

"Yes, ma'am."

"I'm sorry," she said, looking away from him, crossing and uncrossing her arms. She reached up and tucked that strand of brown hair behind her ear again. "This situation . . . I'm a little rattled."

"I understand. It's okay."

She glanced at him out of the corner of her eye. She probably didn't mean for him to see it, but she was wary of him. He got that a lot. Even the most innocent people could become nervous around cops. It went with the territory.

"You're not a suspect," he announced.

The eyebrows snapped downward again. "Of course I'm not."

She sighed again and looked at the ceiling, turning her head as if she was trying to get a kink out of her neck.

"Do you know who she is—was?" she asked.

"Not yet."

"No one has missed her yet. How awful is that?"

The door opened then, and Principal Garnett ushered in a blonde woman and a little girl who was her spitting image in miniature.

# 9

Wendy walked into the big conference room with its big windows and big table, and felt as if she were getting smaller and smaller. Even though she was way over having to hold hands with her mom, she was glad to be doing so in that moment.

Miss Navarre looked angry at first—she was looking at the man at the end of the table—but then she turned and smiled a little.

"Hi, Wendy. Hi, Mrs. Morgan," she said. She had dark circles under her eyes, just like Wendy's mom did. "How are you doing today?"

"I'm okay," Wendy said. "I'm just weirded out, that's all."

"She had bad dreams," her mother confessed. "So did I."

"So did I," Miss Navarre admitted.

"So did I," said the man at the end of the table. He came around and offered his hand to Wendy's mom. "I'm Detective Mendez from the sheriff's office."

"Sara Morgan."

"And you'd be Wendy," he said, offering his hand to her.

Impressed, Wendy shook it. He was very cute. He looked a little like Magnum P.I. with the dark hair and the mustache—only he was shorter, and he probably didn't drive a red Ferrari or live on a fabulous estate. And he was wearing a coat and tie instead of shorts and a Hawaiian shirt. That was the difference between being a TV star and working in Oak Knoll, she supposed.

"I'm the detective assigned to investigate the case," he explained as he motioned for everyone to take a seat. "So one of the first things I need to do is ask you and your friends some questions about what happened in the park yesterday. There's nothing for you to be worried about. You're not in any trouble."

"I didn't do anything to be in trouble for," Wendy said, taking the chair nearest to the detective at the head of the table. She straightened her acid-washed denim skirt and matching jean jacket, wanting to look appropriately grown-up and hip. Copying the style from a picture of Madonna in a magazine, she had pulled half her thick wavy hair up into a ponytail on top of her head.

"Dennis touched her," she said. "He should be in trouble for that, right? Touching a dead person. Isn't that illegal or something?"

"That depends," the detective said.

"It was all Dennis's fault," Wendy said. "If he wasn't such a psycho and hadn't been chasing us, we never would have cut through the woods."

Detective Mendez stopped her to turn on his tape recorder and announce who was in the room.

"Did you see anyone else in the woods, Wendy?" he asked.

"No."

"No one around the area where the body was?"

"No people, but there was a dog. He came out of the bushes and it was like he was guarding her or something."

"What kind of a dog?"

"The scary kind with big teeth and beady eyes. You know."

"A pit bull?"

"Maybe. But he didn't attack us," she hastened to add. "He just growled like he was telling us to stay away from the lady. Dennis said maybe the dog killed her and buried her like a bone, but that's stupid—right?"

Her mother spoke up then. "She tells me that they didn't touch the dog—"

"We didn't!" Wendy insisted, mortified that her mother would bring this up again. Who cared if they touched the stupid dog?

"So it was just the three of you that found the body."

"Four. Me and Tommy, and Dennis and Cody."

"Cody was there too?" Miss Navarre asked.

"Who's Cody?" the detective asked.

"Cody Roache," Miss Navarre said. "I thought of him last night. He's usually wherever Dennis Farman is, but he wasn't in the park when I got there."

"Because he screamed like a baby and ran away," Wendy said with a certain amount of disgust. "The deputies came because of him."

The detective looked at Miss Navarre. "I'll need to speak to him as well."

"Have you found out who the woman was?" Wendy's mother asked.

"Not yet."

"This is so awful. Nothing like this ever happens here."

"The dog knows who she is," Wendy said.

"Wendy," her mother said impatiently, "enough about the dog."

Mendez held his hand up to stop her talking, but his eyes were on Wendy.

"Did the dog have a collar on?"

Wendy shrugged. "I don't remember. He had big teeth. I remember that."

"What color was the dog?"

"White with big black splotches." She turned and gave her mother her best so-there look, then turned back to the detective. "He was black all around one eye and ear."

Detective Mendez scribbled that all down in his notebook. Obviously, these were very important clues.

"Could this really be important?" Wendy's mother asked.

"If we can find the dog, and the dog has tags, maybe the dog belonged to the victim and we can find out who she was through the registration with the city," Detective Mendez explained. "It's probably a long shot, but you never know."

"You've been a big help, Wendy," Miss Navarre said. "It's a good thing you're so observant."

"Thank you, Miss Navarre," Wendy said, beaming.

Detective Mendez reached out his hand to her again. "Thanks, Wendy. If you remember anything else, you can have your mother or Miss Navarre call me."

Wendy had never felt quite so important. This was just like being in a Nancy Drew mystery. Maybe she would write this story herself and become famous. Maybe Tommy would want to be in on it with her. Now that the idea had come to her, she couldn't wait to ask him.

Miss Navarre led the way out the side door to the dark, quiet hall, a place that called for whispers.

"I'm still not sure what we're going to do about counseling," her mother whispered to Miss Navarre.

Wendy intervened. "Mom, I'm fine. I saw a dead person. I'm not warped for life."

"No, I am," her mother said. "Maybe I'm the one that needs counseling."

"Everyone is shaken up," Miss Navarre said. "But if Wendy feels all right to come back to class, then that's probably what she should do."

"Yeah, Mom, don't make such a big deal."

Miss Navarre turned to her then. "It is a big deal, Wendy. So if you're in class and find yourself suddenly feeling scared or upset, you have to promise you'll tell me right away."

"I will. I promise," Wendy said and looked up eagerly at her mother, who was clearly not convinced.

"I'll keep a close eye on her," Miss Navarre promised.

"All right," Wendy's mother said grudgingly. She looked down at Wendy, worried. "But you do exactly what Miss Navarre just told you, and under no circumstances are you to walk home. I will be here to pick you up."

So much for revisiting the scene of the crime so she could make notes about the setting for her story, Wendy thought. Oh well. It wasn't like she was ever going to forget what had happened.

That was for sure.

She couldn't wait to talk to Tommy.

# 10

Jane Thomas always began her day in the garden. This was her quiet time to think and reflect. Working in the garden was her version of meditation and the closest she would ever come to actually stilling her always-busy mind.

Even though she had gotten in late, driving up from LA after a long day of meetings, she had still managed to rise before most of Oak Knoll. The sky was that perfect electric blue of fall, the temperature comfortably in the low seventies. She made her way along the row, deadheading roses while Violet, her black pug, patrolled for mice among the overgrown patch of purple cone flowers.

Jane loved her home in Oak Knoll. She had purchased the 1928 Spanish hacienda–style house nearly five years before, after she had divorced her husband and Los Angeles. Oak Knoll had always attracted her with its interesting mix of people and small-town feel. The college gave it the sophistication of academia and the vibrancy of youth. Its proximity to Santa Barbara and to the northern parts of the LA sprawl made it a doable commute for young professionals with young families, promising a future. All of Oak Knoll's attributes made it a desirable place for retirees with money, bringing affluence and support for the arts.

The college boasted a well-respected music program that attracted talented musicians and singers, both as students and teachers. Every summer Oak Knoll was home to a renowned festival of classical music.

Even though Jane still kept a condo in LA, Oak Knoll was her true home and the Oak Knoll Thomas Center for Women was her focus.

The Oak Knoll center was a scaled-down version of the original Thomas Center in Los Angeles. The centers, brainchild of Jane and her two sisters and started with money from the Thomas family philanthropic trust, were places for women to reinvent themselves.

The clientele was made up of women from all walks of life, women who needed and deserved a second chance. Homeless women, battered women, women with drug histories or police records—all were welcomed and not judged. Each center offered shelter to those who needed it, assistance with health care, psychological and job counseling, and the makeovers of wardrobe and self that would send them out into the job market with confidence and newfound self-esteem.

The Thomas girls had been raised on the ideal of giving back to the community and helping the less fortunate. Forty-one, Jane had found success in the business world and was a well-known patron of the arts. She sat on the boards of several nationally significant charities, but the Thomas Centers for Women were her pride and joy.

Through the open back door of her house she could hear the phone ringing for the third time in an hour. She never took calls during her gardening time, everyone who knew her knew that. But three calls in an hour made it seem like someone was desperate to get hold of her, and a strange uneasy feeling moved through her.

Her parents were both alive and well, but that didn't mean something couldn't happen to them. Her sister Amy was vacationing on a ranch in Idaho. She could have fallen from a horse or been attacked by a bear while hiking.

"You're being ridiculous," Jane muttered to herself, but she was moving toward the house and pulling off her gloves as she said it.

The answering machine had picked up by the time she walked through the kitchen to her antique desk in the front room. Angry red numbers flashed seven messages unheard. She hadn't taken the time to listen to the four that had been there the night before. She had been tired and had gone straight to her room for a bath, bed, and a chapter of *Sense and Sensibility*.

The first message was from her assistant at the center, Tuesday, 10:34 A.M.

"Hi, Jane. Sorry to bother you, but Quinn, Morgan and Associates called to say that Karly Vickers was a no-show this morning. Today was supposed to be her first day on the job. I thought you'd want to know."

Second message: Tuesday at 3:23 P.M.

"Miss Thomas, this is Boyd Ellery from The Nature Conservancy. Could you please give me a call when you have a chance. I want to run something past you with regards to the benefit."

Third message: Tuesday, 5:14 P.M.

"Jane, it's me again. I've been trying to contact Karly, and she doesn't answer her phone. I'm going to drop by her house on my way home and make sure she's all right."

Fourth message: Tuesday, 7:11 P.M. "It's me again. I'm at Karly's. She's not here. I don't know what to think."

Fifth message: Wednesday, 7:27 A.M. Her assistant again. She sounded tired and nervous.

"Jane, I don't know what time you got in last night. Did you see the news? Call me."

Sixth message: Wednesday, 7:39 A.M.

"Jane, it's Mom. We haven't heard from you in a couple of days. We just saw the news. Please call and let us know you're all right."

The news. What news? Why wouldn't she be all right?

Seventh message: Wednesday, 7:52 A.M. Her assistant again.

"Jane, there's been a murder. Answer your damn phone. I have a terrible feeling it might be Karly."

# 11

Tommy hadn't slept very much at all. Every time he had started to fall asleep, he had jerked himself awake, afraid of the dreams he knew would come. But every time his father or mother would come to check on him—which they did several times—he would pretend to be sound asleep.

He had gotten up as soon as it started getting light outside and started the homework he hadn't done the night before. He didn't know what the day would bring. Maybe he would be taken to a doctor or a psychiatrist, or maybe the police would take him in for questioning. The thing he most wanted to do was go to school and carry on as if the day before had never happened. As if.

Now he sat in the school office, waiting, his mother on one side, his father on the other. The secretaries kept looking over at him, then exchanging glances. He felt like a freak in the circus. Murder Boy.

He sighed and shifted on his chair. His father put his hand on his shoulder and gave a little squeeze. His mother got up and went to the counter to ask the secretary how long it would be.

"Are you nervous?" his father asked.

Tommy shrugged.

"All you have to do is tell the detective what happened and what you saw."

Tommy said nothing. He stared at the doorway that led into the hall where the principal's office and the conference room were, willing Wendy to come out and give him some kind of signal.

He heard a door open, but it wasn't Wendy who emerged from the hall. It was a dark-haired man in a coat and tie, and he looked right at Tommy, then at his dad.

"Dr. Crane?"

"Yes," his father said, rising.

His mother turned away from the secretary and stepped forward with her hand outstretched and her smile wide. "Janet Crane."

"I'm Detective Mendez." The detective greeted his parents only briefly, then focused on Tommy, bending over and offering his hand. "Hey, Tommy. How you doin'?"

Tommy shrugged and slid off his chair, sticking his hands in his pants pockets. Adults always thought they could impress kids by pretending to treat them like they weren't kids.

"Tommy," his mother said. "Manners."

"I'm okay," Tommy said. He was fine for having fallen on a dead woman.

They all went down the hall to the conference room, where Miss Navarre was waiting, trying not to look anxious. Pale with dark smudges under her eyes, she smiled at him like she was willing him to be brave.

"Did you get any sleep last night, Tommy?" Miss Navarre asked as they all took seats at the big table.

"He slept through the night," his mother announced. "I gave him an antihistamine before bed. To help him relax."

Detective Mendez raised an eyebrow but didn't look at Tommy's mother. He was messing with a tape recorder and shuffling through some papers.

"Tommy has allergies," his mother went on. "He has a prescription. It's nothing he hasn't taken before."

The detective spoke to the cassette recorder, telling it who was in the room.

"Dr. Crane. What kind of a doctor are you?"

"I'm a dentist. Tommy has a pediatrician, of course."

Mendez pursed his lips and went, "Hmmm."

Tommy's mother frowned, displeased. She thought the detective was disapproving of her. Tommy could tell by the way she narrowed her eyes and pressed her lips together.

"I spoke to his doctor last night," she said. "I was concerned about Tommy having nightmares."

"Tommy, did you have any nightmares?" the detective asked. "You had quite a scare yesterday."

Tommy shook his head and scratched his left forearm where his cuts had begun to itch.

"Really? That's impressive. I had nightmares. Miss Navarre had nightmares."

"I was just asleep," Tommy said, looking down at the tabletop.

"Can you tell me how it went down yesterday?"

"We were running, and we fell down a hill, and I landed by the dead lady." Short and sweet.

"Did you see anyone else around? Any adult?"

"No."

"Do you think the killer could have still been there?" Tommy's mother asked, alarmed.

"I don't know," Mendez said. "I'm just asking."

"He could have seen the kids," his mother went on, her eyes widening. "And now their names will be in the press."

Mendez flicked a glance at her. "They're minors. No one can legally print their names without permission."

"We're certainly not giving permission."

"It wouldn't be very likely that the killer was there," Tommy's father said. "Right? I mean, he would have to be crazy to bury a body in the park in broad daylight."

"Who other than a crazy person could have done this?" his mother asked.

"You'd be surprised, Mrs. Crane," Detective Mendez said. "I've done a lot of research on the subject. This guy could appear as ordinary as anyone in this room. He's not crazy in the common sense of the word. In fact, he's probably of above-average intelligence."

"That's unnerving," Tommy's father said.

"Ted Bundy had been to law school. He was a Young Republican and people in high places believed he had a big future ahead of him. He murdered—"

Miss Navarre cleared her throat the way people do when they want someone to shut up. Mendez looked at her and she tipped her head in Tommy's direction.

Tommy made a mental note to look up this Bundy guy in the encyclopedia.

"Is that what you think is going on here, Detective?" Tommy's father asked. "A serial killer? What would make you think that?"

Detective Mendez looked like he'd gotten caught saying something he shouldn't have. "It's really too soon to say."

"Have there been other cases the public doesn't know about?"

"What's a cereal killer?" Tommy asked.

Miss Navarre looked really annoyed now when she looked at the detective. Detective Mendez turned his attention back toward Tommy.

"Tommy, can you describe to me what you saw, anything unusual you might have noticed at the scene?"

"Well, the dead lady," Tommy said. *Duh.*

"Anything else?"

Tommy shrugged again, then tugged down on the sleeves of his striped rugby shirt and rubbed his arm. "The dead lady. And there was a dog. He was guarding her. He was black and white."

"Did he have a collar?"

Tommy looked up at the ceiling, trying to remember. "Mmmmm. . . maybe . . . I'm not sure."

"Did you touch anything around the dead lady?"

He shook his head emphatically. "No way."

"Did anybody else touch anything?"

Tommy looked at the tabletop again, considering the wisdom of ratting out Dennis Farman. It didn't seem like the thing to do if he wanted to stay in one piece.

"Tommy?"

Miss Navarre. He looked up at her and knew she knew he was stalling. She said a lot with her eyes. He didn't want to let her down, what with being kind of in love with her and all.

"Uh . . . I didn't touch anything. And I know Wendy didn't touch anything." Maybe if he left it at that . . .

Miss Navarre turned then to his parents. "Will Tommy be staying in school today?"

Tommy looked up at his father, willing him to say he could stay. His mother had talked about a psychiatrist. He had seen psychiatrists on television, and Lori Baylor had gone to one after her mother died of breast cancer. From what Tommy had been able to discern, all they ever did was make people lie down on a couch and talk about their feelings. Tommy had nothing to say on that subject. His feelings were not anybody else's business.

"Principal Garnett tells us you've had some training in child psychology," Tommy's father said.

"Yes. Some," Miss Navarre said. "Wendy Morgan is staying, if that helps in your decision-making."

Tommy bugged his eyes out at his father. *Please, please, please, please*. He liked school. School was where he was happiest—except for when he was playing baseball or watching baseball. School was normal. At school he didn't have to be watching adults and trying to figure out what they were thinking and how it would affect him.

"But you don't have a degree," Tommy's mother said.

"No, I don't."

"And the school isn't going to provide someone who has."

"It doesn't look that way."

"And how will you handle the situation, Miss Navarre?" his mother asked, already expecting an unsatisfactory answer.

"We'll talk about what happened with the class," Miss Navarre said. "I think the best thing we can do is be open and honest with the kids."

"Talking about serial killers?" Tommy's mother said, giving Miss Navarre her Cold Eye as Tommy called it. "You think that's appropriate, Miss Navarre?"

"No," Miss Navarre said, raising her chin a little. "But talking about what happened to their classmates, talking about what's going to happen next, talking about how a police investigation works, turning a negative experience into an opportunity to learn—all seems very appropriate. Don't you agree, Mrs. Crane?"

Tommy's mother sighed impatiently. "I think everyone on the school board is going to get a call about Mr. Garnett's poor decision not to call in a professional."

"That's your prerogative," Miss Navarre said. "In the meantime, I'll do the best I can."

"That's not exactly reassuring."

"I want to stay," Tommy blurted out. Now he got the Cold Eye. It might have been better for him if he had ratted out Dennis Farman and kept his mouth shut about this. Oh well. It was too late now. "Please, Mom."

His father spoke up then. "Let's see how it goes. I like your ideas, Miss Navarre. I know you have the kids' best interest at heart."

"I do."

Tommy's mother stood up abruptly, checking her watch."Are we finished, Detective?" she asked. "I have an appointment I have to get to."

Detective Mendez and Miss Navarre looked at Tommy's mother, a little surprised. Tommy wasn't surprised. His mother was mad and she was cutting them off, dismissing them. She was done here and on to other, more important things. She didn't like anything to disrupt her schedule.

Detective Mendez said, "You're free to go."

Tommy's mother turned and walked out. His father put his hand on Tommy's shoulder and looked down at him. "You're sure you're okay with staying, Sport?"

Tommy nodded. He was sure. Especially now. The last thing he wanted was to be stuck with his mother in one of her moods.

His father patted him on the shoulder and stood up.

"Miss Navarre, thank you for your efforts. If there's anything I can do to help, please call." He turned to Detective Mendez. "Good luck with your investigation, Detective. It sounds like you might have your work cut out for you, if this guy is what you think he is."

"They're never so clever that they don't get caught eventually," Mendez said.

"And if they are," Tommy's father said, "I guess we never know it, do we?"

He handed his business cards to Mendez and to Miss Navarre, squeezed Tommy's shoulder one last time, and walked out.

Tommy breathed a sigh and rubbed absently at his arm. "Can we go back to class now, Miss Navarre? I just want everything to be normal."

"Sure, Tommy," she said. "Let's go do something normal."

Of course, Tommy knew nothing would ever feel quite normal again, but he could certainly pretend.

# 12

Karly Vickers was living in a cottage owned by the Thomas Center. The center had placed her in a receptionist position at Quinn, Morgan and Associates, a law firm. She would have a sixty-day probationary trial with full pay. If she succeeded in the job, she would then start paying for her own utilities. At the next plateau she would begin paying a small amount of rent to the center, another step toward self-sufficiency. When she was back on her feet entirely, the center would help her find her own living arrangements, and the cottage would welcome a new woman starting a new life.

Jane drove directly to the cottage. She didn't take the time to phone her assistant. She didn't even take the time to change out of her gardening clothes.

*There's been a murder . . .*

The sense of unease was now like a ball of dough sitting in her stomach.

Karly's car, an old Chevy Nova she owned herself, was not sitting in the driveway.

She could have gotten cold feet about the job, Jane told herself. Karly, twenty-one, had come to the center from Simi Valley with zero self-esteem, a victim of an abusive boyfriend who had beaten her so severely she had been unrecognizable to her own mother. The boyfriend had vanished, escaping justice, leaving Karly in so many shattered pieces it had taken her a year and a half to come this far in her recovery.

Jane had a photograph of the boyfriend imprinted on her brain. As far as she knew, he was still at large. Could he have somehow found out where Karly was living? Upon entering the program at the center, Karly had signed a contract agreeing to reveal her whereabouts to no one, not even her family. Periodic phone calls to her mother were carefully arranged and monitored. The phone service to her cottage was local usage only.

But Jane knew all too well the things women would do to sabotage themselves. She had seen abused women go back to their abusers over and over. The strength it took to break that cycle was sometimes beyond their reach.

The front door of the cottage was locked, suggesting Karly had left of her own free will. Jane had a set of keys to all of the center's properties. Surprise inspections were part of the deal. She let herself in and looked around, careful not to touch anything.

"Karly? Are you home? It's Jane."

The place was as neat as a pin. Only small things indicated anyone lived here at all: a jean jacket

hung on a peg by the front door; a book on sur-
viving abuse sitting on a table next to the sofa;
two pink dog dishes on the kitchen floor. But no
sign of Karly or her dog.

The bed was made. The bathroom was spotless.
The kitchen was sparkling.

Jane let herself out the back door and into the
small fenced yard. The grass needed mowing. A
small round metal table and two chairs sat on the
tiny concrete patio. A huge geranium Jane had
taken from her own garden and potted sat on the
table—a housewarming gift Karly had loved.

Gardening was part of her therapy. It was a
calming hobby and a chance to tend to something
and see a positive result. Nursing plants to full
flourishing health was also a metaphor for the
women's own lives. They should care for themselves, tend to their own needs, with the goal of
coming into their own full potential.

The newly opened geranium flowers were a
vibrant, cheerful red, but the plant needed deadheading and the leaves were starting to brown
and curl. The soil was dry and hard to the touch.
The plant hadn't been watered in days.

Out of habit, Jane picked up the watering can
from the table and went to the faucet at the side of
the cottage near a small potting shed.

Her mind was spinning. Over and over, she kept
hearing her assistant's voice: *There's been a
murder* . . .

A low rumble sounded behind her as she bent to turn the faucet on. A warning growl. Jane turned slowly toward the potting shed. The door of the shed was ajar.

"Petal?" she asked. "Is that you?"

Her answer was another low growl.

"Petal?"

She took a half step toward the shed, trying to peer inside. The slimmest sliver of sunlight penetrated the dark interior. At the base of that line of light, she could see one white paw, then the tip of a black nose.

"Petal? It's me, your auntie Jane. You're okay. Come out and get a cookie, sweetheart. Come on."

Inch by inch more of the dog became visible. She crawled along on her belly until Jane could see her face. "Forlorn" was the only word to describe the look.

*There's been a murder . . .*

Jane crouched down and fished a dog cookie out of the patch pocket of her denim gardening shirt.

"Come on, sweetheart," she whispered, tears rising in her eyes.

Karly would never have abandoned Petal. If there had been a family emergency, she would have called Jane to look after the dog. Even if she had gone somewhere she shouldn't have, she would have gotten word to somebody to take care of Petal.

Of all the dogs in the county animal shelter, Karly had chosen a thin, beaten-down female pit bull, saying they would understand each other. The dog had been the best therapy the girl could ever have had.

Jane held out the cookie, her hand trembling a little, not from fear of the dog, but from fear of what may have happened to the owner. Petal the pit bull inched closer, whimpering.

She looked thinner than the last time Jane had seen her, and she had some nasty scratches on her as if she might have gotten into a fight or had been living rough. Locked out of the house, she didn't have her cushy dog bed or her pink bowl filled with kibble; she didn't have her person to look out for her.

The dog finally, cautiously, stretched her neck out as far as she possibly could, just touching the cookie with the very tip of her tongue. Two tears tumbled over the rims of Jane's green eyes and slid down her cheeks.

*There's been a murder . . .*

# 13

"Mom's a piece of work," Mendez said as the teacher came back into the conference room. "Wound a little too tight, huh?"

She frowned, glancing back toward the door. "A little. When I took Tommy home yesterday she was furious he had missed his piano lesson."

"And what will the neighbors think now?"

Mendez asked, settling in his chair. "Her kid fell on a corpse."

"What would the neighbors think if they knew she was doping him up to make him sleep?"

"A little antihistamine is nothing," Mendez said. "When I was in a uniform in Bakersfield, I saw mothers get their kids drunk, make them smoke crack—"

"That's horrible."

"Makes Mrs. Crane look like the Mother of the Year."

Anne Navarre rolled her eyes as she turned away from him and walked toward the bank of windows. "She probably already has that plaque on her wall, along with Realtor of the Year, Volunteer of the Year, Chamber of Commerce Person of the Year."

"Image is everything," Mendez said.

He was happy to see she sided with the kids, and the kids liked her. There might be a chance they would confide something to her that they might not tell their parents or him. Provided they had anything to tell anyone.

Peter Crane was probably right in assuming the killer had been long gone by the time the kids had come across his handiwork. On the other hand, Vince Leone, one of his instructors at the National Academy and one of the pioneers of criminal pro-filing at the Bureau, had talked about killers who returned to the crime scene either to relive the experience or to watch the police investigation.

Some of them got an ego boost by watching the cops and believing they were superior to the dumb clods trying to figure it out. Some of them got sexual gratification revisiting the scene. Sick bastards.

"Tell me about Tommy."

"Tommy?" Anne Navarre turned her back to the windows, leaned back against the credenza, and crossed her arms—but not as tightly as before. A step in the right direction. "He's very bright, conscientious, quiet, sweet."

"He has a crush on you."

She made a little face and shook her head.

"Yes, he does," Mendez insisted. "He watched you almost the whole time."

"He watched everyone. That's what he does. He takes in everything then decides what to do. He probably watched me more because he feels safe with me."

Mendez chuckled. "Trust me. You might know kids' heads, but I was a ten-year-old boy once."

"I suppose I can't argue with that."

"Why do you think he didn't tell us the Farman kid touched the corpse?"

"Fear of retribution. Dennis Farman is a bully."

A quick knock sounded on the door to the outer office and a uniformed deputy stepped in.

"Farman's not coming."

"The hell he's not," Mendez said.

"He's not coming. He said he'll take his kid's

statement himself. He said it was a waste of everybody's time to come in here and talk to you."

"The fuck!" Mendez caught himself too late and glanced over at Anne Navarre. "Sorry."

"I could call Mrs. Farman," the teacher offered. "Maybe she would come in with Dennis."

"You've got to go now anyway," the deputy said. "Some woman came into the office to report a missing person. Could be our victim."

The woman waiting in Sheriff Dixon's office was in her early forties, tall and slender, and dressed in jeans with dirty knees and a bright green T-shirt with an oversize denim shirt thrown over it and left open. Her long blonde hair was scraped back into a messy ponytail with strands falling loose to frame her pale oval face. She stood in front of the visitor's chair with her arms wrapped around herself. She looked worried.

Cal Dixon was sitting against the front edge of his desk, head down, speaking quietly to the woman when Mendez walked in.

Dixon looked up. "Tony, I'm glad you made it back. I want you to meet Jane Thomas from the Thomas Center for Women. Ms. Thomas, this is Detective Mendez. He's my lead investigator on this case."

Mendez reached out and shook her hand.

"Jane is concerned the murder victim may be someone she knows."

"One of our clients," she said. "Karly Vickers. No one has seen or heard from her since last Thursday night."

"And you just noticed her missing?" Mendez said. "Don't you do a head count or something?"

Many of the Thomas Center "clients" were at-risk women from abusive situations. From what Mendez had heard, they ran a pretty tight ship for security reasons.

"We had recently moved Karly out of the center into one of our cottages. She was ready to transition to independent living."

"What makes you think she didn't take that idea to the next level and just split?"

Jane Thomas shook her head. "No. No. She was excited about starting over. She was a little nervous, but excited about starting her new job. Yesterday was supposed to be her first day."

"But she didn't show up," Mendez said.

"No."

"The employer is . . . ?"

"Quinn, Morgan and Associates. A law firm that helps us out with family court cases."

"When was the last time you saw her?"

"I saw her last week—Thursday morning at the center. I helped her pick out her new work wardrobe. We have our own store in-house, clothing donated from working women here in town, from Santa Barbara, from Los Angeles.

"Thursday was Karly's makeover day. She had

her hair done, her nails, her makeup. I remember her saying she felt like Cinderella."

"Could she have gone out looking for Prince Charming?" Mendez asked. "She had a new look, new clothes. She was feeling pretty—"

"She's shy. She was still recovering emotionally from being beaten nearly to death by her boyfriend."

Mendez dug his notebook and pen out of the patch pocket of his tweed sport coat and started scribbling. "Do you have a name for him?"

"Greg Usher. I have all the information available on him in Karly's file at my office. He has a record."

"And he's walking around loose?"

"The last I heard."

"Do you have a photograph of Karly?" Dixon asked.

"Not with me."

"Do you know if he tried to contact her recently?" Mendez asked.

"She would have told us."

"Maybe she was afraid to."

She didn't have an answer for that. She wasn't sure.

"Does she have a car?"

"Yes, a gold Chevy Nova. 1974 or '75. I have the license plate number in her file."

"Where's the car?" Mendez asked.

"I don't know. It's not at the cottage."

"So she could have gone somewhere on her own."

"No. She didn't just leave."

"You know as well I do, Jane," Dixon said quietly. "How many of these women go back to their abusers?"

"Not our women."

Dixon lifted one white eyebrow. "None of them?"

Jane Thomas scowled. She knew better. "Not this one. She wouldn't. She would never just leave Petal."

Mendez stopped writing mid-word. "Petal? Who's Petal?"

"Karly's dog."

His heart gave a big thump then began to beat faster. "What kind of dog?"

"A pit bull. Why?"

He turned to Dixon. "The kids said there was a black-and-white dog at the scene. It might have been a pit bull."

"Oh my God," Jane Thomas whispered, sinking down onto the chair behind her. She covered her mouth with her hand as her green eyes filled with tears.

"Where is she?" she asked. She didn't look at Mendez or at Dixon but stared at the floor as if her life depended on it. "Can I see her?"

Dixon sighed. "We'll be sending the body to the LA County coroner for an autopsy, but it hasn't left yet. But it might be better just to have you look at some Polaroids from the scene—"

"No."

"Jane—"

"I want to see her." She looked up at Dixon now in a way that made Mendez wonder just how well they knew each other. "I need to see her."

Dixon started to say something, then clamped his mouth shut and looked out the window. The silence hung in the air like fog. The image of the dead woman's face slid through Mendez's memory. He wished he hadn't had to look at it, and that was his job.

Finally Dixon nodded. "Okay. But I'm warning you, Jane, it's going to be hard."

"Then let's get it over with."


The three of them got in a sedan and Mendez drove them to Orrison Funeral Home. No one said anything. Dixon sat in the backseat with Jane Thomas, but neither of them looked at the other, Mendez noted, glancing at them via the rearview mirror.

The funeral home director took them to the yellow-tiled embalming room where their vic was on a gurney in a body bag, waiting for her ride to the city.

Dixon dismissed the man, who closed the door behind him as he left.

"We don't think she had been dead that long when we found her," Dixon said. "Decomposition is minimal, but not absent."

Jane Thomas stared at the body bag. "Just show me."

"I want you to be prepared—"

"Damn it, Cal, just show me!" she snapped. "This is hard enough!"

Dixon held his hands up in surrender. Mendez unzipped the bag and gently peeled it open.

Jane Thomas put a hand over her mouth. What color she had drained from her face.

"Is that her?" Dixon asked.

She didn't answer right away. She stared at the woman on the gurney for a long, silent moment.

"Jane? Is that her? Is this Karly Vickers?"

"No," she said at last, her voice little more than a breath. "No. It's Lisa."

"Lisa?"

"Lisa Warwick," she said, and she began to tremble. "She used to work for me."

"This woman used to work for you?" Mendez said.

"Yes."

"And one of your clients is missing."

She didn't answer. She'd gone into shock. Then she began to cry and sway, and Cal Dixon stepped close and put his hands on her shoulders to steady her.

Mendez looked his boss in the eye. "Three dead, one missing. Do you still think we're not dealing with a serial killer?"

To his credit all Dixon said was, "Call Quantico."

Good thing, Mendez thought, because he already had.

# 14

Vince Leone closed his car door. The sound seemed amplified. He looked up at the sky. The blue was so intense it hurt his eyes. He put his Ray-Bans on and breathed deeply of the crisp fall air. His head filled with the scents of Virginia: damp earth, forest, cut grass.

The academy grounds were alive with people. Young agents going here, running there. Veterans, like himself, hustling between buildings, between meetings.

The sounds of footfalls on concrete, snatches of conversation, a lawn mower, gunfire in the distance: All assaulted his ears. His sight, hearing, sense of smell—all seemed magnified, hypersensitive. It might have been an inner need to absorb as much of life as possible, or it might have had something to do with the bullet in his head.

He went into the building, to the elevators, pushed the Down button. Down. Way down. People got on the car with him. A couple of them looked at him sideways, then looked away. He vaguely recognized faces but couldn't recall names. He didn't know them well—or they him, he suspected, though his short-term memory still had some holes in it.

They knew *of* him, he suspected. He had signed

on with the Bureau in 1971 after a stellar career in homicide in the Chicago PD. He had come to Quantico and the Behavioral Sciences Unit the fall of 1975, just as the unit was beginning to blaze some exciting trails. Being a part of that time had made him and his colleagues legends. He was forty-eight and a legend. Not bad.

Or maybe these people knew *about* him, as in "The guy that got shot in the head and lived." The academy was a small, incestuous community, and like in all small, incestuous communities, gossip ran thick and fast.

The elevator stopped and most of the passengers got off, headed for the cafeteria or PX. The smell of coffee, eggs, and bacon grease hit him like a brick, then the doors closed and the car began to drop another twenty feet to what the agents lovingly referred to as the National Cellar for the Analysis of Violent Crime.

The warren of offices and conference rooms had been a bomb shelter during the height of the Cold War, a hideout for J. Edgar and his cronies in the event of nuclear attack. The Bureau had seen fit to send the Behavioral Sciences/Investigative Support Unit down to the windowless, sometimes musty-smelling, subbasement a year before.

Closed off in their own giant tomb with their cases—the worst of the worst murders and sexual assaults the country had to offer—the agents joked (in the gallows humor that kept them for what passed as sane) that they lived and worked ten times deeper than the dead.

Leone stepped off the elevator.

"Vince!"

He glanced up at his colleague, wearily amused by the expression on his face. "Bob. I'm not a ghost."

"Geez, no. Not at all. I'm just surprised to see you, that's all. What are you doing here?"

"Last I knew, I worked here," Vince said, turning in the opposite direction.

He went into the men's room, went into a stall, and puked, a wave of heat sweeping over him. The meds or maybe nerves, he admitted to himself. He'd been gone six months.

A couple of stalls down, someone else vomited.

They came out of the stalls and went to the sinks together.

"Vince!"

"Got a bad one, Ken?" Leone asked. He ran the faucet, scooped water into his hand, and rinsed his mouth.

Ken's face was gray and drawn, his eyes haunted. "Three little kids, sexually assaulted, their faces blown off with a shotgun.

"We don't know who they are, where they came from. We can't compare dental records to missing kids' because they don't have any teeth left. We keep hearing about DNA profiling as the coming thing, but it can't come fast enough for these kids."

"It's years out," Vince said. It would be a miracle for law enforcement when the technology came, but as Ken had said, it couldn't come fast enough.

Ken shook his head as if he were trying to shake the images from his brain. Ken was a top profiler, but he had never quite mastered the ability to close the door between analysis and sympathy. Therein lay the road to an ulcer, at the very least.

"It's always worse when it's kids," Vince said.

"I don't know how much more of this I can take," he admitted. "The vics were about the same ages as my boys. I go home at night . . . You know how it is."

"Yep."

Vince went home at night to a big-screen TV. He'd been divorced seven years. His oldest was in college now. But he remembered how it had been to try to leave cases at the office so he could go home and pretend to be normal.

"I played golf with Howard on the weekend," Ken said. "IRDU is looking pretty good to me."

"Research and Development. Hmmm . . ." Vince would have sooner stayed home and hit his thumb with a hammer over and over, but that was him.

"Hey," Ken said, as if he had only just realized. "What are you doing here?"

Vince shrugged. "It's Wednesday."

All of the profilers also taught about fifteen hours a week, both in the FBI Academy and the National

Academy for law enforcement officers. But they didn't teach on Wednesday mornings. For those not out in the field on assignments, Wednesday mornings were spent in the conference room, going over case facts, picking one another's brains, bouncing ideas off one another.

BSU had grown over the ten years of its existence to include six full-time profilers, working to assist local law enforcement in solving tough cases. When John Douglas had been made chief of the operational side of BSU, the profilers had been given their own acronym—ISU, Investigative Support Unit—within the BSU. Douglas had wanted to take the BS out of what they did. Ironically, the agents in the unit continued to call themselves BSUers.

BSU. ISU. Another three letters added into the giant vat of alphabet soup that was the Bureau. Unit names seemed to change with every new unit chief, and every new chief seemed to have some pet subgroup to create. IRDU (Institutional Research and Development Unit). SOARU (Special Operations and Research Unit). NCAVC (National Center for the Analysis of Violent Crime). NCIC (National Crime Information Center). VICAP (Violent Criminal Apprehension Program).

Despite John's best hope, BS was the Bureau's specialty.

Vince went into the conference room, turning his back to the long table as he poured himself a cup of coffee to burn the taste of vomit out of his mouth.

The discussion of Ken's case was already under way. Crime scene photos were being passed around and remarked upon. What did this mean? What did that mean? If the children were related, it meant this. If the children had been abducted individually, it meant that. How would authorities go about the task of identifying the bodies? How many children had been reported missing in a two-hundred-mile radius in the past year?

Vince slipped into a chair, reserving comment on any of it. He needed a few minutes to regroup, to build up another charge of energy. The coffee was bitter and acidic, and his stomach lining felt raw.

"There's an NCIC search under way for reports of missing children in the age groups of the victims," Ken said.

"Once VICAP is totally operational, we'll be able to search the database based on the perp's MO," another agent said.

"And once the technology is developed I'll be able to watch the World Series on my wristwatch," said another. "Someday isn't going to help us today."

Had anybody ever heard of anything on a violent child predator with a similar MO? Why a shotgun? Why obliterate the faces? Did that point to murder by a relative or someone else who knew the children? Or was the shotgun a signature meant to make a statement as to the psychological state of the UNSUB (unknown subject)?

Ken stood at the gigantic whiteboard, jotting down ideas being thrown at him on one part of the board and noting pertinent questions on another.

Vince took it all in, his mind half on the case details, half on his colleagues. They were all in shirtsleeves, but the day was young, and all neckties were still neatly in place.

He had known most of these guys a long time. They had worked a lot of cases together and they had a lot in common in addition to backgrounds in law enforcement and years in the Bureau. Three of the five guys in the room right now—including Vince—had been in the marines. John had served in the air force. They had the common experiences of trying to juggle marriage and family with the job—and in several cases the common experience of marriages falling apart because of the job.

"You're quiet, Vince." The voice came from the head of the table.

Vince met eyes with his old friend—who seemed not the least bit surprised to see him. Vince spread his hands and shrugged.

"Sorry, Ken," he said to the agent at the board. "But we're just spinning our wheels until they figure out who these kids are. Unless you want to do two profiles: one for a stranger as the UNSUB, one for a person known to the kids. That's a hell of a lot of work when you've got how many other cases ongoing? Ten? Twelve?"

Ken looked at the end of his rope.

"But hey," Vince said. "What do I know? I'm just an old cop from Chicago. I can reach out to a gal I know at the National Center for Missing and Exploited Children. They're only up and running for a year, but they get a lot of anecdotal information we don't. I can go make the call right now."

Ken nodded. "Thanks, Vince. I appreciate it."

Vince got up and left the room, going directly back to the men's room where he puked up the coffee. He rinsed his mouth out and stood for a moment, assessing himself in the mirror, seeing what his colleagues were seeing.

He had always been a big, good-looking guy: six three, two hundred pounds, built to play football. Now he was a tall, raw-boned man, twenty pounds underweight. He hadn't lost the chiseled bone structure of his face, or his large dark eyes, or his wide white smile, thank God. He had something to fall back on. And there was color in his face at the moment, but when his blood pressure returned to pre-puking normal, his complexion would be a pale reflection of the steel gray heavily threaded through his black hair.

The hair had grown back thick and wavy, thank God. Bald had not been a good look on him.

For a moment he flashed back on that late March evening, walking to his car with his groceries, his mind on a case. That was as much as he had been able to recall. And even that memory had probably been manufactured by his brain. Witnesses had stated a guy in a hooded sweatshirt with a gun in his hand had walked up to him, demanded money. He hadn't reacted quickly enough. The assailant pulled the trigger.

Three weeks went by before he regained consciousness and was told by his doctors that he was a miracle. The .22-caliber bullet had entered his skull and never exited. Only time would tell the extent of the lasting damage to his brain.

He had found it ironic. All his years in law enforcement, and he had never been injured. He, Mr. FBI, had to get mugged in a Kroger's parking lot, shot in the head by a junkie.

Leaving the men's room, he went to his desk. As was his habit since the Marine Corps, it was neat and orderly, and he could have laid his hand on any piece of paper he needed without having to make a mess. An orderly environment spoke of an orderly brain—except for the shards of brass in the middle of his.

After chewing down a handful of antacid tablets from his desk drawer, he made his phone call, got some information, and went back to the meeting where he handed Ken a piece of paper with a phone number on it.

The discussion had moved on to a series of sexual homicides in New Mexico near the Mexican border. The investigation was involving the

Mexican authorities who were asking to send two of their detectives to Quantico for a crash course in profiling.

The morning wore on. Vince bided his time, letting the agents with active cases take their turns. As the meeting wound down, his friend at the head of the table made eye contact again.

"You didn't come in because you missed looking at all these ugly mugs," he said.

"No." Vince cracked a lopsided smile and chuckled. "Where's Russo? I came to look at her."

Rosanne Russo was the only woman in the unit and more than used to taking a rash of shit for it.

"She's at a conference in Seattle."

"Damn. My luck."

"What have you got, Vince?"

He rose to his feet slowly, so as not to touch off a bout of vertigo. "I've got a possible serial killer in Southern California. The guy abducts women, tortures them, and glues their eyes and mouths shut with superglue."

"Pre- or postmortem?"

"I don't know yet."

"What's the victim profile?"

"One of the vics had an old record of arrests for prostitution. No ID yet on the latest one."

"How many vics?"

"Three in two years."

His friend frowned. "That barely meets criteria."

"Tell that to the dead woman they found yesterday. She was buried in a public park with her head aboveground."

Eyebrows went up. Now it was interesting. This was a jaded bunch. There wasn't much in the way of human depravity they hadn't seen. It took something pretty out there to impress them.

"Photos?"

"They just found her late yesterday. No photos yet."

"What about from the other two cases?"

"Were the other bodies buried in the same manner?" another agent asked.

"No and no."

"You don't have any paper on this," his friend said. "*I* haven't seen any paper on this."

"Nope. I was just wondering if anyone had come across this See-No-Evil, Speak-No-Evil thing with the superglue before. Roy?"

Roy was the resident expert on sexual assault and sexual homicide, although they all had dealt with their share of it. Roy shook his head.

"I've seen eyes gouged out, acid poured in them. I've seen lips cut off, objects wedged in the mouth, mouths taped shut. No superglue."

"Okay," Vince said and took his seat again. "I was just wondering."

His friend at the end of the table wore the my-ass expression. Everyone else got up to go to lunch, exchanging handshakes, concerns, and pleasantries with him as they made their way to the door. With him and the boss still sitting at the table, no one bothered to ask if he was coming to lunch.

When the door had closed and they were alone, his friend let his own concern show on his face. He got up and came to Vince's end of the table.

"You grew a mustache."

Vince swiped a hand over the coarse steel gray, not-exactly-regulation hair decorating his upper lip. "You're very observant. You should be a detective."

"Makes me think you're not really back. How are you? Really."

"The meds make me puke up everything I eat," he confessed. "But I hear that's all the rage these days among the beautiful people, so . . ."

"Should you be here?"

"Where should I be? Sitting in a recliner watching the hours of my life tick away? You might as well shoot me in the head. Oh, wait, somebody already did that."

"What's with this case?"

"A kid I taught in the National Academy classes a year or so ago, Tony Mendez, called me at the crack of dawn with this. The crack of dawn *our* time. Had to be in the middle of the friggin' night where he is. He's pretty het up about the case. His first serial killer."

"If that's what it is."

"If that's what it is," Vince agreed.

"Where does the kid rank on it?"

"He's the lead detective. He works for the county sheriff."

"The sheriff gave him the okay to bring this to us?"

Vince made a face. "Not exactly. But the kid's going to convince him."

"And I'm going to learn to speak Italian."

*"Bella!"* Vince said, laughing.

His friend shook his head. "How you still have a sense of humor is beyond me."

"Hey, I'm a living punch line. I got shot in the head and lived to tell about it. That's a big joke on somebody—the perp, God, me."

"What do you want to do with this, Vince? This case won't even come close to the standard. And we've got legit cases coming in for review every day of the week. If I had twenty profilers, they'd all be up to their asses in work."

"This UNSUB has used the superglue at least twice, and probably on a third vic in another jurisdiction," Vince said. "This time he literally plants his handiwork for public display. That's (a) highly ritualized behavior, and (b) escalating in terms of the attention he wants. He isn't going to stop.

"And I like this kid Mendez," he admitted. "He's sharp. He'd make a good agent. I'd like to see him come to the Bureau."

"And let me guess. He's an ex-marine."

Vince grinned. *"Semper fi,* baby. There's no such thing as an ex-marine."

"You want to mentor him."

"He promised he'd take me deep-sea fishing."

"There's no way I get this approved through the unit chief. He'll tell you if you want to teach he'll get you all the class time you want."

"So I go on my own time. I'm still on leave anyway. And then there's the mustache . . ."

"On your own time, on your own dime. No per diem, no hotel room, no nothing."

"Nancy'll let me skip an alimony payment. She's feeling guilty."

"If she hadn't divorced you, you wouldn't have gotten shot in the head?"

"She is all-powerful."

They were silent for a moment. His friend sighed. Vince sighed.

"Look, John, you know how I feel about going to the scene with these cases. For me, being detached from the setting, working out of this friggin' tomb, doesn't give me perspective, it doesn't make me objective. I'd like to teach a hands-on approach to what we do, because for some of us that works better. If I can go out to California, be of some service nicking this dirtbag before he becomes the next Bundy, *and* cultivate a new agent, why not?"

Why not? Because the Bureau had a book of rules and regs, and "why not" was not an approved reason for any action to be taken by an agent. "Why not" would have to go through the channels of ASACs and SACs, unit chiefs, and half a dozen committees on its way to the head of the Bureau. It sure as hell wouldn't happen in his lifetime.

A knock sounded on the door, and a clerk stuck her head in.

"I'm sorry to interrupt, but there's an urgent call on line two for Special Agent Leone."

Vince went to the phone on the credenza and listened, then put his hand over the receiver and turned to his friend. "They just ID'd the vic from yesterday, and they've got another woman missing, both connected to the same women's center."

His old friend shrugged and smiled. "Go with God, my friend."

# 15

"Miss Thomas, does the name Julie Paulson mean anything to you?" Mendez asked.

They had gone into a private family room in the funeral home. The drapes were heavy and the room reeked of stargazer lilies and gladiolas. Jane Thomas had sunk down into a corner of a velvet couch the color of a good cabernet. She was as pale as death, still shaken by the discovery of Lisa Warwick's body.

Mendez had gone into overdrive at the realization that they had both a dead woman and a woman missing, and that both women had ties to the Thomas Center for Women. He had a million questions and wanted to fire them off like rounds from a machine gun, but Jane Thomas was fragile, and he had to be patient. Not one of his stronger virtues.

Jane looked at him, confused. "No. Who is she? Is there some reason I should know her?"

"She was never a client at your facility? She never worked at your facility?"

"Not that I remember. What does she have to do with . . . ?" She turned her head in the direction of the embalming room, unable to say the victim's name.

"Oh my God," she whispered, shaking. "Karly. You think she's with the—the *animal* that did that to Lisa, don't you?"

Cal Dixon put a reassuring hand on her knee. Mendez mentally raised an eyebrow.

"Jane," Dixon spoke quietly, as if he were talking to a nervous horse. "Chances are Karly is with someone she knows. She probably just went—"

Jane Thomas steeled herself, sitting up a little taller. "Don't you dare patronize me. We've been over this. Karly did not *just* anything."

"Miss Thomas?" Mendez tried to bring her attention back to him, a little irritated at his boss for bringing an obviously personal note into the proceedings. "Julie Paulson was a woman found murdered outside of town in April last year. I'm wondering if she might have had a connection to the center."

"April '84? I was in Europe for several months. My parents own horses. Their top horse was competing in Germany and Holland. I went with them . . ."

Mendez knew why people in this situation rambled and digressed. If Jane Thomas was thinking of her parents' show horses, she couldn't be thinking about the horror she had seen in the room down the hall.

"Have there been any threats against the center recently?" Dixon asked.

"The usual kooks and religious fanatics."

"What does 'usual' mean?" Mendez asked.

"The a-woman's-place-is-barefoot-and-pregnant crowd. The whores-should-turn-to-Jesus-or-burn-in-hell crowd. The right-to-lifers, though I'll never figure that one out. We provide our women with access to medical care. We don't advocate abortion."

"Do you keep hate mail?"

"Yes. In a file at the office."

"We'll need to see it."

"Of course."

"You said the victim—Lisa Warwick—used to work for you. When was that?"

"A few years ago. She was an administrative secretary and she volunteered as a victim's advocate in her spare time, hand-holding clients who had to deal with the court system. She still does —did—that from time to time."

"Any cases lately?"

"A few months ago. A client with a drug history was trying to get visitation rights to her children."

"Was there an angry father involved?"

"No. Actually, in the end the father was so impressed with the progress his ex-wife had made, he withdrew his objection."

"Why did Ms. Warwick leave the center?" Mendez asked.

"She went back to college to finish her degree in nursing."

"She left on good terms with everyone?"

"Yes. Absolutely. You can't think someone at the center could have done this."

"We have to explore all possibilities," Mendez said.

"It's standard investigative procedure, Jane," Dixon said. "We never know where leads might come from."

"We'll need to interview the staff," Mendez said. "And the women—your clients."

He could see that was the last thing Jane Thomas wanted.

"These women are fragile," she said. "They'll be scared to death."

"They may have a right to be," Mendez said bluntly.

"That's a little premature, Detective," Dixon said, giving him a steely look. "But we have to err on the side of caution.

"What do you know about Lisa Warwick's background?"

"She's from Kansas originally. I probably have a contact number for her in the old personnel files."

"Ex-husbands? Bad boyfriends?" Mendez asked.

"None that I remember. Lisa was a very private person."

"Did she engage in any risky behavior? Frequent bars? Drinking? Drugs?"

"I can't imagine that she did. She liked to knit."

"When was the last time you had any contact with her?"

"We spoke on the phone from time to time. She dropped in at the center a few weeks ago to say hi."

"Do you know where she was working?"

"The ER at Mercy General, here in town."

She put a hand over her eyes as she started to cry. Dixon got up from the couch and tipped his head toward the door. Mendez followed him out into the hall.

"I'll go to the hospital and see what I can find out about Warwick," Mendez said, still scribbling in his notebook. "I figure I'll send Hamilton and Hicks to the Thomas Center."

"What did your connection at Quantico say?"

"He's coming out."

"He's coming here?"

"Yeah."

"That's not the usual protocol."

Mendez shrugged.

Dixon didn't look happy. "I don't want a circus here, Tony. I don't want this guy talking to the media. I don't want *anybody* talking to the media."

"That doesn't need to be an issue."

"That includes you," Dixon said, thrusting a finger at him. "Dial it down. I know this is a big case for you, and you're excited about it. That'll make you sharp. But I don't want you running off the rails. Understand?"

"Yes, sir," Mendez said, falling back on tried-and-true marine respect for rank.

"I don't want anything said about there being a possible connection between these victims."

"No, sir."

"I've seen a couple of those BSU guys grand-stand and shoot their mouths off. I won't have it."

"No, sir. Absolutely not, sir."

Dixon stepped back, sighed, looked around. "Go radio for a uniform to pick you up. I'm going to take Jane home."

"Yes, sir."

Dixon looked a little sheepish. "We're friends."

"Not my business, sir," Mendez said.

"No, it isn't."

# 16

The Roache home was a modest bungalow in a slightly shabby part of town. The house could have used a coat of paint, but the place was otherwise neat. Someone had put a pot of rust-colored mums on the front step, adding a splash of fall color to the picture.

Anne rang the doorbell and waited. Cody's mother had called the school that morning to say that Cody was ill and wouldn't be in class. Anne had found her thoughts drifting to him off and on all day. He was the only one of the four children who had discovered the body she hadn't seen for herself. At the end of the school day, she got in her car and drove directly to the Roache home.

A small dog yapped its way through the house, followed by Renee Roache. Cody's mother was small and weedy with limp brown hair and a pale complexion. She worked days as a waitress at a diner near the college where the pace was hectic and the tips pathetic. Her husband was a mainte-nance man who worked nights at Mercy General.

"Mrs. Roache, I hope I'm not imposing," Anne said. "I just wanted to check on Cody to see how he's doing."

Renee Roache looked perplexed, as did the dog at her feet, a fat brown-and-white terrier, tipping its head quizzically from one side to the other.

"That's beyond the call of duty, isn't it? It's just a stomach bug."

It was Anne's turn to look puzzled. "Um, well, I had a feeling, after what happened yesterday . . ."

"What happened yesterday? Did something happen at school?"

"Didn't Principal Garnett's office call you?"

"Not that I know of. I ran out to get something for Cody's stomach this morning. Maybe they called then. We don't have an answering machine."

"Oh," Anne said, at a loss. Cody had obviously not told his mother about finding the body in the woods. It was a hard idea to grasp that a child would keep that kind of information to himself.

"What happened?" Renee asked, getting anxious.

Anne took a deep breath. "You might want to sit down for this."

They went into the Roaches' tiny living room where the television was playing a *Star Trek* rerun. Anne expected to see Cody on the couch, watching intently. Spaceships were his obsession. But the couch was empty and Renee offered her a seat there.

Dinner was cooking, the smell of roast chicken drifting in from the kitchen. The little dog hopped up on the couch to give Anne a closer look.

Anne told the story for what seemed like the tenth time in twenty-four hours. Cody's mother sat, stunned.

"Why didn't he tell me?" she asked, her voice as

thin as she was. "He came running home yesterday with a bad stomach. He'd had an accident in his pants. I thought maybe it was something he ate at school, or there's always a bug going around . . . He didn't say a word."

"Did he seem upset?"

"Well, yeah, but . . . He's a ten-year-old boy. I thought he was upset about having the accident. He gets picked on a lot, you know."

That was true. In the jungle that was childhood, Cody Roache was well down in the pecking order. Children could be cruel, their meaner instincts yet to be padded over by the layers of subterfuge, dishonesty, and social niceties adults accumulated over the years. And the kids who were a little different, a little slower, not as hip, took the brunt of it.

Cody was small and homely and a little odd. He didn't really have friends, Anne had observed. He had Dennis Farman, but that relationship was symbiotic, born out of necessity. None of the kids liked Dennis because he was a bully. He had teamed up with Cody to have a sidekick who looked up to him because of his toughness, and Cody had made friends with Dennis because it was safer for him to be for Dennis Farman than against him.

"He was sick all night," his mother said. "And still this morning. He stayed in bed all day. I can't get him to eat anything."

"Would it be all right with you if I spoke with Cody?" she asked. "I've had some training . . ."

She felt like a fraud saying it. She was no more a child psychologist than the man in the moon. But for the time being, she was the closest thing these kids had.

Renee Roache led the way down the short hall to a bedroom with *Star Wars* stickers all over the door, knocked once, and cracked the door open.

"Cody? You have a visitor. Miss Navarre is here."

Not a sound came from inside the room.

Renee opened the door and went in. Anne followed. The room held the musky gym shoes smell of ten-year-old boys—a combination of sweat and dirt and less-than-meticulous hygiene. The room was dark, the shade pulled down on the single window. It took a moment for her eyes to adjust. Slowly she began to make out a small lump in the twin bed that was pushed up against the wall in one corner of the tiny room.

Cody's mother sat down on the edge of the bed, turned on the lamp, and peeled the blankets back, exposing the boy's head. He played dead, squeezing his eyes shut a little too hard.

"Cody, why didn't you tell me what happened yesterday?" his mother asked.

"Nothing happened," he said.

One eye cracked open. His mother handed him his glasses, newly taped together with adhesive tape. He sat up and put them on, blinking at the light.

"Hi, Cody," Anne said softly. "I was worried about you today. How are you feeling?"

He rubbed his nose and scrunched his shoulders up around his ears, then pulled his knees up to his chest and bound them there tightly with his arms.

"Your mom tells me you've been really sick."

She could see the little wheels spinning in his head, wondering just what she knew, what he should reveal, what he should admit to.

"I know what happened in the park yesterday," Anne said. "I talked to Wendy and Tommy."

"Why didn't you tell me, Cody?" his mother asked again, her tone edged with hurt.

Cody looked at her, looked at Anne, looked down and scratched his shin through his red pajamas.

"Mrs. Roache," Anne said. "Would it be all right if Cody and I spoke alone for a few minutes?"

Renee Roache looked uncertain, but she got up and left the room just the same. Anne sat down on the edge of the bed, near the foot, not wanting to crowd the boy.

"That must have been pretty scary finding that body like that. What a terrible thing to see. I think I would have run away if I had come across that like you did. I would have run straight home."

She could see him relax the slightest bit. If she said she would have run away, then maybe it wasn't so bad or embarrassing that he had run away.

"I ran away," he confessed in a small voice.

"I don't blame you. I think I would have gotten sick. I think a lot of people would have."

"Did Tommy get sick?"

"He was pretty upset."

He thought about that for a minute. "I bet Dennis didn't get sick."

"I don't know," Anne said, her mind going to the things Wendy had said, that Dennis had touched the dead woman. She thought about what she had seen in the woods—Frank Farman allowing his son to scamper around the crime scene like it was a playground, taking it all in with great interest. "You don't think so?"

Cody shook his head, his gaze sliding away from her, his mouth turning down at the corners. It wasn't the expression that would have accompanied hero worship, which she might have expected. It didn't say *Dennis is tough, Dennis doesn't get scared, I wish I could be like Dennis.*

"Why do you think that, Cody?"

He gave half a shrug.

She let it go for the moment. "Is there anything you'd like to tell me about what happened yesterday?"

He was thinking about it. He looked down at his bare feet, then pushed his glasses up on his nose.

"We talked about it in class this morning," Anne said. "We talked about how sometimes bad things happen, really bad things. And that's

121

hard to understand—why one person would do something so terrible to another person."

" 'Cause they're crazy," Cody said.

"Sometimes. And when we hear about this scary, terrible stuff it makes us all feel like the world isn't a safe place. You know what I mean?"

Cody nodded slowly. The fat terrier nosed its way into the room, jumped on the bed, sniffed the boy up and down, then went to the foot of the bed, and turned around five times before curling into a ball.

"Is that how you feel?" Anne asked. "Like if you go back out in the world something like that might happen to you?"

He thought about that one for a long time and chose not to answer her, which was an answer in itself. She couldn't blame him. He had caught a glimpse of the worst thing one human being could do to another. Like ripples in a pond, that violence touched everyone who heard of it. Every woman in Oak Knoll would be locking her doors and windows tonight. How could Anne possibly convince a ten-year-old kid that violence couldn't touch him?

And why would he trust her anyway? She barely knew him. If she had to admit it, she knew him less than she knew Tommy or Wendy. He wasn't a good or enthusiastic student. The only attention he drew to himself was when he got caught up in Dennis Farman's disruptive vortex.

She felt guilty for not knowing him better, and wondered how many other kids she was seeing only in the periphery of her vision.

"That chicken smells really good," she said, pushing to her feet. "Think you'll eat some dinner?"

Once again he didn't answer her. She felt his mind was still on the last question she had asked him, that he was still wrestling with something, but she couldn't pull it out of him. He had to want to give it to her.

"If you decide you want to talk about it," she said, "don't be afraid to come to me, Cody. Or tell your mom. You don't have to keep all those feelings bottled up inside you."

Anne turned for the door, took a step, then another. Then Cody Roache said something that ran a chill straight through her.

"Dennis said there were bodies buried in the woods."

Anne turned back around slowly.

"What do you mean, Cody? He said that yesterday? After you found the body?"

Cody Roache was as white as a sheet, his dark eyes huge behind the too-big lenses of his taped-together glasses.

"Before that," he said in a tiny voice.

Anne came back to the bed and sat down. "I don't understand. When did he tell you this?"

"A while ago. We were in the woods playing

commandos and he told me there were dead bodies buried there."

If he had told her this two days ago, Anne would have written it off as something Dennis would say just for shock effect. But as it turned out, there *had* been a body buried in the woods.

Maybe Dennis had been there on his own some other time and had seen something happening. From the corner of her eye she could see Cody staring at her intently, waiting for her to say something, but she didn't know what to say.

"Do you think Dennis killed that lady?" he whispered.

"No," she said. "No, of course not. What exactly did he tell you, Cody? Did he tell you he had seen a body?"

"He said there were bodies buried there and they were rotting in the ground and we were running over the top of them and stepping on them. And then there was that lady!"

She needed to call Detective Mendez. If there was a chance Dennis had seen something . . . She wondered if Dennis had told his father . . . and if Frank Farman had passed that information on to Mendez.

"I'm scared," Cody said.

Anne looked at him sitting there curled into a ball in his red pajamas, his dark hair standing up in tufts.

"What are you scared of, Cody?"

He swallowed hard. "Dennis."

"Dennis didn't kill that lady."

"How do you know?"

Because Dennis was an eleven-year-old boy and certainly not capable of doing what had been done. But Anne said none of that to Cody. Instead, she gave him the pat answer adults always give children when they don't want or know how to tell them the truth.

"Because. I just know," she said. She took a deep breath and let it out, trying to decide what to do next.

"Thank you, Cody," she said, standing up. "You did the right thing telling me this."

Cody didn't look so sure about that. "Don't tell Dennis I said it."

"Don't worry about Dennis," Anne said. "Feel better. I would like to see you back in school tomorrow."

She spent another few minutes with Renee Roache discussing what had happened and the fact that Detective Mendez would probably want to speak to Cody. Then she left the Roache home and the smell of chicken roasting, to go in search of Dennis Farman.

# 17

The Farmans lived not far from the Roaches in a two-story house painted battleship gray. Everything about the exterior was neat and tidy, squared off and symmetrical. No frills. Very military, she thought.

One of the Farman daughters answered the door. Both girls were in junior high school, enough older than Dennis that they probably did all they could to deny his existence. Anne couldn't imagine anything more annoying to teenage girls than little brothers.

There was no sign or sound of Dennis as she waited in the hall for Sharon Farman to materialize. She looked at the family photos on the wall, noting that even as a toddler Dennis had looked like trouble.

*Dennis said there were bodies buried in the woods.*

Sharon Farman came into the hall, wiping her hands on a dish towel. She appeared to be still dressed from work in a skirt and blouse with long sleeves puffed at the shoulder and a ruffled stand-up collar. She had the kind of looks that had probably been quite pretty in high school, but were now worn down by years of smoking cigarettes, raising children, and the disappointment of being married to an asshole.

"Mrs. Farman," Anne said. "I'm so sorry to interrupt your dinner—"

"We haven't eaten yet," Sharon Farman said shortly. "We're waiting for my husband. Why are you here?"

"I wanted to check on Dennis."

"Check on Dennis?" she said, as if that was the most absurd notion she had ever heard. "Why would you check on Dennis? You've just spent the entire day with him. I'd think that would be more than enough of him."

"Dennis wasn't in class today," Anne said. "I assumed you kept him home."

Sharon Farman looked incredulous and exasperated at the same time. "That little shit! His father took him to school this morning."

"Hmmmm," was all Anne could think to say. She'd never heard a parent refer to their child as a little shit, no matter how true it might have been. "Is he here now?"

The woman looked up the staircase and screamed, "DENNIS! Get down here!"

At the same time, the front door opened and Frank Farman walked in. His wife went right to him.

"Dennis wasn't in school today," she said. "Did you drop him off?"

"I got a call," Farman said as he took off his giant cop belt hung with all manner of weapons and handcuffs. He hung it on the coatrack beside the door. "I told him to walk to school."

Sharon Farman rolled her eyes, turned on her heel, and headed back to the kitchen where one of the daughters was yelling, "Mom, it's burning!"

Anne turned to look at Frank Farman.

"I'm Anne Navarre. Your son's teacher," she said, annoyed. She had met him several times and he had yet to recognize her. She was of no importance to him whatsoever. She imagined no woman was.

"You came here to tell us Dennis wasn't in school?" he asked. "You couldn't pick up a telephone?"

"Actually, I came to see how Dennis is doing after what happened yesterday—"

"He's fine."

"I thought he might be upset—"

"He's not."

"Has Dennis talked to you about what happened?"

"The kids were playing and they found a dead body. What else is there to talk about? He's a kid, for Christ's sake."

"Before this happened he told one of the other kids there were bodies buried in the woods," Anne said. "I wondered if he might have seen something before—"

"Look, Miss Navarre, I'm the sheriff's deputy, you're the teacher. I do my job. Why don't you stick to yours?"

Anne pressed her lips together to keep the words she wanted to say from spilling out.

"I'll deal with Dennis," he said, turning to the hall table to go through his mail.

She took a step toward the door then turned back. "If Dennis has an unexplained absence tomorrow, he'll be on probation. If he has three unexcused absences, he'll be expelled for a week."

"Oh, he'll be there," he guaranteed.

Farman looked at an envelope promising he may already have won a million dollars.

Anger flushed through Anne. "Mr. Farman, could I please have your undivided attention for two minutes?"

He set his mail aside and looked at her with an impatient sigh.

"Does it not bother you at all that your son claimed to know there were bodies buried in the park before anyone actually found a body there?"

"Miss Navarre," he said. "Dennis is a boy. Boys make up stories. I'm not concerned that Dennis saw bodies in the park before because there were no bodies. Believe me, if Dennis had seen a dead body before yesterday, he would have told me because that would be a very big deal to him.

"If you believe everything kids say, you're either crazy or unbelievably gullible," he said.

Anne wanted to kick him in the shin. In the span of a few sentences he had managed to make her feel both stupid and furious. She wanted a brilliant, scathing comeback line, but nothing came.

"Go home, Miss Navarre," Frank Farman said.

"And don't read so many mystery novels."

Anne left the Farman house and stormed back to her car—now blocked in the driveway by Frank Farman's cruiser.

*Condescending ass. "There, there, little lady, don't worry, you're just an imbecile."*

With no regard for possible consequences, she got in her Volkswagen, turned around on Farman's neat lawn, and drove down over the curb to the street.

She needed to speak to Detective Mendez.

# 18

"Hamilton and Hicks are getting copies of employee records from the Thomas Center," Mendez said, glancing at Dixon sitting in the passenger's seat. "I reached out to a guy I know on the job in Simi Valley. He's going to find out what he can on the missing girl's ex-boyfriend."

"Good."

"This will be a hell of a lot faster when we can all get computers."

"Dream on, Detective. We're lucky we have ink pens that write. There's no leeway in the budget for toys."

Mendez let it go. The wave of the future would have to crash over Oak Knoll eventually, but it wouldn't happen in time for this case.

"I spoke to Lisa Warwick's supervisor at

Mercy," he said. "She said Lisa was quiet, did a good job, but didn't call attention to herself."

"Was she seeing someone?"

"The supervisor didn't know. But I found a coworker who says Warwick had hinted there might be a man in her life, but she was pretty tight-lipped about it. The coworker had a hunch the guy might have been married, but she's got nothing to back it up."

"When was the last time anyone from the hospital saw her?"

"About ten days ago."

"And no one reported her missing?"

"She had scheduled time off. She said she was going on a trip to the wine country."

"Check that out. Find out where she had reservations and if she was going alone or if it was supposed to be some kind of romantic getaway."

Mendez checked the rearview mirror, signaled, and slowly changed lanes in the choking LA traffic, leaving the 405 freeway for the Howard Hughes Parkway.

He had thought about moving to LA once he had made detective in Bakersfield. He could have gone to LAPD with the goal of one day making the prestigious Robbery/Homicide Unit that worked out of LAPD headquarters downtown in the Parker Center. But it had seemed a better plan to become a big fish in a smaller pond and put in some solid years, then move on to the big pond of LA with an already established reputation as a detective.

When he had the opportunity to go to Oak Knoll and work under Cal Dixon, he had jumped at the chance. Dixon had a solid rep with the LA County Sheriff's office; he had contacts. With this job, Mendez knew he could stand out. If Dixon liked him, this job could provide him a shortcut to bigger things.

So far that plan had worked very well.

As daylight faded into evening, Mendez entered LA International Airport, followed the signs, and parked in the garage opposite the American Airlines terminal.

At first glance through the throng of people arriving into baggage claim from the Dulles/LAX flight, he didn't see Leone. He was looking for a man slightly larger than life, dressed in a flashy suit with a loud tie, a big white grin splitting his face. He scanned the crowd more slowly, spotting a tall, thin man coming toward them with a wheeled suitcase tagging along behind him. The long face broke into a familiar smile.

"Tony! It's good to see you."

Mendez met the handshake. "Jesus, Vince, I almost didn't recognize you. You've lost thirty pounds."

Leone waved off the remark. "It's a long story." He offered his hand to Dixon. "You're Cal Dixon. Vince Leone. It's a pleasure to meet you. Bruce Washington from LA County SO is an old friend of mine."

Leone was a master at disarming people. He greeted every stranger as a long-lost friend. He had gotten a lot of confessions out of suspects that way, luring them in with a smile and a pat on the back.

"I haven't heard from Bruce in a while," Dixon said.

"He's gone into the private sector—executive security. Somehow, he thought making a pile of dough beat the glory and accolades of being a civil servant. Go figure."

He nodded toward the exit doors. "Shall we, gentlemen? I don't want to hold up the show."

What Vince wanted was to lie down on the ground and pass out after the trek through the terminal. He had been determined to get to baggage claim ahead of Mendez and Dixon, so he could have a minute to catch his breath and spot them before they spotted him. The five-and-a-half-hour flight had drained him. He had time to amp up his energy and muster the big grin, even while he questioned his sanity at coming here.

*Show no weakness*, he reminded himself. The first rule of thumb in dealing with the locals.

Exhausting himself doing something necessary was far preferable to lying around thinking about the shrapnel in his brain. So he wouldn't think now about how his head was pounding or how he was beginning to feel edgy and shaky. All he had to do was keep himself together a little longer. All he had to do was get through an autopsy, then the drive up to Oak Knoll, then finding his hotel . . .

Mendez briefed him as they drove across town to the LA County Coroner's facility on North Mission Road. Vince taped the conversation on a pocket-size recorder. He would make notes later. He had already started gathering impressions of the situation.

Dixon had the shield of authority up. He was too smart to drop his guard just because they had one person in common. This case was his baby. He was running the show and he didn't want some G-man coming in and upsetting the balance of power.

That was nothing new. Cops were territorial animals. They all pissed on the fences. Some of them more than others. And no doubt, Dixon had checked him out as well. He could have heard a hundred stories of Vince Leone cutting a wide swath everywhere he went, drawing the media like flies to a rump roast.

He had a certain reputation for being loud and flamboyant, always cracking wise with his unapologetic Chicago accent. What Dixon wouldn't have heard was that he did what he had to do to make his case. If that meant drawing a killer out with a challenge or a taunt or whatever, that was what he did.

They parked in sight of the receiving zone and got out of the car. Vince sucked in the night air, filling and emptying his lungs several times. It was the last fresh breath they would have until the autopsy was over.

"Okay, fellas," he said to Dixon and Mendez. "Before we go in, I have to tell you about my capacity here. ISU can't take your case yet. Right now, it would be a stretch to say it meets the criteria enough to warrant assigning an agent while they're swamped with bigger cases."

Dixon gave him the eagle-eye. "Then what are you doing here?"

"I think it's only a matter of time before you have another body. This latest murder demonstrates your UNSUB has a pretty advanced and sophisticated fantasy he's acting on. That didn't develop overnight. He's killed before. He'll kill again. I'd like to help you nail this creep before you've got a big body count, not after."

"If Investigative Support wouldn't take the case, and you're one of the founding fathers of Investigative Support," Dixon said, "then you're here . . . ?"

"Under the radar," he admitted. "I'll help as much as I can help."

"Out of the kindness of your heart?" Dixon asked.

"Not exactly," Vince said. "I'm exploring the possibilities of continuing education of law enforcement personnel in the field as an extension of what we do at the National Academy."

Sounded good—as long as Dixon didn't have a line to his higher-ups in the Bureau to check it out.

"Correct me if I'm mistaken," Vince said, "but I don't think either one of you has direct experience with this kind of killer. I have more than most people could ever stomach in three lifetimes. I have access to every resource and contact ISU has. I'm just not here in an official capacity.

"So, if you're worried about me attracting attention," he said specifically to Dixon, "trying to take over your case, you can relax."

"Good to know," Dixon said, holding back questions and skepticism. Vince could feel it. He could see it in Dixon's body language. But the sheriff would put it aside for now. He had an autopsy to go to. He turned and headed for the building.

Vince and Mendez fell in half a dozen paces behind.

"So, what's the long story?" Mendez asked. "You look a little rough, Vince."

Vince laughed. He had seen himself in the men's room mirror. "I look like shit, kid. I've got an ulcer." Which was true. He had an ulcer from eating painkillers instead of food.

"Airplane food," he said, rolling his eyes. "It's nothing to worry about. God knows how I managed not to have one until now."

Mendez looked suspicious. "You're okay?"

"Perfect."

"You grew a mustache," Mendez said meaningfully.

"Just trying to blend in with you local boys," Vince said. "Let's go look at your stiff."

# 19

The first impression of the LA County morgue was the smell. The ventilation system wasn't great, but the amount of dead bodies processed through was. No one in the receiving area seemed bothered by it.

Dixon was shooting the breeze with a group of coroner's assistants sitting at a long white table as they waited for their next delivery. When it arrived, the body would be measured, finger-printed, photographed, wrapped in plastic, and put in cold storage, where it would wait its turn for an autopsy if an autopsy was deemed necessary. In the meantime, they took a little break to chat, drink coffee, and listen to the bug zapper sizzle.

"Busy day?" Dixon asked, helping himself to the carton of malted milk balls on the table.

"The usual," said a burly assistant, a bald man the size of a bear, with blue tattoos up and down arms as thick as small tree trunks. He had the demeanor of a man who had been around the morgue for a long time. The kind of guy who could roll in a maggot-riddled corpse, then sit down and eat an egg-salad sandwich.

The lone female assistant, a cute brunette twenty-something, said, "Fourteen field calls, three homicides, four suicides, and six accidental deaths."

"And a partridge in a pear tree?" Vince asked.

The girl laughed.

"Get this," the burly guy said. "Two of the accidental deaths were guys that fell out of trees while trying to rescue cats. Dumb shits. Who ever saw a cat skeleton up in a tree? The damn things will get down when they want."

"They were probably trying to impress their girlfriends," Vince said.

The girl rolled her eyes. "Any woman who wants a guy that stupid should be taken out of the gene pool."

Vince flashed a grin at her. "Now where's your sense of romance?"

She laughed again. "I don't bring it here."

"Anyone seen Mikado?" Dixon asked.

"Third suite," the big guy said. "He's waiting for you."

"Thanks."

"Good to see you, Cal."

"You too, Buck."

Vince winked at the girl, pleased that she winked back. Maybe he didn't look so bad after all.

He fell in step beside Dixon.

"You pulled some big strings to get your vic bumped to the head of the line in this place."

The LA County morgue was legendary. Open 24/7/365, something like twenty thousand autopsies were conducted there every year. There were around two hundred fifty corpses stacked on stainless steel shelves in the crypt on any given day.

"I spent a lot of years spinning those strings," Dixon said. "If there was ever a time to pull them, it's now."

They went into one of the three autopsy suites and slipped into yellow gowns and booties, and white surgical masks so as not to contaminate or be contaminated. The pathologist and his staff were in blue gowns. Some wore goggles or face shields. One wore a small gas mask. Introductions were made by Dixon.

"Mik, this is my detective Tony Mendez and Special Agent Vince Leone, FBI. Tony, Vince: Assistant Chief Medical Examiner-Coroner Dr. Mik Mikado."

Mikado was the one in the gas mask. He raised his eyebrows. "Wow. You're bringing in the BIG guns, Cal." He nodded to Vince. "Pleased to meet you. I'm a big fan."

Vince rolled his eyes. "No autographs, please. I'm just here helping out. There's the star of this show," he said, nodding toward the dead woman laid out naked on the stainless steel table. "Let's see what she has to say."

They settled into the serious business. On the far side of the suite, another autopsy was well under way, the coroner and assistants moving quietly around one another, like dancers performing the same choreography for the hundredth time. A bone saw whined. Steel instruments clanked against steel trays. One of the gowned people approached the table with a huge red-handled tree pruner for cutting ribs.

Mikado began the visual examination.

Lisa Warwick had been a pretty girl in life: dark hair, heart-shaped face, curvy body. The final chapter in her life, however, had not been pretty at all. She had been tortured over who knew how long a period of time. She had been missing as many as ten days. Vince had never known of a serial killer who showed his victims a good time before he killed them. And this one was no exception.

The woman's torso was a macabre artist's palette of purple, blue, green, and yellow—severe bruising, particularly to the breasts and lower abdomen. The beating had been inflicted over the course of days according to the variations in color.

Her tormentor had used a fine-bladed knife to inflict deep cutting wounds all over her body, from the soles of her feet to her fingers to her breasts. The first finger of the left hand was missing. Her nipples had been excised.

Her killer had probably kept the parts to help him relive the event. He may have even incorporated them into his daily life somehow. The infamous murderer Ed Gein, "The Butcher of Plainfield," who had operated in rural Wisconsin in the 1950s, had used the skin of his victims to make lampshades, among other things. Or this killer might have ingested the body parts in a ritual intended to make his victim become a part of himself.

Whatever his intent, the torture appeared to have been very systematic. There were no hesitation marks in the knife wounds, and the cuts seemed deliberately placed, though the pattern suggested nothing in particular.

Crosses cut into victims were always popular among psychotic killers and had the obvious religious connotations. Initials were not uncommon. He had once worked a case in Philadelphia in which a nun had been savagely raped and murdered in the sanctuary of a church, the word "SIN" carved into her forehead with a penknife.

On this victim the lines added up to nothing, but some were vertical and others horizontal, and he had the feeling the pattern meant something to the killer.

The coroner went to raise one of the victim's eyelids.

"They're glued shut," Mendez said. "The mouth too."

"Looks like more than once on the mouth," Vince said, stepping in for a closer look. "Look at the lines, the pieces of flesh missing here and here. I'd guess he glued her mouth shut and at some point during the torture she tore her lips open to scream."

"Jesus," Mendez muttered under his breath.

Vince produced a collapsible Polaroid camera from his coat pocket under his surgical gown and snapped a couple of pictures of the lips and of the cuts on the body.

"Can we get some scrapings of the glue from the eyes and mouth for the FBI lab, please?" he asked Mikado then turned to Dixon. "If they can figure out exactly what kind of adhesive it is, and it turns out to be something unusual, that could be helpful."

Mikado also collected fingernail clippings in a small paper envelope to be sent on to the LA County lab, in case the victim had managed to scratch her assailant at some point. They might be able to get some skin, get a blood type.

"Did you get any trace evidence?" Vince asked.

Mikado cut him a meaningful look. "The body was clean when it got here."

Vince shot a look at Dixon.

"The funeral home thought they were doing a good deed, cleaning her up," Dixon said, clearly knowing they may have lost evidence. Any fibers, hairs, or bodily fluids that may have clung to the body were long gone down a drain.

"No sense crying over what we don't have," Vince said. "After all the publicity on the Atlanta child murder trial and how trace evidence nailed Wayne Williams's ass, the more intelligent criminals have started cleaning up after themselves."

"Maybe we'll get something on the vaginal swabs," Mikado offered.

In fact, the autopsy yielded little in the way of evidence. No bite marks that might be matched with a suspect. No marks from any distinctive type of weapon. Lisa Warwick had been strangled with a ligature of some kind, but it had left no marks save bruising, and no fibers of any kind. Some kind of smooth cloth, Vince figured—a scarf, a necktie, pantyhose. Nothing traceable.

There was predictable deep bruising in the muscles of the neck, but the hyoid bone (a small U-shaped bone situated between the base of the tongue and the larynx) was still intact. To Vince's mind, this, and the lack of bruising caused by fingers, ruled out manual strangulation.

Mikado was unable to raise an eyelid to reveal the almost-certain presence of petechial hemorrhaging in the conjunctivae of the eye—a sure sign of asphyxia. And all attempts to remove the lids from the eyes only resulted in tearing of the eye itself.

"Just send the whole mess to Washington," Vince said, imagining the unpleasant surprise of opening a box to find a pair of mangled eyeballs. "They'll figure out a way to get to the glue."

Separating the lips was an easier job. Inside Lisa Warwick's mouth they found she had bitten her tongue to the consistency of ground hamburger.

Mikado looked inside the victim's ears and swore under his breath. "Her eardrums have been pierced with something. They're destroyed."

"The third piece of our trifecta, gentlemen," Vince said quietly. "See no evil. Speak no evil. Hear no evil."

Mendez turned gray as the images sank in. He went to a trash can marked NO TRASH. ORGANS ONLY and threw up.

Even Dixon, who had seen his share of abject violence, looked undone by this. He turned away, shaking his head. The idea that Lisa Warwick had been literally locked inside her own head with a terror of something so evil was too much to fathom.

Vince would have said a prayer for the girl, born and bred Catholic that he was. But he had not been on speaking terms with God in a very long time. He found a stool off to the side of the autopsy bay and sat down on it, tuning out as Mikado's assistant turned on the oscillating saw to pop the cap off Lisa Warwick's brain.

Over the years he had seen so many cases as brutal as this one, and every one of them left him feeling like ten years had been drained from his life. He felt as old as Methuselah, as brittle as bone. He felt as if he would turn to dust and fall to the yellow-tiled floor to be swept up later with the medical waste.

"How do you get used to it?" Mendez asked quietly.

"Kid," Vince said. "The day you get used to *this,* turn in your shield and your gun. You won't belong to the human race anymore."

# 20

"So what are you thinking, darling?" Franny asked. He handed her a glass of white zinfandel and sat down beside her on her back porch steps. "Are you harboring a fugitive in your fifth-grade class?"

Anne drank a good third of the glass. The evening was chilly. They were both wrapped in thick sweaters. They sat close together to share body heat while Franny's basset hound and cocker spaniel sniffed their way around the backyard, drifting in and out of the pale back porch light.

"Of course not. I just find it unnerving that Dennis may have seen something going on in the woods before yesterday. Are there other bodies out there? What the hell is going on? Now another woman is missing . . ."

"It's like yesterday we woke up in a Disney movie, and tonight we're in a John Carpenter movie," Franny said. "Maybe Jamie Lee Curtis will play you in our movie."

Anne looked at him from the corner of her eye. "Will you be my sidekick?"

"Honey, I AM your sidekick."

"Who will play you in the movie?"

"Richard Gere, of course," he answered without hesitation. "He's secretly gay, you know."

"You think every good-looking man on the planet is secretly gay."

"No, I don't. The hot detective from this morning? Definitely not gay."

"You didn't see him. How do you know he's hot?"

He grinned like the Cheshire Cat. "You just told me."

Heat rushed to Anne's face. She blamed the wine.

"You should definitely take a run at him."

"He's a little busy right now," Anne said. "So am I. I need to find a way to get through to Dennis. Frank Farman tells me Dennis is fine. He found a horribly murdered woman, but why should that bother him? I guess if it wasn't the first dead person he's seen buried in the woods, it's old hat to him."

"He probably made it up, honey," Franny said. "Dennis Farman is a nasty, creepy little shit. He's been looking up his teacher's skirts since he was in the third grade. He's probably got a collection of S and M porn magazines under his bed by now. It's not a stretch to imagine him making up stories about bodies buried in the woods just to scare other kids."

Anne sighed, reaching out a hand to touch the nose of Chester the basset hound, who had lumbered up the steps to check on them. "I guess not. He did try to bring a dead cat for show-and-tell one day."

"No effing way!"

"Oh, yeah. The first week of class. He found it on the road on the way to school, flattened."

146

Anne shuddered at the memory of the incident, and at the memory of the look in Dennis Farman's eyes. She had dismissed it that day, preoccupied with the need to properly dispose of the carcass, but she could see it now in her mind's eye: a weird kind of excitement that went beyond a child's natural curiosity.

"He probably bit it and gave it rabies," Franny said. "Why didn't you tell me about it?"

"You were out sick," Anne said. "The root canal."

"Oh my God!" he exclaimed, dramatically throwing his head back and clamping his hand over his heart. "I thought I would die! That was horrible. I thought I would have to go directly from Dr. Crane's office to the morgue."

"Peter Crane?" Anne asked. "Tommy's father?"

"Yes. Dr. Dream Dentist. He's hot."

"But not gay."

"No. And his wife scares me. Have you seen those shoulder pads? Yikes! Honey, Joan Crawford had nothing on that one."

"So I'm learning," Anne said.

She checked her watch and sighed. She had gone to the sheriff's office to speak personally to Mendez, but had been told he was gone for the day. She had called the number on his card and left a message for him to call her back as soon as possible. She had yet to hear from him.

Now that it was getting late and she was worn out

from the day's events, she began to think maybe she had overreacted, that Mendez would listen to her message and roll his eyes and think she was being hysterical. He and Frank Farman could have a laugh at her expense.

"You know," she said. "I've always felt like I can read my kids pretty easily. I'm a quick study. I meet their parents at conference time and think I have a handle on their home life. Boy, was I naïve . . . or arrogant . . . or something."

Franny put his arm around her and hugged her tight against him. "Put it away for tonight. Tomorrow is another day, Scarlett."

"That's what I'm afraid of. What happens tomorrow? The four horsemen of the apocalypse ride into town? I've lived here my whole life. People don't get murdered in Oak Knoll. Women don't get kidnapped. Fifth graders don't find dead bodies in the park," she said. "*I'm* upset. *I'm* scared. How are my kids supposed to deal with it? How am I supposed to convincingly help them deal with it?"

"You do the best you can," Franny said. "It's easier for me. Five-year-olds are focused on themselves, their immediate little worlds. And their immediate little worlds are safe and mostly happy. They don't really understand death. They don't know what evil is.

"Your kids have started to figure out there's a world out there that isn't always a nice place. I don't think it's a bad thing that you let them know it scares you too," he said.

"Fear: the human condition," Anne said. "Hey, kids, this is what you have to look forward to as you grow up: a world gone mad."

Franny tossed back the last of his wine and set the glass aside. "Enough of your dark thoughts, Negative Nancy. I'm going to pour more wine, and then we're going to talk about my favorite topic: me! I'm going to throw a fabulous party for my fortieth birthday next year. It's going to have a carnival theme. I'm calling it *Franival*!"

Tired as she was, Anne managed to laugh. "I love you, Francis."

He smiled like a saint. "Everyone does."

# 21

Game one of the 1985 National League Championship Series. The St. Louis Cardinals versus the incredibly awesome best team in baseball: the Los Angeles Dodgers.

The day before, Tommy had thought about how much fun it would be: just him and his dad on the couch in the family room, watching the game, eating hot dogs and popcorn, drinking sodas (strictly forbidden by his mother). Wednesday nights his mother had a meeting of one of her many organizations and didn't get home until late.

Now the game was playing, and Tommy wanted

to lose himself in it and get excited and cheer for his team, but he couldn't make himself feel the way he wanted to. He sat on the couch, his too-big Dodgers T-shirt swallowing him up, his scorecard abandoned on the coffee table with his Dodgers souvenir pencil. Fernando Valenzuela was pitching. The Dodgers were up by one in the top of the sixth.

His father sat at the end of the couch, reading newspapers during the commercials. *Los Angeles Times, Santa Barbara News-Press, The Oak Knoll Independent.* Every so often he would look over.

"What are you thinking, Sport?"

Tommy shrugged.

"Are you hungry? I can make the popcorn now."

Tommy shook his head. He glanced over at the paper his dad had put down on the coffee table. There was a photograph of yellow crime-scene tape tied to two trees and uniformed deputies bent over looking at the ground. The headline read: MURDER IN THE PARK. Below it, in smaller bold type: CHILDREN MAKE GRUESOME DISCOVERY.

"I'm just making sure none of these has the names of you kids in the story," his father said.

Tommy said nothing. He didn't want his name in the paper. Unlike Wendy, he wanted this all to go away as quickly as possible.

"Dad? What's a cereal killer?" he asked. "How can you kill someone with cereal?"

"Not cereal, like breakfast cereal," his father

said. "Serial with an *s*, as in a series of events. A serial killer kills a number of people over a period of time."

"Why would anyone do that? Are they mad at the people they kill? Or are they just crazy?"

His father seemed to think about his answer before he gave it. "I don't think people really understand why someone turns out to be a serial killer. I think it's really complicated. But it's not something you need to worry about, Tommy."

"How do you know? What if the killer saw us, and now he wants to kill us too?"

"That isn't going to happen," his father promised. "I'm not going to let that happen. Miss Navarre isn't going to let that happen. Detective Mendez isn't going to let that happen. You don't need to worry, son. You're safe. We're all going to keep you safe. Okay?"

Tommy didn't answer because he didn't want to tell a lie. Instead, he sat closer to his dad and pretended to feel safe while the Dodgers came up to bat.

Later in the evening, a few blocks away, Wendy sat under her covers with a flashlight illuminating her makeshift tent as she scribbled away in a spiral notebook.

She had told Tommy she was going to write their story and sell it to Hollywood for a movie. Maybe they would even get to be in it. She liked the idea of being an actress, as long as it didn't get in the way of her being a journalist. All Tommy had said was that it was going to be a really short story.

"No, it isn't," Wendy said. They had been sitting outside in the sun during the lunch hour, Wendy busily making notes. "Finding the dead body is just the first scene. Now we have to find out who the dead lady is, and who killed her, and why."

"That's the detective's job," Tommy pointed out. "I'm not even allowed to play outside now."

Wendy made a face. "Your mother can't watch you all the time. She has a job. We have to go back to the woods."

"No, we don't."

"Where's your sense of adventure?"

"It's grounded until further notice."

"Don't be such a wuss," Wendy said, annoyed. "In a couple of days our parents won't care anymore. Promise you'll go with me back to the woods."

Tommy looked frustrated with her, as he often did. But he always caved in the end.

She batted her eyelashes like her mom did when she wanted something from her dad. "Come on, Tommy. You said you would protect me. You can keep an eye out in case that dog comes back."

"Or the killer," Tommy said.

"That would make a great scene in the movie!"

She made notes about it now, as she hid under her covers. She and Tommy were in the woods, creeping carefully toward the place where the body had been buried. It would be almost dark. Maybe there would be thunder and lightning. That would add to the excitement. The killer would be creeping through the woods too, watching them. And just as she and Tommy came around a huge tree, the lightning would flash, and THERE HE IS!!!! Looming over them, his ugly face twisted, eyes bugging out of his head, claw-like hands grabbing at them. Their hearts would be pounding as they jumped back and screamed.

Tears filled Wendy's eyes, and she flung the covers back sending pen and notebook flying. *OHMYGOD! OHMYGOD! OHMYGOD!!! WHAT IF IT REALLY HAPPENED THAT WAY?*

Wendy leapt out of bed and beat it out of her room and down the stairs, yelling, "MOM!!!"

In another house, in another part of town, Cody Roache was awake in his bed too. He didn't like being awake at night when his mom was asleep and his dad was at work. He *always* heard sounds in the house. Floorboards creaking. Footsteps coming down the hall. And he would hold his breath and try to listen harder until all he could hear was the sound of his pulse pounding in his ears.

He sat in his bed with the covers pulled up around his chin. He was shaking like crazy. Dennis would have called him a pussy.

Dennis had seen dead bodies in the woods. Cody thought about running through the woods, playing commando, stepping on the dead bodies as they ran. He thought he might never sleep again, because in his nightmares he was running through the woods and a hand reached up out of the ground and grabbed him by the ankle. Then he fell down. Then all the dead people started getting up out of the ground as zombies, their flesh rotting, eyeballs falling out of their heads. And he ran to Dennis for help, but Dennis turned into a zombie too, and came after him.

*Don't worry about Dennis,* Miss Navarre had said.

Miss Navarre was nice. Cody appreciated her coming over just to see him. That had never happened before in his whole life—an adult coming to the house just to see him—and not because he was in trouble, either.

But Miss Navarre didn't know very much about Dennis. She didn't know the kinds of things Dennis liked to talk about, like doing bad things to girls. And she didn't know that sometimes Dennis would just get really mad and hit him for no reason. If Miss Navarre knew those things about Dennis, Cody thought, she would be scared too. And she probably wouldn't want to sleep, either.

Dennis didn't want to sleep. He wanted to be mad. He wanted to hit someone, kick someone. Miss Navarre came to mind. Stupid bitch. It was all her fault his father had come after him with his belt. If she would have minded her own business, but no, she had to COME TO HIS HOUSE to personally tell his parents he had been absent from school.

His back and butt were still stinging like stripes of fire where his father had hit him for lying and for skipping school. He lay now on his stomach because he couldn't lie any other way. He pushed himself up onto his knees, the anger inside him spinning around like a wild animal. He didn't know what to do with it, so he started hitting his pillow with both fists, over and over and over.

He pretended the pillow was Miss Navarre's face, and he punched her and punched her until there was nothing but blood.

*Stupid bitch. Fucking cunt.*

The rage welled up in him again, and he punched the pillow some more until his arms were tired and tears were running down his face.

He would show them all one day. Nobody would push him around or embarrass him or tell him he was worthless. He would be the one doing the pushing. They would all be afraid of him.

Dennis slipped out of bed, got down on the floor, and stuck his arm as far under the bed as he could reach until he got hold of what he wanted. The flashlight he had shoplifted from the hardware store. With the yellow beam of light leading his way, he went to his closet and dug down deep through the pile of dirty clothes to the old cigar box he kept hidden there.

Pride filled him that he had been able to get away with it. No one had seen him take the thing. No one had suspected he had it in his pocket. Cops all around, and no one had caught him.

He took the box over by the window and set it down on the chair. Still holding the flashlight in one hand, he opened the lid and peered inside.

The cigar box was where he kept his most treasured possessions: his pocketknife, the cigarettes he had stolen from his mother, a lighter, the dried-out head of a rattlesnake he had watched a gardener kill, and his newest, most prized addition.

It was squishy and had started to smell, but that only added to the wonderful grossness of it. This was what the corpse would smell like if they had left it in the ground. It excited him to think about it.

He smiled as he carefully lifted the treasure out of the box and held it under the light.

The severed finger of a dead woman.

# 22

Thursday, October 10, 1985
*1:37 A.M.*

Karly Vickers lay in absolute darkness, in absolute silence, in absolute pain, in absolute terror.

Most people would never in their lives know what true terror really is. There were no adjectives to describe it. It was like the hottest, whitest light and the fiercest, highest-pitched sound imaginable put together to assault every part of the brain and nervous system. And even that was an inadequate description.

She remembered very little about her abduction—a moment of recognition, but no memory of a face; a blast of panic, like a bomb going off inside her, then nothing. What had followed was both surreal and too real. Nothing made sense except the pain.

She had no idea when the pain would come, or from where. She had no concept of time, of day or night. She couldn't always tell up from down. Sometimes she felt like she was falling only to realize with a start that she was lying flat. She could see nothing. She could hear nothing. She couldn't open her mouth to speak.

She had no idea how long she had been in this place, or where or what this place was. It was cold. The thing she lay on was hard. She was in too much pain to feel hunger. Periodically, a straw was inserted in the smallest of gaps between her lips, and she was given water, just enough to keep her alive.

The fear would come on her in waves, huge waves that crashed over her, leaving her struggling for air, struggling against her bonds. She had no idea when her tormentor would come, what he would do to her, when he would leave. Because she couldn't hear him, couldn't see him, the only way she knew he was there was to have him inflict pain on her.

When the panic exhausted her, sometimes she would think about the job she was supposed to have started. Had they told anyone she hadn't come to work? Had anyone gone to the cottage to check on her? Had her mother begun to wonder why she hadn't called Sunday night? Was anyone taking care of Petal?

Then she would start to cry, but her eyes produced no tears, nor could she open her eyelids to let them escape if they had come. She could feel the sobs wrack her chest, but if any sound came out at all, she couldn't hear it.

Why would anyone do this to her?

Early on, before her hearing had been destroyed, she had heard another woman struggle, had heard a single, blood-curdling scream that had cut through her like a knife. But that had been what seemed long ago. She had no way of knowing if that woman was still here. She thought not. She felt so alone.

That was the worst thing: the isolation, the sense of being trapped inside her own body, inside her own mind.

She began to pray that the next time her tormentor came he would kill her.

He sat on a stool at the foot of the metal table, watching his victim, wondering what must be going through her mind. Was she still sane? Had she tried to imagine who her tormentor was?

This was his other life, his release from the so-called normal world where pressures built inside him on a daily basis; where the demands on his time, on his energy, on his sense of self came from other people with their own expectations of who he was and who he should be. A husband, a father, a professional, an upstanding citizen.

With his victim, he was in control, he could let loose the self that existed in the innermost part of him.

It excited him that his victim didn't know and would never have suspected who he really was. She had believed him to be trustworthy and deserving of respect. Respect had taken on a whole new meaning in the face of his absolute control of her.

Absolute control. Absolute power.

Absolutely thrilling.

# 23

Thursday, October 10, 1985
*6:15 A.M.*

Mendez and Hicks took the first pass through Karly Vickers's, wanting to see it pristine, exactly as she had left it. It was a small place, neat as a pin. They went carefully through drawers and closets, looking for anything that might have pointed to Vickers having a current boyfriend or a current connection to her past boyfriend, the Simi Valley thug.

She had crossed Greg Usher's entry out of her address book. If she was still in contact with him, the contact probably wasn't being initiated by her. Mendez held the book open for Jane Thomas to see.

"I told you she was through with him," she said.

"People don't always turn out to be as strong as we would like for them to be, ma'am," he said. "That's part of my job."

"Disillusionment?"

"Sometimes. Doubt, always."

He would have preferred not to have her there. He knew she was anxious, and she was undoubtedly feeling violated on behalf of her client as she watched them go through Karly Vickers's things.

That was how he had felt when he was a teenager, and the cops had come to search his family home: violated. They had been looking for evidence against his older brother, a gang member accused of dealing drugs. They had gone through the house like a human tornado, with no regard for personal property or personal feelings. He remembered his mother crying as they riffled through her dresser, touching her clothing, her undergarments, her mementos.

He had never forgotten that when he searched

through the homes of victims and perps alike. A little respect went a long way.

Hicks turned the bedding down and pulled the shades. Mendez turned off the lamp then went over the sheets with a black light, looking for bodily fluids—specifically semen—to fluoresce. There was nothing.

"She isn't seeing anyone," Jane Thomas said. "She's been completely focused on getting her life on track."

"Is she always this neat?" Hicks asked.

"She always was at the center. She's very respectful of the chances she's been given."

"Does she have any close friends that you know of?" Mendez asked. "Any of the other women at the center? Someone she might confide in if she was interested in someone or if someone was bothering her?"

"Maybe Brandy Henson. I saw them together a lot."

This was why he allowed Jane Thomas to hang close. She knew Karly Vickers, knew about her life, her friends. There was a good chance if something wasn't right here, it would jump out at her.

Unfortunately, as they made their way through the tiny house, nothing jumped out. Mendez opened the front door and motioned in the crime scene team.

"They're going to dust for fingerprints," he said as he held the back door open for Thomas. "It'll be a mess. But if there was anyone else in here, we'll know about it. If any of the prints match up with a known offender, we'll have a direction to go in."

Of course, months could pass before they got a match, but he didn't mention that. Comparing latent fingerprints was a manual needle-in-a-haystack process that relied completely on the trained eye of a fingerprint specialist. Someday the system would be automated and offender prints would go into a national database easily accessed. But the prints taken today would be of little use until they had a suspect to compare them with, a scenario that was less than optimal for Karly Vickers if she had in fact been abducted.

"Anything you need to do."

"We'll want to get her phone records. Is the account in her name?"

"No. The account will be in the name of the center with a numeric suffix. That's how it's set up with all the properties we own. The numbers are all unlisted." She forced an ironic smile, looking off in the distance as if she might see Karly Vickers down the street. "We take all the precautions we can to keep the women as safe as possible. The bills come to the center and are on file. But Karly just moved into this house. We haven't had a bill yet."

"We'll get the local usage details from the phone company."

"What about search and rescue?" she asked. "Why aren't there search parties out looking for her?"

"You'd have to ask Sheriff Dixon that question, ma'am," Mendez said.

He was glad to dodge the question himself even though he knew the answer. Dixon hadn't moved on a search because they had no idea where to begin searching. They had no idea where Karly Vickers had gone missing, what direction she might have gone in or been taken. With her car still missing, Jane Thomas or no Jane Thomas, they still had to consider that Karly Vickers might have left of her own free will. She might have received a threat from the ex-boyfriend, panicked, and taken off to parts unknown.

"If she was the twelve-year-old daughter of some professor, he would have called out the National Guard by now," she said angrily.

"I know the helicopter is going up this morning," Mendez said. "They'll be looking for her car, and for Lisa Warwick's car."

They would be looking for a body, as well, but he didn't mention that.

"Miss Vickers's picture will be in every paper and on every news channel in California by tonight. If someone has seen her, then we have a starting point for a ground search."

The sun was a fat orange ball ten feet off the horizon, up but not yet strong enough to burn off the damp chill clinging to the fall air. Mendez was glad for the sport coat he had on. Jane Thomas was wrapped in a hand-knit, moss green sweater that reflected the color of her eyes—except for the red rims from hours of crying.

He felt bad for her. To find out someone you knew had been murdered was a terrible thing. To find out someone else you knew was missing and could very well be the next murder victim . . . he couldn't imagine.

The backyard of the cottage was fenced in to contain the pit bull that sidled up to Jane Thomas, growling low in its throat. Not a warning growl so much as a sound of discontentment. The dog sat and leaned against the woman's legs, looking mournfully up at her.

"This is Petal?" Mendez asked.

"Yes. I took her home with me last night. She's lost without Karly."

He lifted his Polaroid and snapped a shot of the dog. He would take it to Anne Navarre later to see if her students could ID this as the dog they had seen in the woods.

Maybe the dog had jumped the fence and had been in search of its owner when it had come across the body of Lisa Warwick. If this was television, they would give Petal a piece of Karly Vickers's clothing to sniff, and the dog would bark and take off, leading them to her owner who was trapped in the lair of a madman.

Unfortunately, they weren't living in a TV show, and Mendez had never known a pit bull to be much in the way of a hunting dog.

"We'll have deputies interview all the neighbors," he said. "To see if maybe someone saw her leave the house, or saw her with anyone, or saw someone going into the house.

"The fact that her car isn't here makes me think she probably met her abductor elsewhere," he said. "We'll need a list of everyone you know she saw on Thursday."

"I can tell you," she said. "She was at the center. She saw the staff. She had her hair and nails done at Spice Salon. She had her teeth cleaned."

"What dentist?" Mendez asked, pulling out his notebook and pen.

"Either Dr. Pratt or Dr. Crane. They both offer their services to the center."

Petal the pit bull got to her feet and began to growl in earnest. The back door of the cottage opened and Frank Farman stepped out.

"I've got two units here to start knocking on doors," he said. He looked at Jane Thomas. "You'd better have a leash on that dog, ma'am. That's a dangerous animal."

Jane Thomas took hold of the dog's pink collar. "Only to people she doesn't like."

Farman frowned at her.

"Thanks, Frank," Mendez said. "Can you send a unit over to the Warwick woman's residence? We'll canvass that neighborhood as well. Hicks and I will be heading over there next."

"They're already there."

"Great. Thanks."

Farman shot another disapproving glance at the still-growling dog and went back into the cottage.

Petal settled on Jane's feet, grumbling. Thomas patted her big square head. "Good girl, Petal."

Mendez raised an eyebrow. "You know Frank?"

"I know his wife, Sharon. She's a secretary for Quinn, Morgan—the same firm Karly was going to work for. In my humble opinion, her husband is a condescending, misogynistic ass."

He dismissed the remark. Frank being a chauvinist was not news. Farman was old-school and had been vocal in his objection to the idea of hiring female deputies. He had hardly been alone in his opinion. Law enforcement was traditionally the bastion of men. A lot of them wanted to keep it that way.

He left Jane Thomas with Petal the pit bull and drove with Bill Hicks a mile or so across town to the home of Lisa Warwick for their second search of the day.

The address they had been given by the personnel office at Mercy General was a beige stucco side-by-side duplex a few blocks from the hospital in one direction, a few blocks from the college in the other direction. The landlord met them with the key.

"I can't believe Lisa is the woman those kids found in the park," the man said as he opened the front door.

166

Donald Kent, professor of economics, was a neat, distinguished gentleman with a Colonel Sanders goatee and a blue-striped yellow bow tie at the throat of his buttondown shirt.

"How well did you know Miss Warwick?" Hicks asked.

"Enough to say hello, to chat about nothing." He had the kind of well-modulated voice that belonged on public radio. "A very nice young woman. Never a problem. Always pays—paid—her rent early, if you can imagine that. She told me she had family in Sacramento."

"They've been contacted," Mendez said. "They're driving down today. In case they contact you, they won't be able to come in here until we're through with the investigation. The place will be sealed."

Kent seemed troubled at the idea. "I'm sorry for them. I think if I lost someone so suddenly, I would take some comfort being in their surroundings at least."

"I think it's going to be difficult for them to take comfort in much of anything, considering," Mendez said.

"How did she die?"

"I'm not at liberty to say."

"Were you aware of Miss Warwick dating anyone, having company over?" Hicks asked.

The professor shook his head. "I didn't see her that frequently. I live in another building on the next block. She wasn't one to talk about her private life, though, and I'm not one to ask."

He glanced at his watch. "Unless you gentlemen need me, I have a faculty meeting at nine."

Mendez thanked him and let him go.

"Our job would be so much easier if our victims were loud, obnoxious, and talked incessantly about their sex lives," Hicks said as he browsed the contents of Lisa Warwick's bookshelf in the living room. "Like my wife's sister, for instance. Every person who has ever been within earshot of that woman knows all the details about every guy she's ever slept with."

Mendez chuckled. Hicks was a little older than him. Tall, lean, and red-haired, he was a cowboy in his free time. He had an easygoing way about him, and never had a problem with someone else being lead on an investigation. That was not the case with everyone in the department. There were guys with more years on the job who openly resented Mendez for being Dixon's chosen one. All Hicks cared about was working at a case until it was solved. They worked well together.

"Glad I'm not one of them," Mendez said, snooping in a buffet drawer.

"You fail to meet her low standards," Hicks said. "You're employed and have all your own teeth."

They searched in a comfortable silence for few minutes before Hicks went back to his original point.

"We have to have two vics that never said boo to anybody."

"I'm betting that's not a coincidence," Mendez said. "Just like it's not a coincidence they both had some connection to the Thomas Center. I don't think they were random victims, do you?"

"Nope. What's the statistic? Most victims of murder know their killer. Makes you want to put the steak knives away when your relatives come to visit, doesn't it?"

"I wonder," Mendez said, going to the tiny kitchen that was separated from the dining area by a counter. "Did this girl even get a look at him? Or did he grab her from behind and get the glue in her eyes first thing?"

"If he glues their eyes shut to keep them from seeing him, what's that all about? If he knows he's going to kill them, and it seems pretty clear that's his intent, why bother to keep them from seeing him?"

"I don't think he does it for practical reasons."

As they made their way through her house, it seemed Lisa Warwick was private about her private life even with herself. They found no diary, no journal. Her travel plans for her wine country weekend were carefully noted in her day planner on the dining room table, but with no annotations as to a traveling companion.

"Even shy girls doodle hearts on their calendars," Hicks said, paging through the book. "There's nothing in here."

The only photograph they discovered on the first floor showing Lisa Warwick with a man was a framed snapshot of her with her parents at her graduation from nursing school.

Mendez stood in the middle of the living room and took in the space. Lisa Warwick hadn't been as tidy as Karly Vickers. She had clutter, but her clutter was loosely organized all around the place: A pile of magazines on the ottoman, a stack of books on the end table, a bag of knitting on the floor next to the sofa. There was no sign of a struggle, no sign anyone else had been in the house.

"Somebody had to see something," Hicks said. "We just have to find that somebody."

On the other hand, Mendez recalled, Bundy had abducted two of his victims in broad daylight from a crowded lakeshore state park—one within feet of her friends—and no one had noticed anything out of the ordinary.

In the blink of an eye a woman could be gone, sucked into a terrible alternate universe where existence meant unspeakable torture and unbearable pain, a world beyond the darkest imagining, unseen by everyone but the killer and his victim.

They went up the stairs to check out the two bedrooms and the bath. The smaller of the bedrooms was undisturbed. In the bathroom, someone had left a towel on the floor next to the tub. Makeup and costume jewelry littered the vanity. She had been getting ready for something.

In the master bedroom the bed was unmade. Clothes had been tossed over a chair. A framed photo sat on one of the nightstands. Lisa Warwick posing with a small group of people, Jane Thomas among them. Three women and a good-looking man in his mid-thirties, all in business attire, each with a glass of champagne in hand.

A celebration, Mendez thought. A happy moment. But it didn't strike him as the sort of photo a woman would keep on her nightstand. Except for one thing: the way Lisa Warwick was looking up at the man on her left.

"Ten bucks says this is the guy she was having the affair with," he said. "Look how she's looking at him."

"And ten bucks says he's married," Hicks said. "Look at how he's not looking at her."

"Like his life depends on it."

"Or half of everything he owns."

They darkened the room and repeated the black light test they had done on Karly Vickers's bed with no result. This time as Mendez passed the light over the sheets small dots lit up like tiny fluorescent stars. Not many of them, but enough to suggest a story of lovers in bed, a drop of semen here and there—spillage when taking off a condom perhaps, or maybe during oral sex.

"Looks like we've got us a suspect," Mendez said. "Let's bag that photograph and go find out who he is."

# 24

There was a part of him that never wanted to wake up. Vince couldn't decide if it was the damaged part of his brain that didn't want him to wake up, or the rest of his brain that didn't want to wake up and be subjected to the aftereffects of the bullet fragmented in his head.

The doctors, specialists, and neurosurgeons he had seen in the months since being shot had all been stunned by the fact he had survived at all. There were only a handful of cases like his in the world, each of them a little different from the others, dependent on the parts of the brain that had been impacted.

The doctors had no idea what would happen next. They had exhumed what shrapnel they could, but the largest piece of the .22 caliber slug had lodged in a place the surgeons wouldn't go near. There was too great a chance of causing severe brain damage. Yet they couldn't tell him what damage would be caused by leaving a bullet in his head.

They couldn't be sued for that damage, they knew that.

So he was a living, breathing science project, a case study, a freak in the medical circus, an article in *The New England Journal of Medicine*.

The effects of what had happened to him varied. Some days his sense of smell or hearing seemed heightened. Some days he couldn't get the taste of metal out of his mouth. Nearly every day he had a headache that could have knocked a mule off its feet.

In the initial weeks after the shooting he had experienced the frustration of aphasia, a disorder that made it difficult for him to grab the words he wanted from his brain and put them into coherent sentences.

Some days he found himself to be lacking impulse control, but whether that was damage to the frontal lobe or the result of fully realizing his own mortality, he couldn't say. He was a walking, talking second chance. He had no interest in passing up experiences or putting opportunities off to a tomorrow that might never come.

The trauma had left his body weak and lacking the endurance to get through simple tasks. Now, months later, he could get through a day, but stamina was still an issue.

He had been so exhausted by the time Mendez dropped him off at the hotel he'd barely had the energy to try to shower off the smell of the morgue. He had no memory of falling naked across the bed. He had no memory of dreams. He had managed a full seven hours of uninterrupted sleep. That was the first time that had happened in months.

With the phantom smell of morgue still in his nose, he took another shower and made a pot of bad coffee in the little machine on the bathroom counter. Breathing deep the scents of coffee and soap in the steamy bathroom, he wiped off a section of mirror and took his daily inventory.

He had looked worse. He had looked better. If he had been a woman, he at least could have improved himself with makeup.

"You'd be a hell of an ugly woman, Vince," he said, finding a chuckle in that.

He made a mental note to look into visiting a tanning parlor to get some of the gray out of his skin. He was in California, after all. Californians loved their tans. He had no doubt that he would feel like an idiot doing it, but if it kept people from thinking he had one foot in the grave, it was probably worth it.

Room service brought a basket of muffins and toast. He ate what he could just to put a layer of something in his stomach before the first round of pills. The brown prescription bottles were arrayed on the dresser. Painkillers, antiseizure medication, antinausea medication, antipsychotic meds to ward off the paranoia sometimes brought on by pressure against some crucial part of his brain of which he couldn't remember the name.

He had yet to take that one. So far he had managed to fend off the anxiety himself. He looked at the prescription bottle and wondered if he really needed it, would he be sane enough to take it.

As he picked at the food, he listened to his tape

of the conversation in the car from the night before. Mendez had given him an overview of what had happened so far. Three probable victims and one woman missing. He made notes as he listened and mulled over the notes when the tape clicked off. He studied the Polaroids he had taken at the autopsy, particularly intrigued by the cutting wounds that seemed so deliberate and symmetrically placed on the limbs—where there was a vertical cut on one arm there was a corresponding cut in exactly the same place on the other arm. The same with the legs.

He pulled a paper from his briefcase that depicted a simple line drawing of the female human form, front and back, and drew in the marks on Lisa Warwick's body. He would fax the form to Quantico later to find out if anyone in ISU had come across this pattern before.

He would go in to the sheriff's office this morning and go over the particulars of all three cases, with a particular eye out for any similar marks on the previous victims, and begin work on the profile in earnest.

Not that he didn't already have some strong ideas. He had worked enough cases, interviewed enough killers to have the checklist ingrained in his brain. There were maybe nine people on the planet who knew as much about the minds of murderers as he did. They were a small club. Too small for the ever-growing ranks of serial predators.

He picked up the phone and called the sheriff's office.

"Detective Mendez, please."

"What do you know today you didn't know last night?"

"Not much," Mendez said.

"Not much?" Vince said. "What have you been doing all morning? Golfing? And why wasn't I invited?"

"We searched the home of the missing girl, Karly Vickers, and found nothing of significance."

"And *that's* not significant to you?"

Mendez conceded the point. "No signs of forced entry. No signs of a struggle. No indication she was involved with a man. So far, we haven't found anyone who saw anything happen anywhere."

"What does that tell you?"

"He's careful."

They sat in a nice white conference room with big windows looking out on huge, spreading oak trees and green grass. Nice.

"This beats the hell out of the basement at Quantico," he said, getting up from his chair and going to the window.

"You work in the basement?" Detective Hicks asked.

"Deeper than the dead," he said. "I think the Bureau should put that on T-shirts and sell them. BSU could be the next big thing in pop culture."

"Yeah," Mendez said, chuckling. "Behavioral Sciences could be the next *Miami Vice.*"

Vince gave his lopsided grin and shrugged. "Move over, Don Johnson.

"What about your murder victim?" he asked.

"A coworker felt like maybe Lisa Warwick was having an affair, but she never confided in anyone about it," Mendez said. "We found semen on her sheets, and a photograph that may or may not lead us to the guy who left it there."

"Did her neighbors have anything to say about a boyfriend?"

"Not so far," Hicks said. "She lived in a duplex, but her neighbor never saw or heard anything going on next door."

"She was discreet," Vince said.

"Or secretive," Hicks offered. "The guy might be married."

"The guy might be a killer," Vince said.

He went to the long chalkboard that took up most of one wall.

"This is how you build a profile, kids."

He took a piece of chalk and wrote *1. Profile Inputs.* He spoke as he noted pertinent points. "A: What did you find at the crime scene? Physical evidence, a pattern of evidence, body position, weapons."

"We don't have a crime scene," Detective Hicks pointed out. "We have dump sites."

"Make the same notes for dump sites," Vince

said. "And the fact that you don't have a crime scene is highly significant. We'll come back to that.

"B: Victimology. That you have. Age of the victims, occupation, background, habits, family structure, where were they last seen. C: Forensic Information. Cause of death, wounds—are they pre- or postmortem, sexual acts, autopsy report, lab reports. You have everything on two vics except the labs and the official report of autopsy on the Warwick woman. Right?"

Both detectives nodded. Sheriff Dixon sat stone-faced at the head of the table, taking it all in.

"D: Your preliminary police reports. And E: Photographs of the vics, of the crime scene and/or the dump scene."

"We've got photos," Hicks said.

"Let's get them up on the wall, now, and I want a long table situated under the photos where we can organize copies of all the paperwork."

While Hicks went to the large cork bulletin board and began to make room for the photographs, Vince moved to an empty section of chalkboard and wrote *2. Decision Process Models. Homicide type & Style, Primary Intent, Victim Risk, Offender Risk, Escalation, Time for Crime, Location Factors.*

"You've already seen escalation in terms of risk to your offender," he said. "The first victim—first two victims—were dumped in remote locations. The Lisa Warwick scene was staged and in a location right in town, where he ran a much greater risk of being seen. What purpose did that risk serve him?"

"The bigger the risk, the bigger the rush," Mendez said.

"Publicity," Hicks offered.

"Generates greater fear in the community," Dixon said. "It's about power. He can do anything he wants. We can't stop him."

"All of the above," Vince said. "Have you seen any escalation in the violence of the murders?"

"Julie Paulson and Lisa Warwick both died as a result of ligature strangulation," Mendez said. "They had both been tortured. They were both cut up. Eyes and mouths glued shut. The second body was too badly decomposed to get an accurate picture."

"Prior to the Julie Paulson murder, was there any pattern of sexual assaults in the area?"

"Nothing related," Dixon said. "We had six reported rapes in the county in the past year. All solved."

"Congratulations," Vince said. "Let's see what we can do to get your murder clearance rate up to that standard. With regards to the sexual assaults, what about the year before last, and the year before that?"

"The year before was about the same. Before that was before my time here."

"My question is, is this guy homegrown or did

he drop here from somewhere else? Most serial killers start smaller than murder. Fetishism, window peeping, assault, rape. They work their way up over time. On the other hand, though," he conceded, "some just nurse the violent fantasies over the years until they have to act on them to release the pressure."

"We're looking at known offenders," Dixon said.

The door to the conference room opened and a uniformed deputy stepped in.

"You're late," Dixon said. He turned back toward Vince. "Vince, this is my chief deputy, Frank Farman. Frank, Vince Leone."

Vince had specifically asked the sheriff to keep things casual. The less people said those three magic letters, *FBI*, the better.

"Vince is an expert on serial killers," Dixon explained.

The deputy gave him a hard look and said flatly, "You're a Feeb."

Vince smiled like an alligator. "Have a seat, Deputy."

"I'll stand, thanks."

There was one in every crowd.

"I've got feelers out in other parts of the country," Vince said, "looking for any murders with a similar MO and signature. But I'll tell you right now, based on what I've heard and seen so far, this guy is no amateur. He's acting on fantasies he's held for a long, long time, and he's been acting on them long enough to have his routine down pat."

"You talk about this dirtbag like he's some kind of genius," Farman said. "Looks to me like he's just one sick son of a bitch."

"Then why haven't you caught him?" Vince challenged. "I'm assuming you're a top cop, or you wouldn't be in this room right now. If your perp is just some crazy guy, foaming at the mouth, running around attacking women at random, why haven't you caught him?"

Farman had no answer for that.

"I'll tell you why," Vince said. "Because he's not just some sick son of a bitch. Not in the way you mean."

He turned back to the board and wrote *3. Crime Assessment. A: Crime Classification. B: Organized/Disorganized.* (And under that heading) *a: Victim Selection. b: Control of Victim. c: Sequence of Crime. C: Staging. D: Motivation. E: Crime Scene Dynamics.*

He tapped the chalk at B. "A disorganized offender sees a potential victim and commits a crime of opportunity. The crime scene will be sloppy. He'll leave the body there. This guy isn't very smart. He's socially immature. He's impulsive."

"Sounds like you, Tony," Hicks joked.

"Very funny."

"He isn't interested beyond the immediate act," Vince went on. "He isn't looking for publicity.

He's not the kind of creep you're looking for here. And too bad, 'cause he's not that hard to outsmart. If this was your animal, you'd catch him today and we could all go fishing."

"So," Farman said, "are you going to look into your crystal ball and tell us who the killer is?"

"I'm going to tell you *what* he is," Vince said. "If I were psychic, I'd be in Vegas with a wad of cash. I sure as hell wouldn't be here looking at your ugly mugs. Sure, I'd miss all the glamour and adoration . . ."

A single sharp pain pierced his brain like a lance. He hid the automatic wince by turning quickly back toward the chalkboard.

"The organized offender," he said, placing his hand on the chalk tray to counter the vertigo. He held his breath for a second, let it out, raised his hand—willing it not to shake—and started to write again. "The organized offender is intelligent, socially competent, holds down a job. He's likely to be in a relationship. He could have a family, even. No one in his life would look at him and think he might have a second life as a predator."

"Bundy," Mendez said.

He took a slow, deep breath and turned back around slowly to face his audience.

"Bundy. Edmund Kemper up in Santa Cruz. John Wayne Gacy in the Chicago area. Robert Hansen from Alaska is a perfect example of an organized killer."

"Never heard of him," Farman said.

"The guy was a baker by trade," Vince began. "He was a family man, a pillar of the community. He was also a sexual sadist. We think he killed around twenty-one women. His victims of choice were prostitutes. He would engage them for their services, then fly them in his own plane to his hunting cabin, rape them, torture them, then turn them loose in the wilderness, hunt them down like animals, and kill them.

"The Anchorage cops had an escaped victim at one point. The girl had a handcuff dangling from her wrist when she runs into a cop and tells him what happened. She tells how this guy had tied her up in his basement and tortured her, how she got away from him at the airport before he could get her into his plane.

"She identifies Hansen's home as the place where she was raped and tortured. The cops take her to the airport and she identifies his plane. But when the cops go to question Hansen and tell him what the girl said, he's outraged. He produces two business associates who say they had dinner with him the night he supposedly had the girl in the basement. It's his word against the girl's, and he's so freakin' normal, the cops believe him.

"Hansen wasn't charged. He wasn't even arrested. That happened in 1982. It was another year before they finally took him down."

He had the undivided attention of all of them now.

"The organized killer plans his crimes. He chooses his victims. He's more apt to draw out the attack, to restrain the victim, to torture the victim. He's got the whole situation under control. That's what it's about for him: control. And when he's done, he'll transport the victim away from the death scene, then go home and wait to read about it in the papers, see the reports on the news.

"What you're dealing with here, gentlemen, truly is a big-game hunter," Vince said. "He's a killing machine, and he's very, very good at it. Experience tells me he's a white male. Serial killers tend to hunt within their own ethnic group."

"That narrows it right down," Farman said sarcastically.

"He's in his midthirties," Vince went on. "That's when these guys hit their prime. And he believes he's hitting his prime now. He's moving into the big time with this latest victim. He's put her on display so we can all look and see what a badass he is. This victim was his challenge. He's thrown down the gauntlet. He doesn't believe you're smart enough to catch him, and so far he's right."

He gripped the chalk tray with his left hand to ward off another wave of dizziness.

Mendez was watching him like a hawk.

"And I'll take some IV coffee now, if you've got it," Vince said. "This jet lag is a bitch."

# 25

"Dennis, for the tenth time, sit down in your seat," Anne said with more of an edge in her voice than she usually allowed herself.

Her strategy with fifth graders was to maintain self-control at all times. Never let them see you sweat. Today even antiperspirant failed her.

She had been glad to see Dennis Farman in class—for Dennis's sake, and to save herself from having another conversation with his father. She had tried to talk to him about finding the body in the park, but he had no interest in telling her anything. Nor had he had any interest in paying attention to anything she had said all morning.

He sat on his knees, bending over his desktop, intent on drawing in the notebook he shielded with one arm. He was supposed to be reading chapter 12 in his American history book, like the rest of the class was supposed to be doing. But there were plenty of eyes cutting in Dennis's direction—especially those of his fellow corpse finders.

Wendy kept shooting him dirty looks. Tommy watched him from the corner of his eye, pretending not to, not wanting to draw attention. Cody, pale and nervous, kept his nose buried in his book, but hadn't turned a page in fifteen minutes. Dennis sat directly behind him, and would occasionally reach forward and tap Cody on the head with his pen, like a cat toying with a frightened mouse.

Anne got up from her desk and walked purposefully down the aisle. All eyes in the room were now on her. Anticipation rose. She stopped at Dennis Farman's desk.

"Dennis."

He didn't look up. Instead, he ripped a fart that started an avalanche of nervous laughter. The unfortunate girl sentenced to sit behind him leaned back in her chair, her face contorting. The stench was horrific.

"Gross! I'm gonna be sick!"

"Go sit in the next row," Anne said to her. To the rest of the class she said, "You had all better be reading. There's going to be a quiz this afternoon."

Groans of dismay ran through the room.

Anne squatted down beside Dennis Farman's desk and looked at his face. He continued to crouch over his notebook, pretending not to notice her. His eyes narrowed and his mouth puckered into a tight knot of concentration. He looked angry. He flipped to a fresh page in his notebook and started scribbling again, gripping his pen so hard his knuckles were white.

"Dennis," she said very quietly. "Is there some reason you can't sit down properly today?"

He didn't answer her, but his cheeks flushed red and tears suddenly welled in his eyes. He dug the tip of his pen into the paper so hard it tore.

Anne's mind went to the night before, to the Farman household, and Frank Farman's promise that he would deal with Dennis.

She glanced at the clock and stood up. "All right, everyone. *Quietly* go line up in the hall for lunch."

Dennis went to bolt from his seat. Anne put her hand on his shoulder. "Not you."

He winced and jerked away from her touch as if she had burned him.

Wide eyes glanced back at them as the rest of the class filed out the door. The speculation would now run rampant as to the fate of their resident troublemaker.

"Last one out closes the door, please," she said.

The tension in the silence after the door closed was like a balloon filling and filling and filling with air until it was about to burst. Anne pulled the chair away from Cody Roache's desk and sat down.

"Did you get in trouble for skipping school yesterday?"

Dennis looked away from her, his face flushing darker.

"You know, it doesn't help you to keep all those feelings bottled up, Dennis. If you're angry, say you're angry. We can deal with that together. I can't help you if you won't talk to me."

He screwed himself around in his seat until he had all but his back to her. Anne said nothing for a moment, not sure what tack to take. She had a terrible feeling about what might have happened. She had stood up to Frank Farman. He might have even taken it as an embarrassment. And he might have taken that out on Dennis.

Her father had never raised a hand to either her mother or herself, but Anne knew well all other forms of punishment that could be dished out by an angry man with a fragile ego. How many times had her father reduced her mother to a quivering, sobbing mass of inadequacy with his vicious words? And how many times had he tried to do the same thing to her?

Because Anne had detached herself from him emotionally at an early age, his tirades never had the same effect on her as they had on her mother, who loved him. But Anne knew well the anger and resentment that had built inside her like a brick wall. She had figured out ways to deal with it, to release the pressure when she had to. Dennis had not.

"Are you angry with me?" she asked.

The boy's body was rigid with anger. He began to shake under the pressure of trying to contain it, and then suddenly he couldn't. He turned on her, his eyes wild.

"I HATE YOU!" he shouted. "I HATE YOU! YOU'RE A FUCKING BITCH!!"

She hadn't been prepared for the virulence of his explosion. She sat back in her chair, her heart pounding like a trip hammer as he raged at her.

He banged both fists on his desk over and over. "I hate you! I hate you! I wish you were dead!"

*Now what, Miss Child Psychologist Wannabe?*

She had opened the door and let loose a demon. What was she supposed to do? Physically take hold of him? Let the rage pour out of him until it was spent? Make him deny his feelings and shove them back into the box with the now-broken hinges?

While Anne was busy not knowing what to do, Dennis fell forward onto his desk and began sobbing so hard he choked on it.

*Do something, stupid.*

"I'm sorry, Dennis," she said, her voice trembling a bit. "I'm sorry if I got you into trouble. I didn't mean to. I came to your house because I was worried about you."

She had no idea if she was saying the right thing. But then she had no idea if he was even hearing her, he was crying so hard. Despite his outburst against her, Anne's heart ached for him. He was a monstrous, aggravating pain in the ass on a daily basis, but she knew he hadn't gotten that way on his own. And under all the problems, he was just a scared little boy who didn't know how to handle his feelings. He was probably as frightened as he was angry.

Anne leaned toward him and reached out a hand to stroke his head. "I'm sorry, Dennis. You can be as angry as you want with me. We'll work it out. I'm here to help you, if I can."

And just how would she do that? If she could get him to tell her what had happened, then what? If his father had given him the beating she suspected was the reason he wouldn't sit down, then what? She would report Frank Farman to the authorities and open an industrial-size can of worms for Dennis and his family.

"You're safe here, Dennis," she said softly. "I want you to know that. You can come to me and tell me anything you need to, anything at all. I won't get mad at you. I won't punish you. I'll just listen, and then we'll figure out what to do about it."

His sobs quieted slowly to hiccups and sniffles. He wiped his nose on the sleeve of his already dirty sweatshirt. He was embarrassed now. At eleven—a year older than the rest of her charges —he was already edging into that awkward space between childhood and adolescence, further complicating his emotions.

"It's okay," Anne said. "This is between you and me. Nobody else. If anybody asks what went on in here while the rest of the class was out, tell them I yelled at you and gave you extra homework. Does that sound like a plan?"

He didn't look at her, but he nodded. Anne stood up and put her chair back at Cody's desk. "Good. Now go to the lavatory and wash your face, then go to lunch."

All the aggression had gone out of him. He put

his notebook back in his desk and walked away.

She would leave it at that, Anne decided as she watched him go out the door. She wouldn't force the issue. He could think about it, hopefully decide to trust her, and come spill his story when he was ready.

Either that was a great plan, or she was a coward. She didn't know which. If she never pressed him, if he never told her, what happened the next time his father punished him for something?

She wished Mendez would return her calls. He could deal with Frank Farman, and it would be out of her hands.

Almost as an afterthought she turned and looked at Dennis's desk. Guilt scratched at her nerves, but she lifted the desktop anyway, and glanced down at Dennis's notebook, still opened to the last page he had scribbled on.

The paper was tear-stained and some of the ink had smeared on drawings of what looked like thick, angry lightning bolts. Then she turned the page back to the one he had been working on all morning, and her blood ran cold.

He had almost filled the page with childish drawings of naked women with knives in their chests.

# 26

"Tell me about Deputy Farman," Vince said before Mendez could ask him about his health.

They walked across the lot to a car parked under the shade of an oak tree. Vince got in and rolled the window down so he could continue to take in the fresh air and the smells of California nature.

"He's an old-school tight ass," Mendez said.

"You have a real grasp of the obvious there. And I could tell as soon as he stepped in the room you and him probably don't spend a lot of time bowling and drinking beer together. I want to know who he is."

"He's army. Did a tour in 'Nam. He's been on the job here a little longer than me. Dixon hired him out of LA County."

"So they go back."

"Yeah."

"If Dixon brought him here, he must be a good cop."

"Yeah. Commendations out the wazoo. He's a hard-ass, though. If you're two miles over the speed limit he'll pull you over and write you up. No mercy. He's all about the rules. All about the uniform."

"Rigid."

"Like a ramrod."

Mendez started the car and cranked up the air-conditioning.

"He doesn't like me," he confessed. "He sees me as some arrogant affirmative action prick who jumped the food chain because I didn't come up the ranks right before his eyes. And I don't need to tell you, but he doesn't like you either."

"Yeah, I got that," Vince said. "That's nothing new. Every department has a Frank Farman. Some of them have nothing but Frank Farmans. We're ahead of the game here.

"Profiling is still a relatively new tool, and it's subjective. Guys like Farman want hard physical evidence. They don't trust a guy like me who's going to come in here and tell him the killer probably tortured squirrels as a kid and talks with a lisp. They need to see for themselves it's a useful tool. The only way to do that is for me to do my job well."

Mendez turned the car around and headed out of the parking lot.

"Let me tell you something, kid," Vince said. "This will get you further in life and in this business than anything else anyone will ever teach you.

"Leave your ego at home and find a way to make it work with whoever you have to work with. Other cops, witnesses, vics, perps, whoever you're dealing with—learn to figure out in a hurry what makes them tick. If you can do that, you can always get what you need. Even from the Frank Farmans of the world.

"When I was going around interviewing serial

killers for the criminal personality research project, do you think I would have gotten anywhere with those creeps if I had gone in, looked them in the eyes, and told them what I really thought of them? Hell no. I had to figure out in five seconds what each of them was about and adjust my approach accordingly.

"What do I care if some serial rapist thinks I agree with his views that all women are whores? That's his perception; it's not my reality. Get it?"

"Yeah, I get it."

"You may be shocked to know this," he said sardonically. "I'm not by nature the first guy the Bureau goes looking for as an agent. But this is the work I wanted to do, and the Bureau is the place to do it. I learned to navigate the system. Remember that."

Mendez gave him a curious look. "Why are you telling me this?"

" 'Cause you're good, kid. You're sharp. I want you to be all you can be."

"You sound like a recruiting ad. Here's something interesting about Farman: His son was one of the kids that found the body. Frank won't let me talk to him."

"Is it necessary for you to talk to him?"

"Wendy, the little girl of the group, told me Dennis touched the corpse," Mendez said, brushing the question aside. "Frank let the kid hang around the crime scene until Dixon told him he had to send the kid home."

"That's a little odd."

"I mean, he made the boy stay outside the tape, but still. Frank said the kid had already seen the body, why not let him see how a crime scene gets processed."

"How old is the boy?"

"Ten, eleven, something like that. He's a fifth grader. And his teacher left a message for me last night that prior to finding this body, the kid had been talking about there being bodies buried in those woods."

"And your pal Frank hasn't mentioned that?" Vince said.

"No."

"He probably figures the kid was just being a kid," Vince speculated. "But in light of what's happened . . . you need to talk to the boy."

They pulled into a crushed stone parking lot and got out of the car. The sprawling white stucco building in front of them wore a discreet bronze plaque near the main entrance: THE THOMAS CENTER FOR WOMEN.

Inside, the main hall was cool and welcoming, the walls a warm shade of yellow, the old Mexican paver floors polished. They went to the front desk and Mendez asked for Jane Thomas.

"Nice place," Vince said as they waited.

"It's an amazing place," Mendez said. "A lot of the women come from abusive backgrounds, some are coming out of drug rehab, or even jail.

195

The center offers counseling, helps the women prepare themselves to enter the work force. Their program has gotten a lot of national attention."

"With one dead former employee and one missing client, they're about to get more," Vince said.

A tall, well-dressed blonde woman around forty emerged from an office down the hall.

"Detective Mendez?" She glanced from him to Vince and back, clearly worried they were there to deliver bad news.

"Ms. Thomas, this is—"

"Detective Leone," Vince said, offering his hand.

"Can we speak privately with you?" Mendez asked.

"Of course." Now she was really worried. "Come into my office."

They followed her into the spacious office that looked out on a large courtyard and a beautiful garden.

"Do you have news?" she asked, crossing her arms in front of her as if preparing to hold herself up.

"No, nothing," Mendez said.

Jane Thomas sighed in relief. "Thank God."

"We went through Ms. Warwick's home this morning and found a photograph of Ms. Warwick with some friends. I made a photocopy of it," Mendez said, digging the paper out of his coat pocket. "I'd like you to have a look and tell me who the rest of the people in the picture are."

She recognized the photograph right away. "Oh, yes, this was our celebration after one of our clients won her custody battle. The courts had given her children to the parents of her abusive husband temporarily while she went through court-ordered drug rehab, then wouldn't give them back to her when she had finished not only rehab, but our program as well. Lisa was her advocate. She did a lot of hand-holding on that one. In the end Steve was able to persuade a judge to set things right."

"Steve? This is Steve?" Mendez asked, tapping a finger below the man in the photograph.

"Yes. Steve Morgan. Quinn, Morgan and Associates. He donates a lot of time to us."

"Was there anything going on between him and Ms. Warwick?"

"Lisa and Steve?" she said, almost amused at the idea. "Of course not. Steve is happily married. He has an adorable daughter. She must be about ten years old."

"Wendy?" Mendez asked.

"I don't remember her name," she said, handing the paper back to him. "The woman to Lisa's left is Nora Alfano, our client."

"Did Ms. Warwick spend a lot of time working with Mr. Morgan on her various cases?" Vince asked.

"She spent some time with him in client meetings, that kind of thing. But Steve would never cheat. He's not that kind of man."

Mendez said nothing but put the picture back inside his pocket.

"Are you trying to disillusion me for the second time in one day, Detective?"

"No, ma'am. I'm just following leads. Most of them will go nowhere, but we have to follow them to the end."

"I've been out of town," Vince said by way of an excuse, "so I'm not quite up to speed. Have we looked at any hate mail yet?"

"So far nothing has stood out," Mendez said.

"This custody case you talked about—how long ago was that?" Vince asked.

"About nine months ago," Jane Thomas said. "The ex-husband in question is doing a year in county jail."

"We'll check out his friends and family," Vince said. "Just in case one of them is bent on revenge on his behalf."

"Of course." She went to her desk and buzzed her assistant to get the file.

"Then we'll let you get on with the rest of your day," Vince said with a soft smile.

Jane Thomas looked worn-out and stressed out. The Thomas Center was her namesake, her baby by the looks of the framed photos on the walls: Jane Thomas receiving awards from women's groups, photos with politicians, photos with various members of her staff and clients. Her work was being attacked via Lisa Warwick and

Karly Vickers, and she had to be worried what —or who—might be next.

"My day is consisting of fretting," she confessed.

*With good reason*, Vince thought. The center's clients made for a perfect victim pool: women with patterns of abuse in their backgrounds, vulnerable women, women with self-esteem issues. These were the kinds of women predators sought out as being easy to prey on, easy to control. A sufficiently twisted mind would see these women as being less than women living in traditional settings with traditional families, and therefore it was not a loss to society to dispose of them.

Vince had interviewed a number of serial murderers of prostitutes. They had all felt that they had practically done a public service in taking whores off the streets.

"Do you really think this Alfano guy could be behind these murders?" Mendez asked as they walked down the hall to the front doors. "I can see him targeting Lisa Warwick because she helped his wife get the kids back. But we have two other victims before Lisa Warwick."

"It's not likely," Vince said. "But, like you said, follow all leads to the end. I know of a case where an estranged wife's parents stalked and murdered her husband to ensure she would get custody of their granddaughter. "

"Or the guy doing life for a freeway shooting, and his mother builds a pipe bomb, sends it to the key witness against him, and blows half the family to kingdom come," Mendez said.

"People are un-fucking-believable," Vince said, and like every cop he'd ever known, segued from talk of murder to food. "Where are we going? Lunch, I hope."

"The beauty salon," Mendez said. "I thought we could get manicures and bond."

"Very funny."

"Karly Vickers had an appointment the day she went missing," Mendez said. "And there's a sandwich place down the block."

Karly Vickers had spent three hours at Spice Salon on the afternoon in question. She had a haircut and a perm, a manicure and a pedicure. One of the "beauty technicians," as they called themselves, had spent half an hour showing her the latest makeup tricks.

*Three hours of listening to disco's biggest hits pumping over the speakers,* Vince thought as he sat in a vacant stylist's chair. The woman had probably killed herself afterward.

Karly had been excited about the whole process of her makeover, but in a shy kind of way, the hairstylist said. She had talked about the new job she was starting. She hadn't said anything about a boyfriend, had in fact gotten quiet when the stylist had brought up the subject.

Vince observed Mendez at work. The owner of

the salon came over to trim his mustache and flirt with him. Vince asked about their hours and the new addition to the salon—a tanning parlor.

"Vickers left here around three that afternoon," Mendez said as they walked down the street to the sandwich place with tables out front. A waitress took their order and scurried off. "She said she had one more appointment for the day—the dentist."

"How would you like that?" Vince said. "You get nabbed by a serial killer and your last memory of your normal life is going to the dentist."

"Wouldn't be my choice."

"What would be your choice?"

Mendez considered. "Hmmm . . . Heather Locklear. How about you?"

Vince thought about it for a moment. What would he want his last memory to be? Would it even matter? Once you were dead, where did your memories go? He had technically been dead for three minutes when he was shot. He didn't remember anything about it.

"Well?"

"Pitching a perfect game for the Cubs to win the World Series," he said.

Mendez laughed. "Like that will ever happen."

"What? Me pitching in the bigs?"

"The Cubs winning the World Series."

"Hey!" Vince protested with a grin. "A guy's gotta dream. Dream large!"

# 27

"I don't know what to do."

"Jesus, Mary, and Joseph," Franny said, staring aghast at the notebook page depicting one grizzly stabbing death after another. "Call an exorcist."

Anne felt everything inside of her quivering like Jell-O. After seeing Dennis Farman's artwork, she had gone directly from her classroom to Franny's, where he was enjoying his break between his morning kindergartners and his afternoon kindergartners, sneaking a cigarette out by the sandbox.

"You have to come with me," she said. "You have to come with me right now."

She turned on her heel and started walking. Franny jogged up beside her in the hall.

"What's going on?"

She shook her head, tears welling up in her eyes. "I don't know what to do."

"Honey, what to do about what? Have you killed one of them? No one will blame you. They're fifth graders. It's justifiable homicide."

Anne didn't smile. She didn't laugh. She led the way into her classroom, took him straight to Dennis Farman's desk, and opened it.

"He was doing this all morning," she said now, and she told him everything that had happened.

"You have to show this to Garnett," he said, staring at the drawing. "This is really creepy, Anne.

This isn't something to mess around with—not when you add this to him screaming at you that he wishes you were dead."

"If I take this to Garnett, Dennis will be expelled."

"Yes, and . . . that would be bad . . . how?"

"He needs help, Franny," she said. "He's got so much rage inside him, and he doesn't know what to do with it."

Franny's jaw dropped. He grabbed the notebook out of the desk and pointed at the drawings of women with knives sticking into their bodies. "This is what he wants to do with it! Are you out of your fucking mind?"

"He's a little boy."

"He's the son of Satan!"

"He's the son of a man who beat him so badly last night he can't sit in a chair today!" Anne said, keeping her voice down even as her temper rose.

"Did he tell you that?"

"No."

"Did you see any marks on him?"

"No."

"Then tell Garnett, give this to him, and let him handle it," he said, tapping his finger against the notebook to make her look at it. "You have to get this kid out of your classroom before he does this for real."

"But, Franny, if Garnett expels him, what's going to happen to him? He apparently has a difficult home situation. He's socially maladjusted. He has no friends. He found a dead body, for Christ's sake."

"And let's make sure the next one isn't yours."

"He's *eleven*."

"Do you not go to the movies?" he asked, incredulous. "Did you not see *Halloween*? Michael Myers was SIX YEARS OLD when he killed his sister."

"And if we were living in a John Carpenter film, I'd be really scared."

"You *are* really scared or you wouldn't have come running to me. You would have told me tonight over Chinese. 'Oh, by the way, Franny, one of my students did the most interesting thing today. He unleashed the contents of his disturbed mind in a sexually sadistic work of art. And how was your day?'

"And, if you'll remember, last night you were telling me he was talking about other bodies in the woods, and that his only playmate is afraid of him."

Anne sighed. That was all true. But she couldn't help feeling that being in school with supervision and guidance was a better option for helping Dennis Farman than turning him loose, isolating him, giving up on him. Clearly, no one was there for him at home, physically, emotionally, or otherwise. If she could reach him now, maybe she could turn him around.

"And where is Mr. Dream Detective?" Franny asked. "Has he called you back?"

"No."

"Well, he needs to get his tight little ass over here to serve and protect or I'm not letting him have his way with you."

"He's not interested in me."

"And who can blame him, Holly Hobbie?" he asked. "Do you have *anything* in your closet besides these *Little House on the Prairie* dresses?"

Anne looked down at her outfit—a white puffed-sleeve blouse and a loose navy blue dress that hit just above her ankles. "This is a perfectly nice jumper."

Franny rolled his eyes. "Only kindergartners and kinky role-playing prostitutes wear jumpers."

Finally, she found a smile, knowing that had been his intent. Irreverence as diversion.

Sobering, he pressed Dennis Farman's notebook into her hands. "You have to take this to Garnett, Anne Marie. If you don't, and something goes wrong with this kid in your classroom . . . You have to do it."

Anne looked down at the notebook images of women screaming, blood spurting from their wounds. The first bell sounded. Their warning that lunch period was almost over. Her kids had gym first thing. They would go directly to Mr. Alvarez outdoors.

She sighed and nodded, already feeling Dennis Farman slipping beyond her grasp. "I'll go now."

# 28

Steve Morgan looked like he'd had a hard night: dark smudges under his tired blue eyes, pallor a little to the pasty side of healthy. He was taking Tylenol as Mendez and Vince entered his office.

Still, he came around his desk and greeted them with handshakes. He was in his thirties, tall and lanky with a firm grip and a full head of sandy, wavy hair.

"Detectives, what can I do for you?" he asked, returning to his cushy leather chair. "Have a seat."

Vince sat down in one of the two visitors' chairs as if he was settling in for a long stay.

"Jane Thomas called and filled me in on what's been going on," Morgan said. "I've been up in Sacramento since Tuesday morning doing some lobbying for the center. I got back late last night."

"Then you know we're looking into the murder of Lisa Warwick," Mendez said.

"Yes. My daughter was one of the kids who found her body. Lisa was the nicest person in the world. Who would want to kill her?"

"That's what we'd like to find out," Mendez said. "Ms. Thomas told us you and Lisa worked together on some cases involving clients of the center."

"Yes. Lisa used to work at the center. After she

got her nurse's degree, she decided to volunteer as an advocate. She worked the evening shift at the hospital. It left her days free."

"How well did you know her?" Vince asked. "Well enough that she would have confided in you if something had been going on in her life?"

"Like what?"

"Trouble with a boyfriend, someone bothering her at work, that kind of thing."

"One of the ER docs liked to play grab ass with the nurses," Morgan said. "Lisa asked me what to do about it. That was maybe a year, year and a half ago. I had a conversation with the man about what a sexual harassment suit could do to his career, not to mention his marriage."

"And he stopped?" Mendez asked, making notes.

"He left. Took a position on the East Coast."

"That must have been some conversation," Vince said.

"I make a living persuading people to see things my way."

"You must be very good at it."

"I do all right."

"Ms. Warwick hadn't said anything to you about any problems recently?" Mendez asked.

The lawyer shook his head. "I hadn't seen her for a while."

"She never called? You never ran into each other?" Vince asked. "Never met for coffee, anything like that?"

Morgan narrowed his eyes slightly. "What are you getting at, Detective?"

"We have reason to believe Ms. Warwick was seeing someone before her death," Mendez said, watching him.

"I'm a happily married man," Morgan said. "Lisa was a casual acquaintance. I'm very sorry that she's dead, and it tears me up to think of what she must have gone through. She was a sweet, gentle person."

"But you weren't romantically involved," Vince said, finding it curious Morgan hadn't said so himself.

"No."

"You know we have to ask," Vince said apologetically.

"I understand that, yes."

"Can you tell us where you were Monday night through Tuesday midday?" Mendez asked.

"I was at home Monday night. I left early Tuesday morning—around five—to drive to Sacramento."

"We'll talk to your wife, of course," Vince said.

"Of course. I don't have anything to hide."

"You didn't get back until last night?" Mendez asked.

"That's right."

"Did you know your daughter had found the body?"

"Yes. Sara—my wife—called and left messages at my hotel. I spoke with her later that evening."

"But you didn't come home."

"I was in the middle of some very important business regarding funding for women's shelters," Morgan explained. "Wendy seemed to be fine, considering. Sara was shaken up but able to handle the situation. It didn't make sense for me to drop the ball and go home."

"You're very dedicated to the center," Vince said.

"They do important work that saves women's lives and helps them make their lives better."

"But you're a man."

Morgan raised his eyebrows. "Therefore I shouldn't care about battered women? That's a hell of an attitude."

"I only meant that it isn't often men get involved in women's issues," Vince said.

"Abuse isn't a women's issue, Detective. Abuse impacts families. Families aren't gender specific."

"Does it bother your wife that you give so much time to the center?" Mendez asked.

"Sara is very supportive," Morgan said, checking his watch. "I've got a client coming in five minutes. Is there anything else, gentlemen?"

"You know Karly Vickers," Mendez said.

"I've spoken with her. She was supposed to start work here Tuesday as a receptionist and file clerk. We were closed Monday. Don Quinn's mother passed away."

Morgan rose to his feet, signaling the meeting was over. "If I had any idea about any of this—

Lisa's murder, Karly Vickers—I would certainly tell you."

"If anything comes to mind," Mendez said, handing him a business card, "please call."

"What do you think?" Mendez asked as they returned to the car.

"I think he couldn't get us out of there fast enough," Vince said. "I think you need to have a chat with Mrs. Morgan."

# 29

Mr. Alvarez, who had played minor-league baseball, had chosen baseball for their gym unit. Mr. Alvarez liked a theme. During the baseball playoffs, they would play baseball. During the football playoffs, they would learn about football, and so on.

Tommy, who was the ultimate baseball fan, didn't like playing baseball for gym, because they didn't really play. Mr. Alvarez took time with each batter to help improve each one's skills—a tall and tedious order for most of the girls, except for Wendy, who could catch and throw because her dad taught her. For Tommy, it was boring. They mostly just sat around.

He sat on the bench next to Wendy, watching Mr. Alvarez encourage the hapless and scrawny Kim Karloff to try to hold the bat upright. She looked like she was going to fall over from the weight of it.

"This is so lame," he said.

Wendy didn't comment. She had been very quiet all morning. Tommy reached over and poked her to make sure she was still alive. The words "quiet" and "Wendy" didn't go together.

"What's the matter with you?" Tommy asked.

"My dad came home last night."

"You're usually excited when your dad comes home."

"He got home really late," she said, "but I heard him. So I got out of bed, but when I got to the stairs, he and Mom were having a fight."

"Oh," was all Tommy could think to say. His mom was always trying to pick a fight with his dad.

"She was yelling at him for not coming home the night we found the dead lady. And he said he just couldn't. And she said, 'And where the hell were you?' She said she tried to call him at his hotel, and they said he wasn't even registered there. Then he said, 'You know that was a mistake. I called you back.' And then she said that the mistake was his and he should have covered his tracks better."

"What's that supposed to mean?"

"I think she thinks he's having an affair," Wendy said. "You know, a love affair with some other woman, like on *Dallas* and *Dynasty*. People are always having affairs."

Tommy didn't know. He wasn't allowed to watch very much television, and never anything like the shows Wendy was always talking about.

He sometimes got to watch *MacGyver*, but *MacGyver* wasn't interested in girls. He was too busy saving people. "Why would he do that?"

"I don't know," she said, exasperated. "Why do people do anything? Why did somebody kill that lady?"

"My dad says nobody really understands why someone turns into a serial killer."

"That's scary," Wendy said. She looked past the end of the bench to where Dennis Farman was tormenting Cody Roache, poking at him with something. Cody kept trying to get away from him, but he never ran far enough or fast enough. "I think Dennis is going to grow up to be a serial killer."

Tommy looked over at him. "Probably."

"What do you think Miss Navarre did to him?"

He shrugged. "I don't know. Miss Navarre is nice. She probably tried to talk some sense into him."

"Ha! Like that could ever happen."

Dennis caught them looking. Tommy groaned. "Great. Now he's going to come over here and harass us."

"Don't let him, Tommy. Stand up to him."

No sooner had she said it than Dennis made a fist and socked Cody in the stomach. Cody doubled over.

"And get my head knocked off?" Tommy said.

Dennis swaggered up in front of them, a sneer on his face. In his left hand he held something wrapped in tissue.

"Look," he said. "It's the lovebirds. Are you having sex yet?"

Tommy ignored him.

Wendy's eyes flashed. "Shut up, Dennis."

"Is your gay boyfriend gonna make me?" he taunted.

"You're such a moron," Wendy snapped. "You're such a moron even other morons don't want you hanging around." She glanced meaningfully at Cody, who was bent over throwing up on the grass.

Dennis's face began to get red. Tommy swallowed hard, but Wendy was pissed off and kept going.

"If you weren't such a moron that you got held back a year and now you're bigger than everybody, somebody would kick your butt."

Dennis got redder and redder. He stepped in closer. "You're a cunt."

Wendy stood up on the bench so she was taller than he was. Tommy looked to see if Mr. Alvarez had heard the *C* word.

Wendy was furious now, her hands clenched into fists. "You're stupid. You're stupid and everybody hates you!"

Dennis suddenly grabbed her by the arm and pulled her off the bench. He took the thing in tissue paper and shoved it in her face.

"I'm gonna make you eat it!" he shouted.

The tissue fell away, and Wendy screamed. Dennis pushed her backward into the bench, trying to push the blackened thing into her mouth. Wendy frantically turned her head from side to side, trying to escape the thing.

Tommy lowered a shoulder and ran into Dennis Farman like a human battering ram. But Dennis was in a rage now, and even though he staggered sideways a step he continued trying to shove the black thing into Wendy's mouth.

Tommy took his fist and used it like a hammer on Dennis's head. Dennis turned toward him and Tommy clipped him in the mouth, splitting his lip. Blood gushed out.

"You fucking little faggot!" Dennis screamed. He took a wild swing and hit Tommy hard in the face, knocking him off his feet. Dennis's shoe hit him square in the stomach and knocked the wind out of him.

Tommy tried to curl into a ball. He put his hands over his head to protect himself as Dennis kept kicking him over and over.

Then suddenly his assailant was gone, dragged backward by the scruff of his neck by Mr. Alvarez, who was shouting something Tommy couldn't understand. Stars spun before his one good eye.

Wendy hit the dirt beside him. "Tommy? Are you okay?"

Tommy was coughing as he fought to sit up. "No," he croaked.

They both looked over at Dennis, who was in a blind rage, screaming and cursing and hitting and kicking at Mr. Alvarez.

They looked at each other, then they looked at the ground where Dennis had dropped the thing he had been trying to shove into Wendy's mouth: a human finger, blackened and rotted like a bad banana.

# 30

The offices of Peter Crane, DDS, were located in a renovated white stucco, Spanish-style building on a bustling, beautiful, tree-lined pedestrian plaza near the college. Shoppers wandered in and out of upscale boutiques and galleries on the three-block stretch. Sidewalk cafes and coffeehouses were busy with a mix of students, adults, and older people. A guitarist playing classical music sat on a bench outside the bookstore.

*Nice town,* Vince thought, spying an Italian place that advertised Chicago-style pizza. He could smell the olive oil and garlic as if he were swimming in it.

They went inside the dentist's office and Vince took in the waiting area with its leather chairs and a huge saltwater aquarium built into one wall. Even the magazines on the coffee table were upscale: *Town & Country, Architectural Digest, Scientific American*. Mendez showed his badge to the elegant African American woman behind the curved wood counter.

She raised her pencil-thin brows. "How may I help you, Detective?"

"Can you tell us if a woman named Karly Vickers had an appointment here last Thursday?"

She flipped back a couple of pages in the appointment book. "Yes. She had a four o'clock cleaning and exam. She arrived at three fifty-five."

"We'll need to speak with Dr. Crane and whoever did the cleaning."

The receptionist led them into an examination room to wait out of sight of patients. Vince helped himself to a seat in the big chair.

"My mother wanted me to be a dentist," he said, staring up at the mural on the ceiling—a blue sky crowded with plump white clouds. "I've got hands the size of catcher's mitts. Can you imagine having one of these in your mouth?"

A male face loomed over and blocked his view of the clouds. Good-looking guy, midthirties, dark hair, dark eyes.

Vince exited the chair.

"Detective Mendez," Crane said, shaking hands. "And?"

"Detective Leone," Vince said.

"Ava said you had some questions about a patient."

"Karly Vickers," Mendez said, producing a snapshot from his pocket. Karly hugging her dog. "You saw her Thursday afternoon, late in the day."

Crane took the photo and stared at it for a moment. "Her hair was different, but yes, I remember her. I gave her a routine exam after her

216

cleaning, and we took a set of X-rays. She needs a couple of crowns, but that's not a crime," he said, handing the photograph back. "Can I ask why you're asking?"

"Miss Vickers is missing," Vince said. "You may be the last person to have seen her."

Crane was nonplussed. "Missing? And you think I might know something about that? I looked at her teeth."

"We're just trying to retrace her movements that day," Vince reassured him. "Her appointment here was her last of the day that we know of. Did she happen to say if she was going anywhere after she left here? Perhaps dinner with a friend, anything like that?"

"Oh my God," Crane said. "First there's a murder, now there's a woman missing? Nothing like that ever happens here."

"It's disturbing," Vince agreed.

"Are the two things related?"

"We don't know yet," Mendez said.

"Probably not," Vince added. "You'd be talking about a very rare kind of criminal if the cases were linked. It's highly unlikely."

"We've already talked about the possibility of a serial killer," Crane said.

Vince looked at Mendez, who looked a little sheepish. "In theory," he said.

"After we spoke yesterday, I started thinking," Crane said. "About a year or so ago—wasn't there

217

a woman found murdered outside of town? Do you think that murder is connected to this one?"

"I'm not free to speculate," Mendez said.

"I'm not sure which answer would be worse," Crane said. "More than one ordinary killer on the loose, or one extraordinary killer on the loose."

"We're aiming for C: None of the above," Vince said.

"The woman in the park," Crane said, "have you found out who she was?"

"Yes, she's been identified as Lisa Warwick, a nurse—"

"Lisa Warwick?" he said, shocked. "No."

"Did you know her?"

"Enough to say hello. She used to work at the Thomas Center. Oh, man, that's terrible."

"You do a lot of work for the center?" Vince asked.

"I give a break to their clients and employees," Crane said. "It's a good cause. My wife volunteers there as well. She helps with getting donations of clothing for work wardrobes and bringing in successful businesswomen to speak."

"Had you seen Ms. Warwick recently?" Mendez asked.

"No. I couldn't say when."

He leaned back against the counter, crossed his arms, and shook his head. "How did she die?"

"We're waiting on the full results of the autopsy," Mendez said. "But it appears she was strangled."

Crane closed his eyes and rubbed a hand across

his forehead as if the revelation had pained him.

"I hope she didn't suffer," he said quietly. "She was a nice girl."

"How is Tommy doing?" Mendez asked.

"He's pretty undone by the whole thing."

"Dr. Crane's son was one of the kids that found the body," Mendez explained.

Crane looked sharply at Vince.

"I was out of town that night," Vince said easily. "What a terrible thing for kids to have to see."

"He doesn't understand how one human being could do that to another human being," Crane said. "He asked me last night if I thought the man who killed that lady was crazy or just really angry with her."

"What did you tell him?"

"I told him I don't think anyone really understands why someone turns out to be a killer."

"That's not very reassuring," Vince said.

"My son is ten, and he's very bright, Detective. He knows if someone is lying to him. I told him he shouldn't worry about it, that just because a bad thing happened to that woman doesn't mean anything bad is going to happen to him; that he has a lot of people looking out for him, to keep him safe."

"Did he buy that?"

"I don't think so," Crane said honestly.

"Do you remember what time Ms. Vickers left here last Thursday?" Mendez asked.

"A cleaning and exam usually runs around an hour, so it must have been around five. Ava will remember," Crane said. "Ava remembers everything."

"How did Miss Vickers seem to you?" Vince asked.

Crane shrugged. "She didn't make much of an impression on me. She sat with her mouth open and I looked at her teeth. She seemed upset when I told her she would need the two crowns. She was getting ready to start a new job at the Quinn, Morgan law offices. She was worried about having to take time off.

"I told her I doubted it would be a problem. I know everybody at Quinn, Morgan. I told her she should talk to the office manager and we would work something out together. Maybe she went by there on her way home."

"Do you have patient parking here, Dr. Crane?" Vince asked.

"I have three spots behind the building. If those are full, they have to use public parking."

"It's all right if we take a look back there," Vince said. "There's a back door, right?"

"Yes. I'll show you."

He led them down a hall and out a door into the shadowed alley behind the building. Vince took it all in—the surrounding buildings, the lack of activity. The building directly next door had a large FOR LEASE sign up on the wall.

JAMESON REAL ESTATE with the phone number of the agency and a photo of a pretty, smiling agent inviting interested parties to call.

Two of the three parking slots marked for Peter Crane, DDS, were taken. One by a sleek, dark blue Jaguar sedan, and one by a white Toyota Celica.

"I couldn't tell you if Miss Vickers parked back here or not," Crane said. "Ava might know."

"Are there any surveillance cameras back here?" Vince asked, scanning the buildings across the alley.

"I don't know. I don't have one."

The door to the office opened and the all-knowing Ava leaned out.

"I'm sorry to interrupt," she said. "But Miss Navarre called, Dr. Crane. There was some kind incident at school. She asked if you could please come pick Tommy up."

"Incident?" Crane repeated. "What now?"

"She didn't elaborate."

Crane sighed. "I'm sorry, guys. I've got to go."

"By all means," Vince said. "Family first."

Ava held the doctor's car keys out to him, but looked to Vince and Mendez. "Our hygienist, Robin, will be in tomorrow. She did Miss Vickers's cleaning."

"Just for the record, Dr. Crane," Mendez said. "Where were you last Thursday night?"

"Home with my family. Call me if you have any more questions," Crane said, going to the

Jag. "But I honestly don't think I'll be of much help. I'm sure I'm not the last person who saw Karly Vickers that day."

"Why do you say that?" Vince asked.

"Because the last person to see her that day must have been the person who took her, and I know that wasn't me."

He opened the car door but stopped short of getting in. "Is there a search going on?"

"Not yet," Mendez said.

Crane's brow furrowed. "Shouldn't there be? One woman is dead. One woman is missing. It would be terrible if she ended up dead too just because no one was looking for her."

"We're looking for her," Mendez said. "You have my card if you think of anything."

"He's right, you know," Vince said as Crane's car disappeared down the alley. "Karly Vickers could be out there somewhere with the clock ticking down on her life right this minute—if she's not already dead. She's probably wondering if anyone is looking for her, if anyone has even noticed she's missing."

"Lisa Warwick went missing on a Friday," Mendez said. "She was found dead eleven days later. Karly Vickers went missing last Thursday. Let's hope our killer sticks to a schedule."

Vince gave him a sober look. "I wouldn't bet a life on it."

# 31

Mendez stared down at the decayed human finger lying in the dirt near the end of the bench on the third-base line. Flies buzzed around it and crawled on it. The thing was so rotten, the skin had split and started coming off.

He glanced sideways at Vince, who had taken a seat on the bench. They had picked up the call as soon as they made it back to the car from Crane's office. Go to Oak Knoll Elementary immediately. It seemed like an unlikely place for crime. And the crime didn't seem like anything to call the cops over—one kid beat up another kid in gym class.

A severed human finger, Vince conceded, made all the difference. He shook a couple of pills out of a small white bottle and tossed them back.

"You all right?" Mendez asked.

"Headache," he said. Like someone-had-put-an-axe-through-his-head headache.

"What do you make of this?"

"Your vic's missing an index finger. There's an index finger. We don't need Sherlock Holmes for this one."

Hicks bent over the finger too. He shooed the flies off it. They were back on it in two seconds. "Man, that's gross. The Farman kid must have picked it up at the scene Tuesday night."

"The girl told me he touched the body,"

Mendez said. "She didn't say he broke off a finger and stuck it in his pocket."

"Bag the finger and let's go talk to the boy," Vince said, pushing himself to his feet. "I can't wait to hear what he has to say for himself."

They convened in the conference room. Dennis was sitting in a chair, sullen, his lip split, his clothes dirty. He hadn't spoken a word since he'd been dragged indoors by Mr. Alvarez. The gym teacher told Anne it had taken a good ten minutes for him to calm down out on the baseball diamond.

"He just kept swinging and fighting, spewing out the filthiest language I ever heard," he said. "It was like he was possessed or something. I had all I could do to hang on to him."

That in itself was frightening, Anne thought. Dennis was bigger than the rest of her students, but he was still a little boy. Paco Alvarez was built like a fireplug with massive arms.

"I think if I hadn't been there to stop him, he would have killed Tommy Crane," he whispered, glancing over at Dennis as if he were expecting him to leap over the table and charge like a wild animal.

Dennis lifted his head and glared at them, as if to say, "What are you looking at?" then looked down once more at the tabletop.

"That's some serious rage issue," Alvarez said. "The kid had blood in his eye, you know? Like a fighting dog."

Anne knew nothing about fighting dogs. She was beginning to think she didn't know much about anything. Shouldn't she have seen warning signs in Dennis Farman? Or had the warning signs been written off to the easy excuses: Dennis is insecure, Dennis is jealous, Dennis is a garden-variety bully? Maybe there was no such thing.

"I don't know what to say, Paco," she said softly. "He's got bigger problems than I'm equipped to deal with."

The door opened and Principal Garnett came into the room with Detective Mendez and two other men—a redheaded man in his thirties with a badge clipped to his belt, and a tall man in his late forties with chiseled good looks, an air of command, and dark eyes that set their gaze squarely on her.

He broke away from the others and came toward her, holding out his hand.

"You must be Miss Navarre," he said. His hand was big and warm, and swallowed hers whole. "I'm Detective Leone."

Anne turned her head to introduce Alvarez, but the gym teacher had moved on to speak with Mendez. They looked as if they knew each other.

"Detective."

"You've had quite a shock today," he said, still holding her hand.

She didn't object. He was a big man—on the lean side, but still there was a solidness about him that seemed reassuring. Like he was here to take care of everything—a quality that was very appealing to her at the moment.

"Are you all right?" he asked.

"I'm a little shaken up," she admitted.

"Were you on the field when all this went down?"

"No," she said, finally slipping her hand from his. "As it happened, I was in Mr. Garnett's office, having a conversation with him about Dennis. He spent the morning drawing this."

She angled herself so Dennis couldn't see the notebook she had been clutching. She opened it to the page of violent drawings.

Detective Leone frowned darkly as he studied the picture. "He drew these today?"

"This morning," she said. "He's been agitated all day. He's one of the children who found the body."

"Deputy Farman's son."

"Yes. I suppose you know him."

Leone hummed an acknowledgment, but his focus was entirely on the drawing.

"How old is this boy?"

"Eleven. He was held back in the third grade."

"Has he said anything about where or how he got the finger?"

"No. He hasn't spoken at all since Mr. Alvarez brought him in from gym class."

"This is very disturbing," he said softly. Finally he raised his eyes from the drawing to her face. "And it was a young lady he attacked initially this afternoon?"

"Yes. Wendy Morgan. Then Tommy Crane."

"Has he demonstrated violence against girls before?"

"No more than the average fifth-grade boy," she said. "At least not that I've been aware of. But he had quite an outburst with me this morning."

She told him about what had happened in her classroom and what had gone on the evening before when she had stopped at the Farman home.

"I'm afraid he might be blaming me for getting him in trouble," she said. "His parents weren't aware he had skipped school. I think he might have gotten a spanking for it. He wouldn't sit down all morning."

"Could I have a photocopy of this page, Miss Navarre?" Leone asked. "A couple of them, please?"

"Yes, of course."

"The other children who found the body are in your class as well?"

"Yes. This has been a very challenging week."

"I'd like to sit down and talk with you about the kids," he said. "Are you free this evening?"

"Um . . . uh . . . Yes, sure," she said, instantly thinking that Franny would kill her. Thursday was their standing date for Chinese.

"Good. Dinner at seven? Piazza Fontana?"

"Are you asking me on a date, Detective?" she asked, a little shocked at his audacity . . . and a little something else.

"That would be improper of me," he said.

But he didn't say no.

"I've been away," he said. "Just got back last night. I'd like to get a clearer picture of what happened Tuesday. Your insights would be appreciated. Your pleasant company would be a bonus," he added.

Mendez joined them then, and Leone had her show Dennis's drawing to him.

"Jesus Christ," Mendez said, then caught himself. "Sorry, ma'am."

"Has the school notified the boy's parents about this?" Leone asked.

"Deputy Farman is on his way," she said, wishing the principal had called Dennis's mother instead.

Mendez spoke to Leone. "I say we ask the kid about the finger before Frank gets here. If we aren't going to charge him with anything, we don't need a parent present to ask him questions."

Vince shrugged. "Your call. The Cranes might want to press assault charges."

"I'll only ask him about the finger."

He started toward the table then turned back in an afterthought. "Thank you, Miss Navarre. You've been very helpful."

"I'm staying," Anne said firmly.

"I'm sorry?"

"I'm staying while you talk to Dennis," Anne said. "He's my responsibility as long as he's in this building."

Mendez shrugged. "That's fine."

She grabbed hold of the sleeve of his sport coat as he started to turn away again. He swung back around and looked at her.

"And I don't want you asking him about the drawings," she said, keeping her tone low. "He doesn't know I have the notebook. I don't want him to know I betrayed his trust. I want to be able to help him—if I can."

They went to the table together then and sat down to interview Dennis Farman. But Dennis had nothing to say. Not one word. He wouldn't tell them how the finger came to be in his possession. He wouldn't talk at all, and no amount of threats or cajoling could change his mind. He sat mute, staring down at the tabletop with God knew what churning around in his head.

Hicks headed back to the office to see if anything had come in on his background checks of the staff at the Thomas Center. Vince and Mendez walked out of the school and stood on the sidewalk waiting for Frank Farman to show up. The other kids were long gone before they had even made it to the scene—Tommy Crane picked up by his father and taken to the ER, Wendy Morgan picked up by her father also.

"Those are some violent fantasies that kid has running around in his head," Vince said, offering Mendez a stick of Doublemint gum. "He's got some deep-seated anger. Why is that? Kids don't come out of the chute like that. It's learned behavior. Who did he learn it from?"

"Frank's wound a little too tight," Mendez said. "But I don't see him drawing pictures of women with knives stuck in their breasts."

"That boy is a perfect candidate to go all wrong and end up really hurting someone. You'll have to keep your eye on him for years to come."

"Great. I hope the Cranes press charges. We can pack him off to a juvenile facility."

"And he'll be all straightened out when he comes out of there," Vince said sarcastically.

They just stood there for a minute, taking in the momentary quiet, each turning their thoughts over in their heads.

"The teacher's cute," Vince said at last.

"Yeah."

"She's got spunk, sticking up for her kids. I like that," he said. He looked at Mendez out the corner of his eye. "Have you asked her out?"

Mendez startled at the question. "What? No! I'm in the middle of a case."

Vince shrugged. "A guy's gotta eat."

"I just met her yesterday."

"So? I just met her an hour ago."

Mendez stared at him. "You asked her out? She's young enough to be your daughter!"

"Yeah," he said, grinning. "But she isn't."

"I can't believe you asked her out! In the middle of all of that, you asked her out."

"We're meeting for dinner. To talk about the kids," he added.

"She doesn't know it's a date."

"She knows she's having dinner with a charming gentleman at a very nice Italian restaurant."

"I can't believe you asked her out," Mendez said. "She's part of the investigation."

"She's not a vic. She's not a witness. And she's not the perp," Vince pointed out. "There's no conflict of interest. Life is short, junior. Carpe diem."

A county cruiser pulled up at the curb and Frank Farman got out, his face a mask of steel.

"I can't believe this," he said half under his breath. "He had a *finger*?"

"He had to have taken it off Lisa Warwick," Mendez said. "She was missing an index finger at autopsy."

"For God's sake," Farman said, jamming his hands on his hips. "I don't know what's wrong with that boy. I try to set him straight, and he does something like this."

"He beat up the Crane kid pretty bad," Mendez said. "They might want to press charges."

"Jesus Christ." He looked one way and then the other, as if he expected Christ to appear on command.

He didn't get Christ. He got Anne Navarre. The teacher marched out of the building with all the determination of Napoleon.

"Mr. Farman, can I have a word with you?"

"I really don't have the time—"

"You don't have the time to discuss the fact that your son brought a human finger to school today? What could you possibly have going on more urgent than dealing with this?"

"I have a job to do, Miss Navarre."

"Yes. It's called *parenting*. It comes with having children. Does it not mean anything to you that your son is having serious problems here?"

Vince watched Farman's face redden. The deputy wouldn't take being dressed down in front of his peers. Anne Navarre seemed to have no regard. She stood up to him like an angry mouse taunting a lion.

"Dennis needs help. Professional help."

Farman leaned toward her, trying to intimidate her with his size. "I don't need you telling me how to raise my own kid. My wife is coming to deal with Dennis."

"I should be glad," she said. "At least the beating will be postponed."

"How dare you," Farman growled, taking a menacing step toward her.

Vince stepped between them. "Let's take a break here, folks. Cool down."

He herded Anne Navarre a few steps away just as Sharon Farman pulled to the curb behind the cruiser. Frank Farman took a deliberate breath and let it out slowly like releasing steam from a pressure cooker.

"My wife will deal with Dennis," he said, turning to Mendez. "We have to go."

"Where?"

"It just came over the radio," Farman said. "The air search located the two cars: Lisa Warwick's and Karly Vickers's. Dixon wants us on the scene."

# 32

The cars were parked in a field with a hundred others. Hiding in plain sight. The field belonged to a scrap dealer named Gordon Sells.

Mendez got out of his car and walked into a circus. The sheriff's office helicopter had landed, but three other helicopters adorned with logos of LA television stations hovered overhead, blades beating the air. News vans clogged the sides of the country road, and cameramen and reporters were swarming the area like mosquitoes frantic to land on something juicy.

Frank Farman shouted instructions at half a dozen deputies trying to cordon off the scene with yellow tape. Dixon stood near Karly Vickers's gold Chevy Nova, instructing his photographer and videographer as they captured every possible angle of the car, the cars around the car, the ground around the car.

"Tony. Good," Dixon said. "We're going to haul the cars in and process them in our garage."

"Right. Where's Lisa Warwick's car?"

"Two rows back." He pointed in the direction of several deputies, who stood guard around that car. "The chopper pilot said this car definitely came onto the property from a back gate off a dirt road. He could still see the tracks in the grass."

"In the last couple of days," Mendez said.

"And now we've got the press all over us," Dixon said. "Someone heard about the eyes and mouths being glued shut on Warwick and Julie Paulson."

"Shit. We have a leak in our department?"

"I don't know where it came from."

"It could have come from the killer," Mendez said. "Vince thinks the guy wants publicity."

"Where is he?"

"At his hotel. He's working on the profile."

*And a date with Anne Navarre,* he thought, still out of sorts about it, even though it was none of his business, and it wasn't exactly a date. Leone wanted an angle on the kids. Crane's father was the last person to have seen Karly Vickers. Wendy Morgan's father had a connection to Lisa Warwick. And the Farman kid was a budding serial killer who had the victim's severed finger as a souvenir. Any insights she could give them would be welcome.

"Do you think he might have helped out with the publicity?" Dixon asked.

"Vince? Tip the press? No," Mendez said automatically.

"Don't be so sure, Tony. The guy has a reputation."

"As one of the top profilers in the world."

"And one of the most well-known. He didn't get that way being shy and retiring. He might tell us he's gone low profile, but that's not his MO."

Mendez didn't like the assessment. "It's moot now. The press is here. They know what they know. We've got a job to do. Have you talked to the owner of the property yet? What's his story?"

"I've got a couple of deputies sitting on him, they're waiting for you and Hicks. I wanted to get these cars secured first."

"Are you going in with the cars?"

"Yeah."

"And who else?" Mendez asked.

"Why?"

Mendez made a face as if the whole subject tasted bad. "Farman's kid brought Lisa Warwick's severed finger to school for show-and-tell today."

Dixon's eyes went wide. "What?"

"Yeah. It's in a brown bag in my trunk. He tried to feed it to a classmate."

"Oh my God."

"The kid probably picked it up at the scene, but how is that going to look in the press? The boy had the victim's finger and we're letting his father into the victim's car? I don't want to get into it with Frank, but that's going to look improper. A lawyer could use that down the road."

Dixon took a moment to let it soak in. He

would look at the situation from the perspective of nearly two decades spent as a detective himself. It wouldn't matter how well he knew Frank Farman. It wouldn't matter that Farman had a spotless record. This was now a procedural issue.

"Point taken," he said. "Go talk to the property owner. I'll deal with Frank. Does he know about this incident with his son?"

"Yes."

Mendez breathed a short sigh of relief. He walked across the field two rows to Lisa Warwick's car, where Hicks was standing talking with a couple of deputies.

"We're up to speak to the property owner," he said.

"Did you tell Dixon about the finger?"

"Yeah. He said he'll deal with Frank."

"Better him than you."

They took Mendez's car out of the field and down the road to the main entrance of the junkyard, which was blocked with reporters and deputies.

Mendez honked his horn impatiently. Hicks held his ID up. A photographer snapped a picture.

"Guess now we find out what it's like to be in the big time," Hicks said.

"Looks like it's a pain in the ass."

The junkyard office was a rusty trailer house that appeared to be a residence as well. Mendez and Hicks walked in, squinting at the harsh fluorescent lighting that shone down from an acoustic tile ceiling yellowed with cigarette smoke. The place was a mess and stank with the smell of sour sweat and fried onions.

A deputy sat at the kitchen table with the man Mendez presumed to be Gordon Sells. Sells looked a hard midforties, balding, grim-faced. Chest and back hair sprouted out around the confines of his stained wife-beater.

"Mr. Sells," Mendez said, holding out his hand. "I'm Detective Mendez. This is my partner Detective Hicks."

Unmoved by social niceties, Sells scowled up at him and said, "I ain't got nothing to do with them cars. I don't know how they got here."

Mendez took a chair. Hicks leaned back against the cluttered kitchen counter, flushing out a cat that had been busy hunting for food scraps among the dirty dishes.

"You've never seen those cars before?" Mendez asked.

Sells shook his head. Mendez imagined what a woman's reaction would be to this guy. What hair he had was unkempt. What looked like four or five days of beard roughened his jaw line.

"How is that, Mr. Sells?" he asked. "Your property is fenced in, isn't it?"

"Yep."

"So somebody had to open a gate to get those cars in."

"I don't know nothing about it."

Mendez took the snapshot of Karly Vickers out of his jacket pocket. "Have you ever seen this woman?"

Sells barely glanced at it. "Nope."

"Does the name Lisa Warwick mean anything to you?"

"Nope."

"Those are the women who own those cars. One of them is dead. One of them is missing."

"I don't know nothing about that," he said, unfazed by the terrible news.

"Do you have any employees, Mr. Sells?" Hicks asked.

"It's me and my nephew, that's all. He don't know nothing either."

"And where is he?" Hicks asked.

Sells yelled out. "Kenny! Get in here!"

Kenny emerged from the next room, a huge, stupid-looking kid of maybe twenty. He looked like he had walked right off the set of *Deliverance* in his coveralls with one strap hanging down and his mouth hanging open.

Mendez got up and went through the introductions again. Kenny just stared at him blankly.

"Have you ever seen this woman?" Mendez asked, showing him Karly Vickers's photo.

Kenny shrugged.

"He don't know nothing," Sells said impatiently. "He's half a retard."

"Am not," Kenny said in a low dull voice.

"This woman is missing," Mendez said. "The woman that owned the other car is dead. Murdered."

Sells scowled. "He don't know—"

Mendez slammed his hand down on the table and leaned over him. "Shut the fuck up! I don't want to hear how you don't know nothing, you ignorant rube!"

"I ain't under arrest!" Sells shouted back.

Mendez grabbed his cuffs off his belt. "You want to change that? I can change that right now."

Hicks stepped forward calmly and put a hand on his arm. "Tony, calm down. I'm sure Mr. Sells just isn't understanding the seriousness of the situation."

"What part of a murder charge isn't clear to him?" Mendez demanded.

"Take a break," Hicks instructed.

Mendez walked away a few feet to pace restlessly in front of the refrigerator. He grumbled nasty menacing threats in Spanish. Sells didn't have to understand Spanish to know none of it was good.

Hicks took a seat at the table and spoke in a confidential tone. "I apologize for my partner, Mr. Sells, but the woman who was murdered was his cousin, so . . ."

Sells narrowed his eyes, suspicious. "He's a spic. I seen that woman on TV—"

"His cousin by marriage," Hicks specified without missing a beat.

"If I find out you laid a hand on her—," Mendez started, pointing a finger at Sells.

Hicks held his hand up. "Tony, please."

He sighed as he turned back to Sells. "You know, Mr. Sells, if you bought those cars off somebody, you're not in any trouble," he lied. "Our only interest is in finding a killer, and finding that other girl before something bad happens to her."

Sells looked from one to the other of them. Mendez had a feeling he'd seen Good Cop/Bad Cop before. He probably had a record for something.

Sells looked right at Hicks and said, "I don't know nothing about them cars."

Mendez nodded at the deputy, who rose from his seat and turned to the nephew. Mendez went to Sells, opening one of the handcuffs.

"You can stand up, Mr. Sells," he said. "Or I can drag you out of that chair. I don't care which."

"For what?" Sells demanded, but started to get up just the same.

"You're under arrest for possession of stolen property."

They ran Sells and his nephew to the sheriff's office in separate cars. Sells behind a cage in a radio car, the nephew in the backseat of Mendez's sedan. The hope was that separated from his uncle, the kid might have something to say. He didn't.

Hicks put Sells in one interview room and left him there. Mendez stuck the nephew in the room next door. The two of them walked down the hall to get coffee. It was going to be a long night.

"What do you think?" Hicks said.

"The guy gives me the creeps," Mendez said. "You running his record? He's got to have a sheet."

"Not back yet, but I agree."

"Did he ask for a lawyer?"

"Not yet."

"If we can book him for the car theft, we get his prints. I called the ADA for search warrants."

Hicks made a face. "I can't wait to look under the furniture in that place."

"I'll flip you for the bathroom."

"Oh, man . . ."

They doctored their coffees and went to their desks. Sells and his nephew could sit and reflect.

Hicks checked the message slips that had been left on his desk and held one up. "Greg Usher—Karly Vickers's ex—is doing a nickel in LA County for growing pot in his apartment."

"Cross him off the list."

"Here's a good one. One of the maintenance guys at the Thomas Center has a record. His current name is an alias."

"A record for what?"

Hicks raised a brow. "Car theft among other things."

"Anything violent?"

"Domestic violence on a girlfriend six years ago."

"Can we pick him up for something?"

Hicks laughed. "He has outstanding parking and traffic violations to the tune of four hundred and fifty-eight dollars."

Mendez shook his head.

The phone they shared between their two desks rang. He picked it up and listened, and when he hung up he said, "I can trump your car thief. Gordon Sells has a record. As a sex offender."

# 33

"It's not a date," Anne insisted.

"It had better be a date. Chinese night is sacrosanct," Franny said as they walked from the downtown parking lot toward the plaza. "This is Detective Hottie?"

"This is a different detective," Anne said evasively.

"Also a hottie?"

"He's old enough to be my father," she said, even though she certainly hadn't reacted to him that way. Her father had thirty years on Vince Leone.

"Oooh, kinky, but I can totally see it," Franny said.

Anne gave him a look. "Thanks. I'm glad I have such an adventurous sex life in your head."

"You should be. It's the only sex life you have."

She couldn't argue that.

"You're attracted to him," he declared slyly. "You *changed clothes*."

"So did you."

"But I didn't go from Nancy Novice Nun to showing off my perky little breasts in a clingy sweater."

"You're horrible to me," Anne said. "Isn't this what you want me to do? Wear something different?"

"Yes, but you never listened before," he pointed out.

"This is a perfectly conservative sweater," Anne grumbled. And her moss-colored skirt was a perfectly conservative—if slightly form-fitting—skirt that hit just below the tops of her low-heeled brown boots.

The sidewalks and streets were busy. College kids roamed in packs, laughing and talking, heading to the bookstore, to the coffeehouse, to ladies' night at the Buddha Bar. The restaurants were busy. Musicians parked themselves on street corners, playing for change.

"I'm coming to the restaurant," Franny declared.

"No, you aren't. You're going for Chinese."

"I can't go for Chinese without you. It wouldn't be right."

"Don't hold back on my account, really."

"You never answered me," he said. "Is he hot?"

Hot wasn't the right word. Honestly, Mendez was hot. Leone was ruggedly handsome, yet distinguished . . . Anne felt a blush creeping up her neck, much to her consternation. "No."

"Liar!" Franny exclaimed, laughing, highly amused.

Anne stopped and looked at him. "Why am I speaking to you?"

He kissed her on the cheek. "Because I just took your mind off the fact you have the Marquis de Sade Junior for a pupil. Run along now, Anne Marie. Don't want to keep your gentleman friend waiting."

Shaking her head, Anne walked across the plaza to Piazza Fontana, to her non-date.

"It's not a date," Vince muttered to himself as he straightened his tie in the men's room mirror.

What the hell had he been thinking? Anne Navarre probably hadn't even been born yet when he joined the Bureau. He had to be out of his mind. Maybe he should start taking the anti-psychotic drugs, after all.

And asking her in the middle of what had been going on at the school—definitely a sign of brain damage.

It was the bullet's fault. A hallmark of damage to the frontal lobe of the brain: impulsive behavior.

He was feeling edgy, that end-of-the-day out-of-gas nervousness that usually precipitated a big crash. He had managed a short rest after Mendez dropped him off, and he had dozed under the lights of the tanning machine in the salon, but it hadn't been enough. He needed about seventeen hours of sleep. At least he had a healthy glow in his face now thanks to a gazillion watts of fluorescent light and his easy-to-tan Italian complexion.

"Maybe you're just old, Vince," he muttered.

Then again, he should have been dead. So what the hell? Why shouldn't he have dinner with a lovely, intelligent twentysomething lady?

He spotted her entering the restaurant as he stepped out of the men's room. She looked very . . . determined, he decided, determined to be serious, determined to be taken seriously. She also looked a lot less like an elementary schoolteacher in her body-skimming sweater and stylish skirt. Nice.

"Miss Navarre," he said with his most charming smile. "You look lovely."

"Detective—"

"Vince, please. It's been a long day for both of us. Let's shelve the formalities, shall we?"

The maitre d' led them through the restaurant's interior to a quiet booth in a corner. Miss Navarre raised an eyebrow.

"We don't want eavesdroppers," Vince explained. "This isn't a conversation for public consumption, all things considered."

He ordered a bottle of pinot grigio and two glasses—not that he would be able to drink it considering the drugs he was on, but he could pretend to while the lovely Anne loosened up a bit. She looked just this side of suspicious.

"Are you allowed to drink on the job?"

Vince grinned. "Darling, life is too short not to drink wine."

"Okay. Well, I can certainly use it."

"You're not used to having your school overrun with detectives?"

"Not before this week."

"How long have you been a teacher?"

"Five years." It seemed like that was all she was going to say, but then she hastened to add, "But I had a double major in college, which took an extra year, and then a year of grad school."

So she wasn't as close to being jailbait as one might have thought. She had to be twenty-seven or twenty-eight. He wanted to smile at her need to set him straight on that, but he refrained.

"What was your other major?"

"Psychology. I wanted to be a child psychologist, but—" She stopped herself from being so eager. "Life . . . took a different turn."

"Funny how that happens."

Anne looked away, took a deep breath, and sighed. She was embarrassed, he thought. She probably didn't just go around telling her life story to strangers—or to people she knew, for that matter. He pegged her for the kind of woman who confided in one friend, if she confided in anyone, cautious in the way of an old soul—or a wounded one.

The waiter brought the wine. Vince sampled it and nodded his approval. They ordered their meals, sipped at their glasses.

"Anne," he said. "I have a confession to make. I don't work for the sheriff's office. I'm a special agent with the FBI. For now, it's better that isn't common knowledge. My specialty is profiling serial killers."

She said nothing, but her eyes got wider.

"I don't know how much you've been told by Detective Mendez," he went on, "but there is reason to believe Lisa Warwick—the woman your students found in the park—was the latest victim in a series of at least three murders."

"Oh my God."

"Another woman is missing. So, you can see, it's imperative that we try to learn as much as we can from every possible avenue."

"I don't know what I can do," she said. "I teach fifth grade."

"Detective Mendez told me you have a pretty good handle on who your kids are. I saw that for myself this afternoon."

She laughed without humor. "Oh, yeah. I'm so sharp I had no idea Dennis Farman was having homicidal fantasies."

"Why would you suspect that?" Vince asked. "How many people would look at a kid in the fifth grade and peg him for a future killer? Nobody. That's highly aberrant behavior. No normal-thinking person would look for that."

"And that's where you come in?"

He gave her half a smile. "Yeah. I've been experienced right out of normal thinking. I've spent a long time studying murderers and trying to figure out how they got that way and what makes them tick."

"How do you sleep with that in your head?"

"Great," he admitted, "as long as I'm medicated."

"Why do you do it?"

"Because maybe if I'm good enough at what I do, I can prevent some innocent people from dying. Maybe I can spot a kid like Dennis Farman and get the right people to pay attention to him. I'm sure you can relate to that."

She nodded and looked away, a soft sheen of moisture coming into her eyes.

"I'm sorry you have to get dragged into this world, Anne," Vince said, genuinely sorry for her. She probably still had ideals, and she probably still believed the world could hold up to them. "I know this is hard for you."

"I'm afraid the right people *aren't* going to pay attention to Dennis," she said. "Especially not now. He's being expelled from school. He'll be running around loose, with no supervision, no guidance. Who's supposed to police him? His parents work. And even if they were home, they must be terrible parents or he wouldn't be the way he is."

Vince sighed. He would have been agreeing with her if he hadn't wanted to keep her from crying. In fact, if he had been teaching a seminar, using Dennis Farman for an example, he would have said it was probably already too late to save him.

His colleagues back in Quantico would think the same. He had sent them Dennis Farman's drawing by fax. He would talk to them the next day, but he already knew what they would say. They would say Dennis Farman already had well-established violent, antisocial behavioral tendencies. His artwork already showed sadistic fantasies—sadistic *sexual* fantasies in a child who had yet to reach puberty. There probably wasn't going to be any fixing what was wrong with this kid.

But he wasn't about to say any of that to Anne.

"You're right in what you told his father," he said instead. "The boy should have psychiatric counseling."

"And what army is going to make his father believe that?" she asked. "Frank Farman probably thinks he can beat the bad out of Dennis."

The strain of the day's events was taking a toll on her. Vince reached across the table, put his big hand over her small one and gave it a squeeze.

"Don't give up, Anne. Not yet. You fought for that boy today. You stood up to Mendez and me, you stood up to his dad. He needs someone on his side."

One crystalline tear slipped over the edge of her lashes and down her cheek as she looked away from him, embarrassed.

"Hey, come on," Vince cajoled, his voice soft. "No crying. You'll ruin my reputation as a ladies' man."

He won a little smile for that one.

"Are you a ladies' man?" she asked, visibly relieved for the distraction.

"That all depends on the lady," he admitted.

Her cheeks bloomed pink and she glanced away, still harboring the little smile. She extricated her hand from under his, wiped the stray tear away and tucked a strand of brown hair behind her ear.

"I'm sorry," she said. "I don't usually fall apart that easily."

"I'm betting you never fall apart at all," he said. "But you don't usually have a kid bring a severed human finger to your classroom either. I think you can cut yourself some slack."

"Yeah. I guess so."

Their food arrived. Her caprese salad, his baked ziti. Vince pushed his plate at her.

"Eat," he ordered. "Have some ziti. My Italian mother's cure for everything. She would tell you *Avete bisogno della vostra resistenza! Ci e niente a voi!*"

She seemed pleased with his flamboyant Italian. "What does that mean?"

"You need your strength. You're too skinny.

My mother thinks everyone under two hundred pounds is too skinny. Never mind that I can pick her up with one hand."

"How old is she?"

"Eighty-two. And your mother?"

"Passed away." She dropped her eyes and picked at a piece of pasta. "A few years ago. Pancreatic cancer."

"I'm sorry," Vince said. The different turn Anne Navarre's life had taken. Her mother died. She left school. "And your father?"

"Will outlive both of us, despite his alleged poor health."

She didn't seem especially happy about the prospect.

"You still haven't told me how I'm supposed to help your investigation," she said. Back to business.

He stuck a fork in his side of the pasta. "Tell me about Tommy Crane."

She thought he'd thrown her a curve ball. She looked up at him, suspicious again. "Why would you want to know about Tommy?"

"We have to pursue all possible angles in a case like this," he said. "Understand?"

"Yes."

"I'm not saying the investigation is going in one direction or another at this point. We're still trying to piece together the last day anyone saw Karly Vickers, the missing girl. Miss Vickers had a dentist's appointment last Thursday. It was her last appointment of the day."

"With Peter Crane."

"So far, he's the last person to have seen her— that we know of."

"You can't possibly think he's involved," she said. "He's the nicest man. Tommy adores his father."

"I didn't say he was a suspect. He's not even a person of interest at this point," Vince explained. "But he is the last person to have seen this young woman. We have to account for his whereabouts that night. I would like to do that as discreetly as possible."

"I can't tell you anything about that," she said. "But I can tell you he seems to be a wonderful father. Now Tommy's mother, on the other hand . . ."

"Difficult?"

"The Queen of Hearts from *Alice in Wonderland*. Ask Detective Mendez."

"And what's Tommy like?"

"He loves baseball, he plays the piano, and has a better head for math than I do," she said with a crooked smile. "He's smart, thoughtful, quiet. Every mother's dream."

"Outgoing?"

"No. Tommy is an observer," she said, very much in her element talking about her student, analyzing what made him tick. They weren't so different that way. She wanted to get into their little heads, figure them out. "He stands back and watches what's happening before he decides on a course of action."

"He got his butt kicked today."

"He was coming to the rescue for Wendy—the girl Dennis attacked. And he did that knowing full well Dennis would kick his butt."

Vince smiled. "Chivalry lives on."

"That's the kind of boy he is. And by Tommy's accounts, that's the kind of man his father is."

"Fair enough," Vince said. "But would you do me a favor? Would you ask Tommy about last Thursday night? Was his dad home or did he go out that night?"

The idea was leaving a bad taste in her mouth. He could see her resistance rising.

"They're easy questions, and they probably have easy answers," he said. "I just think it's better if they come from you. He doesn't need an FBI agent scaring him, asking him questions about his dad. He trusts you."

She arched a brow. "So I should manipulate him?"

"I'm not asking you to manipulate him. Ask him a couple of questions for me. That's all."

"Why don't you ask Mrs. Crane?"

"The Queen of Hearts?" he tossed her own description back at her. "Wives have ulterior motives. Kids don't."

She thought about it for minute, giving him the I-don't-quite-trust-you eye. She had a shield like a Spartan warrior, this one, and she might guard herself with it, or she might smack him in the head with it if that seemed the more prudent thing to do.

"I'm not asking you to steal trade secrets," Vince said, scooping up some ziti. "Just to ask a little boy where his dad was last Thursday night."

"I guess I could do that," she said reluctantly.

"What do you know about the Morgan family?" he asked.

"They're nice people. The dad—Steve—is an attorney. Sara sometimes teaches art classes for the community education program. She's mostly a stay-at-home mom. They have the one child—Wendy."

"Good marriage?"

She shrugged. "As far as I know. Don't tell me Steve Morgan is a suspect."

"He was a friend of Lisa Warwick. We have to check him out. It's just routine. You could probably get a feeling from the girl if something was off at home, right?"

"And what do I get for interrogating my students?" she asked, surprising him.

"I'll talk to your principal," he offered. "Recommend that he set up some tutoring sessions for Dennis Farman. Maybe the boy could come to school for a couple of hours a day, as long he isn't allowed in the classroom or on the playground. That way you can maintain some contact with him. How does that sound?"

"I would appreciate your support in that."

*Quid pro quo*, Vince thought. Maybe she would

find out something useful, or maybe nothing would come of it . . . except another dinner . . . or two . . .

He reached his hand across the table and she met it with hers. Her hand was small and soft, but strong, like a woman who knew what she wanted. He liked that.

"Deal?" he asked.

"Deal."


He insisted on walking Anne to her car, and she put up little resistance. With a possible serial killer on the loose, it was no time for women to be turning down extra safety measures.

He put her in her sporty little red Volkswagen and leaned down into the open window.

"Lock your doors and don't stop for anybody," he instructed.

"Yes, sir."

"And don't call me 'sir.' You'll make me think I'm too old."

"Too old for what?" she asked with that little Mona Lisa half-smile and a sparkle in her eye.

With no thought process involved, he leaned down and kissed her on the lips.

"For that," he murmured.

Damn bullet.

She didn't slap him. That was a good first step.

"Thanks for your help, Anne," he said.

She was still trying to process the kiss in her analytical little brain.

"Thanks for the ziti," she said.

He watched her drive away into the night, not quite daring to let his hopes go where they wanted. Then he walked across the street and down the alley to the back of Peter Crane's office.

Anne poured herself a glass of wine and went to stand on the back porch, just outside the open kitchen door. She thought of Vince's warning to be careful. There was a killer prowling the streets. But her yard was fenced, and the moon was bright, and she wanted just a few minutes to over-think the evening before she went to bed.

She touched her upper lip, still feeling the brush and tickle of his mustache as he kissed her. She tried to remember the last time she'd been kissed.

Not only did she not have dating life, truth to tell, she was avoiding having a dating life. The men in her social circle weren't men, they were over-grown frat boys who still played video games. The second ring of her social circle was made up of the parents of her students, most of whom were married, not many happily. From her own perspective as a child, she had seen the ideal of being married with children was not all it was cracked up to be. And so she had never been in a hurry to go there.

But she had to admit there was something about Vince Leone that attracted her, beyond his looks. He was strong, intelligent, knew his mind. He saw something he wanted, and he took it.

Too bad he wouldn't be sticking around. He would finish his work here and go back to Virginia, to another round of heinous crime.

She couldn't imagine constantly being immersed in a world of death and evil. Three days of it had been enough for her.

Even as she took a sip of the warm, full-bodied cabernet, she shivered at the idea that evil was not that far away, roaming the streets like a wolf hunting for prey. She thought back to what she had been doing Monday night—grading papers, going over lesson plans, listening to a Phil Collins album—while someone had been torturing and killing Lisa Warwick. She had been sleeping soundly while the killer buried her body in the park, leaving her head aboveground with the idea that someone would see her and be shocked and horrified.

As she stood there on her porch, he was out there with another victim. Things were happening that she would never want to imagine.

She shivered again and goose bumps ran over her in a stampede. She stared out to the darkness beyond her yard and felt as if he might be right there, watching her, the division between her world and his only as thick as the width of her lawn.

She turned then and went into the house, locking the door behind her . . . never aware of the figure standing just out of reach of the moonlight, watching her go.

# 34

"So, Gordon," Mendez said, sitting down across from Gordon Sells at the little table in the interview room.

Sells scowled at him. "I didn't say you could call me that."

"I didn't ask," Mendez said flatly, looking down at the papers he had brought into the room with him. "So, Gordon, you've got yourself a record. You're a pedophile."

"I am not."

"A jury decided you are."

"Them girls lied. I didn't do nothing to them."

"Except expose yourself, fondle yourself, put your hand down their pants—"

"I never did that."

"And you didn't have a collection of kiddie porn stashed in your house either, I suppose. It says here you had a hundred thirty-one pages of photographs of minor girls in various states of undress."

"From the JC Penney catalog!" Sells shouted. "Them were things I was gonna order for my nieces for Christmas presents."

"And the twenty-seven photographs of minor girls engaging in sexual activity with an adult. Whose Christmas present was that collection?"

Agitated, Sells got up out of his chair and started

to walk toward the door. Mendez rose, blocking him.

"Stay on your side of the table, Gordon. And have a seat. We're going to be here for a long time."

He turned to another page in what was supposed to be a thick file on the life and times of Gordon Sells. In reality he had one sheet on Sells. The rest of the file was from an assault case he had closed three months prior.

"You were a guest of the California State Department of Correction for twelve years up in Wasco." Mendez looked up at him, just this side of amused. "I bet that was fun. There's nothing cons like better than raping a child rapist. Or maybe you liked that."

Sells jumped up out of his chair again, his face flushing red. "I don't wanna talk to you! I wanna talk to the other guy!"

Mendez remained calm. "Nobody here cares what you want. Sit back down and stay there or I'll cuff you to the wall."

Reluctantly, Sells took his seat. He was breathing hard.

"You're going back to the can," Mendez said. "But it won't be Wasco this time. They'll send you up to Folsom where a whole new pack of cons can take a crack at you."

"I ain't going to prison," Sells said. "I didn't do nothing wrong."

"The crime scene team isn't going to find any more pictures of little girls when they turn that pigsty you live in upside down?" Mendez asked. "That's a parole violation. We can send you back in just for that. Then there's the grand theft auto, and the murder—"

"I didn't kill nobody!"

Mendez shrugged. "You look good for it to me. You've got her car. If the CSI team comes up with so much as a hair from the head of Lisa Warwick in your home, you're done. And if there's any justice in the world, maybe the death penalty will come back before you go to trial."

Sells glared at him and literally spat out the words, "Fuck you, you fuckin' spic!"

Mendez shot up out of his chair and leaned across the table. Sells went backward so fast, he tipped his chair over and spilled himself onto the floor.

"If you'll excuse me," Mendez said. "I need a cup of coffee. This case is such a slam dunk, I'm bored with it."

With the Sells file tucked under his arm, he walked out the door and across the hall where Hicks and Dixon were watching the video monitor.

"How do you like that?" Mendez asked. "This guy's a member of the master race."

"Unbelievable," Hicks said.

"Did the cars come in?" Mendez asked, pouring himself a cup of coffee.

"Yeah." Dixon nodded. He looked a little frayed around the edges. "I'm mobilizing a ground search for Karly Vickers at first light."

"If she isn't found in a fifty-five-gallon drum in Gordon Sells's garage tonight," Mendez said. "The crime scene unit is still out there, right?"

"It's going to take days for them just to get through the trailer," Dixon said. "The guy is an animal."

"That's an insult to the animal kingdom," Hicks declared.

"How do you think he's connected to the Thomas Center?" Dixon asked.

"Maybe the fact that both women were associated with the center is just a coincidence."

"Three women," Dixon corrected him. "Julie Paulson was there briefly in eighty-four. She washed out of the program. Jane was out of the country. That's why the name didn't ring a bell with her. Can't be a coincidence times three. How could he know these women? How could he abduct three women without somebody seeing something? If you were a woman and this guy tried to get his hands on you—"

"People would hear me screaming five miles away," Hicks said. "But maybe he's not the one who nabbed them."

"Tweedle Dumb in the other room?" Mendez asked. "That's hard to imagine. He probably can't figure out how to roll the window down in a car, let alone persuade some woman to get in with him."

"No," Hicks said. "I'm thinking about this maintenance guy from the center."

"What maintenance guy?" Dixon asked.

"Hamilton found out the guy has a record for car theft and domestic abuse."

"That's impossible," Dixon said. "Jane does background checks on everyone working there. She never would have hired someone like that."

"The guy's been using his brother's name and identity," Hicks explained. "They live together. Hamilton goes to the house to interview the guy—Doug Lyle—but the Doug Lyle he talks to doesn't work at the Thomas Center. The brother, Dave, used Doug's information because he didn't think anyone would hire a car thief fresh out of prison."

"Jesus," Dixon said. "Jane is going to flip out when she hears that story. She goes to such lengths to make sure her women are safe and protected, and it turns out she let the fox in the henhouse herself."

"And how do Doug Lyle and Gordon Sells connect?" Mendez asked.

"My theory," Hicks said. "Lyle steals the cars, takes them to Sells, Sells ships them somewhere, and they split the proceeds."

"And kill a woman or three in the process?"

"Why not? The Hillside Strangler in LA turned out to be two guys working together."

"It's a viable scenario," Dixon said. "See if

you can connect Sells to Lyle. You take a crack at him, Bill. You guys can tag team him until he decides he wants a lawyer."

Hicks took the "Sells file" and went across the hall.

Mendez sipped his coffee, anxious for the caffeine to kick in.

"What do you think, Tony?" Dixon asked. "Do you like this guy for it?"

Mendez stared at the monitor, watching Sells pick his nose until the door opened and Hicks walked in. "That would be an easy solution. If we can tie him to Lyle, and prove that Lyle stole the cars, et cetera."

"But?"

He shrugged. "Sells is a pedophile. They don't usually graduate to crimes against adult women. They go after kids because kids are most vulnerable, kids can't fight back, because something in their own background attaches their sex drive to a certain age group."

"Maybe the other guy is the sexual predator."

"Maybe."

They listened while Hicks questioned Sells about any association to Doug Lyle. Sells denied it.

"You're bringing in the maintenance guy?"

"We sent a unit to pick him up."

"I want to know when he gets here," Dixon said, heading for the door.

"Right. Did you find anything inside the cars yet?"

He stopped in the doorway and turned back around slowly, looking like the weight of the world had descended on him.

"Karly Vickers had a traffic ticket in her glove compartment, dated the day she disappeared," he said.

"Yeah? So?"

"The ticket was written by Frank Farman."

# 35

Friday, October 11, 1985
*12:47 A.M.*

Karly had no idea how much time had passed since she had last been visited. It might have been a day. It might have been a matter of a few hours.

She was losing her sanity. Exhausted and weak, she had begun lapsing into hallucinations. She would see Petal walking around the room, coming over to look at her quizzically. Karly would go to pet her and realize she couldn't move her hand, though she didn't understand why. Then Petal would speak as clearly as any person.

"You can't get up. We have to kill you." And the dog would lunge for her throat and tear it out.

This time when the hallucination came and she went to pet the dog, her hand was free. If only that was true, she thought. Then the dog vanished and darkness descended, and she began to think she might actually be conscious. And her hand was still free.

And her other hand was free.

And she was able to move her legs.

Was this really happening or was it another dream? Slowly, carefully she tried to sit up. The pain was terrible in her stomach, her ribs, but she sat up. Dizziness swirled around in her head like water in a toilet bowl. She waited for it to pass. When it had, she carefully turned herself until her legs dangled over the side of the table.

Was she alone? Was she being watched?

She had no way of knowing if her tormentor ever left. He could have been right there, sitting at a table, eating his breakfast, casually watching her, knowing she would never be able to get away.

But that didn't mean she wouldn't try. She had fought so hard to rise above her past. Having her future snatched away from her wasn't fair. She had to get angry. She had to try to help herself. Miss Thomas always said, "God helps those who help themselves."

She had to try to help herself.

Having no idea how far it might be to the ground, she started to slide off the table, reaching downward with her toes. And there was the floor. It was cold. Pain bolted up her legs, up her spine to her brain. The soles of her feet had been cut numerous times. The half-closed wounds burst open as she put weight on her feet. It had been so long since she had been upright, her legs felt as if they didn't really belong to her.

She gripped the edge of the table, fighting not to pass out or collapse to the floor. She couldn't think about the pain. She had to fight.

Slowly, she began to walk. One step and then another. She clutched the edge of the table as she inched along. If she could make it to a wall, she would follow the wall around until she came to a door. When she found a door, she would go through it.

Without sight or hearing she had a difficult time trying to balance. Her head felt as huge and heavy as a bowling ball perched on top of her neck. As she moved it would feel as if the bowling ball began to roll one way and she would overcorrect and tip in the other direction.

She began to panic when she realized the table was not sitting against a wall. She would have to walk across open space.

Three steps and she couldn't tell up from down. She stumbled and flailed with her arms, pitched forward. She didn't realize she was falling until she hit the hard floor. Because she was disoriented, she didn't even try to break the fall with her hands. She hit the floor headfirst, her skull hitting so hard it bounced twice before she lost consciousness.

She didn't know how long she had been out when she came around again. It didn't matter. She had to get out. Maybe she would walk out a door into a neighborhood and someone would see her and call for help. Or she might walk out into the wilderness, wander aimlessly, and die of exposure. At least that would be on her own terms.

Karly pushed herself up onto her hands and knees and began to crawl. Better to stay on the ground, and still she lost her balance and fell again and again. She ran into a cabinet and slowly felt her way up the front of it until she was standing again.

Her hands swept over the surface—a counter, cluttered with things, tools maybe. Maybe she could find a weapon. Each object she picked up she carefully studied with her fingers until she found a screwdriver. That would do. She could stab someone with a screwdriver. Maybe she could gouge his eyes out, blind him as he had blinded her. Maybe she could sink it into his body and tear at his internal organs as he had torn at her.

Adrenaline came with the ideas of revenge. She began to feel giddy. Laughter bounced up and down inside her chest. The laughter segued into hysteria. She was losing it. She had to pull herself from that mental ledge. She had to keep going. She had to keep moving. She had to get out.

Now that she had found a wall, she lowered herself back down to the ground and began to crawl again. There had to be a door. And she had to get out.

# 36

Dawn was a pale sliver of color on the eastern horizon when Mendez pulled into Gordon Sells's salvage yard. Despite the hour, the place was a hive of activity.

Crime scene teams from two counties and the state Bureau of Forensic Sciences were working over the property. Besides the trailer house, the place was cluttered with garages and sheds half falling down—all packed with machinery, parts, cars, and junk of all varieties. Behind the salvage business was a dilapidated barn and a pen full of twenty to thirty hogs. As if the place wasn't disgusting enough to begin with.

Mendez went on in search of Dixon. In an hour the main investigative team would meet and they would be briefed as to what had been found so far during the search.

He walked down the field of cars, the dew-damp grass soaking his shoes and wetting the hem of his pants. A crowd had gathered at the end of the first rows. Deputies, people in street clothes, forty or fifty volunteers in search and rescue windbreakers, all milled around, waiting for something to happen.

Photographers and camera crews from half a dozen television stations recorded the event while on-air reporters stood in front of blinding portable lights relating the latest to viewers of the early morning news programs in LA and Santa Barbara and who-knew-where.

Jane Thomas and Steve Morgan stood in the flood of harsh light with Petal the pit bull sitting at Jane's feet. Dixon stood behind the camera crew with his arms crossed over his chest. Mendez stepped up beside him.

". . . as you can see," Jane Thomas was saying to the blonde with the microphone, "a ground search has been organized and will be getting under way shortly. I encourage any of your viewers who might be able to join the search. Karly Vickers has been missing now for an entire week. It's imperative that we do all we can to find her."

"And I understand your center has posted a reward," the blonde said.

"Yes, the Thomas Centers for Women have established a reward of ten thousand dollars for information leading to Karly's recovery and to the conviction of the person who took her."

"A tip line has been set up . . ."

"How's she holding up?" Mendez asked quietly.

"She feels better doing something," Dixon said. "She's got the women at the center helping with the hotline, running off posters, helping organize food and beverages for the searchers."

The reporter introduced Steve Morgan. He spoke about the importance of the Thomas Center to the community, and about the professionals—

like himself—who donated their time and services to the center.

"I hope to God they don't find a body out there," Dixon said.

"The odds of finding this girl alive are getting longer by the day," Mendez said.

"It's not impossible. Maybe Sells—if Sells is our man—decided he had to lay low for a while and he's got her stashed. Maybe he was enjoying this girl more than the other. Maybe he decided to keep her."

None of that seemed very likely to Mendez but he kept that to himself for now.

"Sells hasn't said anything yet?" Dixon asked.

"He told me to go fuck myself, but that's not what you wanted to hear."

"What a nightmare," Dixon said. "I moved up here to get away from this kind of craziness."

"Bad is everywhere, boss."

The sky was brightening enough to see beyond the lights. The field beyond the cars was tinted green from rain they had had the week before, and studded with the big spreading oak trees the area was known for. It was a pretty place, a place where people might want to have a picnic, not to search for a corpse.

"Did you talk to Farman?" he asked.

"Yeah."

"How did that go?"

"About how you'd think," Dixon said. "I

assigned him to desk duty. He's not a happy camper. But I didn't have a choice. I can't have any hint of impropriety in this investigation. When these cases go to trial, I'm not going to have some defense attorney get up and point out that we had a potential suspect working the investigation."

"Are we supposed to consider him a suspect?"

"No, of course not."

"His wife has a connection to the Thomas Center."

Dixon looked at him. "How?"

"She's a secretary at Quinn, Morgan."

Dixon frowned darkly. "I asked him about the ticket he wrote Karly Vickers. He says he didn't remember her, which is why he didn't say anything about it."

"He didn't remember stopping a woman that we're now looking for?" Mendez said. "We've all been looking at her picture for two days. We're looking for a ten-year-old gold Chevy Nova. He stopped *that* car with *that* woman in it, and he *didn't remember?*"

Dixon sighed and rubbed his temples. "I know. It's lame. There's no reason he shouldn't have mentioned it, though. Frank writes half a dozen citations every day. That's part of his job."

"What did he stop her for?"

"He stopped her for doing twenty-nine in a twenty-five zone."

"What an ass," Mendez said. But that was just

like Farman—by the book, no mercy. "What time did he write the ticket?"

"Fifteen thirty-eight."

"Before her dental appointment. That's good."

On their time line, Farman wouldn't be listed as the last person to have seen the woman. Not that it should have mattered. Farman had a clean record. There was no reason for anyone to look at him as a suspect. The fact that his son had been in possession of Lisa Warwick's finger was the complicating factor.

Any defense attorney worth his salt would use that to plant the seeds of reasonable doubt. What if the kid didn't pick up the finger at the scene? What if he found it at home hidden among his father's things?

Defense attorneys loved nothing better than trying to make cops look dirty. They would find someone who had overheard Frank make a derogatory remark about women—not that difficult to do, him being the chauvinist he was. They would look at every traffic citation he had ever written and manufacture a pattern of harassment against women. They would drag in Anne Navarre and get her to say she believed Frank beat his kid, that he had a volatile temper.

Mendez could see Frank spanking his son for skipping school—and who was to say that was so wrong? Mendez had suffered a couple of good strappings as a boy bent on mischief, and he had straightened up because of it. And Farman could certainly come across as a bully, but brutally murder a woman? Mr. Law Enforcement? No.

Dixon sighed and shook his head. "Maybe Sells will confess today."

*And maybe pigs will fly*, Mendez thought, as he walked back to his car, passing the hog lot.

An hour later the team of six detectives and Vince Leone met in the conference room that had now been fully converted into their war room. Photographs had been moved from the smaller bulletin board and tacked up on a freestanding corkboard at one end of the room. A time line had been drawn out on the big white board.

Mendez took a marker and added to the line for the day Karly Vickers disappeared: 15:38 traffic ticket issued by F. Farman.

He added to the line for Thursday: L. Warwick index finger in possession of D. Farman.

Leone came over, tapped a finger on the line about the traffic citation, and raised his eyebrows.

"Yeah," Mendez said. He looked his mentor over. "You look good today. You've got some color."

Vince grinned. "I had a lovely evening, thanks for asking."

"I didn't ask," Mendez said, cranky. "Spare me the details, please."

"The food was excellent. Miss Navarre was a lovely dinner companion. We talked about her students. I walked her to her car, then I took a walk back down the alley behind the dentist's office."

Mendez chose to skip past the date part and jump right back into the case. "Yeah? What did you find?"

"The vacant building next door has a big roll-up garage door, like you could back a truck through. Could be a good place to stash a victim say from five until dark."

"I don't see the dentist as a suspect," Mendez said. "The only thing we have on him is that he saw Vickers late in the day. Anybody could have grabbed the girl in the alley. And Sells had the cars."

"What does your gut tell you about Gordon Sells?"

Mendez rolled his shoulders, as if physically uncomfortable defending the Sells theory. "There's definitely something wrong about the guy. But his record is as a pedophile. These victims are grown women."

Leone nodded, satisfied. "And back to your dentist: Yes, anyone could have snatched the young lady in that alley. And anyone could have stashed her in that empty building. There's a padlock on the door, but it doesn't work. But if she was a specific target, then her abductor has to be someone who knew she had that appointment."

Mendez thought about it. Karly Vickers on her way to the dentist, Farman pulls her over. Why is she going so fast, he asks her. She tells him she's on her way to a dentist appointment . . . Obviously, Crane knew where she would be, and people from the center, and people from the hair salon . . .

Dixon came in then and briefed the group regarding Frank Farman's necessary departure from the case. No one seemed to know what to say.

"He happened to make a traffic stop the day Karly Vickers disappeared," Dixon said. "He filed the citation, in no way tried to conceal that, and the time noted was fifteen thirty-eight. More than an hour before Ms. Vickers went missing."

"His kid was running around with a dead woman's finger in his pocket," Detective Hamilton said. "That's fucking screwed up."

"The boy has some behavioral issues," Dixon conceded.

"Deputy Farman has been put on administrative duty until further notice. Meanwhile, we have a legitimate suspect. Let's concentrate on Gordon Sells."

"Has the search of his property turned up anything yet?" Mendez asked.

"So far, nothing to connect him directly to any of the victims." Dixon said. "The trailer is a hazardous waste dump of biological material. It'll take months to process the samples."

"He hasn't said anything to incriminate himself," Mendez said. "He's uncooperative, to say the least."

"How long did you interview him last night?" Vince asked.

"Six hours. Hicks and I took turns."

"And he hasn't asked for an attorney?"

"No," Hicks said. "He doesn't trust public defenders. He claims the last one he had sold him down the river."

"Maybe he's right," Vince said. "He's a pedophile. How any decent person can defend a turd like that is beyond me."

"What decent person?" Detective Trammell asked. "I thought we were talking about lawyers."

They all got a laugh out of that. Nothing like slamming lawyers to lighten the mood for a bunch of cops.

"He did time," Vince said. "What was the charge?"

"He was accused of abusing three different twelve-year-old girls, but only one case went to trial. Sells pled out on lewd acts on a minor and possession of child pornography," Mendez said. "The deal was for eight-to-twelve. He did every day of it. The mother of the victim came to every parole hearing."

"Was he violent?" Leone asked. "Did he use a weapon?"

"Each time he threatened his victim with a knife."

"No actual rape?"

"Oral sex was his thing, but he's had twelve years to sit and think about it."

"Twelve years of taking it up the ass from every bubba in the joint probably," Trammell said. "That's a lot of motivation for revenge against women."

"That's true," Vince said. "But guys like Sells don't usually change targets. He was locked in on twelve-year-old girls long before he got put away—probably since his teens. His sexual attraction is to pubescent girls he can easily manipulate and intimidate. Molesting children is generally an unsophisticated crime."

"You don't think he's our guy?" Dixon said, annoyed.

"From what you've told me, he doesn't fit the profile. I think you're looking for a white male in his midthirties, educated, intelligent, methodical. I think he holds a position of respect or authority, or these women knew him personally. So far it looks like the victims just vanished, no commotion, no witnesses. That suggests they went with him willingly. They didn't think he posed a threat."

"Or he incapacitated them quickly and efficiently," Dixon countered. "He stalked them to a secluded location and grabbed them. No witnesses."

"That's possible," Vince conceded. "But with the way he staged Lisa Warwick's body in the woods, this killer is looking for attention. He wants an audience. He wants credit for his work. He's got an ego. He's liable to try to insinuate himself into the search for Karly Vickers, attend the funeral of Lisa Warwick. That kind of involvement will be part of the power trip for him.

"With the exception of the missing finger, everything about the Warwick dump site was neat and tidy. The cutting wounds on the body were laid out in a specific pattern. Your victim number one—Paulson—had similar deliberate marks on the body. But you're telling me Gordon Sells isn't organized in any way. He lives in a hovel, out in the country, away from people, not attracting attention."

"He had both women's cars in his possession," Dixon said.

He looked like he was feeling persecuted, Mendez thought. No doubt he was as exhausted as everyone else, maybe more so considering his personal connection to Jane Thomas. She had to be hammering on him to solve the case. Mendez could see Leone taking the same reading on his boss.

Vince held his hands up. "Hey, Sheriff, I appreciate your position here. You're under a lot of pressure, and you've got a bird in the hand with Sells. But it's not my job to agree with you. I'm no help as a yes man.

"I'm telling you what I know based on my experiences," he said. "That doesn't mean this guy couldn't be the exception to the rule. I'm just telling you what I know. You've got him with the cars. Hold him. But I would strongly advise you to continue to develop other possible suspects."

Dixon sighed and nodded and rubbed his hands over his face. "Does anybody else have anything?"

"Lisa Warwick's vacation plans didn't turn up anything," Hamilton said. "But her phone records show a lot of calls to the law offices of Quinn, Morgan and Associates. Two calls the day she disappeared."

"She volunteered as a court advocate to women from the center," Mendez said. "Morgan handles most of the family court cases. I think she might have had a thing for him. He's tougher to read. I haven't spoken to his wife yet."

"Steve Morgan is as straight an arrow as they come," Dixon said.

"He's the guy in the photograph?" Trammell asked.

"Yeah," Mendez said.

"I finally talked to the next-door neighbor last night," Trammell went on. "Nosey old bat. She said she saw a man coming and going from Lisa Warwick's house from time to time at odd hours, late at night. She—the neighbor—is up at odd hours on account of her sciatica, she told me. I showed her the photo. She couldn't swear he was the guy, because it was always dark, but she thought it could be. Right height, right build."

"When was the last time she saw him?" Mendez asked.

"She wasn't sure—I think she drinks for that sciatica—but she thought it was maybe the night before Warwick went missing."

Dixon swore under his breath. "Tony, talk to Morgan again."

"We've got the maintenance man from the Thomas Center in," Hicks said. "He denies any connection to the stolen cars or to the women, but Miss Vickers's friend told us he had his eye on Karly and she didn't like it."

"He did five in Wasco for stealing cars—"

"That's where Gordon Sells was," Mendez said.

"Lyle claims he didn't know Sells there, but he has been to Sells's junkyard."

"And Lyle had charges on him for abusing a girlfriend?" Dixon asked.

"Six months' worth."

"He's still here?" Dixon asked.

"Holding him on a bench warrant for outstanding traffic violations. But unless we come up with his prints in one of those cars, we've got nothing to charge him with. He can pay his fines and go."

"Talk to him again," Dixon said. "If nothing turns up, kick him loose. Hamilton and Stuart, I want you to canvass the businesses around Peter Crane's dental office. So far, that's still the last place anybody saw Karly Vickers. Trammell and Eaton, knock on every door within half a mile of Gordon Sells's place."

Mendez turned to Leone. "You coming with me? I'm stopping at the elementary school to talk to the Crane boy and Wendy Morgan to see if they know how the Farman kid got that finger."

"No," Vince said. "I have to make a call to Quantico. But do give my regards to Miss Navarre," he added with a smug smile.

"Yeah," Mendez said, rolling his eyes. "I'll get right on that."

# 37

Tommy hurt all over. He had a whopper of a black eye. The back of his head hurt from where it had bounced off the ground when Dennis knocked him down. The doctor at the emergency room had taken X-rays and said that his ribs weren't broken, but they sure were bruised. His whole stomach was black and blue from where Dennis had kicked him, and it hurt like crazy when he tried to breathe.

Still, he felt pretty proud of himself for going after Dennis. There was no way Dennis was going to do anything but kick his butt, and still Tommy had taken him on. His dad had told him he had done the right thing defending Wendy. A man should always defend women.

His mother, of course, had flipped out about the whole thing. She had spent much of the evening screaming about Dennis Farman and Dennis Farman's parents, and how she was going to press charges AND sue—sue the Farmans, sue the school, sue Mr. Alvarez.

His father had been calmer, but still upset. He had gotten on the phone with Principal Garnett after Tommy's mother had finished screaming at him, and asked a lot of questions about what would be done about Dennis.

His mother was voting for prison, but Tommy knew they didn't send kids to prison for fighting during gym class. Tommy figured Dennis would get expelled, which was good, except that that left Dennis free to harass and attack people when school was out. And he had no doubt that Dennis would come after him.

Dennis would blame him for everything. Never mind that Dennis had tried to shove a rotten finger from a dead person down Wendy's throat. That right there was enough to get him expelled. But Dennis wouldn't see it that way.

Tommy and Wendy sat in the outer office while their mothers were in with Principal Garnett. Tommy could hear his mother's voice as she ranted and raved. She was down a hall and behind a closed door, and he could still hear her. He felt bad for Principal Garnett.

He felt bad for himself too. He was afraid his mother would come storming out of the principal's office and drag him home with her just because she was mad. She had already made threats about moving him to another school, which he didn't want at all.

He looked at Wendy sitting next to him and made an impatient face, rolling his eyes. She just looked at him.

"Are you all right?" Tommy asked.

"No!" she said, her voice lowered so as not to attract the attention of the secretaries. "I'm mad! Dennis tried to stick the finger of a dead person in my mouth! He touched my face with the finger of a dead person! I'm still totally grossed out!"

"Oh." He knew better than to say too much when a girl was really mad.

Wendy's expression softened. "Are you all right? You look like you hurt all over."

"Yeah, but I'm pretending I don't or my mom will make me stay home. I don't want to stay home with her. She's crazy mad."

A door opened back in the depths of the office. Tommy snapped his head around, wincing at the pain. His mother came storming out of the hall, her face as red as the suit she wore, her eyes bugging out of her head.

Tommy cringed, waiting for her to grab his arm and haul him off. Why hadn't he had sense enough to hide in the lavatory?

But she went right past him, her high heels clicking against the floor. She didn't even look at him.

Open-mouthed, Tommy watched her go. He and Wendy exchanged a look.

"You lucked out," she said.

He had, but they hadn't, he thought as Detective Mendez came out of the hall and crooked a finger at them. He got up gingerly, trying not to suck in too big a breath.

"Hey, Tommy," the detective said as they followed him down the hall. "I hear you can take a punch if you have to."

What was he supposed to say to that? "I guess so."

They went into the conference room. Principal Garnett was standing by the door, red-faced and breathing too hard.

"I'm going to leave this to you, Detective," he said. "I have to call our attorneys."

"That doesn't sound good," Wendy whispered.

Wendy's mom came over to her. She looked upset too.

"Have the office call me if you decide you want to come home," she said.

Wendy nodded. Her mother kissed her cheek and started to leave the room.

"Mrs. Morgan?" Detective Mendez said. "Can I have a word with you in private before you go? We'll be finished here in a few minutes, if you don't mind waiting."

Wendy's mom looked unhappy, but she said, "I guess so. I'll be out here."

Miss Navarre came over then, turning as white as a sheet as she looked at Tommy.

"Tommy! Oh my God," she said. "Should you be here?"

"I'm okay," he said. "I went to the doctor."

"You don't look okay. You look like you should be home in bed."

"Tommy's tough," Detective Mendez said. "He did what he had to do, and he took it like a man."

Miss Navarre looked at him with narrowed eyes and said half under her breath, "Men are stupid."

They all sat down at the table.

"Detective Mendez has a few questions for you both about what happened yesterday," Miss Navarre said.

"Yeah," Detective Mendez said. "Did you guys know Dennis had that finger?"

"No!" they said in unison.

"Wendy, you told me before that you saw Dennis touch the body in the park. Did you see him take that finger?"

"Gross!" Wendy exclaimed. "No! I would have told you that for sure!"

"How about you, Tommy?"

Tommy shook his aching head so hard he saw stars.

"Dennis didn't say anything about it? Not at the park, not since?"

"We try not to talk to Dennis," Wendy said primly.

"Because he's a bully?"

"Because he's gross AND a bully," Wendy said. "He always smells bad, and he uses bad language, and he's always carrying around something disgusting like a smashed frog or some part of a dead animal he found in the road. He's weird and sick and gross," she declared. "And stupid."

She shot a quick, nervous look at Miss Navarre, like maybe she would get in trouble for that last part.

"You would say the same thing, Tommy?"

"Not out loud," Tommy admitted. "Or I'll end up like this again."

"Neither of you saw him take the finger," Detective Mendez said, but more to himself than to them. He sighed. "Does Dennis talk much about his father?"

"Yeah," Wendy said. "Like, *My dad's a deputy and he can arrest you. My dad's a deputy so he can drive as fast as he wants.*" She rolled her eyes. "Gag me."

"Has Dennis ever said anything about his father punishing him?" Miss Navarre asked.

They both shook their heads.

Detective Mendez looked at his watch.

"All right. Thanks, kids, Miss Navarre," he said, getting up from the table. "I have to go."

Miss Navarre said nothing, but watched him go out the door. Then she turned back to them.

"You guys have had some week," she said. "Good thing it's Friday. I just want to say how proud I am of both of you. You've gone through things this week that most adults would have a hard time handling, but you've handled it all really well. You've been very brave.

"Still, if there's anything you'd like to talk to me about, I'm here for you."

"Can the cops put Dennis in jail?" Wendy asked.

"Dennis is not going to jail," Miss Navarre said. "Dennis is a very troubled boy. Hopefully, he'll get some good counseling."

"He's not coming back to school?" Tommy asked.

"No. He's been expelled for the rest of the semester."

"Oh, great," Tommy muttered.

"You didn't want him to be expelled?" Miss Navarre asked, looking confused.

"He'll blame Tommy," Wendy said.

"He'll blame Tommy because he got expelled for beating up Tommy?"

"He hates Tommy," Wendy went on. "He thinks Tommy has everything. Tommy's smart. Tommy lives in a big house. Tommy plays the piano. Tommy has cool parents. They have cool cars. Blah, blah, blah."

"He's jealous," Miss Navarre said. "And everybody came to Tommy's rescue while Dennis got suspended."

"Right."

"Tommy, how do you feel about that?"

Tommy shrugged. People did stick up for him. Nobody stuck up for Dennis. Teachers always liked him; they never liked Dennis. Tommy's dad was cool. And maybe Dennis's dad hit him. Maybe Dennis had a right to be jealous, but that didn't give him the right to beat people up.

"Dennis doesn't know anything," he said.

Miss Navarre left it at that. She looked to Wendy. "That was pretty creepy yesterday with the finger. Did you have trouble sleeping last night?"

"A little," Wendy admitted.

"How about you, Tommy? Are you sleeping at night?"

Adults were obsessed with sleeping, he had decided. Like, if everybody slept more the world would be a better place or something. His mother was crazy about him getting enough sleep. She gave him allergy medicine to make him sleep. Sometimes he swallowed it, sometimes he didn't.

"I'm fine," he said.

He wanted to get out of this chair, out of this room, and go be a normal kid. He didn't want all this attention and all these questions. He wished his dad had picked him up from school Tuesday and he never would have fallen on that dead lady. But his dad played golf on Tuesday afternoons, and his mother was busy.

"Okay," Miss Navarre said. "Wendy, why don't you go back to class? I have a couple of things to talk to Tommy about."

Tommy felt like a big rock dropped into his stomach. Him alone in a room with Miss Navarre. Oh, brother.

Wendy left. Tommy's eyes went everywhere but to Miss Navarre.

"Tommy, look at me and tell me the truth now. You feel well enough to be in school?"

He looked straight at her and tried not to blink. "Yes, ma'am."

"No running around at lunch and no gym class today. And if you don't feel well, you tell me right away."

"Yes, ma'am."

"Your mom is really upset about what happened."

"I know," Tommy said. "She was yelling last night. She was yelling this morning. Sometimes I think her eyes are gonna pop out of her head when she yells like that."

"Does she do that a lot at home?"

Tommy shrugged. "It depends."

"Does she yell at you like that?"

He shrugged again and looked down. "Sometimes. When I do something wrong, or mess up the schedule."

He thought his mom was really mad at him this week on account of him finding that body, and him getting beat up, and her having to change her schedule to come to school where she always felt like she had to scream at people.

"I wish none of it ever happened," he said, and to his horror, he felt like he might cry.

Miss Navarre came around the table and squatted down beside him, her pretty flowered skirt floating into a puddle around her feet. She looked up into his face like she was searching for something.

"I wish that too, Tommy. But you know none of it was your fault, right? You didn't cut through the park expecting to find that body. You didn't miss your piano lesson on purpose. You didn't ask Dennis Farman to beat you up. It's not your fault."

Tommy didn't argue with her, but he knew it *was* his fault. He had decided to cut through the park. He had looked at Dennis when he shouldn't have. His mother was upset because of all of this trouble he had fallen into.

Miss Navarre stood up and crossed her arms and walked around in a little circle. From Tommy's observations that usually meant the person was working up to saying something nobody wanted to hear.

"Do you remember last Thursday night?" she asked. "Do you remember what you did that night? Were your mom and dad home?"

"I think so," Tommy said, puzzled. "My dad and me watch *The Cosby Show*."

"I like that show too," Miss Navarre said with a little smile. "Does your mom watch with you?"

"No. She doesn't think anything is funny."

"That's too bad for her."

"She's not a very happy person," he said.

"How about your dad? He seems like a happy person."

"Most of the time," Tommy said, but he didn't say anything about how it was when his mother was on one of her rampages and yelling at his dad. He didn't say that sometimes his dad would just have to leave, and how he wouldn't come back for hours.

It didn't feel right to tell anybody things like that. Not even Miss Navarre. That was family stuff. You weren't supposed to tell other people family stuff. It was like a code. You had to be loyal to your family first.

"My mother used to say 'This too shall pass,'" Miss Navarre said.

"What does that mean?"

"It means even bad times will go away. All the crazy stuff that happened this week already happened, it's behind us. We should look forward. Next week could bring something really great."

*I hope so*, Tommy thought as he slid off his chair and followed her out of the room, holding his arm against his aching ribs. *I sure hope so.*

# 38

"I can't believe any of this is happening," Sara Morgan said, pulling her pink sweater around herself as if she was freezing, even though the morning was warming up quickly.

She was a pretty woman in a wholesome athletic sort of way, dressed like maybe she was on her way to aerobics class in black leggings with gray leg warmers slouching around her ankles. She had a head of hair a man would like to tangle his hands in—thick with curls and waves. She had caught up a couple of sections in barrettes in a halfhearted attempt to keep it under control.

They stood on the sidewalk in front of the school. Mendez flipped his Ray-Bans down against the bright sun.

"We had such a nice life a week ago," she said. "Suddenly everything is wrong."

She was on the verge of tears—out of proportion to what had gone on in the conference room. Although, Mendez thought, Janet Crane was almost enough to make him cry.

"You've had a lot to deal with," he said. "I spoke to your husband yesterday. I understand he was out of town when the kids found the body."

"Yes," she said, suspicion creeping into her expression. "You talked to Steve? Why?"

"The murder victim, Lisa Warwick, volunteered at the Thomas Center as a court advocate. She and your husband had worked together frequently. We thought she might have confided in him if someone had been giving her a hard time. Did you know her?"

"Yes," she said. "I met her a couple of times."

"Is that all?" Mendez asked, feigning surprise. "They never met at your home to talk about a case?"

"Steve doesn't bring his work home with him."

"Hmmm. Well, I suppose that's good, but it

makes for a lot of late nights at the office, doesn't it?"

"Steve's very dedicated," she said, her voice cool.

"To his work," Mendez said. "Does it bother you that he gives up so much time to the Thomas Center?"

"It's a worthy cause."

She looked away, pulled a pair of aviator sunglasses from on top of her head and settled them in place to hide the stress in her cornflower blue eyes.

"You volunteer as well?" Mendez asked.

"No. I'm busy with other things."

Like holding herself together, he thought. *We had such a nice life a week ago.*

"Mrs. Morgan," he started, "there's no delicate way of asking this question. Was your husband involved with Lisa Warwick? Romantically?"

"No!" she said, too quickly, hugging herself tight.

"We've looked at Ms. Warwick's phone records. There are a lot of calls to your husband's office. A lot of after-hours calls."

"You said yourself, they worked on a lot of cases together."

Mendez didn't press for more. Browbeating Sara Morgan into saying it aloud would only have been cruel. Her husband was unfaithful to her. She was suffering enough keeping the secret to herself.

"One other thing," he said. "Do you happen to

remember where your husband was last week, Thursday, late in the day?"

"He was in town," she said. "I remember that. I teach an art class every other Thursday evening. He was home when I got back."

"What about from, say, five to seven?"

"He rarely gets home before seven. I leave for my class at six."

Which meant she couldn't account for his whereabouts during the time period Karly Vickers went missing.

He waited for Sara Morgan to ask why he wanted to know, but she had had enough.

"Thank you for your time, Mrs. Morgan," he said. "I'll let you go. Have a nice day."

She laughed without humor, already on her way to her car.

"I spoke with Sara Morgan," Mendez said, walking into the war room, where Vince had carved out a spot for himself at a small table in one corner.

He glanced up from making notes, reading glasses perched on the end of his nose. "And?"

"It's a good bet Steve Morgan was having an affair with Lisa Warwick. Mrs. Morgan was very uncomfortable with the topic," Mendez said, pulling up a chair.

"She didn't come right out and say he was cheating on her?"

"No. She couldn't deny it fast enough. She's trying to hold together what she has," Mendez said. "It's a sore point with her that he dedicates so much time to the Thomas Center."

"With other women," Vince said. "Vulnerable women, women in need of heroes. That's a rich prowling ground for the wrong kind of guy."

"Everybody says he's a Boy Scout."

Vince arched a brow. "What kind of merit badge do they give out for adultery these days?"

"A scarlet letter?"

"Good one," Vince said. He pulled his glasses off and set them aside. "So, let's say he's having an affair with her. That's a long way from doing what was done to her."

"Maybe she was threatening to tell the missus, giving him an ultimatum he couldn't live with."

"Motive for murder, yes. But a guy murders his mistress in the heat of the moment. He gets rid of the body. He doesn't carve it up like a totem pole and plant it in a public park for school kids to stumble on."

"Maybe he wants to make it look like some maniac did it."

"How much information about the Paulson murder was made public knowledge?" Vince asked. "The strangulation? The cutting? The mutilation? The glued eyes?"

"Almost none of it," Mendez admitted. "And the wife couldn't account for his whereabouts when

Karly Vickers went missing, either. Guess we'd better find out if he ever met Julie Paulson."

"She had a record, right?"

"A couple of old prostitution charges in another jurisdiction."

"See if she got busted with a john. Maybe you'll get lucky."

"I'll make some calls. Did you get anything from Quantico?"

"One of the agents knew a case in Ohio where a guy went away for killing a ten-year-old girl. When he got out, he switched to killing prostitutes of small stature—childlike. He figured when a kid goes missing, people notice. When a hooker disappears, *c'est la vie*."

"Karly Vickers is small," Mendez said. "But Lisa Warwick was pretty curvy. No mistaking her for —or pretending she might have been—a child."

"Let's go see your Mr. Sells," Vince said, getting up slowly. He stuck his reading glasses on top of his head and picked a folder from a neat stack on the table. "Dixon gave me the go-ahead to interview him. I want to know what pushes his buttons."

Gordon Sells looked at Mendez as they entered the room, and jabbed a finger in his direction. "I got *nothin'* to say to *you*, you fuckin' spic."

Mendez looked at Vince and shrugged. Vince tipped his head toward the door. He didn't want

Sells pissed off just because he didn't like Mendez.

Vince sat down, perched his reading glasses on his nose and paged slowly through the notes that had been made thus far regarding Gordon Sells. Sells watched him suspiciously and fidgeted in his chair as the minutes ticked past.

Finally Vince sighed and looked up.

"Mr. Sells," he said with a friendly smile. "I don't care how many stolen cars you've shipped to Mexico."

Sells didn't deny it.

"That's not important. Not to me, not to you. You've got other issues," Vince said. "I've talked to a lot of guys like you over the years. Guys who had that same . . . attraction . . . you have. None of them wanted to have it, you know. You probably don't want to have it either. I mean we all know it's against society, but you didn't ask to be that way. It's not your fault you like girls younger than other people think is right."

"Who are you?" Sells asked. "Are you a shrink?"

"Something like that," Vince said. "I'm Vince."

He reached across the table to shake the grubby hand of Gordon Sells.

"Now, Gordon. May I call you Gordon?"

Sells shrugged. "I guess."

"So, Gordon, Detective Mendez thinks you have something to do with the murder of a woman—Lisa Warwick."

"Never heard of her."

297

"And the disappearance of another woman—Karly Vickers."

"Don't know nothing about it."

Vince got up, went to the wall, and taped up three black-and-white crime scene photos. The partially decomposed remains of Julie Paulson. "Come have a look."

Sells came over and looked at the gruesome pictures, held his hands up and turned away. "That's sick. I got no stomach for that. I maybe have done some things in my time that ain't right, but nothing like that."

"See? That's what I figured," Vince said. He went back to the table and took a couple more photos out of the file, pornographic images of well-endowed women in their twenties. He stuck them up on the wall beside the others.

"I need coffee," he said. "Would you like some coffee, Gordon?"

"Yeah, sure."

"I'll be right back."

He went out the door and across the hall.

Dixon looked at him as he strolled into the monitor room and went to the coffeemaker. "What's the point of that?"

"The porn?" Vince said, pouring two cups of black coffee. "You'll see."

He doctored his coffee with four plastic thimbles of fake cream, stirring as he came over to the monitor. In the other room, Sells went over to the wall, looked at the porn for a minute, looked at the other photographs, and walked away.

Mendez opened the interview room door and let Vince back in. Vince handed a cup to Sells. "I brought it black. I didn't know. Me, I've got to load up the cream. Bad stomach."

Sells took the coffee and sipped at it.

"See, I said to Detective Mendez you wouldn't be interested in anything like that," Vince said, hooking a thumb toward the photos. "That's not what you're about. You're not a violent man. You don't want to hurt women."

"That's right," Sells said. "I never hurt nobody."

Vince went back to the wall and took down all the photographs. He replaced them with three photographs of a twelve-year-old girl, her unripe body naked, just beginning to bud into something more. She looked at the camera as she touched herself provocatively.

Vince went back to the table and promptly knocked over his coffee.

"Oh, shit! Look at that! Oh, man . . ."

He scooped up the file, the jacket dripping coffee. "Shit. Excuse me. I've got to get some towels."

He went back out the door and across the hall, dropping the file jacket into the trash. He joined Dixon, Hicks, and Mendez at the monitor, and they all watched as Gordon Sells went to the door and glanced out to see no one in the hall. He went back to the wall to stare at the photographs. Not thirty seconds had gone by before he began to fondle himself through his baggy pants. Another thirty seconds and he was fully aroused.

"Barnum and Bailey could pitch a tent on that pole," Vince said. "He's not your guy."

But before Dixon could say anything, Detective Trammell hustled into the room.

"We've got something at Sells's place," he said. "Bones. They look human."

# 39

The search for Karly Vickers ceased to be the lead news story of the day. Word that skeletal remains had been found in the hog yard behind Gordon Sells's salvage business shot through the media like a bolt of lightning. Mendez and Hicks had to fight through the crush of reporters and their support staff to get to the yellow-tape barrier.

The hogs were highly interested in the fuss and in the people in crime scene jumpsuits and knee-high rubber boots wading through their territory. They stood off to the side with individual members of the herd occasionally rushing toward the people, snorting bravado then rushing back to the safety of the group. Their squeals were ear-splitting.

"This smells almost as bad as the trailer," Mendez said, wrinkling his nose.

"I'm glad I have a badge," Hicks said, watching

the crime scene techs systematically raking through the inches-deep muck of mud and feces and pig urine. "My granddad up in Sacramento used to raise hogs. When I was a kid, in the summers, I used to have to help him move them from one pen to another. You don't shake that smell fast."

Dixon motioned them over to a table set up along the back of a shed. The findings had been washed and laid out on a tarp: what appeared to be a human femur and several rib bones.

"What do we do now?" Mendez asked. "We have no way of knowing who these belonged to. Unless they can find a pelvis, we don't even know if we're looking at a male or a female."

"The BFS team will take them," Dixon said. "They'll call in an anthropologist to have a look."

Mendez picked up the femur and looked at it more closely. What appeared to be knife marks scarred both ends of the bone. "Whoever it was, Sells cut them up before he threw them out there."

"And he did a neat job of it," Hicks observed. "That was severed at the joint."

"Let's hope the victim was dead when he did it," Dixon said. "He may not fit Leone's profile, but we've definitely got ourselves a killer."

"*A* killer," Mendez said. "But is he *the* killer?"

"We've got the cars here. Now we've got remains here."

"We don't have Sells's fingerprints on those cars yet, do we?" Mendez asked.

"The comparisons are being made," Dixon said. "We'll know this afternoon."

He shook his head as he looked out at the crime scene techs raking through the shit. "The bastard has no respect for human life at all. Kills someone, cuts them up, throws them out like trash. In a hog yard."

"You know why, right?" Hicks said.

Dixon just looked at him.

"Hogs will eat anything."

Mendez put the femur down and walked away.

A call came from the crime scene techs. "We've got a skull!"

Vince avoided the scene at Sells's junkyard. They didn't need him there to look at bones. They certainly didn't need him there to be recognized by the media.

Dixon would have his hands full now as it was. His case had just taken on Hollywood movie status: a creepy convicted pedophile living in a creepy junkyard on the outskirts of the idyllic college town, murdering people and throwing their corpses out to be devoured by farm animals.

All he needed was to have a top profiler step in from the FBI and he would have a blockbuster on his hands.

And all Vince needed was for the powers at the Bureau to see his face on the nightly news in the middle of it.

Bones or no bones, he still didn't think Gordon Sells was the man who had murdered Lisa Warwick. Guys like Gordon Sells tried to fly under the radar as much as possible. He was by nature a pedophile. It was Vince's theory that the majority of pedophiles were ashamed of what they did no matter how long they were at it or how prolific they were. What they did never became okay—not even to themselves.

Men like Sells operated in secret, in hiding. They asked their victims not to tell—or made sure that they couldn't. They covered their tracks and disposed of all evidence.

The Gordon Sells theory of Lisa Warwick's murder and Karly Vickers's abduction could be packaged and wrapped with a big red bow for the press, but in reality that box was going to be empty.

He wondered how his UNSUB would take it when the press made Sells out to be the big bad serial killer. Would it amuse him? Piss him off? Drive him to do something to prove them wrong? In Vince's experience, this kind of killer had an ego that needed feeding and stroking. He wouldn't like someone else getting credit for his work.

That could be a good thing for the investigation, forcing him to make a move.

It could be a very bad thing for Karly Vickers, if she was still alive.

Vince pulled Mendez's car into the field where the searchers were parked, across the road from

Gordon Sells's property. Sunglasses in place, he pulled a Dodgers' baseball cap on. He shucked his tie and sport coat in exchange for a windbreaker from the Oak Knoll Softball League, grateful Mendez was broad-shouldered.

Tables laid out with drinks and snacks sat under a couple of pop-up tents. Under a third tent, another table held flyers with a photo of Karly Vickers.

*Have You Seen This Woman?*

She was young. Pretty in a simple way. Permed blonde hair with a fountain of bangs sprayed in place. She wore a necklace with a small pendant —the figure of a woman with her arms raised in victory—the logo of the Thomas Center.

She had been missing nearly eight days. She was probably dead.

A woman asked if she could help him. She was in her midthirties, wearing a pink Thomas Center T-shirt, slender with a big head of auburn hair.

"I'm looking for Steve Morgan," he said, setting the flyer down. "Have you seen him?"

"Steve and Jane are giving an interview in the media tent," she said, looking off to her left to another pop-up tent set off by itself, maybe fifteen yards away. "They should be finished soon. Is there anything I can help you with?"

"Do you work at the center?" Vince asked.

"Are you with the sheriff's office?" she countered.

Vince flashed her a smile. "What gave me away?"

"The mustache," she said, loosening up a little. "I grew up in a family of firemen and police officers."

"Then we're not exactly hard to spot."

"No. I'm Maureen Collins."

"Detective Leone. How long have you worked at the center?"

"Three years. I do family counseling."

"You know Miss Vickers, then."

"Yes. She's a nice girl. I can't believe this has happened to her."

"Did you know Miss Warwick?"

"Yes. I knew Lisa fairly well. I'm sure you're aware she was volunteering as a court advocate. We worked together on several cases."

"With Steve Morgan?"

"Yes. Steve is our hero," she said with a smile.

"Do you know if Miss Warwick was seeing anyone?" he asked. "We have reason to believe that she was, but we haven't found anyone to confirm that, let alone tell us who she might have been involved with."

She hesitated just a fraction of a second before saying, "I have no idea. Lisa was a very private person."

"I find that strange," Vince confessed. "Why be so secretive? Unless the guy wasn't supposed to be seeing her."

The woman looked over at the media tent and said, "It looks like they might be finished."

"Thanks."

Vince walked to the tent with his head down as the interviewer and photographer went past. Jane Thomas went in another direction. Steve Morgan stood looking at some papers on a clipboard.

"You're getting a lot of media attention," Vince said, strolling under the canopy of the open-sided tent.

Morgan glanced up. "The more, the better, right? Somebody had to see something. If just one person comes forward with a lead . . ."

"Sometimes that's all it takes," Vince said. "One person who saw something that struck them as odd. Like a man coming and going to and from a woman's house at late hours of the night."

"Is that supposed to mean something to me personally, Detective?"

"A neighbor of Lisa Warwick thinks she saw you."

"In the dark. In the middle of the night."

"If you had a relationship with her, better for you to come clean now and tell us. We'll find out eventually, and it won't look good that you tried to hide it."

Morgan went back to studying the papers on the clipboard.

Vince took a seat in one of several tall directors' chairs that had been positioned for interviews.

"We've got semen on her sheets," he said. "That gives us a blood type."

"I didn't kill Lisa," Morgan said.

"I'm not saying you did. Just because you were sleeping with her doesn't make you a murderer."

"I wasn't sleeping with her."

"Your wife thinks you were."

Morgan looked at him with a gaze that could have cut steel. "You talked to my wife?"

"I told you we would."

"And she told you she thinks I was sleeping with Lisa."

"Does that surprise you?"

"You're lying. Sara wouldn't say that."

Vince let him wonder for a minute. Finally he sighed.

"You know, Steve, man to man, I don't care if you were sleeping with her. You want to screw up your family situation—that's none of my business. I care that you're wasting our time by denying it. I care that you're going to make us waste man hours looking into every goddamn day of your life for the past six months, digging through your financials, comparing hotel receipts with calendar dates with trips to Sacramento and trips you said you made that you never did because you were really in town fucking your mistress. I care about that."

The muscles in Morgan's square jaw flexed. "Are you finished?"

"No," Vince said, leaning forward. "I care that if you were involved with this girl, and now she's dead, that you're that big an asshole you would waste time we could be spending finding her killer just because you don't want to step up and be a man. You would do that to try to cover your own ass. Didn't you care about her at all?"

Steve Morgan said nothing for several minutes. He turned and looked out across the field with no expression whatsoever. What he was seeing, what he was thinking, Vince could only imagine.

Maybe he saw his family slipping away from him, his wife divorcing him, his daughter hating him. Maybe he was remembering Lisa Warwick and how much he had loved her. Maybe he was looking back on his last visit to Lisa Warwick's home, wondering if he had really been so careless as to leave traces of himself at the scene.

"Look, Steve, I'm not trying to bust your ass here. Maybe you really loved the girl, but now she's gone and you don't want to lose your family too. Unless you killed her, it's nobody's business. We can try to keep it quiet."

"In the middle of a media circus." Morgan laughed.

"I hear you have a suspect in custody," he said quietly. "You found Lisa's car, Karly's car here on this property. Remains have been found."

"We have a person of interest," Vince said.

Morgan nodded. "Then I guess you'd better check his blood type," he said, and walked away.

# 40

The lower jaw was missing from the skull, still lost in the filth of the hog yard. But the upper part of the skull was intact with what looked to be a full set of teeth.

Mendez and Hicks took the thing in a brown paper bag and went back to their car, ignoring the shouts and calls of reporters being held at bay on the far side of the crime scene tape. A virtual motorcade followed them back to the sheriff's office. As they pulled into the parking lot the television reporters and cameramen rushed the lawn to lay claim to the prime backgrounds for their remote reports.

*Vultures*, Mendez thought, as he and his partner cut through the maze of hallways in the building, and went out into the garage where the cars of Karly Vickers and Lisa Warwick were being gone over a second time.

"Anything new?" Mendez asked.

"Two sets of prints off both cars," said the brunette from Latent Fingerprints—Marta. She stood beside Karly Vickers's Nova, watching as someone else combed the carpet in the driver's side foot well. "Two identical sets of prints from both cars, and nothing else. Not so much as a partial from any other party."

"Sells and Doug Lyle?" Hicks ventured. "Sells and his nephew?"

"Walter is doing the comparisons now."

"The victims' prints?" Mendez asked.

Marta shook her head. "Nada. Already eliminated."

"Somebody wiped the cars clean," Hicks said.

"What's in the bag?" Marta asked. "Did you bring me lunch?"

"You don't want to know," Mendez said as he started for the side door.

"Why would Sells get rid of the victims' prints but not his own?" Hicks asked.

"He wouldn't. Someone else brought the cars there, wiped them down, and left them."

"Sells and his nephew find them in the field, think Christmas has come early, and put their hands all over them. You know what that means?" Hicks said as they got into a sedan parked behind the garage.

"If Sells didn't kill Lisa Warwick or grab Karly Vickers, but he killed whoever we have in this bag, then we've got more than one murderer," Mendez said.

"It's a banner day for the chamber of commerce."

They drove to the back door of Peter Crane's office and blocked in his Jaguar.

"You just caught me," Crane said, leading them down the hall to an empty examination room. "I told Steve I would close for the afternoon and join the search party."

"Steve Morgan?" Mendez asked.

"Yeah. I'm sure you know Steve's spearheading the search effort and helping Jane Thomas deal with the media."

"You're good friends?"

"Yeah. We golf when we can. Our kids are friends. Steve got me involved with the center," Crane said, leaning back against the counter, crossing his arms over his chest.

"Do you happen to know if he has a girl-friend?" Mendez asked.

Crane's expression seemed carefully arranged. "Steve's married. Happily."

"Yeah, we know that. But that doesn't change the question. We have reason to suspect he and Lisa Warwick might have been seeing each other."

"Steve and Lisa?" The dentist looked at the floor as if he might be trying to picture the couple there. "I wouldn't know anything about that."

He was a poor liar.

"We're not looking to bust his balls over it," Mendez said. "We need a clear picture of what was going on in her life before she was killed. That's all."

Crane shrugged. "Sorry. I can't help you with that. So, what *can* I help you with, detectives?"

"Some remains were discovered this morning during a search," Mendez said. "A skull, to be exact. We were hoping you could compare the teeth against the X-rays you took of Miss Vickers's mouth last week."

Crane eyed the brown paper bag Hicks set on the counter. "Let me get the X-rays."

Mendez took the skull out of the bag and set it on the counter. The bone was dingy white, clean of all flesh. It seemed unlikely the person it belonged to had been alive a week past, that this shell had been filled with a brain, covered by a face, crowned with hair. It had been attached to a living breathing human, a person with thoughts and opinions and goals for a life that was then abruptly ended.

Crane returned with the X-rays and clipped them to the light box on the wall, then he took a deep breath, sighed, and carefully picked up the skull, turning it upside down to look at the teeth.

"No," he said almost immediately. "Miss Vickers had several amalgam fillings in the upper molars. See here?" he said, pointing to the X-rays of individual teeth.

"These teeth," he said, looking at the thing he held in his hands like a halved cantaloupe, "were in need of attention. There's significant decay in a couple of them. This filling in the premolar needed replacing. This bicuspid is chipped."

"How much can you tell about the person by looking at the teeth?" Mendez asked. "Can you tell their age?"

"Like a horse?" Crane asked. "Not exactly. But this is a full set of teeth, so the person had to be at least a teenager. The teeth aren't worn down, so not an older person. They haven't been cared for, which would tend to make me think of someone in a poor financial situation. The teeth are on the small side, the jaw is relatively narrow, the skull is smallish with no pronounced brow ridge, so I'd guess it was a woman."

"How about a name and address?" Hicks asked.

Crane gently set the skull down. "That's your department, gentlemen. Can I ask where this came from?"

"Sells Salvage Yard, outside of town."

"That's the man you have in custody, right? That's where you found the women's cars? I saw it on the news this morning. You think he's the killer."

"He's being questioned," Mendez said.

Crane shook his head, staring at the skull. "This woman wasn't Karly Vickers. So who was she? Is there another woman missing?"

"Not that we're aware of," Hicks said. "The remains will be sent to the Bureau of Forensic Sciences for possible identification."

"So there really is a serial killer," Crane said. "Thank God you have him in custody."

"Yeah," Mendez said. "Thank God."

"Thanks for your help, Dr. Crane," Hicks offered.

"Anytime."

"So, you're off to join the search?" Mendez asked.

"Yes." Crane looked at the skull again. "You see that . . . I hope we're not too late."

• • •

"This is a nightmare," Dixon said. "They're absolutely sure about the prints?"

"They're a match for Sells and his nephew," Hicks said, reaching for tuna salad on rye. They had called out for lunch and sat at the conference table, eating and catching up on the latest details.

"Someone brought those cars out to Sells's field, through the back gate," Mendez said, "wiped them down and left them."

"And then what?" Dixon asked. "Walked back to town? Had an accomplice drive back? Or is Sells the accomplice?"

"You have to take Sells out of the equation with Warwick and Vickers," Vince said. "He's not the kind of guy who has a partner. Him doing his own thing, at his own place, disposing of his victim in his own backyard—that I can see. But that kind of murder and Lisa Warwick are two entirely different things."

"We've got two killers," Dixon said. "Un-fucking-believable."

He got up to pace. He was in uniform and still looked starched and pressed, despite what the day had already put him through.

"We do everything in our power to keep this out of the media," he said. "Gordon Sells is in custody. The press can keep their eye on him for now."

"And you have to hope your UNSUB doesn't

get pissed off by that," Vince said. "Sells getting credit could push him into something."

"It's a no-win situation," Dixon said. "If we admit there's still a serial killer out there, he gets his ego fed, then he wants more. He wants more, he does more—right?"

"Probably," Vince conceded.

Dixon swore under his breath and shook his head. "We're working three murders and a missing person with at least two different perps in a county that doesn't see three murders in a year. We've got to break this down.

"Trammell and Campbell, check all missing persons reports from a five-county target area then work your way out if you have to. We've got to try to put a name to the victim at Sells's. The Bureau of Forensic Sciences has a forensic artist who can come up with a likeness of the victim from the skull. And put some pressure on the nephew, see if he won't crack."

The two detectives grabbed their lunches and headed to their desks to start making phone calls.

"If we take Sells off the board, that leaves us where with Lisa Warwick?" Dixon asked.

"Nowhere," Mendez said. "But I'm pretty stuck on the idea she was having an affair with Steve Morgan. We asked Peter Crane about it this morning—he and Morgan are buddies—and he about turned himself inside out trying to deny it."

"I spoke to Morgan this morning," Vince said.

"He's not interested in owning that. He's a cool customer. I told him you've got semen on Lisa Warwick's sheets. He said then you'd better test Gordon Sells's blood type."

Brow furrowed, Hicks abandoned his sandwich and dug through a stack of papers that had been left on the table over the morning while they were out.

"Here's why," he said, holding up a report. "I asked for labs back ASAP on the semen stains. No blood type available. Whoever left that sample for us is a nonsecretor. He wouldn't be worried we'd match his blood type if he knew his blood-type antigens didn't carry into his semen."

"How many people know if they're secretors or nonsecretors? Most people don't even know what that means," Mendez said. "And only twenty percent of the population are nonsecretors. It's not like he had a fifty-fifty shot at being right. He had to know."

"Having an affair doesn't make him a sexually sadistic homicidal maniac," Dixon said.

"Have you done a thorough background check on him?" Vince asked. "Has he been in any kind of trouble with the law? Where did he come from? What do you know about him? He spends a lot of time with at-risk women. That could make him the Man of the Year, but that same set of circumstances could attract a predator. Has he been involved with other women associated with the center?"

"Jane would never have it," Dixon said. "If she

caught a whiff of impropriety, he would have been out of there. It's not like the world is short on lawyers."

"When we asked Dr. Crane if he knew where Karly Vickers was going after her appointment, he suggested she might have stopped by the Quinn, Morgan offices to find out about getting time off to have her dental work done," Vince said. "Has anybody checked that out?"

"If she left the dentist at five o'clock, the law office was already closed," Mendez said. "The sign on their door says they close at four thirty."

"They lock the door at four thirty. That doesn't mean there might not have been someone still there," Vince pointed out. "Appointments run late. Lawyers love to rack up those billable hours."

"Check it out," Dixon said.

"She probably never made it out of the dentist's office. Janet Crane probably killed her and ate her," Mendez said. "That's the meanest woman alive. I don't get why he would be married to her. He's a successful, educated, good-looking guy. Why would he hook up with a ballbuster like that one?"

"Maybe he sees another side of her," Vince offered. "Or maybe he's a masochist. Can you picture her wearing leather and spike-heeled boots?"

"If I want to have nightmares."

"Don't add another killer to the mix," Dixon

said. "We've got enough trouble. If you can't find anyone at Quinn, Morgan who saw Karly Vickers after her appointment, find out where Peter Crane was."

"Home with the family," Mendez said. "That's his alibi. We're not going to break that unless someone saw him somewhere else."

"I'm meeting his wife this afternoon. I'll see what I can find out," Vince said, drawing a stunned look from Mendez. "I'm curious. What can I say? And she's the agent representing the vacant building next to her husband's office. A great place for a newcomer to start a business—or for a kidnapper to stash a victim while he establishes an alibi. I'll scout it out for you."

"I've made a call to the Oxnard PD," Mendez said. "That was where Julie Paulson had her last two arrests for prostitution. They'll get back to me if they can connect her to any johns who might have gotten caught up in a sweep with her."

"Steve Morgan spends a lot of time in Sacramento," Dixon said, grim-faced. "I can reach out to a friend in the PD, see if they've had anything going on up there. I hope to God not."

"If we're dotting *i*'s and crossing *t*'s," Mendez said, "Someone has to account for Frank's whereabouts last Thursday night. Otherwise it'll look like we gave him a pass."

"Talk to his wife," Dixon said, checking his watch. "I told him we have to do this by the book, and no one is more by the book than Frank. He'll deal with it."

Famous last words, Mendez would think later. For the moment it was just one more thing on the endless checklist of a murder investigation.

# 41

Vince popped a couple of pills and washed them down with a locally bottled orange cream soda. *Nice town,* he thought again, as he walked down the pedestrian plaza. *Nice place to settle—except for the serial killer.*

He tossed the soda bottle in a trash can camouflaged with decorative wrought iron, and checked himself in the window of a parked car. In a smart dove gray suit with an orange Italian silk tie, he looked pretty damn good for a guy who had been raised from the dead.

Janet Crane was waiting for him when he arrived at the building next door to her husband's dental office where a sign on the door declared the office was closed. A HAVE YOU SEEN THIS WOMAN? poster of Karly Vickers hung below the CLOSED sign.

She was an attractive brunette in her thirties with a head of puffed-up, sprayed stiff hair, red suit, red heels, and a thousand-watt smile.

"You must be Vince," she said, shaking his hand. She tilted her head just so and batted the eyelashes. She seemed a little too excited, a little too eager, her grip was a little too strong. "I'm Janet Crane. It's so nice to meet you, and so nice to be able to show you this *fantastic* space."

"Lovely to meet you, Ms. Crane. Any relation to the dentist next door?"

"Peter is my husband," she said, letting go of his hand. The smile lost a couple of watts as he took away her tool of flirtation. "Do you know him?"

"I saw the name on the door."

"Well, he's the best dentist in town, in my humble opinion. If you were to lease this space, you could just pop next door when the need arose," she said.

"I'll hope that doesn't become necessary, no offense," he said, flashing the big white smile. "So let's see what the place has to offer."

"As you can see, this is the main retail space," she said as they walked inside. "Like most of the buildings on the plaza, this building dates back to the mid-1920s and has all of the original detail such as the cove molding and the tile floors. But the electrical and plumbing is all up to date," she said. "You're new in Oak Knoll, Vince?"

"Visiting, actually, but I'm very taken with your little city. I can see myself staying."

"Where are you from?"

"Chicago."

"Well, you'll miss the winters, I know," she said, laughing at her own joke. "But this is a wonderful community. We have the college, a very good small hospital, wonderful restaurants, cultural opportunities. We're convenient to both Los Angeles and Santa Barbara."

"What about crime?" Vince asked.

The smile became a little brittle. "Generally, there isn't much to speak of."

"But I saw something on the news about a woman missing, and another woman being found dead in a park," Vince said. "That's pretty serious."

"Yes, but the exception, not the rule," she said. She didn't like him steering her off her sales pitch. "What kind of business are you thinking of for the space?"

"Italian imports. Olive oil, gourmet foods, pottery," he said as if he had given the idea a lot of thought. "The police are looking for a serial killer, I heard."

"We also have an excellent sheriff's office that takes care of the city as well as the county," she countered. "Are you married, Vince?"

"Single, but I have two daughters. How are the schools?"

"Excellent. The top in the state for their size."

"Nothing strange goes on there, I guess," he said jokingly, even as he recalled Dennis Farman and the severed finger.

A muscle in Janet Crane's jaw pulsed. "Not at all."

"So it's just the serial killer we have to worry about."

Now she was getting pissed off. He could see it in the set of her shoulders, the quickness of her breathing, the little line of frustration that made an *L* between her eyebrows. He wasn't letting her manipulate him, and she didn't like it.

He chuckled. "Don't worry, Mrs. Crane. I'm not going to be frightened away. After all, I'm not exactly a part of the target group of victims, am I?"

The brittle smile reappeared. "No, you aren't."

"Still, it's a terrible thing to think about."

"I heard the man responsible is in custody."

"They called him a 'person of interest' on the news, not even a suspect. I don't know that they believe he did it," Vince said. "I've read about serial killers. They're very clever, you know, practically chameleons. This guy could be a businessman, someone respected in the community, but with a dark side. I've heard of women being married to serial killers and not having a clue about their husband's other life."

"That seems hard to believe."

"I know, but it makes you want to know if your husband really plays poker on Thursday nights, doesn't it?"

"I trust my husband implicitly," she said, tension pulling on the natural downward curve of her mouth.

"But should you?" Vince asked. "That's the question."

"You're making me uncomfortable, Mr. Leone," she said curtly.

Vince feigned shock. "Oh, no! I'm so sorry! I didn't mean to—Oh my gosh, no! I'm the last guy . . . Really." He started to laugh at the very notion. "Believe me, Mrs. Crane, I'm a lover not a fighter."

"I didn't mean to imply—"

"No, no, of course not," he reassured her.

"What with everything that's been in the news . . ."

"I understand. And if you don't want to go on—"

"No, no, I'm fine, really," she said, a little embarrassed. She tried to cover it with a little joke that wasn't a joke. "But for the record, my boss knows I'm here with you!"

She laughed. He laughed.

But having spent too much time with killers, Vince couldn't help thinking, *How did she know he hadn't given her a phony name?* As he followed her into the back of the building, why would she think she wasn't in danger just because he was friendly, had a sense of humor, apologized for frightening her? It only took about four minutes to strangle someone to death. He could have done the deed, left her in the back of the store, and walked out via the alley. No one would have been the wiser.

She opened the overhead garage door and sunlight spilled into the dark space.

"As you can see, there's plenty of storage space back here, and easy access for delivery trucks."

"And another door over here—"

"To access your parking spaces. I'm afraid there are only two. That's the only drawback to being on the plaza—the lack of parking. But the pedestrian traffic more than makes up for the inconvenience."

The door also led to Peter Crane's parking spaces, Vince noted. Karly Vickers could have come out the back of the dentist's office, been grabbed and dragged into this storage space. No one could see back there from the front windows of the vacant building. The walls of the building were brick with a thick coating of old-fashioned plaster—virtually soundproof.

Vince walked around the empty space looking for something, anything a victim or her abductor might have dropped. A gum wrapper, a cigarette butt, a stray hair. Nothing. The concrete floor had been stained over the years by oil and paint. A splatter here, a drip there. Did anything look like blood? No.

Industrial shelving lined two walls. Former tenants had left behind old paint cans, rags, assorted odd boxes of stuff. Nothing that looked useful to a killer.

He asked a couple of routine questions and listened to Janet Crane with one ear while he pictured what might have happened if Karly Vickers's abductor had approached her in the alley.

She knows him. She feels safe, happy even. She's had an exciting day. She has no idea she's in danger until he puts a choke hold on her and pulls her into the vacant building.

It takes him a matter of a few seconds to accomplish the deed. He pulls her inside the building and ties her up. He glues her mouth shut to keep her from screaming. He leaves her until dark, when he comes back and takes her to the place where he will torture, rape, and eventually kill her.

It was a workable theory—provided Karly Vickers had exited out the back of the dental office. But Dr. Crane's ever-efficient receptionist had stepped out of the office to take some bills to the corner mailbox that day, and hadn't seen the young woman leave.

If Vickers had left out the back, and the assailant was as organized and methodical as Vince believed, Karly Vickers had not been a victim of opportunity. He had chosen her. Which meant he had to know she would be there.

That had to be a short list of subjects. Someone connected to the Thomas Center; someone who overheard her at the hair salon; the dentist; Frank Farman, who had written her a ticket on her way to the appointment. She might have told a friend, could have been overheard at a restaurant or standing in line at the supermarket . . .

Maybe not such a short list after all.

The garage door rolled down.

"And the lease is six hundred a month," Janet Crane said.

"Great. That seems very reasonable," Vince said, flashing the big smile. "Thanks for your time, Mrs. Crane," he said, shaking her hand again. "I'll definitely give it some thought."

"Good!" she said, back to being a little too animated. She needed to leave him with that last good impression. "Your business would be a wonderful addition to the plaza. And I would be more than happy to show you some beautiful homes in town as well. I hope to hear from you again. Soon!"

She led the way to the front of the store, and Vince looked around at the space. Some warm yellow paint, old wooden display shelves filled with products imported from Italy, an espresso bar in the corner . . . As fantasies went, he thought, it was a good one.

# 42

Anne followed her students out of the building and watched them climb onto buses or into waiting cars. Not one child was being allowed to walk home.

Wendy's father had come to pick her up. Janet Crane had come for Tommy. Anne ducked back behind the door to avoid being seen.

"Chicken," Franny said. He grabbed her at the waist from behind and Anne gave a squeal of surprise.

"You're just lucky I haven't taken up a martial art," she scolded. "You shouldn't sneak up on women when there's been a homicidal lunatic on the loose."

"He probably doesn't work at Oak Knoll Elementary," Franny said. "Who were you hiding from?"

She rolled her eyes. "Janet Crane. I have never seen anyone more vicious or, frankly, out of her mind as she was in the office this morning. Shrieking about everyone she's going to sue—including me, by the way."

"You? What did you do?" Franny asked, out-raged at the idea. She could have murdered someone with an axe and he still would have been the first to rush to her defense.

"I happened to be standing in the room."

"She should kiss the ground you walk on!" He cupped a hand around his mouth and pretended to shout after the cars driving away. "C U Next Tuesday, Janet Bitch Queen!"

Anne elbowed him in the ribs, giggling. "Hush! What if Mrs. Barkow heard you?" she said, refer-ring to the third-grade teacher pulling sidewalk monitor duty.

"Oh for God's sake," Franny said. "She's a hundred and twelve. She'd probably die of excite-ment if somebody called her that. It's been so long since she's used hers, I'm sure it's grown over by now. The Land That Time Forgot."

"Oh my God. You are horrible!" Anne said, trying—and failing—not to laugh. "I love you!"

"Will you love me drunk?" he asked.

"Did you have a long day?"

"Honey, I teach kindergarten. Every day is a long day," he joked. "Today I had one eat a crayon, one barf on the art table, and one poop in the sandbox and cover it up like a cat. Arnie the janitor had to put on his hazmat suit to clean it up, and then I had to explain to Garnett why we need all-new sand by Monday. How was your day?"

"Besides being threatened and verbally abused, I spent the day trying to explain to seventeen ten-year-olds why their classmate would have a severed human finger in his possession, and why people kill each other, and try to reassure them that they don't have to worry," she said, feeling the weight of every minute press down on her. "I spent the day wondering about Dennis Farman and what happened to him last night, and where was he today. Who's with him? Is he alone? Is he going to get help?"

"There's nothing you can do about Dennis Farman, honey," Franny said soberly. "It's not up to you."

"But I seem to be the only one who cares," she said. "And that breaks my heart. Garnett and the school board are only worried about liability. The sheriff's office only deals with punishment. His parents created who he is. And social services probably won't do anything because there's no proof of abuse."

"You called social services?" Franny said. "On the Farmans?"

"I felt like I had to do something," Anne said. "At least if there's a complaint, and they see Dennis and talk to him, maybe eventually someone will do something to get him some help."

"You called social services on a sheriff's deputy?" Franny said. "Are you out of your mind? Have you never seen a Women in Prison movie?"

"I'm not afraid of Frank Farman."

"Well, you probably should be. He'll bankrupt you with speeding tickets at the very least. Does Garnett know you did this?"

"No."

"You need hard liquor," Franny declared. "*I* need hard liquor. And lots of it."

Anne nodded and tried to muster a smile, knowing her other option was to just lie down on the ground and cry.

"Margaritas at Cantina Maria?"

"I might have to catch up with you," Anne said as Vince Leone pulled up to the curb and got out.

Franny sucked in breath. "Ohmygod, that's HIM!"

Anne rolled her eyes. "Don't wet yourself, Francis. How will I explain you?"

"Very dapper," Franny declared, eyes on Leone. "Handsome. A little on the rugged side, but distinguished. Sharp dresser."

"Old enough to be my father."

"No, he isn't. Your father is a fossil. Besides, you don't even like guys your own age," he reminded her. "May-December—no, really, May-mid-September. It's romantic! You should totally sleep with him."

"I met him yesterday!"

"Come on. Be a skank-o-potamus for once. Have some fun before Frank Farman gets you thrown in the slammer. That's all's I'm sayin'. You don't have to keep him, honey, but for God's sake, kick the tires and take a ride around the block!"

Anne gave him a stern look. "Shut up and do *NOT* follow me."

She had to admit, as she walked toward him, the man was attractive. He needed to put on a few pounds. The gray suit was a little loose, but it draped expensively over his lanky frame, and the color complemented the steel gray in his hair and mustache.

He was also an FBI agent using her to spy on a family via a ten-year-old boy, she reminded herself.

"Agent—Detective—"

"Vince," he said, stopping just a little too close to her, his dark eyes sparkling with amusement.

"I'm surprised to see you here," Anne said. "We have no dismembered body parts today."

"I'm glad for you. How was your day?"

"I'm planning to take up drinking—only because

it's cheaper and more socially acceptable than heroin."

"And legal," he added. "Provided you don't try to operate heavy machinery. Do you need help with that? I can drive a Volkswagen as well as anybody."

"Hello! Francis Goodsell. Anne's sidekick and best friend in the whole wide world."

Anne felt herself blush as Franny stepped between them to shake Leone's hand.

Vince grinned. "Nice to meet you, Francis. Vince Leone. Anne's would-be suitor."

"How have I missed seeing you around town?" Franny asked. "I know absolutely everybody worth knowing in Oak Knoll."

"I travel a lot," Vince said.

"Domestically or abroad?"

"Franny . . . ," Anne said through gritted teeth.

Vince seemed happy to play along. "Both."

"An international man of mystery," Franny said. "I like that. And are your intentions honorable?"

"Franny!"

"Absolutely."

Franny frowned. "Well, we'll have to do something about that. This girl needs to have some fun."

Anne turned him by the shoulders and gave him a push toward the building. "Good-bye, Francis."

Franny grinned over his shoulder, his eyes disappearing into twin crescents above his cheeks. "Nice meeting you, Vince!"

"Likewise."

He looked entirely too amused when Anne turned back to him.

"Take a walk with me," he said as he put his hand on the small of her back and started down the sidewalk away from the building. "I want you to show me where the kids found the body."

"Can't Detective Mendez do that?"

"He's otherwise engaged and not nearly as pretty."

"What's going on?" Anne asked, falling in step with him, ignoring the compliment. He was a natural flirt. He couldn't help himself. "Have they found the missing woman yet?"

The weight of his hand felt good against her back, but shouldn't have. She wasn't in the habit of letting people touch her, but she made no effort to stop him.

"No," he said. "Not yet."

"But someone's been arrested, right?" she asked looking up at him. "I saw that on the news this morning."

"Yes," he answered, his face carefully blank.

"But?"

He cocked a brow at her. "I'm not at liberty to discuss an ongoing investigation."

"Oh. But you can feel free to recruit me into it."

He dodged the barb. "Did you speak to the boy?"

"Yes, and I feel like a creepy sneak, thanks for asking."

"I wouldn't ask if it wasn't important, Anne."

"He thinks his father was home that night because they watch *Cosby* together. A boy and his loving, caring father sit down together and watch a wholesome family comedy."

"What about Mom?"

"She has no sense of humor. But I would certainly buy her as a serial killer before her husband."

He chuckled at that. "I heard she was a little upset this morning."

"I've discovered this week that Janet Crane does not become *a little* upset."

"Gee, and she was so pleasant to me today. Must be my charm and stunning good looks," he teased.

A little smile tugged at the corner of Anne's mouth as she looked up at him. "Must be. Here we are."

The area around where the body had been buried was still corralled with yellow tape. Vince ducked under it and walked into the shallow grave. He stood there for a couple of minutes, saying nothing, looking very serious as he surveyed the area for 360 degrees around the spot.

"How well do you know this park?" he asked.

"I grew up six blocks from here."

"Is there another way to get to this spot other than the way we just came?"

"There's a service road about twenty yards over that rise," she said, pointing in the general direction behind him. "The sheriff's office is maybe a quarter of a mile beyond that."

Even though there was probably two hours of daylight left, it was growing dark in the woods. And cold. Anne hugged herself and tried not to imagine what it would be like to have some evil monster carrying her in here to plant her body in the ground.

"I'm sorry," Vince said, coming back to her. He shrugged out of his suit coat and draped it around her shoulders. It swallowed her up and smelled pleasantly of sandalwood soap and man. "You're cold. Let me get you out of here. You've had a long week."

"Yes. Starting right here."

"It must have been quite a shock to you."

"I suppose you're used to it."

He shook his head. "You never get used to it. You learn to close a door on it emotionally, but it's never easy. I don't want it to ever be easy."

Something rustled in the dead leaves that covered the floor of the woods. Anne strained to see into the gathering gloom on the far side of the grave. She thought she could almost make out a shape half-hidden by a tree trunk.

"Somebody's watching us," she murmured. *Probably Franny,* she thought, though the feeling that crawled over her skin was creepy, and that wasn't right.

The somebody must have felt their stares as well. There was another rustling sound and a figure darted from behind one tree to behind another. A smallish figure. A child.

"Dennis?" she called out, walking toward the grave. "Dennis, is that you?"

More rustling, and the figure streaked behind another tree. Anne started to jog, Vince's jacket slipping off her shoulders.

"Dennis, come out! It's all right. Come out!"

Another flash of movement. She was picking up speed, dodging branches. Her heart was pounding out of proportion to her effort. She wanted to catch him—needed to catch him—figuratively, literally, before he got away.

"Dennis!"

She caught a glimpse of him, never more. He kept running. She ran harder.

"Anne!" Vince called, gaining ground on her. "Anne, let him go!"

It seemed everyone had let Dennis go, not for the good of Dennis, but because it was too hard to deal with him. Someone needed to hang on to him or he would truly be lost.

"Anne!"

The toe of her loafer stubbed an exposed root, and she found herself falling. Losing him. She hit the ground.

"Anne!"

Vince was beside her instantly. "Are you all right?"

*No*, she thought. She began to tremble as the weight of it all settled hard on her shoulders—a rotten week culminating with the suspension of the one child in her class who needed the most help. And that child was now running in the woods like a wild animal, haunting a gravesite where he had somehow managed to steal the finger of a dead woman.

"Hey," Vince said, his hands cupping her shoulders as he helped her up. "You're shaking."

"I'm fine," she murmured.

She was fine, but tears rose in her eyes and she wished to God it was too dark for him to see them.

"Let me take you home, honey," he said softly, brushing leaves and twigs from her hair. "You're exhausted."

His kindness was her undoing. She could be as tough as she had to be, but kindness . . . she couldn't manage that. No matter how hard she squeezed her eyes shut, the tears still came.

"Come here," Vince whispered. He slipped his arms around her and drew her close as carefully as if she were made of fine porcelain. "It's all right. This shoulder has been cried on before."

For the first time that week Anne let go. She let the fraying ends of control slip through her fingers, and let loose the pressure that had been building and building inside her.

She let Vince Leone hold her and cradle her head against his chest and tell her she would be all right, that she would make it through this. She took the comfort of a stranger and somehow she didn't feel like she was free-falling. She felt . . .

protected, safe. It took a moment for her to even realize what the feeling was.

Vince came up with a pristine white handkerchief and dabbed gently at the tears on her cheeks, but he seemed in no hurry to let her go. And Anne felt in no hurry to leave.

She tilted her chin up and looked at him, no longer caring what he saw in her eyes—sadness, vulnerability, longing. He settled his mouth on hers for a kiss that was long and deep. And when it was finished, she pressed her ear to his chest and listened to his heart beat for a long while.

# 43

"Are you and Mom getting divorced?"

The question just came out, like a hiccup or a cough. Wendy opened her mouth and the words just tumbled out. They were in the backyard, beyond the swimming pool, away from the house where her mother was fixing dinner. Her father had picked her up at school and suggested a game of catch because they hadn't played in a long time.

"Because you're never home," she had said.

She was tired and in a bad mood. It seemed like life was never going to be the same again since they had found the body in the park. School wasn't the same. Tommy wasn't the same. Nobody treated her the same. Her parents weren't the same. It sucked.

Her dad stopped his throwing motion as her question hit him. He looked shocked, which just went to show how oblivious adults were. Like they didn't think their kids could hear, or that they didn't live in the same house, or had no clue what was going on around them.

"No," he said, coming over to her. He tried to laugh it off—as if that question could ever have been part of a joke. "No. What would make you think that, Wendy?"

Wendy rolled her eyes. "Dad, I'm not a baby. I know what goes on."

"What goes on?" he asked, sitting down on a stone bench. He pulled his fielder's glove off and set it aside. Wendy did the same.

"People have affairs," she said. "I know all about it."

Of course, she didn't. Not exactly. It made no sense to her. You only married someone if you loved them, and then why bother with having an affair? From what she'd seen on television it was never worth it, and everyone involved was just miserable.

Her father scratched his head, trying to think of what to say. "Did your mother say something to you?"

"No, because all she does anymore is cry and try not to let me know it."

"Honey, your mom is upset about the things that have happened this week: you finding that body, and what that Farman kid did to you—"

"I heard you fighting," she said, playing her big card. He couldn't know exactly what or how much she had heard.

He closed his eyes and sighed, leaning his forearms on his thighs and letting his hands dangle between his knees. He looked tired and maybe a little angry.

"There are things your mom just doesn't understand," he said, his tone of voice short, almost businesslike. "Things I need to do. Sometimes I have to be away. That's just how it is. She should be used to it by now, but this week has been difficult. It's not something you need to worry about, honey. All right?"

Wendy wanted to say no, but she had the feeling he would get mad at her. Besides, her mother had come onto the patio to call them in for dinner.

Tommy wandered into the small office down the hall from the family room. He liked being in this room with his father's desk and the leather chairs. The bookshelves were full of all kinds of books. He liked to climb up and pull them out at random just to see what was inside.

His favorite was the *Encyclopaedia Britannica*. Page after page, volume after volume with all the knowledge in the world practically. He would pick a letter at random and sit in the big fat leather chair in the corner and examine every page.

His father sat at his desk now, going through

the newspaper, sipping on a drink, while his mother worked in the kitchen fixing dinner.

"What are you reading?" Tommy asked as he walked around the desk, running his finger along the carved edge.

His father didn't look up. "The news. You want to see? Here's a picture of where I was this afternoon."

Tommy came around to his father's side and looked at the photograph. A bunch of people standing around in a field. The headline above read: SEARCH CONTINUES FOR MISSING OAK KNOLL WOMAN.

"There's Wendy's dad," Tommy said, putting his finger on the image of Wendy's father in serious conversation with a blonde lady.

"Yep."

"Who is that lady?"

"That's Jane Thomas. She runs the women's center."

"Did you find the missing lady?"

"No. Not yet."

"She's probably murdered," Tommy said gravely. "That's what serial killers do."

"Hopefully not," his father said, taking a sip of his drink.

Whiskey. Tommy liked the smell and the color of it, but he had once tasted some left in the bottom of a glass on the blotter, and it was gross. He had coughed and choked and gagged on it until he ran into the kitchen and got a drink of water.

"Dad? Did we watch *Cosby* last week?"

"Last week? I don't remember. Why?"

"I don't know," Tommy said. "Miss Navarre asked me today if we were home last week on Thursday. I think we were."

"Why would she ask you that?"

Tommy shrugged and winced because it still hurt his ribs to move. His attention was already on to something else. He had started to read the article about the search. He recognized the place in the picture. He and his father had gone there once to look for parts to the old Mustang convertible that sat in the garage in a million pieces. It was a cool place in a kind of a creepy way.

"That's a strange question," his father said. "Did she ask the whole class?"

Tommy shook his head. "Nope. Just me."

"Huh."

He turned and looked at his father. "Dad, I'm not going to have to go to another school, am I? I like Miss Navarre. She's a really good teacher."

And pretty. And she smelled nice. And she really cared about him. But he said none of that to his father. Being married and old and all, he probably didn't remember what it was like to like a girl.

"No, son. Your mom was just upset about what happened yesterday. She'll calm down."

*How does she think I felt?* Tommy wondered. His mother had been all worried about him at the emergency room after Dennis beat him up—when there were people all around making a fuss—but she hadn't had much to say to him since then. She was too caught up being mad at people. But Tommy said none of this to his father, either.

"I think the Dodgers'll win tomorrow, don't you?" he said instead.

His father got up from the desk, went to the bookcase, and poured himself another drink. "I hope so."

"If they win tomorrow, then it's only one more game and then they're in the World Series!" Tommy said, thrusting his fists into the air like a champion—then quickly bringing them down because that hurt like crazy. He turned around in a couple of tight circles until he started to get dizzy.

"I'm going to check on dinner," his father said. He ruffled Tommy's hair absently and walked out of the room.

Tommy wasted no time scrambling into the big leather swiveling desk chair. Someday he would have a desk and a chair like this one, and he would do something important, like his dad.

He went back to reading the article in the newspaper to see if his dad's name was in it.

Karly Nicole Vickers, 21, originally of Simi Valley, California, was last seen around 5:00 P.M. on the afternoon of Thursday, October 3, in the office of local dentist, Dr. Peter Crane . . .

# 44

It took Sharon Farman nearly five minutes to come to the door. Mendez and Hicks stood on the front steps, periodically ringing the doorbell, then knocking. They had been told at Quinn, Morgan that Mrs. Farman had stayed home for the day to look after her son. Her maroon minivan was parked in the driveway.

"Why doesn't the kid answer the door?" Hicks asked.

"He's probably chained to a radiator," Mendez said.

"Maybe he slit his mother's throat and took off."

Mendez rang the bell again and banged his knuckles on the door.

"Frank is going to shit a brick over this," Hicks said.

"We don't have a choice. If he's got nothing to hide, then he should shut up and let us do our jobs."

"Yeah. That'll happen."

The door opened then. Sharon Farman had clearly been asleep. Her puffed-up hairdo was lopsided, squished flat on the right, and there were creases on her cheek. Her eyes were a little bleary. Her lipstick was smudged.

"Mrs. Farman? Detectives Mendez and Hicks," Mendez said, holding up his ID. "We need to ask you a few questions."

She stared at them, confused. "What's this about? Dennis?"

"No, ma'am. Would it be all right if we came in for a few minutes?"

Still slow to react, it took her several seconds before she stepped back from the door. Mendez watched her closely. She seemed a little unsteady on her feet, and he began to wonder if it wasn't something other than sleep impairing her reaction time.

She led them into a dining room.

"Are you feeling all right, ma'am?" he asked as they all took seats at the table.

"I was having a nap," she said, reaching for a pack of cigarettes. Her hands trembled ever so slightly as she lit up.

"We're sorry to interrupt your day," Hicks said. "We have just a couple of questions and we'll let you go."

"Questions about what? Are the Cranes going to press charges?" she asked, irritated. "Kids get into fights. Maybe they should teach their precious little angel to stick up for himself."

The longer sentence gave her away. Her speech slurred ever so slightly. She'd been drinking.

"This isn't about your son, ma'am," Hicks said. "We need to clear up a couple of things as to your husband's whereabouts last week Thursday evening."

"My husband? Frank? You work with him, for

heaven's sake, why don't you just ask him?"

"This is a bit delicate," Mendez admitted. "Because your husband made a traffic stop on Karly Vickers the day she went missing, we have to make sure his time after that is accounted for so he can officially be ruled out as a suspect."

Sharon Farman sobered at that. She sat up a little straighter. Her cigarette burned down in her fingers. "A suspect? You think Frank had something to do with that?"

"Not really, ma'am," Mendez said. "Deputy Farman's reputation speaks for itself. The timing was unfortunate, that's all. This is a formality."

Hand shaking again, she put the cigarette in the ashtray.

"I'm not comfortable with this," she said. "Maybe I should speak to my husband first."

"It's really not a big deal, ma'am," Hicks said easily. "We just need to nail down his time line. Do you remember what time he got home that evening?"

"We eat dinner at six thirty sharp," she said. "Every night."

She glanced at her watch then and what color she had left her cheeks. "Oh my God. Look at the time! I had no idea how late—Oh, no. I haven't even taken meat out of the freezer! Why didn't the girls wake me? Where are they?"

She looked around the room, as if they might appear.

It was 5:09, Mendez noted. Sharon Farman was genuinely distressed, not just ready to give them the bum's rush out the door.

"Has Frank seemed different in any way this past week?" Hicks asked. "Stressed?"

"Of course he's been stressed," she snapped. "Look at what's gone on: a murder, a kidnapping, our son finding that body. We're *all* stressed, Detective."

"Yes, ma'am."

"Do you remember if your husband was home all evening, or if he might have gone out after dinner that night?" Mendez asked.

"I don't know," she said impatiently. "It was a week ago. And I have meetings on Thursday nights. I'm sure he was here when I left and when I came home. He always is."

She looked at her watch again and got up from her chair. "I have to start dinner. Is there anything else?"

"No, ma'am," Mendez said, rising. "Thank you for your time. We'll show ourselves out."

Without a word Sharon Farman turned and disappeared into the next room, leaving her cigarette smoldering in the ashtray.

"Well, that was weird," Hicks said as they walked out to the car. "What do you suppose happens if she doesn't serve dinner at six thirty on the dot?"

"I don't know," Mendez said. "Court-martial?

But I bet I know where she goes on Thursday nights."

"Where?"

"AA meets at the Presbyterian church on Piedra Boulevard Thursday nights. That's my jogging route. They're usually all out smoking on the lawn when I run by."

"She had definitely had a few before we got here."

"Yeah. Nap my ass. Sleeping it off is more like."

Hicks shrugged as they reached the car. "If I was married to Frank, I'd drink too."

Farman was in Dixon's office when they got back. He did not look happy to be there.

*Join the club*, Mendez thought as he and Hicks walked into the room.

"It's just a formality, Frank," Dixon said.

"It's an insult," Farman snapped. "How many years do we go back, Cal?"

"A lot."

"A dozen. A dozen years, and you're doing this to me? This is bullshit."

"I'm not doing anything to you, Frank. We're following procedure to the letter. If I had written that girl up myself, I'd have the detectives do the same thing. If Mendez had written the girl up, I'd be doing the same—and you'd be saying it was the right thing to do."

Farman had nothing to say to that because it

347

was true. He would have been the first one in line demanding to treat Mendez like any other person of interest. But he was embarrassed and his pride was hurt, and Mendez could understand that too. A guy like Frank lived for the job. His reputation was everything to him.

"It's nothing personal, Frank," he said. "We're dotting *i*'s and crossing *t*'s, that's all."

Farman wouldn't look at him. Mendez sighed.

"You wrote up the Vickers girl at fifteen thirty-eight that day," Hicks said, getting on with it. "We'll just need to see your logbook for the rest of the shift."

Farman crossed his arms over his chest. Dixon motioned to the logbook sitting on his desk. Hicks picked it up and paged through.

"You'd never met the girl before, right?" Mendez asked.

"Do you remember every citation you ever wrote?" Farman demanded.

"No," Mendez said calmly.

"I didn't remember the girl ten minutes later. It was just another ticket."

Mendez had a hard time believing that, but he let it slide. "You'd never met her before that."

"No."

"I don't want to go through the DMV records and find out you wrote her up before."

Farman looked at him then. "You're a prick."

"Frank," Dixon cautioned.

"I'm just saying, Frank," Mendez said. "Better if you tell me now than have it be a surprise."

"Fuck yourself."

Mendez held his temper, remembering what Vince had told him about getting what he needed out of people—even the Frank Farmans of the world. From the corner of his eye he saw Hicks frown as he read the log entries.

"Frank, it says here you took dinner from five to six that day."

"So?"

"Your wife told us you're home for dinner at six thirty every night."

Farman got to his feet, his face turning dark red. "You spoke to my wife? You went to my home and spoke to my wife without telling me?"

"Standard op, Frank," Mendez said.

"Have you ever heard of common courtesy, you arrogant little shit?"

Dixon stood up. "Frank, that's enough."

Mendez took a step toward Farman, feeling the need to draw a line.

"I've taken enough abuse off you, Frank," he said, keeping his tone calm and even. "I'm bending over backward to do this right. You want to make it hard? That's your choice.

"I can take the gloves off and make this hard for you. I can call in every person you know, all your neighbors, the people you go to church with, and ask them all about you. Does he drink? Does he fuck around on his wife? Does he beat his kids?

"Is that what you want?" Mendez asked. "Or we can turn this over to another agency and really do it right. You can have some arrogant little shit you don't know and who has no loyalty to this office digging through your life. Would you rather we do that?"

Farman looked like he might blow an aneurysm. So much for getting what he needed.

"Frank, sit down," Dixon ordered. "Let's get this over with."

Farman sat and stared at the front of the desk.

"I worked late that night," he said. "I had paperwork. My wife is mistaken."

"You were here?" Hicks said. "Okay."

But as he said it, he cut Mendez a look.

Farman caught it from the corner of his eye. He turned on Hicks. "What?"

Hicks looked uncomfortable. "You were off the clock at four thirty. You're salaried. You don't get overtime. Why put it in your logbook that you went to dinner?"

"Habit," Farman said.

Hicks looked to Dixon. "Can I keep this for a couple of hours?" he asked, lifting the logbook.

"Un-fucking-believable," Farman muttered, shaking his head. He stood up. "I'm done here. I'm going home."

Mendez checked his watch. 6:26. He hoped for Sharon Farman's sake dinner was ready.

# 45

"You received a traffic fine in the mail."

Anne looked at her father as she dropped her book bag and purse inside the front door. "What?"

"It says something about reckless driving and destruction of property. I taught you how to drive better than that."

"I learned to drive from Mom," Anne said, taking the citation from him. Frank Farman had written the ticket because she had turned around on his lawn after he parked behind her and blocked her in. Jerk. "You must be thinking about some other daughter you had with some other woman."

"What's that supposed to mean?"

"You know exactly what it means. It means you don't get to reinvent my history."

"You don't have to worry about it, anyway," he said, waving at the ticket. "I give to the sheriff's charity every year. They know me. They'll look the other way."

"I don't think that's how it works, Dad."

Fine: $150!

"Of course that's how it works. What were you doing behind the wheel? Drinking and driving?"

"No, but I'm thinking about taking that up."

He didn't react because he never listened to her. The other person's role in a conversation with

Dick Navarre was to kill time while he was deciding what to say next.

In all their years of marriage he had probably heard about 3 percent of what her mother ever had to say. Her opinion had meant nothing to him, nor had Anne's. She remembered when she was nine years old her mother telling her to go into the living room and talk to her father before dinner. Even then Anne had seen the futility of that exercise.

"Really, honey," her mother had said. "Daddy wants to hear about your day at school."

Anne had looked up at her mother, perfectly coiffed, perfectly made up, all for her husband who treated her like a servant, and said, "Mom, he doesn't even know what grade I'm in."

She regretted saying it instantly only because her honesty had hurt her mother. Her father probably couldn't say what grade she taught now because what she did was of no interest to him, even though he had been a teacher himself. The ultimate narcissist, it only mattered to him that she took care of the things he needed taken care of.

"You're late," he said. "Again. What's your excuse tonight?"

"I've been recruited by the FBI to work undercover in this murder investigation."

He looked annoyed. "The FBI doesn't hire women."

"Yes, they do. It's 1985, Dad. We have the right to vote and everything."

"Ha. Very funny," he grumbled, walking away. "The right to vote."

Anne dropped the citation on the dining room table and headed for the kitchen, calling, "Did you take your meds?"

"Of course I did. I'm not senile. I don't need you to tell me what to do."

"Good. In that case, I'll be moving out next week."

She looked into the plastic case that held his pills for the day. He hadn't taken half of them. If she asked him why not, he would undoubtedly tell her it was because he once read an article in *The New England Journal of Medicine* while waiting for his dermatologist to remove a mole, and therefore knew more about the subject of pharmaceuticals than any one of the three medical specialists he saw.

"Maybe you can get a girlfriend," Anne called out, dumping the pills into her hand. "It'll be just like the old days."

"I don't know why you go on like that," he groused. "I was a very good husband."

"Really?" she said, coming back into the dining room. "To whom?"

"You always took your mother's side."

"Yes. Damn but that I didn't inherit that amoral gene of yours. My life would be so much easier."

"Are you finished?" he asked coolly. "I'm going next door to watch *Jeopardy!* The Ivers are such a lovely family."

Anne rolled her eyes. "You hate Judith Iver. Tuesday night you called her a stupid cow."

"Not to her face."

"Well, that makes all the difference. Here," she said, handing him a fistful of pills and a glass of water. "I'm not letting you out the door until you take those."

"I don't know why you bother," he complained. "You'd be happier if I was dead."

"Yes, but I'm such an obvious suspect."

"I'm sure your new friends at the FBI would take care of you."

"It would make a better story if I called in all your markers for donating twenty dollars a year to the sheriff's annual circus day fund."

Her father sniffed and struck a pose like a Shakespearean actor on stage. Sir Richard of Bullshit. "How sharper than a serpent's tooth it is to have a thankless child!"

"Oh, please," Anne said, quickly thumbing through the rest of the mail. "I'm completely thankful to my parent. That just doesn't happen to be you, that's all."

"I'm leaving," he announced, offended. It would give him something to talk about when he sat down with Judith Iver and her nephew. He could lament his daughter's low treatment of him and elicit half an hour's worth of sympathy while flogging them at *Jeopardy!*

Anne hurried to her room to shower and

change clothes. The Thomas Center was holding a candlelight vigil for Karly Vickers and in memory of Lisa Warwick, and she felt a need to be there. She refused to recognize the fact that she expected to see Vince there, just as she refused to think too hard about the fact that he had kissed her. She had allowed him to kiss her.

It was only because she had felt weak and vulnerable, and he had felt so strong and safe by comparison. And she wanted to trust him. The deepest, most private part of who she was had existed in emotional isolation for most of her life. But in that one moment of weakness she had wanted to drop those shields just to feel the comfort of another soul next to hers for a little while.

The sound of his low, rough voice was warm in her head as she stood in front of her bathroom mirror.

*It's all right. . . . This shoulder has been cried on before.*

She ached all the way through at the memory of how much she had needed to hear someone say that.

Now she pushed the feeling away as something impractical and a waste of time. She had things to do and needing was not high on the list of priorities.

The Thomas Center was a collection of white stucco buildings that had been a private Catholic girls' school from the early twenties into the sixties. Modeled on the style of the old Spanish missions, the buildings formed a courtyard between them with a fountain at its center and stunning, simple gardens rambling along the stone walkways.

It was a beautiful place by daylight. By candlelight it was magical. Hundreds of tiny flames seemed to dance on the dark night air. The courtyard was nearly full. Franny had scoped out the scene before Anne got there and had chosen a spot with the optimum potential for eavesdropping.

"This is my entertainment for the evening," he said as she joined him. "I'm giving up *Miami Vice* to be here."

"Well, I hope for your sake a car chase ensues at some point," Anne said.

"I'd settle for a Don Johnson sighting. Or a sighting of your Mr. Leone," he suggested, raising up on the tiptoes of his Top-Siders to survey the crowd. "What were you doing out there in the woods all that time, Anne Marie? A little horizontal hokeypokey?"

"Oh, yeah. In a shallow grave," Anne whispered. "Have some respect, please. We're at a vigil."

"We should hold a vigil for your vagina if you take a pass on the Italian Stallion."

A couple of heads swiveled in their direction. Anne grabbed his arm and pinched him hard. "Behave yourself!"

"I liked the way he put his hand on your back," he said. "Very proprietary. BIG hand, I might add."

Anne shushed him and told herself the flush of heat that washed through her was embarrassment and had nothing to do with the memory of Vince Leone touching her.

Jane Thomas stepped up onto a small stage that was positioned at one end of the courtyard and thanked everyone for coming. The program was short. A poetry reading in memory of Lisa Warwick. A plea for information from the public regarding both cases. An announcement about the reward the center had posted. Donations from the public would be accepted in memory of Lisa. A local folksinger got up and sang a song that made everyone tear up. The end.

They shuffled toward the exit with the rest of the crowd. Talk of the findings at the salvage yard that afternoon rippled through. Speculation about the sudden series of crimes ran the gamut from evil seeping north from Los Angeles to an obvious decline of a once-great society.

"I need an espresso," Franny declared as they made it to the sidewalk. "All this melancholy has worn me out."

As they turned in the direction of the plaza, Anne caught a flash of red from the corner of her eye.

Janet Crane was bearing down on her like a

charging tigress. Her eyes were so wide-open the white was visible all the way around the iris. Her lips pulled back in a grimace that showed gritted teeth.

Anne's heart plunged into her stomach and bounced back up to the back of her throat.

*"Miss Navarre,"* she spat each word as if it tasted bad. "I would like a word with you."

Anne swallowed hard. *Show no fear*. She stepped out of the flow of human traffic and faced the woman, hoping she appeared calmer than she felt. Janet Crane didn't stop until no more than a foot separated them.

"Mrs. Crane—"

"How *dare* you!" Her voice was lowered to a harsh whisper to keep from being overheard, but carried all the strength of a shout. "How dare you try to use my son."

Caught mentally flatfooted, Anne couldn't think of a response. She was guilty as charged. She didn't deserve to defend herself.

She glanced at Tommy, who looked both mortified and hurt, and wouldn't make eye contact with her. His expression was a harder punch in the stomach than any verbal attack his mother could launch.

Janet Crane's words broke up like bad radio reception in Anne's head. She wanted to drop down on her knees and beg Tommy's forgiveness.

". . . making a little boy think his father might be

some kind of-of *monster* . . . absolutely *outrageous* . . . My husband is a highly respected member of this community. How *dare* you insinuate . . ."

Anne felt like she was having an out-of-body experience. Or maybe she wished that she was. She couldn't seem to move or speak. She was aware of people staring at them, Franny looking like a deer in headlights.

Then a man's voice came from her left. Low, rough, familiar. "Is there some kind of problem here, ladies?"

It took a minute for the rage to clear from Janet Crane's eyes. She blinked at Vince like he had dropped out of the sky.

"Oh. Oh! Mr. Leone," she said, scrambling. Anne could practically see the wheels in the woman's brain brake to an abrupt halt and struggle to start turning in another direction. "Mr. Leone. What a surprise to see you here!"

"If I'm going to be part of the community, I thought I should start participating," he said smoothly. "Is everything all right? This looked like a bit of a disagreement," he said, wagging a finger from one to the other of them.

"No. No!" Janet Crane said, flashing the too bright smile. "Not at all. Everything is fine. Mr. Leone, this is Anne Navarre. Anne teaches at Oak Knoll Elementary."

"We've met, actually," he said.

"Oh. Well. That's wonderful!"

He smiled down at Anne, a thousand watts of pure charm.

"I certainly hope it will be. In fact, I was hoping to catch up with you tonight, Miss Navarre," he said, settling his hand on the small of her back once again. "I need to discuss something with you. If you'll excuse us, Mrs. Crane?"

Janet smiled the brittle smile that made Anne think the fine veneer of her face was about to shatter to pieces and reveal the reptilian alien beneath the facade.

"Of course," she said. "My son and I were just on our way home. Have a lovely evening. Good to see you, Anne."

A chill ran down Anne's back.

"Oh my God," Franny said, finally regaining the ability to speak as Janet Crane walked away. "I think you were just saved from having your soul liquefied and sucked out of you."

"That was your fault," Anne said, angry and upset as she turned to Vince. "Do you have any idea what just happened? I just lost that little boy's trust. Do you have any idea what that means to me?"

He had the grace to look contrite. "I'm sorry."

"You should be. She's going to get Tommy taken out of my class," she said, swiping angrily at a tear that dared to fall. "I'm someone he should be able to trust and she's going to take him away, and who will he have then?"

"Anne—"

"I'm going home," she announced, and started walking toward the public lot where she had parked. She felt like Janet Crane had reached right into her chest and torn her heart loose. And it was her own fault. She should have gone with her gut.

"Anne," Vince said, taking hold of her arm. "Wait."

"No," she said, jerking away from him, not slowing down. "I'm upset, and I'm going home before I make a complete spectacle of myself in the street."

"I'll fix it," he said.

"You'll fix it?" she turned and stared at him, incredulous. "How will you fix it? How will you get that little boy to trust me?"

"He'll trust you again," he promised. "He wants to trust you. He needs to trust you. He sure as hell can't trust his mother. He'll turn back to you. And he won't be going anywhere. I'll take care of Janet Crane."

Anne arched a brow. "Take care of? That sounds like something a gangster would say."

"Well, I am from Chicago, but I promise I only work on the right side of the street."

"Don't try to be amusing," she snapped. "I'm in no mood to be amused."

"Sorry."

"And what makes you think you can stop Janet Crane from doing something if she's made up her mind?" she demanded, jamming her hands on her hips.

"I don't *think* I can. I *will*," he said. "Janet Crane has a lot, which means she has a lot to lose. Her status, for instance. Her standing in the community. I have the ability to make those things go away simply by having a conversation with a reporter."

Anne's eyebrows went up. He meant it. Seriously.

"I owe you," he said. "Besides, people can't mess with people I like. And she can't screw with me because she's got no currency with me. She's got nothing to threaten me with. I've got the big stick, and I'll use it."

Anne thought about that for a moment. She had never had anyone rush to defend her before, let alone promise annihilation of the enemy. And she had no doubt that he would do exactly what he said. His expression was just this side of fierce. He radiated power. She felt a little like she had poked a stick at a lion.

"Let me see you home," he said, dialing down his intensity a notch.

"I'm capable of driving myself home," Anne said.

"I'm well aware you're capable," he said, brows lowered over his dark eyes. "I would feel better seeing you home. You're upset. You're not going to be paying attention. There's still a killer on the loose. Now that I've fucked up—pardon my

French—your relationship with your student, making sure you're safe seems like the least I can do. Is that all right with you?"

Without examining her reasons too closely, Anne handed him her car keys.

# 46

Anne led the way up the sidewalk to the home she had grown up in, a sturdy Craftsman-style house of dark painted wood and stone. Soft amber lights flanked the front door. Rosebushes lined the front walk. The roses glowed white in the moonlight.

Vince followed her up the steps, admiring her behind in a pair of blue jeans. "You live here alone?"

"With my father. He allegedly needs a keeper."

"Right. You said his health is poor. What does he have?"

"His heart is bad," she said. "Literally and figuratively."

"How old is he?"

"Seventy-nine," she said, unlocking the front door and letting them in. She glanced up at him, catching the surprise on his face. "My father was an English professor with a wandering eye. My mother was his much-younger student."

Vince kept his mouth shut. He had to be happy her father was seventy-nine and not forty-nine. Anne started to go down a dark hall, and he caught her gently by the arm.

"Whoa, sweetheart. Don't go charging down dark hallways," he cautioned. "Do you keep all your doors and windows locked?"

"As of this week I do," she said.

Vince flicked on the hall light. "You can't be too careful. We still don't know who this killer is, but he's not the guy sitting in jail. He could be someone you know."

"I can't imagine that."

"And that's what this kind of predator counts on. He hides in plain sight and gets a rush out of knowing no one suspects him."

"That's unnerving," she said, that emotion plain in her pretty brown eyes as she looked up at him.

"Better that you know it than not. You don't exactly fit the victimology, but you're the right age, and God knows you're pretty," he said, tracing a blunt-tipped forefinger down her pert little nose. "You don't have a connection to the Thomas Center, but I don't have a crystal ball, either. He could know you some other way and decide you meet his profile well enough."

"You're scaring me," she whispered.

"I just want you to be careful, honey. If you're in a situation that doesn't feel right to you, there's a reason you feel that way. Get yourself out of it and call me. Day or night. Or call the sheriff's office and ask for Mendez. Okay?"

She nodded solemnly as she looked up at him. His gaze lingered just a little too long on the full soft bow of her lower lip. The memory of the taste of her was still in his mouth. Electricity hummed in the scant distance between them. It made her skittish.

"I'll give you the nickel tour," she said, her voice a little breathless as she turned and started down the hall.

The first door they came to was a cozy library/office with a big old mahogany desk and heavy leather chairs. A masculine room. Her father's study, the built-in shelves crammed to the ceiling with books. Vince checked the window to make certain it was locked.

Amber light shone under the last door on the hall. Her father's bedroom.

Anne knocked and cracked the door open. "I'm home."

Her father was sitting up in his bed in maroon pajamas, reading. An oxygen tank sat beside the bed, clear tubing conducting the air into his nostrils. He didn't even look over at his daughter, but merely grunted his acknowledgment.

"Did you take your meds?"

He made a sound in his throat that might have meant anything.

"If you didn't, I have an FBI agent here with me, and he'll make you take them."

Even that got no response from the old man. Anne shut the door and rolled her eyes. "The love is overwhelming, isn't it?"

She said it with such dry sarcasm, Vince thought she must have long ago stopped caring whether her father felt anything for her.

"Does he have a problem with speech?" Vince asked as they started back down the hall.

"No," she said. "He's an ass."

"Oh."

And yet, she had given up finishing her education and going into her chosen field to come home and take care of him. When her mother died. It wasn't difficult to piece the story together from what she had said at dinner the night before and what he had just seen for himself. She must have come home because her mother had asked her to. The fact that she had, despite her feelings for the old man, spoke volumes to the kind of woman Anne Navarre was.

"Do you think I'm a terrible daughter?" she asked.

"No. Actually, I was just thinking you're pretty remarkable."

She wasn't comfortable with that and dodged his gaze. "Damn, I forgot to ask him if he'd seen any homicidal maniacs in the house."

"That's my job, anyway," Vince said.

She showed him through the rest of the house, hesitating a little when they came to her bedroom.

"Afraid to go in there with me?" he teased as they stood outside the door.

"No! Of course not," she protested.

He liked watching her when she got rattled. She made him think of an annoyed little cat, ready to get her back up and hiss at him.

He leaned down a little too close to her ear and murmured, "I promise to be a perfect gentleman."

Brows low, she huffed an impatient sigh and pushed the door open.

The room was neat and tidy, feminine but not frilly. Vince wanted to take time and absorb the surroundings, knowing what he found here would speak volumes about her, but she wasn't having it. She backed out of the room before he could say anything and started down the stairs.

"Looks like the place is all clear, ma'am," he said, following her.

"That's a relief," she said, leading the way back into the kitchen. "I'm not a very good hostess. I should at least offer you a drink for making sure I'm not going to end up a corpse tonight. Would you like something? Wine? Tea? I have arsenic, but I'm saving it for my father's birthday."

"A little wine is never a bad thing," Vince said.

"I don't have anything chilled, but I have a nice cabernet from a local vineyard."

Vince flashed the big grin. "I love California."

She got a couple of glasses out, uncorked the bottle with efficiency, and poured the drinks.

"I like the look of that porch out back," he said as she handed him his glass.

"Will we be safe?" she asked, glancing up at

him from under her lashes. *Almost flirtatious,* he thought. He wondered if she realized it.

"You're with me," he said. "I have a gun."

She smiled that crooked little smile. "What more could a girl want?"

The back porch was a mirror image of the front, but filled with well-used green wicker furniture strewn with thick flowered cushions; an outdoor room with armchairs and a coffee table and big lush ferns on plant stands.

Anne curled up in the corner of a wicker sofa at one end of the porch where the illumination was as soft as candlelight. Vince took the other end, letting her have some space.

"What did you mean when you told Janet Crane *if you were going to be a part of the community?*" she asked.

"Presently she thinks I'm a businessman looking to relocate here," he explained. "I had her show me a piece of property today."

"No wonder she was so happy to see you."

"You think she's just after my money? I'm crushed."

"You should be relieved she doesn't want to hang you upside down in her lair and deposit her eggs in you."

Vince chuckled a little under his breath. "She's a case study."

"Not what I prefer to call her, but whatever." She sipped at her wine, growing serious. "What's going on here, Vince? Last week this was Ozzie and Harriet–ville. Now you think there are two killers operating here?"

"It looks that way."

She shook her head. "Things like this don't happen here."

"But they do, honey," he said quietly, reaching a hand out to stroke the back of her head. Her hair was like silk. "They happen everywhere."

"I feel like I've been looking at this lovely jewel box garden all these years only to find out there are snakes in the grass."

"This too shall pass," Vince said. "These cases will be solved and closed. There are still more good guys than bad guys."

She smiled to herself, not a happy smile, as she turned the stem of her glass back and forth between her fingers. The wine swirled gracefully against the sides of the glass, glowing like liquefied rubies in the amber light.

"I said that to Tommy today: This too shall pass."

Vince shifted a little closer to her. Close enough that he could rest his hand on her shoulder in a reassuring touch. "You'll get him back, Anne. He doesn't have a lot of stability in his family life with that piece of work for a mother. He needs you."

She nodded, but didn't look convinced. She didn't want to talk about it anymore or the emotions would come back, and she had no doubt had it with feeling upset and vulnerable. She was a person who kept her emotions as neat and tidy as she kept her house, he suspected. And she probably did that because she hadn't had total stability in her own life as a child. That explained her emotional tie to Tommy Crane. She looked at the little boy through the eyes of the little girl she had been.

The idea of her as a lonely little girl made him want to scoop her up in his arms and hold her close, make her feel safe.

She looked at him from the corner of her eyes. "So tell me about you. All I know is you work for the FBI, and you're on the fresh side."

He smiled. "Me? I'm an old cop from Chicago. I come from a big, loud Italian family. I have an ex-wife and two daughters—Amy and Emily."

"How old?"

"Fifteen and seventeen." He leaned a little closer, like he was going to tell her a secret. "And I'm forty-eight, and it doesn't matter."

Even in the soft porch light, he could see her blush and smile nervously. "And I'm twenty-eight, and I met you yesterday."

"Yes. And tomorrow, either one of us could be hit by a bus. Life is unpredictable, honey. We should live every day like it might be our last."

As if he needed a reminder of the truth of that statement, a small explosion took place in his brain, like an electrical circuit shorting out spectacularly. His breath caught in his throat and he had to bend over and put his head in his hands.

Anne was beside him instantly, her hand on his back. "Are you all right? Vince? What is it?"

"Headache," he said tightly. "Wow."

"Is there something I can do? An ice pack? Aspirin?"

"I'll be fine."

He breathed slowly and shallowly through his mouth, willing off the nausea that was sure to come, and the next wave of pain that was sure to come after that. Damn bullet. Damn bad timing.

"You don't look fine."

"Just give me a minute," he said, rubbing his fingers back through his hair, massaging his scalp in an attempt to relieve some of the tension.

"Is it a migraine?" Anne asked anxiously. "You shouldn't be drinking red wine."

"It's a bullet," he said, relaxing as the pain ebbed away. A wave of weakness washed over him in its wake. He leaned back against the cushions and turned his head to look at her.

She looked confused. "I beg your pardon?"

"It's a bullet," he repeated. "Last winter I became a crime statistic. A junkie trying to rob me, shot me in the head."

"Oh my God!"

"Most of the bullet is still in there. Lucky for me I never used that part of my brain anyway."

"You have a bullet in your head," she said, as if hearing it from her own lips would somehow help her make sense of it. "How can that be? Shouldn't you be dead?"

"Yep. I should be," he said. "But I'm not. Instead, I'm just a guy with a headache, and I get to go on living."

"They can't take it out?"

"Not without turning me into a drooling vegetable."

"But what will happen with it in there?"

He shrugged. "Don't know. There aren't a lot of cases to study, as you might imagine. So far the worst side effect is the pain. It comes and goes. It's nothing I can't handle. The point is I should have died that night.

"I have a very different perspective on life now. Now, I look around me, I see what I want, I'm going to make it happen. There is no someday. We have here, now.

"I spent a lot of years buried in my career—not that I don't love it—but I put off a lot of stuff I shouldn't have, assuming there would be time for it later. I regret that," he admitted. "I lost my marriage. I know my daughters like I'm a distant uncle, not their father.

"I won't live like that anymore. You shouldn't either," he said. "You've got twenty years on me. You can skip a lot of mistakes."

She sat facing him, one leg curled up on the sofa, the other foot on the floor. She had put on a thick sweater to ward off the chill of the evening. She wrapped it around herself now as she met his gaze, her dark eyes full of sadness.

"My mother was forty-six when she died," she said quietly. "I never thought she would be gone so soon. I always assumed my father would go before her, and I would have her all to myself for a long, long time . . . I always believed she would be there for my wedding, for my children, for me . . . And then she was gone. Just like that."

"Life is what happens while we're making other plans," Vince said.

Even from a distance, he could feel the ache in her heart. He reached out for her and whispered, "Come here."

She came to him deliberately. Coming to him, not running from her feelings. Vince took her in his arms and lowered his mouth to hers. He kissed her to offer comfort, to distract her from sad memories, to fill a lonely corner of her heart.

He kissed her slowly, deeply, savoring the taste of wine on her tongue, drinking in the feeling of her body against his. She melted into him, surrendered willingly, accepted what he had to give her, and gave back in return.

Gradually comfort gave way to desire, distraction to sharp focus and keen awareness.

Vince stroked her hair back from her face, his big hand taking in the delicate lines of her cheek, her jaw, her throat. Her breath shuddered softly as his lips followed the same path.

Her sweater fell open and his fingers found the buttons of her blouse, loosing them one by one. She gasped as his hand cupped her breast and his thumb brushed across the nipple, and gasped again as he closed his lips around the tight bud of flesh.

Anne lifted her hips to let him draw down her jeans and moaned his name as he gently opened her legs, settled his mouth against her, and kissed deeply the most feminine part of her. Her hands tangled in his hair, holding him to her, then tugging him back up to share the taste of her on his lips.

Vince shed his jacket, his gun, his clothes, never separating from her for more than a few seconds. He wanted nothing between them but flesh and desire. And when he came to her, naked, she reached out and closed her hand around him, and he thought he might die on the spot.

They made love by turns both slowly and urgently; without words, but in full communication in a language of gasps and groans and eyes locked on each other. Their bodies moved together, arched against each other, tangled and tugged and stroked. She was tight and hot and wet around him. He pushed deep, deep inside her, and they went over the edge together, reality giving way to bliss.

Afterward, they lay tangled together, sweating, panting, communicating entirely with tender looks and soft smiles and sweet kisses. Vince had worried Anne might now recall they hadn't known each other two days ago, and would retreat into regret, but she didn't. He certainly didn't.

Maybe the bullet made him impulsive. Maybe a year ago he wouldn't have pressed her so hard, so soon. But he sure as hell didn't regret it. He hadn't felt anything so satisfying and right in a long time.

Her hair was damp against her cheek. He brushed it back and kissed her softly. She brought her hand up and touched his face. Her small foot slowly rubbed up and down the back of his calf.

"That was highly improper of you," she whispered, eyes sparkling. They shared a soft chuckle and a softer kiss.

"You're so beautiful, Anne," he whispered. "So special."

He drew breath to say something more, but the sound of his pager bleating broke the spell.

Swearing under his breath, he reached over the side of the sofa to grab his jacket. Pulling the pager out of the pocket, he hit the display button and swore again.

"Mendez." He looked down at Anne and sighed. "I'm sorry, honey. I have to take this."

"It's all right."

"No, it's not," he growled. "I want to hold you all night long. I want to make love to you again . . . and again."

She smiled at him in a way that was knowing and sexy and absolutely female, and he felt himself getting heavy and hot.

The pager trilled again.

"Duty calls," she said.

"Can I use your phone?"

"In the kitchen."

Reluctantly, he got up off the sofa and pulled on his clothes. Anne sat up and drew her heavy sweater around herself, curling her bare legs beneath her. She tucked her hair behind her ear and gave him that little half smile that quickened his heart a beat. He contemplated throwing his pager into the neighbor's yard when it went off a third time.

He went into the kitchen, found the phone, and dialed Mendez back.

"What?" he said impatiently by way of a greeting.

"Did I interrupt something?"

"This had better be good."

"It's good," Mendez promised. "I just got a Telex from Oxnard PD. Julie Paulson's last arrest for prostitution happened in a vice sweep. Guess who else got caught in the net?"

"Who?"

"Peter Crane."

# 47

He watched from the oleander bushes to one side of the backyard. From his angle he was able to see right onto the back porch. He was able to see where they sat down. He was able to see everything.

He watched them kiss. He watched the man take her pants off, watched him go down between her legs to eat her pussy. He watched the man take his clothes off, get on top of her, and fuck her.

She let him. She let him do all of that. And she liked it. He could hear the sounds she made.

She was supposed to be perfect. The perfect teacher. The perfect example. The perfect woman. But she was just another whore . . .

# 48

"Someone has some 'splainin' to do," Mendez said as Vince got into the car.

"Yeah. I wouldn't want to be in Dr. Crane's shoes."

Mendez gave him a look. "I wasn't talking about the dentist."

Leone scowled a bit and made no eye contact. He had the grace to look a little embarrassed at least.

"Just how did you end up here with no car?" he asked, pulling away from the curb in front of Anne Navarre's home. "And why did it take three pages before you called me back?"

"I saw Miss Navarre home from the vigil downtown, and none of your goddamn business," Vince answered, a big self-satisfied grin splitting his face.

Mendez groaned. "I don't want to know."

"A gentleman doesn't kiss and tell, junior."

"You just did," Mendez groused. Damn, the

man moved fast. He had homed in on Anne Navarre like a fucking heat-seeking missile. And she had clearly welcomed him. "You're a dog."

"No," he said, dead serious. His expression held a hint of warning. "No."

Mendez raised his eyebrows. "Okay."

"Tell me about the dentist."

"So the Telex came in, then I called Oxnard PD and talked to one of the detectives there. They were running a series of sweeps for drugs and prostitution. This would have been fall eighty-three. Nothing fancy, just normal street sweeps. Round 'em up and herd 'em into the paddy wagon kind of thing."

"Did they put Crane with Julie Paulson?"

"Interestingly, no. But Crane was among the johns, and Paulson was one of the hookers. He sat in the clink overnight, posted bond in the morning. He showed up for his court date later on, pled no contest, and paid his fine."

"The detective remembered him?"

"In that Crane was the only one who wasn't whining and crying and trying to get out of it when they busted him."

"It wasn't his first time then."

"I've requested his record. We'll see."

"How big was this bust?"

"Twenty-five arrests. There was some kind of festival going on. I guess they get up to some mischief down in Oxnard. Who knew?"

"How far is that from here?"

"Thirty-five, forty minutes, depending on traffic on the 101."

"It's not in your jurisdiction."

"No. It's Ventura County."

"And that bust was how long before the Paulson murder?"

"Seven months. Then Paulson showed up at the Thomas Center about six weeks before her death. She washed out of the program pretty quickly, which is why it's taken us this long to find out she was ever there."

"Crane goes to another county to have his fun," Vince speculated. "It won't make the papers here if he gets caught. He's just another john in Oxnard. Then the hooker shows up here. At the Thomas Center, no less."

"Blackmail?" Mendez suggested.

"Maybe. Or maybe Ventura County should be going back through their missing persons reports and unsolved homicides. The second homicide was in another jurisdiction too, right?"

"Yeah. To the east of here."

They pulled up in the Cranes' driveway. There were no cars parked in the driveway, but lights were on in the downstairs windows. Someone was home.

"Hicks called a while ago and asked for Dr. Crane," he said. "Janet Crane said he wasn't home and she isn't expecting him until late."

"That's all right," Vince said, getting out of the car. "That's fine, actually. I have a thing or two to say to Mrs. Crane."

"Should I call you an ambulance now or wait?" Mendez asked.

"Don't worry about it, kid. Let me show you how to handle Janet Crane."

"Better you than me," Mendez said as they started up the sidewalk.

"Walk up right behind me," Vince instructed. "I don't want her to see you when she opens the door. After that, just follow my lead."

Vince went to the Crane's front door and rang the bell. Beautiful home. Mr. and Mrs. California lived here. The perfect couple with the perfect home and perfect jobs and a perfect child; perfect tans and perfect white smiles. A pretty facade. The thing Vince had learned over the years was that a lot of not-so-perfect things often lived behind a beautiful exterior.

Janet Crane peeked out the sidelight, her face switching from annoyed to overjoyed in the blink of an eye. *Welcome to the borderline personality disorder*, Vince thought.

"Mr. Leone!" she said, opening the door. She was a little confused, an emotion that didn't sit well with her. How did he know where she lived? Why would he come by at such a late hour? "What a surprise!"

Vince smiled the big smile. "Mrs. Crane, sorry to bother you so late, but we have some questions for you."

"We?"

He stepped to the side enough that she could see Mendez behind him. Now she smelled a rat, and the nice smile hardened.

"Detective." Her gaze darted back and forth between them. "What's this about?"

"Well, I have a small confession to make," Vince began amiably. "It would probably be better if we came inside and sat down for this. You don't want your neighbors looking out and seeing a couple of guys on your doorstep at eleven o'clock at night."

She hesitated just enough to let him move toward her, then automatically stepped back, and he easily stepped into the foyer. Mendez stepped in behind him.

She had changed out of her red power suit into a pink jogging suit, but the makeup was still in place and the brown hair was still starched stiff.

"I'm a little confused, Mr. Leone. Why would you feel the need to bring a detective with you to my home?"

Vince played contrite, ducking his head. "That's where the confession comes in. I'm afraid I wasn't entirely forthcoming with you earlier today."

She was working up to disliking him now. She wouldn't take kindly to being played.

"I'm not really just visiting," he admitted. "I'm here on business."

He pulled out his ID and held it up for her to see. She peered at it, her face frozen carefully blank.

"I'm with the FBI," he said. "I'm here helping out with the investigation."

"What could you possibly want with me?" she asked, crossing her arms tightly against herself.

"We just have a few questions," he assured her.

"About what?"

"Is your husband home, ma'am?" Mendez asked.

"Not at the moment. Why?"

"Do you know where he is by any chance? We have a couple of questions for him as well."

"He's playing cards. Friday is his night to play cards."

*Lie,* Vince decided from her body language and the way she repeated the statement as if to confirm that it sounded good.

"Who does he play cards with?" Mendez asked, pen poised over his notebook.

"Friends. Men he plays golf with. I don't know them."

Vince arched a brow. "You don't know your husband's friends?"

"Not all of them," she said defensively. "I don't play cards, and I certainly don't have the time to play golf. Those are Peter's hobbies and Peter's friends."

"You must have met them, at least," he said.

"Don't they ever come here to play cards? You don't stick around to serve them snacks?"

She was getting her back up now. Her eyes narrowed ever so slightly. "I'm not a barmaid or a waitress. I make a point of not being here when Peter entertains his male friends."

Mendez bobbed his eyebrows and hummed a little while he made notes.

"So you must have hobbies of your own," Vince said. "That's very healthy, I think. Couples don't have to do everything together."

"I serve on a number of committees and boards here in town," she said. "I don't have time for hobbies."

Vince frowned. "All work and no play—"

"I don't understand why you're asking me these questions," she said abruptly. Her tone of voice was changing, the cadence of her speech becoming more clipped, curt. "I heard you have a suspect in custody."

"We're really not at liberty to discuss the case, Mrs. Crane," Vince said.

"I don't see how I can help you."

"Where was your husband on the night of Thursday, the third of October?" he asked.

"He was here. He and our son like to watch a television program together Thursday nights."

"Yes, *Cosby*. We know," Vince said. "Your son mentioned that to his teacher, Miss Navarre."

"She had no business asking Tommy those

questions," she said, her temper rising another notch. "He's terribly upset."

"Why is that, Mrs. Crane?" Vince asked. "It seems an innocent question to me. Why would your son think it was anything else? I wasn't there, but I feel safe in assuming Miss Navarre didn't ask Tommy if his father is a serial killer."

"He found out that was the night that girl went missing. He's a bright boy."

"I guess so," Vince said. "I should start recruiting him for the Bureau now, because that's quite a leap in a ten-year-old's logic system. How did he know anything at all about the disappearance of Karly Vickers?"

"He saw it in the newspaper."

"Your fifth grader sits down and reads the newspaper in the evening?"

"His father was reading it."

"Does your husband have an unusual interest in following these cases?"

"No more than anyone else in town."

"Has he been keeping the articles?"

"Why would he do that?"

"He was the last person to see Miss Vickers that day," Mendez said. "You're aware of that, Mrs. Crane?"

"Yes. That doesn't make him guilty of anything."

"And you don't remember if he was home that evening?"

She glared at him. "I told you he was."

"But you don't remember if he went out of the house later that evening."

"No. I'm sure he didn't," she said. "Peter doesn't go out that much."

"Except to golf and play cards with people you don't know in places you have no idea about," Vince said, his own tone of voice becoming harder, colder. "Now that seems odd to me, Mrs. Crane, because you strike me as the kind of woman who would keep a short leash on a man."

The whites of her eyes showed all around the iris. "I beg your pardon?"

"You're controlling," he said without rancor. "You want to be in charge. I'll bet if I go into your kitchen or laundry room you'll have a big whiteboard calendar and everything on it will be color-coded. Am I right?"

She was getting angrier by the second now. "There's nothing wrong with being organized."

"Not at all. Controlling, however, is a different thing," he said. "Controlling is getting pissed off at people who don't toe your line, people who don't follow your script, people who ask questions you don't want to answer."

He let the last shred of the Mr. Nice Guy act fall away. "That's the flip of the switch that sets you off and makes you think you can scream at people and threaten them, and be a Class A bitch to anyone who crosses you."

Her jaw dropped, astonished anyone would

speak to her that way. "I beg your pardon?" she said again.

"You don't want my pardon," Vince scoffed. "You want to kick me in the balls right now, don't you? Because I won't do what you want, and I won't believe what you want me to believe just because that's your agenda.

"I'm bigger than you, and meaner than you, and I'm not going to take your bullshit," he said. "I'm not some little fifth-grade teacher you can push around and try to intimidate."

Janet Crane's face was nearly purple, her eyes popping. Vince expected her hair to stand straight up. She pointed to the door.

"Get out! Get out of my house!"

Vince laughed at her. "Or what? You'll call a cop?" He hooked a thumb at Mendez. "I brought a cop with me. Where's your witness? Who's going to testify on your behalf? The child you drugged to make him sleep so he won't bother you?"

She turned on Mendez. "Aren't you going to do something?"

Mendez was the picture of disinterest, so unconcerned with her needs he couldn't be bothered to raise more than one shoulder to shrug. "He outranks me."

"I'm calling my husband," she announced, storming down the hall to a beautiful study with two desks and white bookshelves that climbed to the ceiling.

"So you *do* know where he is," Vince said.

She glared at him as she snatched up the receiver of the phone. "He has a cellular telephone in his car."

"Really? What for? So he can be available for all those urgent emergency teeth cleanings?" Vince asked. "That's an extravagant toy—"

"So what?" she snapped back at him, punching numbers.

"So he works all day in an office ten minutes away from here. Why does he need a cellular telephone? You're telling us he rarely leaves the house if he's not working. When is he not at your beck and call?"

"But he's not here now," Mendez pointed out.

"True," Vince said. "But I doubt he and his cronies are playing cards in his car, and why would he lug that phone into his card game with him? You have to carry the damn things around in a suitcase."

"Doesn't make a lot of sense," Mendez agreed. "Unless he's just that whipped."

"Is that it?" Vince asked, depressing the plunger on the phone and disconnecting her call. "Do you have your husband that cowed, Mrs. Crane?"

She was so angry now there were tears in her eyes and her mouth was quivering as she tried to hold back the vitriol she wanted to spew at him. She made a strangled gurgling sound in her throat.

"Because that kind of domineering, controlling behavior can create some pretty nasty recoil on the other end of a relationship," Vince said.

"Edmund Kemper," Mendez offered.

Vince nodded. To Janet Crane he said, "Edmund Kemper endured so many years of domination by his mother, he ended up murdering college coeds and cutting their heads off to relieve his psychological pressure."

"My husband is NOT a MURDERER!" she screamed.

"You're that sure?" Vince asked quietly. "He was the last person to see Karly Vickers the day she disappeared. He knew Lisa Warwick from the Thomas Center. And it turns out he was arrested in Oxnard for soliciting Julie Paulson for sex. Those women are all dead or missing."

Janet Crane slammed the receiver down on the phone and stood absolutely rigid beside the desk. "You're lying. My husband is a pillar of this community. He is well respected. He is admired. He is the perfect husband and father."

"Is he?" Vince said. "Because down in Ventura County he's just another john that comes to Oxnard to fuck hookers."

"That's outrageous! How dare you say that!"

"And if I opened one of his desk drawers here and showed you newspaper clippings from all three of these cases, what would you say then, Mrs. Crane?"

"Get out of my house," she said. "Get out of my house or I'm calling our attorney."

Vince exchanged a look with Mendez.

"You'd better be on good terms with that attorney," Vince said. "You never know how soon you might need his services."

He let the silence between them hang for a moment. She was breathing hard, starting to hyperventilate. Even clenched into fists at her side, her hands were shaking. Good.

"Think about that, Mrs. Crane," he said quietly. "Every time he's out of your sight. Every time he doesn't answer that cellular telephone. Every minute he doesn't have to listen to you harping and harping and harping. Where is he? Every time he brings you a little gift of jewelry, where did he get it? Every time he goes out to be a part of the search for Karly Vickers or man the phones on the hotline. Why is he *really* doing that?"

She said nothing, just continued to stare at him, glassy-eyed and trembling with rage.

"One more thing," Vince said, taking a step toward her, and then another. He lowered his voice to just above a whisper. "If I hear you're trying to take your son out of Anne Navarre's class, or that you're going to sue her, or that you accosted her on the street, you'll answer to me, Mrs. Crane.

"All I have to do is make one hint to a reporter that you know something you shouldn't about that murder victim in the park, or that your husband has a predilection for prostitutes, and all that status you prize so highly comes tumbling down," he said.

"You're threatening me?"

"No," he said, taking another step into her personal space, leaning toward her so that she had to tilt her head back to look him in the eye. "I'm telling you how it is. *I'm* the big dog in this fight, *Janet*. Don't piss on my fences."

He didn't wait for a reaction from her. He had accomplished exactly what he had set out to do. How she reacted now was irrelevant. He turned his back on her and walked out.

He didn't realize how hot he'd gotten until he stepped out into the cold. He was sweating and breathing hard. He felt more than a little primitive. The male of the species defending his mate, testosterone running like a flood through his veins. His pulse pounded in his head, and he worried for a second he might have a stroke.

Jesus H.

When they reached the car, Mendez opened his door and paused to look across the roof at him.

"Man, just so you know," he said. "I am NEVER getting on your bad side."

Vince forced half a grin. "Like we say in Chicago: She had it coming."

# 49

As Detective Mendez and the other man went out the door, Tommy scurried back up the stairs— just far enough to be out of sight. His heart was beating so fast he thought it might burst and send blood gushing everywhere.

His mother would be mad at him then for getting blood all over her carpet. Everything about their house belonged to her.

*Don't get blood on my carpets.*
*Don't spill juice on my clean floor.*
*Don't get dirt on my sofa.*

A lot of the time he felt like he and his dad didn't belong there at all.

He sat now on the stairs just out of reach of the light from below. He was shaking and scared and mad all at once. He had so many crazy, mixed-up feelings tumbling around inside of him he thought he might throw up again.

This had been the worst night of his life. Worse even than finding the dead lady, though he couldn't help thinking if he hadn't fallen on the dead lady none of the rest of this would be happening.

His mother had exploded over Miss Navarre asking him questions. Miss Navarre was no friend to him, his mother had told him. She was a lot of bad names Tommy would have gotten his mouth washed out with soap for using.

And he was in trouble too—for answering Miss Navarre. But what else was he supposed to do? She was his teacher and she asked him a question. And why was it such a bad question anyway?

Because Miss Navarre was practically accusing his dad of being a serial killer.

Tommy didn't believe that, but what if she was? Then he would feel like Miss Navarre had betrayed him. That idea hurt him like getting cut with a knife.

He wished he could talk to Miss Navarre now. She was smart and caring, and usually knew what to do. She kept telling him she wanted to help him, that if he needed to talk about anything, anything at all, he should call her.

He wanted to call.

He was scared to call.

She had said to call. Anytime.

He thought of all the times this week Miss Navarre had been there for him, to help him, to comfort him. And even though he was kind of in love with her, he knew the way she treated him was more like if she was his mother.

How he wished he had a mother like her, or like Wendy's mom. Mrs. Morgan was always full of smiles and laughter, and she hugged and kissed everybody for practically no reason at all. That was what a mother should be like, he thought, and then felt guilty. His mom was a very unhappy person, and he should be sad for her. She told him that herself every once in a while when she was in one of her blue times.

Lately she was on the rampage more often than not. She had carried on for a long time before dinner, mad at Tommy, mad at his father. Then she wouldn't speak at all during dinner. She clanked her silverware together and against her plate like she was angry at the tuna casserole. She sighed and tsked over and over, waiting for someone to ask her what the matter was. No one did. Both he and his dad knew if they asked her, she would go off again.

When they were finished with dinner she ripped the plates off the table and practically threw them in the sink. Then his father had made the huge mistake of telling her to calm down because it didn't matter what Miss Navarre thought.

Oh, brother! That had set her off. What was wrong with him? How could he think it didn't matter? Why wouldn't he stand up for himself, for *her,* for HIS FAMILY!

It was never a good thing when his mother started speaking in capital letters and exclamation points. That meant she would keep going for a long time.

And she had.

His dad had finally had enough and just walked out of the house, got in his car, and drove away, leaving Tommy alone again to deal with his mother. That wasn't fair to him. He was just a kid, after all. Even grown men were afraid of his mother.

She had gone into one of her hyper moods and dragged him downtown and paraded him around like a prize dog. She went from being so angry to being too happy to see people, too eager to show him off as her perfect son.

That always made Tommy uncomfortable. He was sure people looked at him and figured he was a dork for going along with it.

And then she had gone off on Miss Navarre. Right on the street with people all around. By that point Tommy had been so tired and confused and had listened to so much of his mother's ranting, he didn't know what to think.

What he had known was that he didn't want to be there. He was embarrassed and hurt and mad and wanted to run away and go join someone else's family.

When they got home he had been sent immediately to his room to put his pajamas on. Then he had to take the allergy medicine, sickeningly sweet and purple, and he was so stupid that he had told his mother he didn't want to take it. She had screamed at him so loud it hurt his ears.

In the end, he had taken the medicine, but as soon as she had gone out of the room Tommy had gone back into his bathroom and stuck his toothbrush down his throat until he threw up.

Now he wished he had taken it after all and that he had slept through everything that just happened.

When he heard the voices downstairs he had

crept down the steps to see what was going on. The bigger, older man was from the FBI! The FBI had come to his house to ask questions about his father. And Detective Mendez too.

Tommy had listened as the FBI man had made his mother angrier and angrier. She had lied and told him Tommy's father was playing cards. She sure wouldn't have told him the truth, that she was such a terrible person his father could only take so much of her.

When they had all disappeared down the hall, Tommy had hurried down the upstairs hall and down the back staircase, through the kitchen to the little bathroom that shared a wall with the study. There he had sat on the toilet, listening to everything that was said.

It was terrible. The FBI man believed his father was a killer. His dad was no serial killer! His dad was the best dad in the world. So what if he had been the last person to see that lady? Someone had to be the last person to see her before the kidnapper got her. And besides, his dad had been home that night.

Tommy hadn't been very sure of that before, but he was sure now. His dad had come home and they had played catch in the yard, and they watched *Cosby* together and had fun, and it was the best night. That's how he remembered it now, and that's what he was going to tell anyone who asked him—even the FBI.

● ● ●

Wendy stood in the dining room, pressed up against the wall next to the French doors that went into the living room. No one knew she was there. It was dark in the dining room, and her parents believed she was asleep upstairs. They were too wrapped up in their argument to notice anything else anyway.

Adults were foolish, she had decided. Or naïve— that was a word Tommy had taught her. They thought they could put on nice faces and phony voices and make a kid believe anything. That was about as stupid as she had been when she was little and believed if she pretended to be a cat, she would actually look like a cat to people watching her.

She listened now to the things they said to each other. Hurtful things. Sad things. Things that would add up to nothing good.

"What do you want me to do, Sara? Go to a hotel? This is my home. You're the one who's not happy. Why don't you leave?"

"You're the one who's cheating—"

"That's bullshit! You don't trust me. How hurt do you think *I* am? You think you're the wounded party here, Sara. What about me?"

"You're the one the detectives are asking questions about! How well did you know Lisa Warwick? Where were you when that other girl went missing?"

"So you just go ahead and believe I'm a killer?"

"I don't! But—"

"That's insane! They're asking questions because they don't have the answers! It's called an investigation. That's what they do."

"I know you had feelings for Lisa. I know she had feelings for you—"

"So you think I had feelings for her, that I was cheating on you with her, but I also murdered her? That doesn't make any sense!"

"Nothing makes sense! We had such a good thing. We had such a nice family—"

"We still do if you would stop being such a crazy jealous bitch!"

"Stop it!" Wendy shouted, running into the living room. "Stop it! Stop it! Stop it! Stop fighting!"

Stunned to silence, both of her parents stared at her.

"You're never here, Daddy!" she said, then turned to her mother. "And when he's home all you do is fight! Stop it!"

Her mother put her face in her hands and started to cry. Her father looked from one to the other of them.

"I'm sorry, honey," he said to Wendy. "But I think it's better if I just go tonight. Maybe you can talk some sense into your mother."

Wendy's mom looked up at him, shocked and angry. She got up from the sofa and walked right up to Wendy's dad.

"How dare you do that to your daughter," she

said, her voice tight and controlled, the way it got when she was *really* mad. "How dare you?"

Her father got a hard, cold expression that scared Wendy deep inside. "It takes two, Sara. Think about that."

He turned and walked out of the room. A minute later, the front door slammed. And just like that, he was gone.

# 50

"What the hell is the matter with you?"

Dennis could hear his father's voice as soon as he snuck in the back door. It was like he had hit the Pause button on his way out. His parents were still having the same conversation they had been having when he had snuck out of the house earlier.

He had somehow managed to slip away from the supper table without attracting his father's attention, which had been a minor miracle—especially because his stupid sisters weren't there for a distraction. They had gone to the football game at the high school and then to a sleep-over. Stupid lucky cows. Dennis couldn't imagine why they had friends and he didn't. They were so stupid.

Anyway, Dennis had managed to slide out of his chair and out of the room without attracting attention. His father was too busy going on about how he was being betrayed at work, and how Dixon didn't appreciate him. He seemed to be just talking out loud, like he was trying to figure it all out, and it didn't really matter if anyone was listening or not. Then every once in a while he would direct something at Dennis's mother, and she would have to say something to prove that she was paying attention.

Dennis had gotten enough of his father's attention the night before, getting punished for taking the finger to school. His dad had been furious about that. Dennis had embarrassed him and made him look bad at work.

He had made Dennis take off all his clothes except his underpants and stand in the corner of the dining room while everyone else ate dinner.

"You humiliated me," his father said. "Now I'm going to humiliate you."

He had been made to stand there for hours, until he had to go to the bathroom so bad he wet his pants.

After he cleaned up the mess, he had been sent to bed. He had waited until he got checked on, then climbed out his window and down the oak tree that grew beside the house.

He spent hours looking in people's windows. They never saw him, but he saw them do all kinds of things. It was like having his own television with no channels he wasn't allowed to watch. Mostly he looked for bedroom windows where he watched girls and ladies take their clothes off. He liked to look at their boobs, all different shapes and sizes.

Sometimes he got to watch people having sex,

which he found both gross and weirdly exciting. He mostly liked it because the man got to grab the woman and push her around, and make her do things he wanted, and she couldn't say no. A lot of the women screamed and stuff while the guy was doing it to them. Dennis liked that part.

It had been weird to watch Miss Navarre and the old detective. Dennis had never really thought about his teacher having breasts or what she would look like with no clothes on. He hardly thought of her as a woman at all. He had never thought of her kissing a man or letting a man do stuff to her. But she sure had. What a whore.

Now Dennis stood in the dark kitchen, watching his parents in the dining room. He couldn't get to the stairs without going past the dining room and having his father see him. He would have to go back outside and climb the tree to get to his room. But for the moment he stood watching his parents framed by the doorway like they were on a stage or something.

His father was still sitting at the dining room table, still in his uniform, still drinking and talking. His mother still sat in her chair. All the plates and pots and food and stuff were still on the table.

His father had started drinking as soon as he had gotten home from work. That was never a good thing. Then supper had been really bad. Half-frozen meatloaf. His dad had taken one bite of it, got a face, then got up from the table, took the plate with the meatloaf to the back door, and threw it out in the yard.

He worked hard. All he wanted at the end of the day was a decent meal. Was that too much to ask? he demanded of Dennis's mother. She had been home all day. Was she so lazy she couldn't bring herself to do the one thing he needed?

"Are you stupid?" he asked now.

Dennis's mother was crying very quietly. "I'm sorry, Frank. What was I supposed to do?"

"Not talk to them without talking to me first!" he said, his speech barely slurred despite the fact that he had been drinking for hours.

His dad knew how to hold his liquor.

"Now I look like a fool in front of that prick Mendez."

"I'm sorry, Frank."

"And Dixon turns on me like a snake! All these years, and he turns on me like a fucking snake!"

"He should have more respect for you."

"My record is spotless! Spotless! And that's not going to count for a goddamn thing because I stopped that stupid little whore and gave her a speeding ticket!" he said. He looked stunned, shocked at the idea that something so meaningless could have such an impact on his life.

"I know, Frank. It's not fair," his mother murmured.

"Dixon took me off the investigation," his father said to the whiskey in his glass. "Because of Dennis having that finger. And because I wrote

401

that stupid slut a ticket. She was a whore. Bad things happen to whores."

He turned and looked at Dennis's mother. "Isn't that right, Sharon?"

"Yes, Frank."

"They have it coming."

"Yes, Frank, you're absolutely right."

"And now you make me look bad. All because you can't keep your stupid mouth shut."

"I'm sorry, Frank. I was stupid. I didn't think."

"You never think."

His mother was so stupid. His father was very proud of who he was. He was proud of being chief deputy. People respected him and looked up to him. His mother should have known better than to make him look bad.

His father poured more whiskey into his glass and sipped at it.

"'Standard procedure,'" he muttered. "'Don't take it personally, Frank. It's just standard op.'"

He pushed back from the table and got up to pace back and forth, his too-full glass in his hand. The whiskey sloshed out of it as he moved, spilling onto the hardwood floor.

"Standard operating procedure," he said. "Fucking spic. I don't want you *ever* talking to that fucking little prick again. Do you understand me?"

"Yes, Frank." His mother's voice was so soft and trembling so badly, it was hard to hear.

"What?" His father cupped a hand to his ear, sloshing more whiskey onto the floor. "I can't hear you, you stupid fucking cow. Answer me so I can hear you!"

"Yes, Frank!"

"That little bastard is going to try to pin that murder on me. You wait and see," he said. "Do you think I'm murderer?"

"No!" she said on a gasp, her eyes going round as she stared down at her plate.

"Look at me and say it," he ordered. "Do you think I'm a murderer? Huh? ANSWER ME!"

She looked at him, shaking and afraid, tears streaming down her cheeks. "No!"

There must have been something about her face that wasn't right, because Dennis's father cursed and went to backhand her. He took a step toward her, stepping in the whiskey he had spilled. His foot slid out from under him, and he went down hard on the floor, banging his elbow and his head. His glass crashed and shattered.

"FUCK! FUCK, FUCK, FUCK!" he raged.

As he lifted his head, he looked straight into the kitchen—right at Dennis—and saw him plain as anything.

"What are you doing in there?" his father snapped, struggling awkwardly to get to his hands and knees. He never took his laser gaze off Dennis. Dennis seemed frozen to the spot.

"What the fuck are you doing in there?"

"N-n-n-nothing."

"Are you spying on us?"

"N-n-n-no!"

Dennis was shaking his head so fast he felt like the bobblehead doll he got the time he went to the Dodgers game with his cousins. He was scared now. He knew that look in his father's eyes when they got dark and flat and cold, like a shark's eyes.

His father got to his feet and came toward him.

"Don't lie to me, you rotten little shit. You're standing in here listening. What the hell's the matter with you?"

"I-I-I don't know," Dennis stammered, tears running down his face. He wanted to turn and run, but he was afraid to. Maybe if he stood very still, his father would calm down. Maybe if he ran, his father would chase him down and beat him to within an inch of his life.

"You good-for-nothing little smartass brat. I try to set you straight, and you take the finger off a dead woman. What the fuck is wrong with you?"

Dennis didn't answer him fast enough. Or maybe it wouldn't have mattered. His father was past calming down. The rage was in him now. There was no stopping him.

"I asked you a question!" he shouted. "Answer me!"

But he didn't let Dennis even try to answer. He slapped him across the face so hard it knocked Dennis off his feet, then kicked him once, twice, the toe of his boot like a sledgehammer against Dennis's back and buttocks.

"Frank! Stop it!" Dennis's mother yelled. "He's just a little boy!"

His father spun around, redirecting his fury.

Dennis scrambled to his feet and ran out the back door. He was trying to run faster than his legs could go, and he tripped himself and went sprawling down the concrete back steps. *BAM! BAM!* His chin bounced off one step and then another, skin scraping off. He bit his tongue hard and tasted blood as he landed at the bottom.

From inside the house he heard his mother cry out and the sound of plates crashing off the dining room table to the floor.

Dennis didn't move for a minute. He lay there in the damp grass, thinking he would start to cry. But it was like something had broken inside of him, and he couldn't feel anything. He got to his feet and limped around the side of the house to the oak tree.

It was harder to get up into the tree than it was to get down. He tried three times to jump up and catch hold of the lowest branch, finally getting hold of it with his fingertips. Groaning and twisting he struggled to get a better grip and pull himself up. If his father came out of the house now he would be dead.

Fear helped launch him up to where he could get his leg over the limb. Then he was in the tree and climbing. It didn't matter that it was dark. He knew every branch.

He needed to disappear. He needed to go to a place his father couldn't find him. He would go to his safe place and wait out the storm.

He had to stretch out over space to get hold of the windowsill into his bedroom. If he slipped and fell he would probably die. He didn't know if he cared.

Flopping through the open window like a seal, he fell to his bedroom floor with a thud. The sounds of a beating came up through the floor. His father yelling, his mother crying. *SMACK! SMACK!*

Dennis scraped himself up and went into his closet. In the ceiling was a trapdoor with a pull-down ladder leading up into a section of attic. He climbed up the ladder and pulled it up behind him, closing the trapdoor. From the attic he could go out a dormer window onto the roof.

Finally he made it to his hiding place. He could sit behind the old brick chimney, tucked up against the slope of the roof, and no one could see him from below. His father would never think to look there. At least he never had before.

Dennis sat there for a long, long time, cold and shaking. He had wet his pants when his father hit him. His lip was split and his chin was bleeding, but he didn't care. He didn't think about anything. He didn't think about what was going on inside the house below him. He just stared at the moonlit speckles in the shingles on the slope of the roof.

After a long while he heard the back door, then heard his father in the backyard, calling for him and cursing at him. Then his father went back inside the house, and a few minutes later Dennis heard him moving around in his bedroom, still cursing.

Dennis could hear the thumps and crashing as his father searched through his room, tipping over furniture, breaking things, screaming at him to come out. But Dennis never moved, and he never made a sound. He never thought, and he never felt. He never wondered why his mother didn't come looking for him.

The noise in his bedroom died down. Time passed. He heard the back door slam and, a moment later, a car start in the driveway. His mother's minivan. The engine sounded like a toy compared with his father's cruiser. Maybe she was leaving and would never come back. What would it matter to him? Nothing.

When the car had gone, and silence fell and everything was still at last, Dennis climbed a little higher to the ridge of the roof where he could see as far as he could see, and wish himself just as far away.

The world was a pretty place at night and from far away. You couldn't see bad things happen. You couldn't see what was ugly. When you looked in people's windows at night every family looked happy, and every child loved.

If only . . .

# 51

Saturday, October 12, 1985
*1:47 A.M.*

Karly had crawled around and around the perimeter of the room so many times she had long ago lost count of the corners she had turned. The space seemed to be one large square. Left turn, left turn, left turn. She had crawled around and around—crawling, then passing out, crawling some more, then passing out—in search of the way out of this hell, only to learn there was no way out.

She was exhausted, dizzy, emotionally drained, and so, so cold. The concrete floor had sucked every drop of warmth from her naked body. It felt as if she had grown into the floor, as if tissue and sinew had sunken down and taken root. She thought she might not be able to move from where she lay. And maybe it wouldn't be the worst thing if the next time she lost consciousness it simply never returned.

The despair was overwhelming. She lay there imagining that she was crying, imagining that Petal came to her and licked her tears away.

Thirst nagged at her. It felt as if the walls of her throat kept closing and sticking together. Then instinct would kick in and she would cough and choke and struggle against the feeling of not being able to breathe.

If her tormentor didn't kill her soon, she would die of hypothermia and dehydration. She wouldn't last long enough to starve to death.

If only she had the strength to stand, maybe she could feel her way to a faucet or a container with water in it. Maybe if she could get a drink, she would think more clearly. If she could think more clearly, maybe she could at least fight her tormentor when he came back. If she could fight him, maybe he would kill her outright, and she would at least die trying instead of wasting away like an abandoned caged animal.

Gathering every last ounce of will in her, Karly curled herself into a ball then rolled onto her hands and knees. She pulled one foot up under her and started to rise up, doing her best to shut out the pain that cut through her like a thousand razor blades along her nerve endings. The screwdriver still clutched in her right hand, she reached out to find the wall.

As she gained her feet, she put her left arm out in front of her, and touched evil.

# 52

He watched her struggle, amused at her will to survive. The last one had given up too easily. This one had been more sport.

She got to her feet and stretched her left arm out in front of her, the fingers of her hand spread wide.

He stepped closer, leaned down, and licked her palm with his tongue.

She tried to scream, her voice too hoarse to make much of a sound. But then she wouldn't know that because she couldn't hear.

She jerked her hand back as if he had burned her. She turned in a panic and ran into the wall. When he grabbed hold of her shoulder, she turned back toward him, swinging at him with her right arm, a screwdriver clutched in her hand.

He jumped back in the last instant, the flat tip of the screwdriver just missing cutting across his chest.

Amused no longer, he pulled the silk scarf from his pocket and wrapped both fists into the ends of it.

She was stumbling blind, running into the table, tripping over a chair, swinging the screwdriver out in front of her as if she might get lucky and strike him. But her luck had run out.

As deliberately as a tiger stalking its prey, he went behind her and moved in for the kill.

# 53

At 3:23 in the morning Jane sat bolt upright in bed, awakened from an exhausted, restless sleep by an unearthly, blood-curdling howl. For an instant, she thought her heart would explode, it was pounding so hard, so fast.

Violet, her pug, launched herself off the bed and ran barking from the room.

Jane got up, grabbing the Lady Smith & Wesson from her nightstand. She had left every light in the house on every night since Lisa's body had been found. Her outdoor lights blazed bright. A county cruiser prowled past every hour. And still she kept the gun handy.

Petal and Violet were both at the back door, barking incessantly, Petal jumping up and hurling herself at the door again and again in a vain attempt to break out.

"Girls! Girls, calm down," Jane said, setting her gun on the washing machine.

She caught hold of Petal's collar and nearly had her arm pulled out of the socket as she tried for three seconds to restrain the pit bull. The dog was like a torpedo of solid muscle.

"Calm down, sweetheart!" Jane shouted, her ridiculous words falling on small deaf ears.

Petal lunged at the door again and again, snapping, fangs bared, ready to tear to pieces whatever—or whoever—was outside.

Jane stood back, shaken by the dog's ferocity. She looked out the window above the washing machine, seeing nothing in the arc of lighted lawn. Taking her gun with her, she went into the kitchen, cut the light, and went to the window above the sink. She opened the window and strained to listen, hearing only the barking of the two dogs in the laundry room at first. Then came an eerie accompaniment in the distance: Coyotes yipping wildly down in the arroyo behind her property, celebrating the death of some unfortunate creature.

She hated that sound. It was not the semi-romantic howl of the wild people most often associated with the animals. It was a frenzied, hysterical cacophony of voices that preceded prey being ripped apart and devoured by the pack. It made the hair stand up on the back of her neck and ran goose bumps down her arms.

The dogs went wild to hear it, but Jane never allowed them outside at night off leash. Violet would have made a nice appetizer for a coyote. Even Petal wouldn't have been a match for a pack of them. Bold and criminally clever, coyotes routinely lured dogs away from safety with one member of the pack dancing and bowing, inviting the dog to play, only to draw the dog into an ambush by the rest of its cohorts.

Breathing a sigh of some relief, she closed and locked the window and went back to bed, not to sleep, but to sit and fret and pretend to read. Violet joined her eventually, jumping on the bed to spin around like a tiny whirling dervish before settling in her spot to sleep. Petal remained at the back door, her barking gradually subsiding to a piteous whining.

Jane debated breaking down and calling Cal, deciding against it. The dogs were calming down. The coyote victory party had died down. Her doors and windows were locked. She had her gun. What did she need with a man?

Reassurance and strong arms around her.

Her relationship with Dixon had teetered off and on between friendship and something more for a long time, never entirely tipping one way or the other. Her choice. She chose not to push it over the edge tonight . . . again.

At some point exhaustion won the battle, and Jane fell asleep only to be tormented by dark dreams of captivity and torture at the hands of a madman. When the alarm went off, she was relieved to be dragged up out of that hell.

Still wearing the sweatshirt and leggings she had fallen asleep in, she got up and went into the bathroom to splash cold water on her face and brush her long hair back into a loose ponytail. Violet came to the doorway and began hopping up and down like a flea.

"I know, I know," Jane said. "I'm coming."

Dogs were the great levelers of life. It didn't matter what had happened the day before. When the sun came up, the dogs would always need to go outside. Life would go on.

The doorbell rang as she walked through the house. She could see Steve Morgan through the glass in the front door. What a godsend he had been through this ordeal, taking some of the weight of managing the press off her.

They had agreed to meet early to go over everything that had gone on, every scrap of information that had come in to date on both Lisa's murder and Karly's disappearance, in preparation for a press conference set for nine.

"Hi, Steve," she said, opening the door. "Come on in. I have to let the dogs out. Sorry."

"No problem," he said, following her back through the house. "I brought doughnuts. I figured we could both stand a big jolt of fat and sugar to start the day."

"I'll supply the coffee," Jane said as they walked through the kitchen.

Petal was still sitting by the back door and had scratched the paint to shreds overnight. Both dogs flew out into the yard like a mismatched pair of rocks from slingshots, disappearing into the wilds of the garden.

Jane walked out onto the stone patio, crossing her arms over her I SLEEP WITH DOGS sweatshirt. The sun was barely up, and the air was cold. She glanced at Steve, taking in the dark circles under his eyes, the lines creased around his mouth.

"You look like you got about as much sleep as I did last night," she said.

Somewhere at the back of the garden the dogs were going crazy, barking, howling, yelping.

"What in the world?" Jane asked, heading back toward the commotion. She grabbed a hoe away from the potting bench as she went. She glanced back over her shoulder. "If this is a snake, I'm calling on you."

"I'll pass, thanks."

She took a right at the iceberg roses and stepped into a waking nightmare.

There, at the very back of the garden, planted among the calla lilies was Karly Vickers.

# 54

Jane didn't hear her own scream. The shock had rendered her deaf and weirdly numb. She knew she was running, but couldn't feel her legs. She flung herself down on overturned soil of the shallow grave and began digging frantically with her hands, but couldn't feel the earth between her fingers. She stared at Karly Vickers's face, pale blue-white against the dark earth, but couldn't feel the horror of that reality.

"Oh my God!" Steve Morgan exclaimed behind her.

"Call for help! Call for help!" Jane shouted, digging and digging like a frantic animal. She uncovered the girl's throat, part of one shoulder. She glanced back over her shoulder to see Steve standing, flat-footed.

"Call 9-1-1!" she screamed at him.

"She's dead, Jane."

"No!"

"She's dead."

"No!"

Like in a nightmare, he didn't move, didn't seem to grasp the urgency of the situation.

Jane pushed to her feet and ran past him back to the house.

It wouldn't penetrate her brain that Karly Vickers was dead. Hands trembling wildly, she grabbed the phone and dialed 911.

"I need an ambulance! I need an ambulance at five eighty-nine Arroyo Verde. Hurry!"

"What's the problem, ma'am?" the operator asked with a sense of calm that struck Jane as being insane.

"I need an ambulance! Are you deaf? Send the damn ambulance!"

She didn't wait for an answer, but ended the call and dialed Cal Dixon's pager number, leaving her number and 911 for the message.

Operating purely on instinct, she ran back outside and grabbed a spade as she passed the potting bench.

"Jane, we shouldn't disturb the scene," Steve said, trying to block her from the grave.

Without hesitation she swung the spade and hit him in the shins with the business end of it. He jumped back, shouting something she didn't hear.

She turned the loose earth as quickly as she could, exposing an arm, a leg. In the distance she could hear a siren wail.

*Oh my God, oh my God,* she chanted inside her head over and over. Had this been what the dogs had gone crazy for in the night? She had believed it was just the coyotes. Had some madman been back here doing this? Why hadn't she gone to look? Why hadn't she called Cal? What if it was too late because she had done none of those things?

*Oh my God, oh my God, oh my God.*

The EMTs came charging around the rose hedge, skidding to a stop at the sight.

"Jesus Christ!"

"Holy shit!"

Jane threw the shovel down and shouted at them, "Help her! Help her, damn you!"

The two men moved hesitantly closer. She grabbed hold of one of them by a fistful of uniform. "Help her!"

"There's no helping her, ma'am," he said. "She's gone."

The other one got down on the ground and put two fingers on the side of Karly Vickers's bruised throat.

"Oh my God," he said. "I think she might have a pulse."

"No way."

"Way. Get down here!"

Jane stepped back, shaking uncontrollably as she watched the two men go to work.

"What the hell?!"

She turned to see Cal Dixon, his face a mask of shock and horror as he ran to her. Somehow she managed not to faint until he was close enough to catch her.

# 55

Mendez abandoned his car at the curb in a red zone and ran into the ER at Mercy General Hospital. An ambulance had delivered Karly Vickers ahead of him. There was a chance she might be alive.

He held his badge up to the staff, not listening to them and not speaking.

It was plain where the action was. Half a dozen people in surgical scrubs swarmed around the bloody, filthy, naked woman on the table in the first exam room. The doctor in charge was shouting orders like a field general. Hang this, push that, get labs stat. The girl had been hooked up to an array of beeping, buzzing machines. She had tubes and wires coming and going. One person stood squeezing the big blue ball of a ventilator bag, sending air into her lungs via the hole that had been cut in her throat. The floor of the room was awash with debris—bloody gauze, discarded packaging, tubing, syringes.

"She's in V-fib!"

"Paddles! Charge! Clear!"

*BAM!* Her body jumped on the table.

"Charge! Clear!"

*BAM!*

The process was repeated again and again with the staff swearing and begging in between jolts.

"Come on, damn it!"

"Hang on, Karly!"

*BAM!*

"We've got a sinus rhythm!"

"All right, Karly, don't die on us now!" the doctor shouted. "I've got money riding on you. Stats!"

Pulse. Blood pressure. Respiration. Numbers all too low.

"We need another liter of ringers, wide-open!"

Mendez turned to one of the EMTs standing at the nurses' station, scribbling on paperwork.

"Is she going to make it?"

"I doubt it," the guy said. "But she shouldn't have been alive when we picked her up, either. Guess it depends on whether or not she wants to fight for it."

*Not an easy answer to that,* Mendez thought. He had yet to get a close look at Karly Vickers, but if their killer had followed form, she had been blinded and her eardrums destroyed. She would have multiple stab wounds. She would have been sexually tortured and mutilated. Would she want to live? He hoped so. At least long enough to tell them who killed her.

Dixon was in the next exam room with Jane Thomas, who sat on the exam table wrapped in a blanket and shaking like a seizure victim. If she had been any paler she would have become invisible.

"What happened?" Mendez asked, pulling his notebook out of his coat pocket.

"The girl was buried in Jane's garden," Dixon said. "Same as Lisa Warwick, with just her head exposed."

"Jesus."

"Lucky for the girl Jane didn't just assume she was dead."

"The dogs were barking," Jane Thomas said, her voice soft and tremulous. She looked at the floor as if that might help her concentrate. "Last night. Petal woke me up. I looked at the clock. It was three twenty-three. She was beside herself, howling and wanting out. I thought it was just that there were coyotes in the arroyo. I never imagined . . . If only I had gone to look—"

"Jane, we've been over this," Dixon said, his hand on her shoulder. "You couldn't have known, and you sure as hell shouldn't have gone out to look."

"I could have called you," she said, big tear-drops tumbling down her cheeks. "But I didn't do that, either."

"It's not your fault, Miss Thomas," Mendez said. "This is the fault of the man who took her and abused her, no one else's."

"Thank God I had to get up early to meet Steve," she said. "Where is he? Did he come?"

She looked around as if he might suddenly materialize in the room.

"Steve Morgan?" Mendez asked.

"Yes. He came over at seven. We had a meeting scheduled to plan the press conference." Her eyes went round. "Oh my God. The press conference! What time is it?"

"I wouldn't worry about the press," Dixon said. "Whenever you're ready, they'll come running. It's more important for you to be here. Right? If Miss Vickers comes around, you'll want to be the first to know."

"Yes, right," she murmured, shivering inside the blanket again. "But someone will have to call them."

"It'll be taken care of, Jane. And I want you looked at," he said, giving her a warning eye.

She didn't object as another tremor rattled through her. "He didn't help me," she said.

"Who didn't help you?"

"Steve. It was like one of those nightmares where you're trying to tell somebody something, but they don't understand you. He just stood there."

Dixon stepped away from her. Mendez moved with him.

"I want everyone in the war room in an hour."

Mendez nodded. "The media is going to be in a feeding frenzy over this."

"And we've got nothing to tell them. Do we?"

"Is that a question or an order?"

"A question."

"Leads are being followed. We have no comment to make on persons of interest at this time," Mendez said. "Vince was right. This guy wants credit for his work."

"He wants to make us look like fools."

"So far, he's succeeding."

"She didn't have her necklace," Jane said, seemingly talking to herself.

Dixon looked at her. "What?"

"Karly," she said. "She didn't have her necklace. Her graduation necklace from the center. She would never have taken it off. I have to get her another one. I have to go to the office."

"That can wait."

She shook her head and climbed down off the table. "No. No, it can't. I have to go get her another one."

"You have to sit down, Jane. You fainted."

"I can go pick it up," Mendez offered. "If you can call someone to have it at the desk."

Dixon sighed. "Thanks, Tony."

"*De nada.* That's the least I can do for the heroine of the day."

On his way back out to his car, Mendez spied the front page of the Saturday *LA Times*. The headline read: CASE CLOSED? SUSPECT ARRESTED IN OAK KNOLL HOMICIDE.

# 56

Dennis got up early and dressed in jeans and a long-sleeved rugby shirt. He went into his closet and dug through the dirty clothes to find his cigar box. From the box he took the pocketknife he had stolen from his dad's dresser and shoved it deep into the front pocket of his jeans.

The knife was his most prized possession. He liked to pretend his father had given it to him for his birthday. He wished that was true, but his father never even remembered his birthday.

He took the lighter he had stolen out of his mother's purse, and put it and the half-dozen cigarettes into a zippered pocket on his backpack. He hadn't tried to smoke before, but he thought maybe he would start.

Almost as an afterthought, he tossed the dried-out rattlesnake head in there too—just because it was his. Then he put on his blue jean jacket, hiked his backpack up over one shoulder, and headed downstairs.

The house was completely quiet. Usually,

Dennis's mother was up by now to make breakfast. Even on the weekends, his father liked breakfast early. His father was a busy man, and had a lot of important things to do, even on his days off.

But there was no sign of his mother.

Dennis had never heard her car come home, and he had been awake all night. Even when he had finally climbed back down from the roof to his bedroom, he hadn't wanted to sleep. Not because he was afraid of bad dreams, but because he just didn't feel anything. He didn't feel pain. He didn't feel sadness or anger. He didn't feel tired.

He had crept through the house like a burglar to see what he could see. The downstairs looked like a bomb had gone off with broken stuff all over the floors of the dining room and kitchen. His mother was gone. His father too. Dennis was all alone.

He lay on his bed all the rest of the night, just staring at the ceiling.

Now, in the light of day, the kitchen was a terrible mess. Dirty dishes had been thrown in the sink. A pot with macaroni and cheese in it had been knocked off the stove and spilled all over the floor. There must have been a thousand ants crawling on the gooey pile. There was red stuff smeared on one wall by the light switch. *Blood,* Dennis thought. He stared at it and felt nothing.

The dining room was no better. There were broken glasses on the floor, and a couple of broken plates.

For sure his mother had not come home. She would never have gone to bed and left the place like this. She kept everything clean and tidy because that was the way his father liked it.

Dennis got a bowl and fixed himself some cereal. He was halfway done when his father came walking in, looking like he hurt all over. He had a hangover. Dennis could tell by the color of his skin and the bags under his eyes.

His father didn't get drunk very often, and when he did he didn't try to hide it like Dennis's mother did. He knew his mother drank almost every day on account of he knew where she hid her bottle. But it was her secret, and most of the time even his father couldn't tell.

Dennis stopped chewing and just stared at his dad now, not sure what to expect from him. Would he be normal? Would he still be mad?

His father made a face like his mouth tasted bad, went to the coffeemaker, and stared at the empty pot.

He looked at Dennis. "Where's your mother?"

Dennis shrugged.

His dad went to the window and looked out at the driveway. "Her car's gone. I never heard her come home last night."

*I never heard you come home last night, either*, Dennis thought, but he just shrugged again. He fully expected his dad to explode and belt him one for not answering, like he had the night before, but he didn't.

"I think she left," his father said, still staring out the window.

Dennis said nothing. He still couldn't feel any emotions. In a weird way, it was like he was wrapped up in a cocoon. He could see the world around him, but it couldn't touch him. He liked it that way.

His father turned and left the room. Dennis could hear his footfalls going up the stairs. When he couldn't hear them anymore, he put his backpack on and left the house with no intention of ever coming back.

# 57

"Mimosas," Franny told the waitress. "And keep them coming, honey."

On Saturdays they met for breakfast at the Ivy Garden, a favorite place off the plaza where tables spilled out of garden-inspired rooms into the garden itself. A fantastic spreading oak tree grew like something from a fairy tale right in the center of the space, shading the tables in daytime and providing a canopy of twinkling lights at night.

"I need the alcohol," Franny said, fussing with the bright yellow bandana he wore twisted at the open throat of his purple Ralph Lauren polo shirt (collar turned up, of course). The bandana matched the little polo pony embroidered on the chest. "I'm still shaking from last night. Are you all right? I knew that woman was a bitch, but MY GOD! She's bat-shit crazy!"

A pair of older ladies at the next table looked over from their French toast. Franny rolled his eyes at them.

"I'm worried about Tommy," Anne said.

"Can you imagine having that F-U-C-K-I-N-G C-U-N-T for a mother?"

"Kind of."

"Your mother was a saint."

"But my father is Dick."

"Your father is *a* dick, but he's not crazy," Franny said. "I was stunned speechless last night, and that hasn't happened since . . . ever. Thank God for Vince!"

*Vince*. His new best friend.

"Where is he?" he asked. "Did he take you home last night? Did you sleep with him?"

Anne blushed and ducked her head.

"Oh my God, you DID!" he exclaimed, delighted. "You vixen! I'm so proud of you!"

"Stop!" she hissed, swatting at him with her napkin. "Stop it!"

"Tell all!"

"I'm telling nothing. We are in a public place and I teach the fifth grade. And I wouldn't tell you anyway, because I'm not that kind of girl."

"Well, apparently you are."

"It wasn't like that."

He put his elbows on the table and leaned forward, eyes bright. "So what *was* it like? Sweet and romantic or hot and wild with animal passion?"

"It was none of your business," she said bluntly.

"This is very interesting," he said. "You haven't slept with a man since Jimmy Carter was president."

"That is categorically untrue. It was the first Reagan administration—and that wasn't that long ago."

"So what now? Where is he? Did he spend the night?"

"He's working, and this part of our conversation is over," Anne declared as the waitress returned with their drinks.

"I'll have the lemon blueberry ricotta pancakes," Franny said, handing his menu over. "And so will my friend. She worked up a big appetite last night."

Anne let that one go. If she didn't rise to the bait, he would get bored.

He raised his glass in a toast. "Here's to ya, Anne Marie. That's all's I'm sayin'."

"Good. Then the rest of the meal will be pleasantly quiet," Anne said, picking a cornbread minimuffin from the basket on the table.

She had no big revelations to make on the subject of Vince Leone at any rate. She had to sort through her feelings about what had transpired between them the night before. She didn't regret it, she knew that. Strange as it sounded to her own ears, it felt right and good to share herself with a man she barely knew, who would probably be gone in a week. It was going to take a while to make sense of that.

"I'm worried about Tommy," she said, going back to her original topic of concern. "I want to talk to him, but how am I supposed to accomplish that?"

"You can't go to their house," Franny said. "That creature will pull you into her cave, suck all the blood from your body, and pick her teeth with your bones."

"I know. But am I just supposed to wait until Monday? He looked so hurt last night. It broke my heart. Who knows what his mother put in his head? She said I made him think his father might be a serial killer."

"Did you?"

"No! Vince asked me to ask Tommy if his father was home the night Karly Vickers went missing. That was all I did."

Franny's eyes got big. "Does Vince think Peter Crane is a k-i-l-l-e-r?"

"You do realize most adults can spell, don't you?" Anne said. "Spelling doesn't prevent eaves-dropping."

"But they have to work harder at it," Franny said loudly, squinting at the old ladies.

"I don't know what I'm going to do, Franny."

"Call Vince. He might not have an answer, but you can always screw his brains out."

"Don't try to distract me just yet," Anne said, too

familiar with his MO. "I have a real problem here."

"But I don't know how to help you, sweetheart," he confessed. "I don't want you involved in this mess at all."

"Mr. Franny!"

One of Franny's kindergartners came charging over to the table. A bright-eyed, adorable moppet with a head of curly brown hair.

Franny went instantly into kindergarten-teacher mode, making a face of wild surprise and slapping his hands against his cheeks. "Oh my gosh! It's CASEY! How are you today? Are you having breakfast?"

"I already did. I had pancakes!" As evidenced by the syrup smeared on the face and fingers that grabbed hold of Franny's hands.

"I'm having pancakes too!" Franny said.

The parents stopped by and exchanged pleasantries. As they left, Franny turned back to Anne, made a wacky face, and said, "Poop-in-the-sandbox kid. I'm going to go disinfect myself. And when I come back you're going to get your mind off this for an hour, young lady. Drink up!"

# 58

"The girl is in critical condition," Dixon said. "She's not expected to make it. Just like Lisa Warwick, her eyes and mouth had been glued shut. She was strangled. Somehow he didn't quite finish off the job. Who knows how long her brain was deprived of oxygen. She's severely dehydrated and suffering from hypothermia."

He stood at the front of the room, the eyes of all of his detectives, along with personnel from two neighboring counties, riveted on him. Mendez passed out new flyers with a close-up photo of the necklace Karly Vickers had probably been wearing at the time of her abduction.

"We believe she was wearing this necklace," Dixon went on. "It's the logo from the Thomas Center. All women who graduate the program get a gold one. Staff have the same necklace in silver. Karly Vickers was not wearing hers when she was discovered. The perp might have kept it as a souvenir."

"Did the Warwick woman have one?" Hamilton asked.

"She was an ex-staffer. She would have owned one. Go back into her apartment to see if it's there."

"He took the time to bury the Vickers girl, but not to make sure she was dead?" Hicks said. "That doesn't make sense."

"She barely had a pulse," Dixon said. "He probably just didn't pick up on it."

"Or it might not be an accident," Vince said. "He could have left her alive as part of a taunt. He leaves a living victim and we still can't find him. Proves his omnipotence."

"How are we supposed to respond to that?"

Dixon asked. "This guy's running around thinking he's God."

"Tell him he made a mistake. Go in front of the press and announce that he made a crucial mistake and it's only a matter of time before you close him down."

"A bluff," Mendez said. "But what if he calls us on it?"

"It's got to be a damn good bluff. Something he can't prove or disprove, something that gets under his skin and starts to make him worry a little.

"He's intelligent. Hard science will get his attention. Something to do with trace evidence or we tell him the FBI has come up with a new method of lifting fingerprints from a human body or that he can be linked to a victim through DNA. We don't quite have that technology yet, but it's coming soon. We can certainly talk a good game about it, enough to make him worry a little.

"That's what we want," Vince said. "We want him either careless or worried. That's when he'll make a mistake."

"But at whose expense?" Mendez asked. "He's going to be trolling for another victim, isn't he?"

"He will be whether you challenge him or not. He's at a place where he's sure he's smarter than all of us combined. He'll get drunk on that power."

"Let's table the idea for the moment," Dixon said. "We need to finish processing the scene at Jane's. Maybe the CSIs will come up with some actual forensic evidence and we can make a bluff with some teeth in it."

"A little truth sells a lie every time," Vince agreed.

"What's going on with Gordon Sells?" Dixon asked.

"He's still not talking," Trammell said. "The nephew lawyered up last night, but we've got him talking deal with the DA's office. I think we'll get something out of him soon. He's not liking what he's hearing about prison."

"What about the victim?"

"There are about half a dozen possible victims among the missing persons we've looked at within the target area," Campbell said. "Based on gender —we're assuming female; based on size—relative to the length of the femur found; and looking at an age range from twelve to thirty. BFS will be doing the comparisons of dental records."

Detectives were assigned to canvass Jane Thomas's neighbors in the event anyone might have been up at three in the morning to see a car drive by. The deputy assigned to patrol the neighborhood had been called to report in.

It probably hadn't been dumb luck that their UNSUB had happened into that yard to bury a body just after the prowl car had left the street not to return for an hour. He had to have been watching from somewhere.

"Tony," Dixon said. "What's your agenda?"

"I want to go to the scene, then talk to Steve Morgan, and I want to bring Peter Crane in and question him about that solicitation bust and Julie Paulson. He also needs to account for himself for last night."

Dixon nodded. "I'm going to make a statement to the press regarding Karly Vickers at noon. We'll do it here out in front of the building. Try to get them away from the hospital. I've posted deputies at all entrances to Mercy General, and I have no doubt they'll still try to get in."

"Where's Miss Thomas?" Vince asked.

"She's still at the hospital. Sedated for the time being. She was pretty shaken up."

"Have somebody keep an eye on her, Sheriff," Vince said. "If this guy decides to make a big gesture with his next victim, she's the obvious choice."

Vince, Mendez, and Hicks rode together to the Thomas home where news vans lined the street, and reporters crowded the front lawn.

Ball cap pulled low over his eyes, Vince hung back, letting the two detectives take the attention of the media, then slipping past while they barked out " 'No comment's." If Dixon decided to go along with the idea of challenging their killer, Vince would be stepping into the spotlight soon enough. But the disclosure of his involvement would come on his terms, not the media's.

Jane Thomas's property was slightly larger than the average lot, and bordered on two sides by a narrow, shallow ravine, thick with trees. Their killer could have made his way around to the backyard garden this way without risking a neighbor seeing him. Karly Vickers was a small woman—105 pounds according to her driver's license—easily carried by an average-size man in good shape.

He wouldn't have been visible from the house, digging at the back of the garden. If he knew the garden was there, he wouldn't have even had to bring his own shovel. One had been generously provided for him by the garden owner.

Still, it was a bolder move to bury a body here than in the park where Lisa Warwick had been found. Cocky. Theatrical. Personal? Did he have some axe to grind with Jane Thomas? Maybe she was the one with the enemy, not the victims.

It was interesting to him that the victims had been women trying to make their lives better, not women stuck on the low end of society.

Prostitutes were always favorite victims of serial killers because they were considered by the killer to be despicable, disposable, and easy prey. The other end of that spectrum was the killer who hunted young women perceived to be of good virtue, for lack of a more modern word. High school girls, college coeds, young single women.

This killer chose women trying to move up

from poorer circumstances. Trying to fool people into believing they were something they weren't? Was that it? Or were they simply vulnerable and accessible through the connection to the center?

Nothing was ever that simple.

Steve Morgan sat at a table on the stone patio, watching the swarm of law enforcement going over the yard. Vince walked over and sat down across from him.

"Hell of a thing, huh?"

Morgan looked at him, his expression unreadable. "Not the way you want to start your day: finding someone half-buried in your friend's yard."

"But she's alive."

"Unbelievable." He shook his head at some private thought. "I heard Jane scream. She had gone to see what her dogs were barking at."

"Where are the dogs now?"

"Jane's assistant came and got them. Why?"

"We'll need to collect hair samples from them, in the event hairs were recovered from Miss Vickers. A stray hair from an unknown source could open the investigation in a different direction. Maybe the perpetrator owns a dog or a cat. One stray hair could make a connection. It only takes one loose thread to unravel a cheap sweater."

"The science is that sophisticated?" he asked.

"You can't imagine the things they're doing at the FBI lab in Washington, the advances in analyzing trace evidence, DNA evidence. One day soon there'll be a national DNA databank with the DNA codes of every convicted criminal in the country."

"That's a little Orwellian, don't you think?"

"Big Brother is sure as hell going to be watching the criminal population," Vince said. He shrugged. "It's nothing to worry about if you haven't done anything wrong."

He sat back and squared his left ankle over his right knee, settling in as if watching evidence collection at a crime scene was all part of a normal, relaxing Saturday morning.

"Good thing you were here so early today," he said.

"Jane and I had scheduled a meeting. We were supposed to be having a press conference this morning."

"Another five, ten minutes, that girl probably would have been dead. Now there's a shot she can tell us who abducted her."

"I read the man glued Lisa's eyes closed," Morgan said. "So she couldn't see him. Did he do that to Karly?"

"I don't think that's why he did it," Vince said, watching him carefully. "I think it has to do with his fantasy. See no evil, hear no evil, speak no evil. I think the women become objects to him— pretty to look at, but no trouble. A lot of guys would say when a woman opens her mouth it spoils everything."

Morgan tipped his head in acknowledgment.

"How's your family, Steve?" he asked, surprising the man a little. "Your daughter—how's she holding up after what she saw?"

"Wendy is very resilient."

"How about yourself? Now you know exactly what it was like for her, stumbling on that body in the woods."

"I certainly wish that hadn't happened to her."

"Yeah."

Mendez wandered over from the gravesite, scribbling in his notebook. "They found a couple of good shoe prints in the arroyo."

"In the what?" Vince asked. "I'm from Chicago here. Don't go throwing language at me."

"The arroyo. Down the hill in the trees. There's a stream. The ground is just damp enough to hold a good impression."

"Great."

"Mr. Morgan," Mendez said. "I have to ask you where you were last night."

"In bed like any sane person. Jane thinks she might have heard the guy back here—or that the dogs did—sometime after three."

"And you arrived . . . ?"

"Just before seven."

"Hell of a deal, huh?" Mendez said. "Finding that girl alive."

"Hell of a deal," Morgan said. He pushed to his feet with the effort of a much older man. The dark circles beneath his eyes spoke of another long night. "Unless you gentlemen need me, I'm going out to the search site and let people know what's happened. The search is over."

They watched him round the corner of the house and disappear.

"You know," Mendez said, "he didn't lift a finger to help her—Jane. She came out here and found that girl half buried, and started digging her out, and Morgan just stood there and watched her. I find that odd, don't you?"

"Yes." Vince said. "But he might have been in shock."

"Or he might have been enjoying the show."

Vince slapped him on the back. "Now you're thinking like a profiler, kid."

# 59

Wendy had gotten up early and dressed for the day in a baby blue turtleneck and bib overalls. She put her hair in two thick braids, the way her father liked it.

Her plan had been to bounce downstairs and help her father make breakfast as he always did when he was home on a Saturday. They got up early and made breakfast while Wendy's mom slept in. They made crazy kinds of pancakes, like pumpkin or butterscotch, and cut them into shapes with cookie cutters. She loved Saturdays with her dad.

Then she remembered that her dad had left.

But surely he would come back this morning because it was Saturday and they had their tradition. He might have been mad at her mother, but he wasn't mad at her. Of course he would come home to make pancakes.

Then she would talk him into going with her to the park. She wanted to show him where everything had happened. She wanted to tell him about her idea to write a book and/or a movie about the experience.

That had been her plan.

But her father wasn't in the kitchen when she got downstairs. The house was quiet, the only sound the hum of the refrigerator.

Wendy's heart felt like a thousand pounds in her chest. It was so unfair. They were a great family. All her friends said so. They all envied her her parents. Her mom was so artsy and funky and cool. Her dad was so handsome and so much fun.

*We had such a nice family*, her mother had said.

Had—like in the past.

They were being so selfish, Wendy thought. They yelled at each other, hurt each other, but neither of them thought about her.

Fine then. If they wanted to be selfish, they could be selfish on their own. Let them realize she's a person too, she should have a say too. Let them find her gone and see how selfish they were then.

She went back to her room and got her back-pack. Then she tiptoed down the stairs and slipped out the front door and headed for the park.

In another part of town, Cody Roache was being pushed out of his home by his mother. One of the neighborhood dads was taking kids to the park. Not to the part where they had found the dead lady, but to the part where the fun stuff was—the swings and monkey bars and tetherballs.

Cody didn't want to go. He felt nervous. But his mother said he would never get over it if he didn't go out and do normal things and play like a normal kid.

There were about ten kids piling into the neighbor's van. He would feel safe with ten other kids and a dad there. So Cody glanced back at his mom and climbed into the van. It never once occurred to him that he might never come back.

# 60

Anne begged off from a ride to Santa Barbara for an afternoon of shopping and meeting some of Franny's friends for wine in the afternoon.

"I've had enough excitement for one week," she said as they parted company outside the restaurant. "And I really need to figure out the situation with Tommy."

Franny frowned at her. "Please stay out of

trouble. And promise me—if you aren't busy tonight—and by busy, I mean having mad hot sex with Vince—promise me you'll come over and watch *The Golden Girls* with me."

"*The Golden Girls*?" Anne raised her eyebrows. "Can we play mahjong after?"

"Don't make fun of my favorite show."

"I wouldn't dream of it." Anne kissed his cheek and promised to call.

Franny headed off to the parking lot. Anne walked up the street to the plaza, thinking some mindless window shopping would allow her brain to sort through the trouble with Tommy Crane . . . provided she could keep thoughts of Vince from creeping in. Easier said than done.

Preoccupied, she almost walked past Peter Crane without seeing him. He was taking the MISSING poster of Karly Vickers off the door of his office.

"Did they find her?" Anne asked, hopeful.

Crane stopped, poster in his hands. "Yes. The same way Lisa Warwick was found."

"Oh, no."

"But she's alive. It's quite a story."

Anne looked at the photo of Karly Vickers on the poster in Peter Crane's hands as he told her what he had heard. She looked shy but happy. Like everyone else, Anne had read Karly's story in the papers. The young woman had fought hard to overcome adversity in her life. The gold necklace she wore with the Thomas Center logo of a woman with her arms raised in triumph spoke to just how far Karly had come. Now she would have to fight hard to just stay alive at all.

In light of Karly's story, Anne was embarrassed to feel anxious at all about what was going on in her life.

"I'm glad I ran into you, Dr. Crane," she said. "I think there's been a misunderstanding, and I would really like to clear it up."

God knew what his wife had told him about the night before. The best thing Anne could do would be to set the record straight.

"Sure," Crane said. "Why don't you come into the office?"

He opened the door for Anne, followed her in, and locked the deadbolt behind them. Anne's heart jumped.

"No walk-ins," he said by way of explanation.

They seemed to be alone. There was no receptionist, no lights on except in the enormous aquarium in the waiting room.

"You're not usually open on Saturdays?" she asked, feeling vaguely uncomfortable.

"Emergencies only," he said as he bent to pick up the mail that had been shoved in through the slot in the door. For the first time, Anne realized he was in jeans and a denim shirt, and sneakers. "I came in to catch up on paperwork. Why don't we have a seat?"

He gestured toward the waiting room where they each took a comfortable leather chair.

"The detectives asked me to ask a couple of questions of the kids involved in finding the body in the park," Anne said, going straight to the heart of it. "The questions seemed harmless enough, but—"

"You don't need to apologize, Miss Navarre," he said. "I did think it was odd, coming from you, but, as you said, harmless enough."

"Mrs. Crane didn't seem to think so," Anne said. "I ran into her after the vigil last night. She was very upset with me. She said I made Tommy think you might be a suspect. I'm not sure how he would have gotten that idea from me. That certainly wasn't anything I was thinking."

"I'm glad to hear that," Crane said with a charming smile. "People have enough fear of the dentist without thinking he might be a serial killer."

Anne relaxed a little.

"Really, I'm not upset or offended," he said. "Janet is much more apt to take offense. She's had a hard time dealing with everything that's happened this week. I know she's been difficult."

"I'm not going to try to tell you that isn't true," Anne said honestly. "We're all in uncharted territory, dealing with the things that have happened this past week. Everyone at the school is doing the best in a bad situation."

"I know that," Crane said. "I think you've done

an admirable job, all things considered. I appreciate that you take a real interest in my son, Miss Navarre."

"Thank you."

"As for my wife . . . Janet is a person who needs to be in control of her environment. She has good reasons for that. Obviously, I can't elaborate, but she had to overcome a lot in her early life, and in times of stress . . . She doesn't always handle that well."

Anne had no interest in understanding Janet Crane. No matter what she'd had to overcome in her life, Janet was an adult and should have been able to conduct herself in a better way than she had. But she wasn't Anne's focus.

"I'm actually worried about Tommy," she admitted. "I'm afraid he somehow thinks I betrayed his trust."

"Tommy thinks the world of you."

"I would feel better seeing that for myself. I would really like to be able to sit down with him and have a talk, one-on-one. I want him to know he can rely on me. Do you think there would be any way we could arrange that without upsetting Mrs. Crane?"

He thought about it for a moment, no doubt weighing the benefit for Tommy against the risk of incurring his wife's wrath.

"I'll see what I can do. Can I call you?"

"Of course. I would really appreciate that."

"I'm sorry if Janet has made your life difficult."

"I'm fine," Anne said, getting to her feet. She felt worse for him and for Tommy. Janet Crane could attack her and Anne could still go home at the end of the day. Peter Crane and his son had to live with the woman. "My concern is Tommy."

The buzzer at the front door sounded, making Anne jump. Crane got up and went past her. When he opened the door the space was taken up entirely by Detectives Mendez and Hicks. Mendez flicked a glance at Anne.

"Dr. Crane," he said. "We have a couple of things we need to discuss with you. Would you mind coming down to the station with us?"

# 61

Dennis went into the woods, not from the park entrance, but from the back, from the service road. On the other side of the service road was the sheriff's office. Where the good guys worked. That was what his third-grade teacher had told the class when they had all walked over, hand in hand, from school for a field trip.

Mrs. Barkow hadn't known Dennis's father beat his wife, beat him. Dennis had always believed his father was a good guy, anyway, that there had to be something wrong with him that he made his father so angry. He was bad, he was stupid, he was brain damaged, and his mother was just a drunk, stupid cunt, and she deserved whatever happened to her.

Maybe that was all true, but he didn't think the same way about his father anymore.

His backpack was heavy with stuff he had taken out of the kitchen—cans of soup, tuna, beans—stuff he needed to live on his own. He trudged along, kicking through the fallen leaves, thinking of nothing but his destination.

The yellow tape had started to fall down, making it look like a place nobody cared about anymore. That was good. Then no one would come there and bother him. Dennis dropped his backpack on the ground and sat down on the rock where the dead lady had put her head.

It was time for lunch, and this was where he wanted to have it: in a grave.

Wendy didn't go into the woods. She stayed in the park where the grass was mowed and there were no fallen branches or thornbushes, or graves. She sat on a bench with her legs crossed, doodling in her notebook.

It was quiet here, the kind of quiet with birds in the background and the sound of running water from the fountain across the path. Not the kind of quiet at home.

She wondered if her dad would move away or just out of their house. It seemed like he was going to Sacramento a lot, but maybe that was just what he said when he went to have his affair.

She wondered if the Other Woman had kids, and if she had kids, did Wendy already know them? What if they were kids in her school? What if they were kids she didn't like? What if Dennis Farman was going to be her stepbrother?

These were things adults never considered, things that didn't matter to them.

Of course, she would live with her mother. They would stay in their house. Maybe her mom would have to get a job. She had had a job before Wendy was born. There was a picture in their family room of her mom and dad in graduation caps and gowns, getting their diplomas from college. That meant she could get a good job.

Or, Wendy thought as she looked out into the woods, she could write her book about her and Tommy finding the dead body, and it could get made into a movie, and she would be rich. Her father would be sorry then.

Cody flipped himself around the monkey bars, pretending he was really a monkey. Monkeys had it good. They were always his favorite animals at the zoo in Santa Barbara—especially the white-handed gibbons with their long, long arms, swinging them from limb to limb. He pretended now that he was a white-handed gibbon, and he started making loud monkey noises as he negotiated the bars.

The thing he wanted to do most in the world—next to being an astronaut—was to go to the San

Diego Zoo. His mother had told him maybe next summer they could have a real family vacation and go there. The San Diego Zoo had every kind of monkey there was, he bet.

Cody was glad he had come to the park. He didn't feel nervous anymore. Hopping down from the monkey bars he ran over to the tetherballs and started a game with a younger kid from down his street.

Yep. He was glad he had come to the park.

Out in the woods, Dennis dug a can of beans out of his backpack and got out his pocketknife. He couldn't figure out how to work the piece that was supposed to be the can opener.

It didn't look like any can opener he had ever seen. He tried and tried to work it, but all it did was make a dent then slip off to the side. And every time that happened, he became more aware of being hungry. And then he began to feel something else.

He began to feel.

Fingers fumbling, he cut himself closing the can opener. Bright red blood welled up out of his finger. He stared at it for a minute, then licked it off.

He opened the big blade on the knife, and stabbed it hard into the top of the can. He stabbed it again, and liquid from the beans squirted out through the holes.

He stabbed it again and he began to feel something bigger growing in his chest. All the pain, all the anger started coming out as he stabbed the can with the knife.

So he stabbed it again and again and again . . .

# 62

"Oh God, this is embarrassing," Peter Crane groaned, looking at the arrest report—complete with mug shot—Mendez had put down on the table in front of him. He sighed and looked away.

"What you do in your free time is your business, Dr. Crane. I don't want an explanation," Mendez said. "I'm not going to tell your wife. I don't need another homicide to investigate. You seem like a nice enough guy.

"My problem with this is that on that same night, in that same vice sweep, Julie Paulson was arrested."

"Who's Julie Paulson?"

"Julie Paulson was a prostitute. Not long after her arrest in Oxnard, she turned up at the Thomas Center. And not long after that, she turned up dead."

"I don't know anything about that!" Crane said, shocked.

Mendez made a pained face. "But you do, Doctor. Actually, you brought that murder up the first day we spoke."

Crane looked confused for an instant. "The girl that was murdered last year? The one found outside of town? I read about that in the newspaper!"

"I have a hard time with that," Mendez said. "I don't believe in coincidences—especially not when they start to pile on top of each other.

"Julie Paulson was a prostitute in Oxnard. You were arrested for soliciting a prostitute in Oxnard. Julie Paulson comes to Oak Knoll. You live in Oak Knoll. She gets in the program at the Thomas Center. You work with the women at the Thomas Center. She ends up dead. Karly Vickers goes missing. You knew Lisa Warwick . . .

"Can you see where all these things might lead me, Dr. Crane?"

Crane rubbed his hands over his face. "Oh my God."

Mendez let him stew for a minute, tapping his pen on the tabletop slowly as the seconds ticked past.

"I didn't know Julie Paulson," he said at last. "The girl I got arrested with in Oxnard, Candace, I used to see her from time to time."

"You were a regular customer is what you're saying?"

Crane closed his eyes like he had a bad headache. "I'm not proud of it. And it's not that I don't care about my wife. It's just . . . Janet has some . . . issues—"

"I really don't want to know about that," Mendez said. "Really."

"I know you've only seen the worst of her," Crane said. "This week has been a nightmare. She's really not a bad person. I don't cheat on her in the truest sense of the word—"

"Don't care. *Really.*"

If Peter Crane wanted absolution he was going to have to consult a priest. Mendez had no interest in arguing the definition of adultery. The man was fucking women other than his wife—that pretty much defined the word for him.

Crane sighed. "After I got arrested, I stopped going down there."

"And Julie Paulson moved here," Mendez said. "You're not helping yourself here, Dr. Crane."

"I'm telling you what happened," he said, exasperated. "I can't help it that that girl moved here. It's a free country. Maybe she had a friend here, but it wasn't me."

"And you stopped going to Oxnard."

"Yes."

"And . . . ? What? You gave up prostitutes? You gave up sex?"

"I . . . have . . . Oh Jesus," he muttered, looking down at the floor. "I have an . . . arrangement . . . with a woman in Ventura."

Mendez slid a paper and pen across the table to him. "I'll need her name and phone number."

Crane looked like he wanted to be sick. Mr.

Respectable Upstanding Citizen frequenting prostitutes.

When he had written the information Mendez took the paper. "I'll be right back. You want a coffee or something?"

"No. Thank you," Crane said, staring at the table.

Mendez went across the hall and handed the paper to Hicks. Vince and Dixon were watching the monitor. Crane sat with his head in his hands.

"Good job, kid," Vince said. "You've got him twitching."

"Man, he's sweating like a horse," Mendez said. "Can you imagine what his wife would do to him if she found out where her pillar of the community has been?"

Hicks laughed. "Yeah, his pillar's been all over the place."

"Although, you can hardly blame the guy," Mendez said. "That wife of his . . . She'd be like fucking a bear trap."

"Press him about last night," Vince said. "Ask him how his card game went."

Mendez poured himself a cup of coffee and went back into the interview room.

"So how was your card game last night?"

"My what?"

"Your wife told us you weren't home last night because you were playing cards."

"Oh."

"Where were you? Ventura?"

"No. Janet and I had a fight."

"What about?"

"She was angry that Tommy's teacher had asked him some questions about our home life. I'm sure I don't have to tell you, my wife can be a formidable character in an argument," he said. "It's been a long week. I'd just had it. I didn't want to hear any more, so I went out."

"Out where?"

"I had dinner at O'Brien's Pub, watched the American League Championship game. Around nine Steve came into the bar—"

"Steve Morgan?"

"Yeah. We sat around and cried in our beer until closing time."

"What was his problem?"

"A fight with his wife. What else? She kicked him out."

"Why did she throw him out?"

"She accused him of having an affair, which has gotten to be a routine thing with her."

"Is he?" Mendez asked. "Where there's smoke, there's usually fire."

He didn't answer for a while, turning words over in his head, trying to choose them carefully. "Steve's a complicated guy."

"I don't care," Mendez said. "I want to know: Was he having an affair with Lisa Warwick?"

Peter Crane rested his elbows on the table and hung his head, looking defeated.

"Don't fuck around with me, Dr. Crane," Mendez said sharply. "The woman was murdered. Was he having an affair with her?"

"Yes."

# 63

Dennis crept through the woods like a commando, crouched low, sometimes crawling on his belly. He had smeared dirt on his face for camouflage and tied a rag around his head like Rambo.

He could hear voices in the park. People talking, kids laughing. People with normal lives. He hated them.

He could see them from the edge of the woods, where he hid behind a tree. Little kids, bigger kids, a couple of adults. He crept a little closer.

They were having fun. They were happy. And there was Cody, who was supposed to be his friend, playing catch with a kid from the fourth grade.

"Hey, Cody," he said, standing at the very edge where the park became the woods.

Cody glanced over at him and frowned.

"Hey, Cockroach, come 'ere."

Cody pretended not to hear him.

"Come on," Dennis said. "I have something cool to show you."

Cody came a little closer, looking at him kind of suspicious through his stupid, crooked patched-together glasses. "I'm not supposed to play with you, Dennis. My mom said."

Dennis rolled his eyes. "Oh, come on. I found something. It's really cool."

Cody glanced back at the people who had brought him to the park. The kid he had been playing catch with ran over to the swings.

"Come on. Don't be such a wuss," Dennis said as he took a step back into the woods.

"I'm not supposed to go in the woods."

"You're such a mama's boy."

"Am not."

"Are so."

Cody looked tempted but unsure.

"I thought we were friends," Dennis said.

"You're mean."

"You're stupid." Dennis shrugged his shoulders. "Suit yourself. You'll just miss it, that's all."

He turned sideways and started to walk away, back into the woods. Cody looked back at the playground, then back at Dennis, then back at the playground. Dennis took a few more steps, turning his back. Then footsteps came behind him in the fallen leaves.

Dennis glanced at Cody and started to jog. Cody broke into a trot. They went over a little rise and out of sight of the playground.

Dennis stopped, laughing. Cody ran up on his heels. He was laughing too. Then Dennis turned, still laughing, and plunged the knife into Cody Roache's belly as deep as it would go.

# 64

Wendy sat on the park bench looking out into the woods. She had made a sketch in her notebook showing the scene of the crime—the hill they had jumped off and tumbled down, the rocks and trees, and the grave at the bottom. She was afraid to draw the head of the dead lady, like the drawing would somehow come to life and the head would start talking to her.

That was stupid, of course. If Tommy had been there, he would have told her what a stupid idea that was. Although it might be a good, really creepy thing in their movie: If the head of the dead lady haunted them and followed them around in ghost form, and talked to them about what had happened. And no one would be able to see her except Wendy and Tommy. Unless she wanted to be seen in order to scare people, like Dennis or the killer.

Or maybe, in the movie, Dennis would be the killer. THAT would be really weird. There was nothing scarier in a movie than an evil kid. Dennis wouldn't even have to be acting, she thought.

She wished now she had called Tommy and prodded him into coming with her to the park. Now, in the full light of a beautiful day, the woods didn't seem so scary, and she wanted to go back in and retrace their fateful journey from school that day. But it would have been much better if

Tommy had been there to help her recount the tale.

It made Wendy mad that Tommy's mom was so strict. He always had to go to this lesson or that recital. He couldn't just be a normal kid and play. He had to be here by a certain time and there before dark, and he couldn't this, and he couldn't that.

And he wasn't like Harlan Friedman, who pretended to be weak and allergic to everything so he didn't have to do gym class or go on field trips. Tommy liked to do stuff. He just didn't like to get in trouble.

Wendy was in no mood to be that careful. Her parents were already going to be mad at her because she had left the house without permission. She might as well do what she wanted before she got caught. And even when she got caught, what were they supposed to say to her? How could her father talk to her about not breaking the rules, when he was breaking the biggest rule of all himself?

Emboldened by her temper, Wendy hopped off the bench, tucked her notebook under her arm, and started walking. It wasn't far before she veered off the path and into the part of the woods they had run through on Tuesday with Dennis and Cody chasing them. She remembered calling Dennis *Fart*man, and wondered if she would be allowed to put that in the movie. Probably so. They let people swear in movies—not movies she was allowed to see, but still . . .

Here she remembered looking back over her

shoulder and Tommy yelling, "Jump!" And down the bank they went, skidding and sliding and tumbling. Wendy took the long way down this time then looked back up the bank. It was like they had fallen into a bowl, she thought, and she opened her notebook and scribbled that down, sticking her tongue out the side of her mouth as she tried to write and walk and look around all at the same time.

Tommy had rolled the farthest, stopping right—

The scream that split the air came so fast and so instinctively that Wendy didn't even realize it had torn up from her own lungs. There in the grave, half-covered with dead leaves and branches, Cody Roache sat crying, with blood all over his hands and his stomach and his face.

He looked right at Wendy and sobbed, "Dennis killed me!"

Dennis bolted out from behind a tree. He grabbed at Wendy, catching hold of one braid and yanking her off her feet as she tried to run. Her notebook went flying. She landed on all fours and barely managed to dodge sideways enough that Dennis missed her back as he plunged down with the knife.

Scrambling to get up, looking over her shoulder at Dennis, she ran smack into Cody, and they both fell flat. Wendy was covered in blood as she rolled off him and started running, Dennis Farman right on her heels.

Dennis was bigger and stronger, but Wendy was

quick. Every time he lunged for her, she managed to arch her back and evade his grasp—until the toe of her sneaker hit squarely on the exposed root of a tree.

She fell hard, the wind going out of her in one big, painful *whoosh!*

"I hate you! I hate you! I hate you!" Dennis screamed over and over.

He fell to his knees on top of her, the knife flying out of his bloody hand as he drew his arm back to stab her. He didn't seem to notice it was gone and kept bringing his arm down again and again, as if he was driving the knife into her, his fist thumping so hard against her chest she saw stars with each contact.

Wendy's vision filled with black lace. She couldn't get a breath. Dennis was on top of her. She was going to die.

# 65

Tommy spent the day walking on eggshells. It was something he was very good at because he had a lot of practice doing it. He had always known how to read his mother's moods—or anyone's for that matter. He never understood people who couldn't.

His father had left the house very early to help with the search for the missing lady. Tommy had asked to go along, but his dad had explained they didn't allow kids to be there.

That didn't make sense to Tommy, since kids could look for things just as well as adults—and probably better. They were closer to the ground and they paid more attention to what was around them. And besides that, he had already seen a dead body before, so it wasn't like he would be afraid if he saw one again.

But it didn't matter, because his dad left him once again to deal with his mother, who got out of bed mad, slamming doors and drawers, muttering to herself. That was the worst thing: when she talked to herself under her breath, so angry, her eyes hard and cold.

She went through the house "cleaning," as she called it. Throwing things left and right, out of drawers, onto the floor—magazines, newspapers, mail. She went through the kitchen throwing out food, throwing things out of the refrigerator into the sink.

Later, when she had calmed down, she would go through the house again, following the trail of destruction, making sure there would be no signs left of what she had done. By the time his father got home, the house would be perfectly neat and clean, like nothing had ever happened.

Tommy stayed in his room for most of her tirade, but knew that eventually she would come in there as well, and if he hadn't done a perfect job of keeping his room neat, he would have a BIG problem. His mother would tear the sheets from his bed, throw his toys in the garbage, tear up papers he had brought home from school to save because he had gotten stars on them from Miss Navarre, or she had written a note on them saying how well he had done.

He knew how his mother would particularly be after those because she was still angry at Miss Navarre. More than ever after Detective Mendez and the FBI man had been there.

Tommy made a special effort to hide the things he valued most, pressing papers between the mattress and box spring of his bed.

He wished he dared to just leave, but he didn't. Instead he slipped from his room and followed two rooms behind his mother, going through the mess to make certain she hadn't thrown out anything of value. He sometimes found things like watches and jewelry, money, checks, all kinds of things that his mother would never throw away if she hadn't been in one of her moods.

Today was no exception. Tommy sorted out the good things and put them back where they belonged. Books, magazines, and drink coasters in the family room. Figurines and photographs in the living room. In his parents' room—where he had to be extra careful not to be caught—he saved his father's ring from college and a tangle of jewelry his mother had thrown in the wastebasket.

When she finished her tirade, she was in the study, sitting on her knees sobbing amid a pile of papers, letters, newspaper clippings. And like always when she started crying, Tommy went in and sat with her, and held her hand. He told her that he felt bad for her, and he was sorry for her, and he hoped she would feel better soon.

It wasn't a job a kid should have, but that was just his life.

He wished he could have just gone to the park on a Saturday like everyone else.

# 66

"Steve wouldn't kill Lisa," Crane said. "He cared for her."

"So much that he would only see her in the dead of night?" Mendez asked. "Wouldn't admit it to anyone, wouldn't let her tell anyone?"

"He's a married man."

"He should have thought of that before he unzipped his pants," Mendez said.

Crane got up and started pacing, his hands on his hips. "I'm really not comfortable talking about this."

"You said Steve is a complicated guy. In what way?" Mendez asked. "He's your friend, man. Tell me about him."

"I just meant that Steve is very driven. He's passionate about the work he does for the center. Steve comes from a tough background—single mom, not much money, desperate times. He had to fight his way to get where he is—including being married to Sara. She's from a good family, educated, beautiful."

"She's a trophy for him?"

"No! I don't know." He shook his head and closed his eyes. "I should have kept my mouth shut. Why don't you talk to Steve? I'm sure he'll tell you anything you want to know. He doesn't have anything to hide."

"Except a mistress," Mendez said. "What time did you leave O'Brien's?"

"One thirty, quarter to two."

"Where did you go from there?"

"I went home. Steve was going to check into the Holiday Inn."

"All right," Mendez said, getting up from his chair.

Crane looked at him, a little suspicious. "I can go?"

Mendez spread his hands. "Sure."

Peter Crane breathed a sigh of relief and started for the door. Pausing with his hand on the knob.

"How is Karly Vickers?" he asked. "Has there been any news?"

"Much better," Mendez lied. "She's a tough cookie. The doctors are pretty confident she's going to come around soon."

"Really?"

"I guess there won't be any questions left then."

"I guess not."

The door opened from the outside then, and

Hicks leaned into the room, a grim look on his face. "We've got to go. There's been a stabbing in Oakwoods Park. Multiple victims."

The EMTs were already on the scene and loading a gurney into their bus when Mendez and Hicks pulled into the parking area.

"Who's our vic?" Mendez asked, running up to the back before they could close the doors.

"A kid. He's bleeding out! We gotta go!" The tech shouted at his driver. "Go! Go!"

A couple of deputies slammed the back doors shut, and the rig turned around, siren bleating, scattering onlookers like sheep.

"What the hell's going on?" Mendez called out, holding up his shield.

One of the deputies said, "The call-out was a stabbing with multiple victims—both children. They're both on their way to Mercy General."

"Does anybody know what happened?" Hicks asked.

"Several people reported hearing a little girl scream. They ran over here," he said, pointing to the woods in the direction of the place where Lisa Warwick's body had been found. "And they found the subject attacking the little girl. Blood was everywhere."

"Mother of God," Mendez said. "And the subject?"

"You aren't gonna believe this," the deputy said, leading them over to his cruiser.

Sitting in the backseat with his hands cuffed together with zip ties was Dennis Farman, covered in blood and staring blankly straight ahead.

They drove directly to the hospital. Hicks got on a phone to call Dixon. Mendez watched the medical team working frantically on the boy. The same doctor who had worked on Karly Vickers barked out orders the staff jumped to carry out. There was blood everywhere. Too much blood to have come from so small a patient—and have him live, Mendez thought.

Jesus. He had already known Dennis Farman was a disturbed child, but who the hell could have predicted this? Kids beat each other up on the playground; they didn't pull knives and go berserk.

What could drive a child to that kind of violence?

There had to be a lot more to the story of the Farman household than a mother who drank a little and a drill sergeant for a patriarch. Dennis hadn't gone off this deep end because he got spanked for cutting school.

Suddenly the doctor was shouting at his staff to GO! and half a dozen people bolted into action, wheeling the gurney out of the exam room and down the hall. Mendez had to jump back out of the way.

The doctor pulled off his bloody gown and gloves and threw them on the floor in disgust.

"How does it look for him?" Mendez asked, holding up his shield.

"He's lost a lot of blood and he's still bleeding. I think the blade might have nicked his spleen."

"Will he make it?"

"He's on his way to surgery. He can live without a spleen. He can't live with less than half his blood supply. We'll know within the hour. Do you have any idea who did this to him?"

"Another kid," Mendez said. "Where's the other victim?"

"Room three. Another kid? What's the world coming to?"

"Nothing good. Have you had any word on Karly Vickers?"

"She's up in ICU. Stable."

"Conscious?"

"Don't get greedy. She's in a coma. She should be dead."

The big glass doors whooshed open and a panicked couple—Renee Roache and her husband—rushed in, Mrs. Roache sobbing hysterically.

"That'll be the Roaches," the doctor said. "I'd better go talk to them."

Mendez turned to go down the hall.

"Frank's not working today," Hicks said, joining him. "Dixon's got everyone looking for him. How's the kid?"

"We'll know within the hour. He's on his way to surgery. The other vic is down here."

Wendy Morgan sat on the table looking like a refugee from a horror movie with blood on her face, on her clothes, on her hands. Mendez showed his badge to the nurse standing beside her, holding her hand.

"Wendy," he said with genuine concern. "How are you, sweetheart? Are you hurt?"

Big tears welled up in the cornflower blue eyes. "Dennis killed Cody!"

"No, honey. Cody's hurt pretty bad, but he's not dead."

"Dennis had a knife!" she exclaimed. "He tried to stab me with it, but I think he dropped it or something because he was just hitting me over and over with his fist, and I couldn't breathe, and then I saw—like—stars, and I thought I was going to die, but then somebody grabbed Dennis and dragged him away, and I really wish my mom would get here!"

"She's on her way, honey," the nurse said.

"And my dad too."

"I don't know if they've found him yet, Wendy," the nurse said. "But your mom will be here any minute."

"You hang in there, Wendy," Mendez said, giving the little girl's shoulder a squeeze. "We'll check back with you later."

"The world's going to hell on a sled," Hicks said as they went back out into the hall.

"Before it gets there, let's go upstairs," Mendez

said. "Maybe we'll witness a miracle and Karly Vickers can name our killer. I want that guy in hell before Armageddon."

They took the elevator to the fourth floor and went through the glass doors into the intensive care unit. The only sounds were the beeps of monitors and the sighs of respirators. As they approached the nurses' station, Mendez felt compelled to speak in a hushed whisper as if he were in church or the library.

They both held up their badges. Mendez said, "We're here to check on Karly Vickers. Is her doctor available?"

"He's with another patient at the moment."

"We'll wait."

"Her room is right over there. You can wait with her friend."

"Her friend?" Mendez asked, immediately thinking Jane Thomas.

But when they turned in the direction she indicated the person staring in at Karly Vickers through the glass partition was Steve Morgan.

# 67

"No law enforcement agent can legally talk to the boy without a parent or guardian present," Dixon said. "I've got everyone looking for Frank, but no sign of him. And no sign of Mrs. Farman, either."

They stood in the coffee room watching Dennis

Farman on the monitor. The boy had not moved since he had been put in the room.

Anne stared at the black-and-white image of Dennis, thinking he looked very small from the point of view of the video camera high up on the wall. He sat drawing with his finger on the table-top, looking strangely calm.

Vince had come for her, catching her just as she had been leaving the house to go grocery shopping. There she had been, trying to do one normal thing, and suddenly an FBI agent was asking her to come to the sheriff's office to speak to her student who had allegedly knifed two kids in the park.

She was beginning to think she would never know "normal" again.

"I've called Child Protective Services, but Vince suggested you're probably more qualified than anyone to try to communicate with him," Dixon said. "You certainly know him better than anyone here."

Detective Hicks had called with the names of the two children Dennis had attacked: Cody and Wendy. Cody had been taken to surgery. Anne could only imagine how terrified he must have been. Wendy had no life-threatening wounds. She had been lucky by comparison. But she had already been through an ordeal with Dennis trying to shove a dismembered finger down her throat. Now this.

"I'm not qualified for this," she said. "I can

handle a fight on the playground. But this . . ."

"You're more qualified than any of the rest of us, Anne," Vince said. "The boy needs someone to try to reach out to him. At least until his parents get here. He hasn't said a word to anyone."

Anne stared at the monitor, at Dennis. He was eleven years old and he had tried to murder two other children. "What if I say the wrong thing? What if I make it worse?"

"He knifed a ten-year-old boy," Vince said. "How much worse could you make it?"

Anne thought back to Thursday—God, was that all? Two days ago?—to Dennis's outburst and what she had told him as they sat together, alone in the classroom. She had told him she would be there for him. She knew he had no one else on his side.

"All right."

She went into the hall with Vince, then took a deep breath and let it out as he opened the door to the interview room for her.

"I'm right out here if you need me," he whispered.

Anne nodded and went into the room.

Dennis wouldn't look at her. He stared down at the blank tabletop, drawing patterns on it with his finger. Anne studied him, wondering if she had ever really noticed that his hair was so red, or that his ears sat a little too low on the sides of his head. Someone had taken him out of his blood-stained shirt and jacket and put him in a man's sheriff's office T-shirt that swallowed him up.

"Dennis," she said softly, carefully easing herself down onto the nearest chair as if she was afraid he might spook like a wild pony.

"I know something really bad happened today. I don't know exactly why." Her voice was gentle, quiet, the kind of voice she might use to tell a bedtime story or confess an innocent secret to a friend. "I won't pretend that I understand what you're going through. I don't have any idea. I have a feeling you've seen things and been through things I wouldn't want to imagine."

He lifted his head then and looked at her. A bruise was spreading across his left cheek, blackening the skin beneath his eye. Coagulated blood knit together his swollen lower lip.

"When can I go home?"

The question was stunning. He wasn't joking. He wasn't being sarcastic. An hour ago he had stabbed a playmate so seriously the child could die, and Dennis just wanted to go home.

"Dennis, you won't be going home," she said. "You hurt somebody really badly."

"Just Cody," he said, as if Cody Roache was no more important to him than a toy he had broken.

Anne didn't know what to say. She didn't know if this was a hard-wired part of Dennis Farman's psyche or a by-product of the day's trauma. Could he really care so little about the only boy who had ever tried to be his friend?

"I'm so sorry, Dennis," she said. "I wish I could have helped you sooner. I wish I had a clue how to help you now, but I don't. All I can do is sit here with you until someone who knows more than I do can come and try."

"What'll happen to me?" he asked.

As horrible as his crime was, Anne felt her heart break for Dennis Farman. She didn't know if it was a trick of the harsh lighting or the dimensions of the room, but he seemed smaller to her now than he had in her classroom. And she had the strangest, saddest feeling as she sat there watching him that he was getting smaller and smaller before her very eyes, that the light inside him was getting dimmer and dimmer, and before long he would disappear altogether.

"The sheriff is trying to find your mom so she can come and be with you," she said. "Do you know where she might be?"

He looked up at her for the first time since she had walked in.

"She's dead," he said without emotion. Then he looked past her to the glass inset in the door.

Anne turned to see Frank Farman's face in the window.

"He killed her."

# 68

"I thought the rules up here were: authorized personnel and family only," Mendez said.

Morgan turned and looked at him. "Detective. Jane needed a break. Or, I should say, I made her take a break. She's down the hall in the family room resting. She made me promise to stand here and come get her if anything changed."

"Miss Vickers's family hasn't arrived yet?" Hicks asked.

"Not yet." He turned and looked at the girl in the bed again. "It didn't seem right to just leave her. That doesn't make sense, does it? I mean, she doesn't know we're standing here. She's not aware of anything at all as far as we know."

"Or maybe she's playing it all through her mind," Mendez suggested. "What happened to her, who did this to her. And if she can just fight her way up through the fog, she'll tell us everything."

"What are the odds she'll remember anything?" Morgan asked. "The doctor said it'll be a miracle if she survives at all. I wouldn't hang your hat on getting the story from her."

"But here's the thing with my job, Mr. Morgan," Mendez said. "Even dead victims tell their stories, one way or another. It just takes longer."

"You always get your man? We'll all hope so."

"We'll have to spell you here, Mr. Morgan," Hicks said. "You're needed in the ER."

They accompanied Steve Morgan to the ER and hung back at the edge of the Morgan family drama. Sara Morgan had arrived to comfort her daughter. The parents managed to hide all but the edge of the tension between them as they let Wendy take center stage and tell her story.

Mendez answered what questions he could as to what would happen to Dennis Farman, though he admitted he had never come across such a young violent offender. He had no idea if there was any precedence to guide the powers of the judicial system on how to deal with him. The only thing he knew with certainty was that Dennis Farman would not be going home that night, or any night soon.

The doctor informed them that Wendy could go home. She had a badly bruised sternum and ribs, but considering what had happened to Cody Roache, she was a lucky girl.

"Will Cody be all right?" Wendy asked.

"He'll be in the hospital for a few days, but he'll be all right," the doctor announced to the relief of everyone. The surgeons had managed to repair the damage to his spleen and stop the internal bleeding. He was a lucky little boy.

"This guy has a damned strange definition of luck," Hicks commented as they loitered in the hall, waiting for the Morgans to leave. "Luck would have been never running into Dennis Farman in the first place."

They followed the Morgans out to the parking lot where Steve lifted Wendy out of the obligatory wheelchair and into her mother's minivan.

"Daddy, are you coming home?" the little girl asked, her cornflower blue eyes as big and hopeful as she could make them.

"I'll be along soon, honey. Don't you worry."

But as Sara and Wendy Morgan drove away, and Steve Morgan turned to go to his own vehicle, Mendez stepped in his way.

"We have a couple more questions for you, Mr. Morgan."

Morgan only hesitated a second, then walked around him. "It's been a long day, Detectives. I'm going home."

Mendez fell in step beside him. "When I asked you this morning where you were at three A.M., you failed to mention the bed you were supposedly sleeping in was at a hotel."

"You didn't ask."

"It's really not a good idea for you to blow us off, Mr. Morgan," Hicks said, striding along on Morgan's other side. "It gives us the impression you're being arrogant in a situation that calls for cooperation."

"I'm not being arrogant. I'm irritated," Morgan said. "I give a big part of my life to the Thomas

476

Center and the clients there. I don't appreciate being considered a person of interest because of my generosity."

"That's not why we're looking at you, if that makes you feel any better," Mendez said. "We're looking at you because you're being less than cooperative and because we know you were having an affair with one of the victims."

"You don't know—"

"Yes, we do. Peter Crane confirmed it for us. He also told us you were planning to spend last night at the Holiday Inn because your wife threw you out."

Morgan stopped beside a low-slung black Trans Am. "My marriage is not your business."

"Could be a good motive, though," Hicks said. "If Lisa Warwick was putting pressure on you, threatening to tell your wife—"

"And what's my motive for attacking Karly?"

"Maybe you just plain enjoy it," Mendez suggested.

He looked through the back passenger window into the car. There was a black Members Only jacket on the backseat, and a couple of baseball caps. A box holding MISSING posters of Karly Vickers. On the floor was a dusty pair of hiking boots. There were no instruments of torture, no obvious souvenirs from victims, nothing that could have given him probable cause to search the car.

"I understand you have a job to do," Morgan said. "But you're wasting valuable time on me when maybe you should be looking a little closer to home."

"What's that supposed to mean?" Hicks asked.

"Ask Dixon. Let's just say the interest some of your deputies take in the women from the center is less than altruistic in nature."

They watched him drive away, both of them at a loss for words.

Finally, Hicks said, "What now?"

"I think if Dixon wanted to tell us something, he would have told us already."

"Right," Hicks agreed, and started back toward the hospital. "Let's ask Jane Thomas."

# 69

"He's lying!" Farman shouted.

"Frank, sit down and shut up," Dixon ordered.

They had gone into the interview room next door to where Farman's son had just declared him a murderer. Despite Dixon's order, neither of them sat. They were two broad-shouldered men with their arms crossed, each of them laying claim to his section of the room.

Vince watched them on the monitor, knowing this wasn't going to go well.

"I was told he'd been in a fight," Farman said. "Was that just a lie to get me down here so you could accuse me of something, Cal? What the hell?"

"Dennis wasn't in a fight, Frank. He attacked two kids in Oakwoods Park. He stabbed a boy. The child could die. Dennis is under arrest."

Farman's face dropped. "What? He did what?"

"He stabbed a boy. The boy is in surgery. He might not make it, Frank."

Now Farman sat down as if his legs wouldn't hold him up any longer. He looked dazed.

"I don't understand," he said, almost to himself. "I don't understand what's wrong with him. You know Sharon was drinking when she was pregnant with him. He's never been right."

"I brought his teacher in because I know she has some rapport with the boy," Dixon said.

"Oh, great!" Farman said. "That snotty little bitch. Who knows what she's put in his head. She's got a problem with men—"

"Can it, Frank," Dixon snapped. "Stay on point here. We're talking about your eleven-year-old son committing a felony. I'm trying to decide where to house him. He's too young to go to juvenile detention, let alone jail."

"This is . . . I can't believe this is happening."

"Where's your wife, Frank?" Dixon asked. "We've been trying to reach her. Now your son tells us she's dead."

"That's ridiculous."

"Why would he make that up?"

"Why would you believe him?" Farman countered angrily. "Jesus, Cal! We've known each other a dozen years. We've been through it together. And you turn on me like a fucking snake! I don't get it. A week ago we were friends. I was your goddamn right hand!"

"I haven't turned on you, Frank," Dixon snapped back. "I'm doing my damn job! How hard do you think this is for me? My right-hand man is acting like a suspect. My right-hand man can't account for himself when a girl was abducted. My right-hand man can't tell me why his kid was in possession of the finger of a murder victim! Don't give me all this wounded-friend bullshit!"

Vince went across the hall and knocked on the door before sticking his head into the room. "Sheriff, you have a phone call. It's urgent."

Dixon gave his right-hand man a final scathing look and exited the room. He was red in the face and breathing too hard.

"What's the call? Is it Mendez?"

"The call is, You need to step out, boss," Vince said. "This isn't going anywhere good."

Dixon jammed his hands at his waist and breathed in and out, visibly reining himself in.

"Let me talk to him," Vince said. "I got no stake in him. I don't know him from anyone. It'll be easier for me to get what you need."

Dixon nodded.

Vince walked into the interview room, coffee in hand, and took a seat at the table, turning his chair a little sideways so he could comfortably cross his legs in front of him.

Farman glared at him. "What the fuck are you doing here?"

"You should be happy to see me, Frank," Vince said evenly. "I'm fucking Switzerland. I don't know you. I got no history with you. I got no beef with you. There's nothing personal going on here. I've got some questions. You've got the answers. It's all good."

Farman said nothing, but Vince could see him settle with the idea somewhat. He was going to have to answer these questions. Better to answer them with no emotion involved.

"So where's your wife?" Vince asked. "She should be part of the discussion about your son. Let's just get hold of her and clear this up."

"She left," Farman said.

"And went where?"

"I don't know. We had an argument last night, and she left."

"See?" Vince said, lifting his hands. "There's always an explanation. Was that so hard?"

Farman said nothing.

"So, what happened?" Vince asked. "She got pissed off, took off, went to her mother's, something like that?"

"I don't know where she went. I admit I had too

much to drink at dinner. I was an ass. Later I passed out. When I woke up this morning, she was gone."

"Does she have a friend, a sister, or someone nearby?"

Farman shook his head, but to himself, as if he was having an internal conversation, considering and discarding answers. "I don't know her friends."

"Do you have kids besides Dennis?"

"Sharon's two girls from her first marriage. They're staying with friends or something. They're teenagers. I don't try to keep track of them."

"You can see here, Frank, where this gets sticky," Vince said reasonably. "Nobody knows where Sharon is, and your son is saying she's dead and you killed her. If you weren't in a uniform, what do you think would happen about now?"

"If I was smart, I would ask for a lawyer," he said quietly.

"Is that what you want to do? You know what happens then, Frank. Everything goes totally by the book. You know the book inside and out. The lines of communication shut down. Or you can let your people go to your house, have a look around, see that everything is fine. You dig up the phone numbers of Sharon's friends and family, and she's contacted and everything is good.

"You shut it down now, you know where everyone's head goes. You had too much to drink, you were pissed off about Dixon taking you off the team. You got into it with the missus, she said the wrong thing, you lost your temper. One thing led to another, things got out of hand, you panicked . . ."

Farman took a big breath, heaved a big sigh, put his face in his hands for a moment.

*Come on, come on* . . . Vince could feel he was on the edge of saying something. The moment hung there, getting heavier and heavier. And then it was gone.

"Dixon wants to search my house, fine," he said, though he clearly was pissed off at the idea. "I've got nothing to hide."

Vince nodded. "Okay."

"But he has to do it himself. I don't want Mendez in my house again."

"Fair enough."

"I want to see my son now."

"You know that's not going to happen until your wife shows up."

"Then I'll go," Farman said, standing up. "I've got to get the boy a lawyer."

Vince nodded and rose from his chair. "This is a tough situation, Frank. I'm sorry."

Maybe the guy was a dick. Maybe he was worse than a dick. That didn't make what was going on with his son any less a tragedy. If the man had any humanity at all, that had to hurt.

Farman nodded and walked out into the hall where Anne had just stepped out of the room next door.

"You put that in his head, didn't you?" Farman said to her.

Anne stood right up to him. "Yes, because you wrote me a ticket for driving on your lawn, I got your son to stab another child and then accuse you of murder."

"I told you before to mind your own business," Farman growled, stabbing a finger at her.

"Your son *is* my business, and somebody should have stepped in a long time ago and done something. Now look what's happening to him."

"That's not my fault," Farman argued.

"He can't be *your* son without *you* taking responsibility," she said fiercely. "He didn't turn out this way by accident."

"You fucking little bitch," Farman said quietly, backing her into the wall.

Adrenaline surging, Vince stepped in between them, put his hands on Farman's shoulders and shoved him back against the opposite wall hard enough that he banged the back of his head.

"I was nice to you in there, Frank," he said, pointing toward the interview room as he advanced on the deputy. "You give this lady a hard time, I'm not gonna be nice. I'm gonna kick your ass up between your ears. You should leave now before that happens."

"Leave?" Anne said, incredulous, as Farman stalked off. "Isn't he under arrest?"

"They don't have anything to hold him on

besides the say-so of a mentally disturbed eleven-year-old child," Vince said. "We don't know Sharon Farman is dead, or even missing. Did Child Protective Services get here?"

"Yes, they're in with Dennis now," she said and sighed. "He wants to know when he can go home."

She wanted to cry for the boy, Vince could see. He walked her down the hall and they went out the end door to the side yard. They stood in the shade on the far side of an oak tree and he put his arms around her and just held her—and she just stood there and let him hold her, slipping her arms around his waist as if that was the most natural thing in the world.

"I'm proud of you," he said quietly.

"Proud of me? For what?" she asked, slipping out of his embrace as easily as she had slipped into it.

"You're a tough little mouse, standing up to Farman like that."

She frowned. "Look at all the damage he's done. Dennis is never going to have a normal life, is he? Whether he's in prison or not. He's never going to get over this, is he?"

Vince shook his head. "No. I'm sorry, honey. I wish I could say different, but in my experience . . . He's broken, and there's probably no fixing him."

"So what are we supposed to do?" she asked. "Throw him away? I don't like that answer."

"I know, but I don't have a better one." He reached a hand out to her and she took it without hesitation. "Maybe someday you could be one of the people who figures that out."

"Someone has to try," she said stubbornly.

"I know. I mean it. You're great with your kids. You're passionate about figuring them out and helping them. Not that teaching isn't an important job, it is. But you could be making an even bigger impact on kids that need serious help."

"I just want to do the best I can for them," she said.

Vince leaned down and kissed her softly.

"You are one incredible lady, Anne," he said, settling for those words instead of the ones that sat on the tip of his tongue—*I'm falling in love with you.*

He was forty-eight with a bullet in his head, falling in love on the third day of knowing Anne Navarre. That sounded a little crazy, even to him. But it was true . . . and he was going with it.

# 70

"I did complain to Cal about it," Jane Thomas said, pouring herself a cup of coffee. "I felt that the women from the center were being stopped with inordinate frequency. He told me I was imagining things."

"What did you say to that?" Mendez asked.

"I told him he needed to go look up the records and then he could accuse me of having a persecution complex, not before."

"When was this?" Hicks asked as they left the family waiting room and started back down the hall toward the ICU.

"Oh, we revisit this subject every eight or nine months," she said. "He claims the numbers are normal, and that maybe I have an inordinate number of bad drivers among my clients."

"Have your clients complained about any one deputy in particular?" Mendez asked.

"There are two or three regular offenders. Ask your boss."

"Did any of the women complain about the deputy that stopped them being inappropriate in any way?"

Thomas looked at him sharply. "Are you thinking one of your own people . . . ?"

"No, ma'am," Hicks said. "We're just following up on a remark someone made in passing."

She frowned and started moving slowly toward the door. "I want to go back and check on Karly."

All three of them went to stand outside Karly Vickers's room, looking in at her through the glass. Nothing had changed. The young woman lay on the bed with tubes and wires attaching her to machines and bags of fluids and blood. She looked as thin and pale as an apparition, like a vision that might fade away to nothing in the blink of an eye.

"The doctor told me she probably won't be able to see or hear," Thomas said quietly. "Can you imagine how alone she must have felt? How terrifying that must have been never to know if that monster was there with her or not, never to know what he was going to do next."

She shivered and sipped her coffee to ward off the inner chill. In her left hand Mendez noticed she held the gold necklace she had asked for that morning. She rubbed the figure of the woman between her thumb and forefinger the same absent way he had often seen his mother rub at her rosary beads, a gesture that offered a certain amount of comfort or perhaps hope.

"Her mother should be here soon," she said, glancing at her watch. "She had to wait for a friend who could drive her up here. What am I going to tell her? Your daughter came to me for help, and this is what happened?"

"You can't blame yourself, ma'am," Hicks said. "You saved her life today."

"I hope so," she murmured.

A nurse went into the room to check the monitors and make notes. When she put her hand on Karly Vickers's arm to check her IV, all hell broke loose.

The comatose woman came alive violently, arms and legs thrashing. Monitors went wild. The nurse shrieked and jumped back.

Jane Thomas ran into the room, calling out to Karly Vickers, forgetting her voice would fall literally on deaf ears.

Staff came running. A doctor called out for a sedative.

*Panic,* Mendez thought as he watched. Karly Vickers had come out of her coma and entered a state of panic. She couldn't know where she was. She couldn't see who was touching her. She couldn't hear them tell her she would be all right, that she was safe.

The thing that finally seemed to calm her was Jane Thomas pressing the gold necklace into her hand, closing her fingers over the figure of the woman with her arms raised in victory.

# 71

The Dodgers lost that day 4–2 to the St. Louis Cardinals in game three of the National League Championship series. For some reason that would stick with Tommy for the rest of his life as being his clearest memories of that day.

Bob Welch was the losing pitcher. Danny Cox got the win and Ken Dayley got the save. St. Louis second baseman Tommy Herr hit the only home run of the game in the bottom of the second inning.

None of it seemed that important at the time, however. The Dodgers were still up in the series two games to one, and Tommy had a date—sort of. His father had told him a secret while they watched the game: that they were going to see Miss Navarre while Tommy's mother was at one of her endless meetings.

This was highly exciting news because Miss

Navarre had sought out his father and asked him especially if she could meet with Tommy to talk about the things that had been happening. She was worried he might have gotten some wrong ideas. And it wasn't even a school night. Miss Navarre was making a special effort to see him on the weekend. Tommy hadn't felt that special since he won the fourth-grade science fair.

He waited until his mother was well into her preparations for her meeting before he quickly took a bath and got dressed in his good gray pants and a shirt and sweater. This was a special occasion. Miss Navarre was taking time out of her weekend for him, the least he could do was look his best.

He even had a present for her, although he wasn't sure he would be brave enough to give it to her.

He had thought and thought about what had happened the day before, and he had decided the fault was with his mother, not with Miss Navarre. His mom had twisted Miss Navarre's intentions into something bad because that was how his mother's mind worked.

Miss Navarre didn't think his dad was a serial killer or else she wouldn't have even talked to his father today. Therefore, everything his mother had done the night before—yelling at Miss Navarre in public—had been bad and wrong.

She deserved a special present as an apology. And it made sense that it should come from his mother—sort of.

He put it in a little square box like a ring would come in, and wrapped it himself with a piece of colored paper he found in a kitchen drawer where his mother kept greeting cards and stuff like that.

He hid it in his coat pocket so his mother wouldn't see it before she left, on account of she would have been REALLY mad at him. It wouldn't matter to her that it was something she had thrown out herself. She had decided Miss Navarre was her enemy, and if he didn't think the same thing, then HE was the enemy too.

Nobody knew how complicated his life was because of his mother. Although, he thought Miss Navarre would understand if he told her.

He watched from the upstairs hall window as his mother drove away for her dinner meeting. A few minutes later his father called up the stairs.

"Hey, Sport, are you ready to go?"

And a million butterflies took flight in Tommy's stomach.

# 72

"They had to restrain and sedate her," Mendez said. "She was so combative there was a chance of her disconnecting the respirator. She has too much swelling in her throat from the strangulation. The doctor doesn't think she would get enough oxygen on her own."

"Jesus," Dixon whispered, shaking his head.

"Restraints. I'm sure Jane was happy about that."

"No, but she got it. She and the girl's mother are going to take turns sitting with her. They aren't going to risk her waking up alone or with a stranger again."

"I guess we should just be relieved she's out of the coma," Dixon said. "But how the hell are we supposed to get answers from her if she can't hear the questions?"

Mendez shrugged.

They had taken over a corner of the family waiting area down the hall from the ICU— Mendez and Hicks, Dixon and Vince.

"So she's out right now?" Vince asked.

"Yes."

"I want to take a quick look at her, if that's possible. I want to see if she has the same pattern of cutting wounds as Lisa Warwick. If the pattern is consistent, then it means something specific to the offender. If we can figure out what it means, it could lead us somewhere."

"Have at it," Dixon said. "If you can get past guard dog Jane."

Leone left the room. Mendez wanted to follow him, to pick his brain as he gathered details from looking at the victim, but there was still an issue to discuss with Dixon.

"Why didn't you tell us Miss Thomas had complained to you about her clients being stopped for traffic violations?" he asked.

Dixon looked at him, taken a little off guard by the question, as if the subject was something he filed away long ago.

"There was nothing to it," he said.

"She told us she's had this discussion with you on more than one occasion. How is that not significant to us?"

"If I thought there was anything to it, I would have said so, Detective," he said, getting irritated. But he got up from the arm of the sofa he had been sitting on and started to pace, arms crossed over his chest—which told Mendez he wasn't comfortable with the subject.

"Did Jane bring this up to you?" Dixon asked.

"Actually, Steve Morgan brought it up," Hicks said.

"Don't you think Jane would have been the first person to say something about it if she felt it was significant?" Dixon said.

"Except that she trusts you. She trusts your judgment," Mendez said.

Dixon glared at him. "And you don't?"

"Don't jump on me, boss. I'm doing the job you hired me to do."

"A couple of the deputies seem to have a written a lot of stops on women from the center," he conceded. "But they're deputies who write a lot of tickets across the board. The numbers didn't bother me. And I'm sure as hell not going to tell them to treat Thomas Center clients any differently from the rest of the population."

"I just want to know one thing," Mendez said, dreading asking the question, already knowing the answer. "Is one of those deputies Frank?"

Dixon sighed heavily. "Yes. Of course. Frank leads the league in traffic citations—and in complaints from the people he's written up. That's hardly news."

"I want to see his file," Mendez said.

"I've reviewed his file."

"Yeah, well, I want to see it."

"You think I'm trying to protect him?"

"I think you and Frank go way back, and it's not appropriate or fair to you to make a call on him. Sir."

He half expected Dixon to blow a gasket. His boss was a by-the-book kind of guy, and he had toed that line so far with Frank Farman, but friendship and history could make that line blur, even with men like Cal Dixon.

But Dixon held his temper. He stopped his pacing, staring down at the gray industrial-grade carpet on the floor.

"Frank's wife is missing," he said quietly. "His son is saying Frank killed her."

Mendez felt all the blood in his body free-fall to his feet. Hicks got up from the arm on the other end of the sofa and said, "What?"

Dixon filled them in on what had transpired that afternoon while they had been at the hospital with Wendy Morgan and Cody Roache.

"Where is he now?" Mendez asked.

"Home," Dixon said. "We don't know that Sharon is dead or even missing. I've got Trammell and Hamilton calling her friends and relatives. Frank claims she left on her own. And the boy is less than reliable. I don't even know if he has a firm grasp on reality. He seems almost catatonic for the most part."

"Except the part where he said his father killed his mother," Mendez said.

"Frank let me have a look around his house. Nothing seemed out of the ordinary."

"Or he wouldn't have consented," Mendez pointed out.

"It's a catch-twenty-two," Dixon conceded. "And you know damn well I wouldn't cut him any slack on a charge like this. We simply have nothing to indicate a crime has been committed. We've got nothing to hold him on."

Mendez put his hands on his head and turned around in a circle. "What a fucking mess."

Vince approached Karly Vickers's room with the same kind of quiet respect he would have used in church. Jane Thomas sat beside the girl's bed, holding her hand, the gold necklace laced through fingers entwined.

"She's lucky to have you on her side," he said softly.

"I don't know how she's going to make it through

this," Thomas confessed. "She'd been through so much before she ever came to the center."

"She wants to live," Vince said. "Or she wouldn't be here now. She'll find a way to make it, and you'll find a way to help her."

Tears glittered in her green eyes as she looked up at him as if he might actually have an answer. "Why does it have to be so hard?"

"I don't know. I only know my part, and that's helping find the animal who did this to her. Can you help me with that?"

Jane Thomas helped him catalog the wounds Karly Vickers's tormentor had carved into her, and Vince left her with a promise to do everything in his power to bring a madman to justice.

And he walked out of the room and away from the ICU thinking the same thing she had asked him: *Why does it have to be so hard?*

# 73

When Anne saw Tommy waiting outside the pizza place it was all she could do not to break into a big smile. He had dressed up in what had to be his best outfit: smart gray pants with a buttondown shirt and a navy blue sweater under his open Dodgers jacket. If he'd worn a tie he would have looked like a miniature prep school candidate. Only the black eye Dennis Farman had given him spoiled the image.

"You look very nice tonight, Tommy."

"Thank you. So do you, Miss Navarre," he said, terribly serious.

"Thank you."

"You're welcome."

He had run out of things to say. He sighed and tried not to fidget.

Anne looked up at his father, handsome and relaxed, a pleasant smile curving his mouth. "Dr. Crane, I want to thank you for making this possible."

"Not a problem," he said. "I appreciate your concern for setting the record straight. Why don't we go inside? The smell of that pizza is too much to resist."

They went into the restaurant and found a booth. The place was booming with Saturday night customers—college kids, families, teenagers traveling in packs. Video games bleeped and growled in their own alcove at the rear of the place. Tommy was wide-eyed, taking it all in.

"We don't get to come here very often, do we, Tommy?" Peter Crane said.

Tommy shook his head.

"Tommy's mom is a member of the food police," Crane explained. "All healthy, all the time."

"And as a dentist, you must agree with that," Anne said.

"I don't think the occasional pizza is such a bad thing. Tommy and I sneak in some fun stuff every once in a while, don't we, Sport?"

Tongue-tied, Tommy nodded.

"What do you like on your pizza, Tommy?" Anne asked.

"Cheese."

"Me too. What about pepperoni?"

The shy smile tucked up one corner of his mouth as he nodded again.

"What about Brussels sprouts?"

"No!" he said emphatically, shaking his head so hard his whole body swung from side to side.

Anne laughed. "All right. No Brussels sprouts."

A waitress came and took their order for pizza with no Brussels sprouts. When she had gone, Anne looked across the table at Tommy, growing serious.

"Tommy, after seeing your mom last night, I just want to make sure you don't have the wrong idea about something," she began. "When I asked you those questions I never meant for you to think that your father might be involved in what happened, or that I might think that. Do you understand?"

"I guess," he said in a tone of voice that was less than convincing.

"You know the detectives have to ask a lot of questions when they're investigating a crime," Anne said. "They ask questions of a lot of people. That doesn't necessarily mean they believe everyone they talk to might be guilty. But they have to ask a lot of questions to try to get a clear idea of where people were when a crime was being committed. They want to know who couldn't have committed the crime as well as who might have.

"Detective Leone asked me to find out from you if your dad was home that night. And you told me he was. That's all they wanted to know."

Tommy's brow furrowed. "But why didn't they just ask my dad?"

"They did ask me," Peter Crane said. "But not everybody tells them the truth. They need to get confirmation from other people—like you or Mom."

"My dad would never kill anybody," Tommy said. "He's a good person. He doesn't even ever yell—not even at my mom. And even if he wasn't home, that doesn't mean he would kill somebody."

"No, it doesn't," Anne agreed even as she found his statement odd. *Even if he wasn't home . . .*

"My dad helps people," Tommy said. "That's what he does. Even when he doesn't have to."

"That's great," Anne said. "Your dad is a really good example for you."

"My mom says he's a pillar of the community," he said, not exactly sure what that meant, but certain it was something very admirable.

"I'm sure he is. And I'm sure you will be too, when you grow up," Anne said. "You've been through a lot this week, and you've handled it all with a lot of courage. I've been very proud of you and Wendy."

At the mention of his friend's name, Tommy's

face went very sober. "Dennis Farman attacked Wendy and Cody in the park today."

"Yes, I know," Anne said, wishing they could have gotten through the evening without this conversation. She had decided it would take her until Monday to come up with a way to explain to her students what had happened to Wendy and Cody, and what would happen to Dennis. She couldn't make sense of the senseless to herself. How was she supposed to make sense of any of this madness in a way ten-year-old children would understand?

"Wendy called and told me," Tommy said. "She said Dennis had a huge knife and he tried to cut Cody's heart out!"

"He had a knife," Anne said. "And he hurt Cody with it, but Cody is going to be all right. So is Wendy," she added, in case Wendy had taken the opportunity to embellish her part in the story as well.

"My mom says Dennis is evil and he should be locked up like an animal."

"Dennis has done a lot of bad things," Anne said. "He's a very troubled boy, Tommy. As easy as it is for us to just be angry with Dennis, we need to feel bad for him too."

"Why?" Tommy said with all the brutally honest incredulity of a child.

"Son, we can't know what makes other people do bad things," his father said. "We can't make excuses for them, but we have to understand that there are probably a lot of complicated reasons Dennis is the way he is."

Tommy made a face. "I just don't want him to be around me, that's all. If he was a grown-up and he tried to cut somebody's heart out, he would have to go to prison, wouldn't he?"

"Yes," Anne said. "And Dennis will have to pay for what he's done. But at the same time, I hope someone can help him understand why he did it."

" 'Cause his brain doesn't work right," Tommy said matter-of-factly as the waitress brought their drinks.

He was bored with the subject now, having stated unequivocally the root of the problem. He took a big gulp of his Pepsi and looked up at his father.

"Dad, can I go play Pac-man until the pizza comes? Please?"

"Sure," his father said, digging quarters out of his pocket. "Excuse yourself from the table."

"Excuse me, please, Miss Navarre."

"Have fun," Anne said, watching him dash for the arcade machines. "You have a very special little man there, Dr. Crane."

"He's a good boy. I'll thank my lucky stars today especially, after hearing about what the Farman boy did. It's difficult to imagine a child that young having that much rage inside him."

"I don't think Dennis has had the best childhood," Anne said. "We really can't know what goes on in someone else's family."

"No," Crane agreed. "Every family has its secrets, and those secrets can run deep—deeper than lies, deeper than death. And they impact every member of that family in ways we can't know."

"True enough," Anne said, thinking of her own family secrets. Her father's philandering and callous treatment of her mother had left lasting scars on her, though certainly no one outside the Navarre household knew anything other than what a model family they had appeared to be.

"I worry a little about Tommy," Crane admitted. "His mother can be a very negative influence on him. I do my best to counterbalance that aspect of my wife's personality. But will it still have an impact on Tommy? Probably. Will it drive him to knife a playmate? I don't think so, but with all this talk about serial killers this past week, you can't help but wonder what drives someone to do that."

"Hopefully the killer will be caught soon, and we won't have to think about it at all," Anne said, steering the conversation on to activities coming up on the school calendar for Tommy and his classmates, including a field trip to the Griffith Observatory in Los Angeles, which Tommy had seemed especially excited about.

She felt relieved to have set things straight with Tommy. One burden off her shoulders. She tried not to think about Dennis Farman, who was spending the night on a cot in the same interview room where she had seen him that afternoon. Instead, she tried to enjoy the pizza and the company.

As they left the restaurant and said their good-byes, Tommy's eyes suddenly got big.

"Oh! I almost forgot!"

He dug a hand in the pocket of his jacket and came up with a small, gift-wrapped box, which he presented to Anne.

"That's for you."

Anne bent down next to him and accepted the gift with a soft smile. "Thank you, Tommy. How sweet of you! You didn't have to bring me a present. Should I open it now?"

"No!" he said, blushing furiously. "Not until you get home."

"Okay." Anne leaned over and kissed his cheek. "Thank you. I'll see you Monday."

She tucked the little box in her purse and walked down the plaza thinking maybe there was hope for humanity after all.

# 74

"How do you usually spend your Saturday nights, Vince?" Hicks asked.

They were in the war room, a couple of boxes of decimated pizza spread out on the table in between stacks of files and reports. Dixon had remained at the hospital as Karly Vickers's mother had finally arrived.

"Oh, well, Saturday nights I usually take the

Concorde to Paris for dinner, then pop over to Monte Carlo for a little gambling."

"Our tax dollars at work," Mendez said.

"Seriously."

"Seriously?" Vince thought back over the last year. Most of his Saturday nights had been spent in bed, recuperating. And before that? "Pretty much the same thing we're doing here."

"That's grim, man."

"I don't have a wife. I don't have a life. I'm the perfect man for the job. How about you, Detective Hicks?"

"The second Saturday of the month is jackpot calf roping at the rodeo grounds. I'm usually winning me some money right about now."

"How about you, Tony?" Vince asked.

"Nothing special."

"Sign that man up for the FBI."

"Watch out, old man," Mendez teased. "I'll take your job."

"You're welcome to it, junior. I've done my time. I'm about ready to move on."

"You? Quit the Bureau? No way, man. You're a freaking legend."

"I'll trade places with you. I'll move here and live the good life. You head east and take up the mantle."

"If it was that easy . . ."

"You'd have to pay some dues, but hell, you're young—as you keep reminding me."

As if to punctuate the fact, his brain began to throb. He was about done in for the day, and odds were the pizza wasn't going to taste as good the second time around. He dug in his jacket pocket for the pill bottle.

Antinausea. Antiseizure. Antipain.

He tossed them back and washed them down with cold coffee.

"You pop those things like breath mints," Mendez said. "What are they?"

"Breath mints."

"Bullshit."

"Better living through chemistry," Vince said, shrugging off the topic of his health. "What have you found out about the traffic stops?"

"If Frank got a dollar for every ticket he wrote, he'd be driving a new Cadillac every year," Hamilton said. "But we all knew that."

"Complaints filed against him?"

"A few."

"By women?"

"Most of them."

"Allegations of inappropriate conduct?"

"Several," the detective said, flipping through Farman's personnel file. " 'He's rude, he's condescending, he's a bully, he's a chauvinist, he's a sexist, he made me feel uncomfortable, he made a remark about my ass.' "

"He likes to push women around," Vince said. "Any sign of Mrs. Farman yet?"

"No. We called everyone in her address book. No one has seen or heard from her."

"Wouldn't that be a hell of a deal, if Frank turned out to be See-No-Evil?" Hamilton said.

"If Frank was See-No-Evil," Vince said, "the last thing I would expect him to do would be to kill his wife. This killer is getting off on the fact that no one suspects him."

"What about his need for publicity?" Mendez asked.

"He's getting plenty. 'Investigators Baffled in Oak Knoll Murders.' 'Serial Killer Stumps Sheriff's Department.'" He held his hands up to frame the imaginary headlines.

"Meanwhile, he's walking around like the guy next door," Vince said. "He's probably bringing up the case to his neighbors, talking about it over coffee with business associates. He's loving it. Everybody looks at him and sees the perfect citizen, the perfect husband, the perfect family man, whatever. He's not going to kill his wife."

"Maybe he just lost control," Mendez ventured. "Bundy's killings at the Chi Omega house in Tallahassee, Florida, at the end of his career. He lost it. Took a stupid amount of risk. Killed in a frenzy. Kemper's last victim, the motivation for all of his murders: his mother. He killed her symbolically over and over, until he finally did it for real."

"Then why hasn't anybody found Sharon Farman?" Vince asked. "If your theory holds, he should have planted her right out in front of the building. His last grand gesture. Ed Kemper's mother was a ball-busting man hater who ragged on him so incessantly that his final act of revenge was to shove her larynx down the garbage disposal.

"Now, I haven't met Mrs. Farman," he said, "but let me take a shot in the dark here, based on what I know of her husband.

"She's on the small side. The looks are showing age because she's a nervous sort. Smokes—maybe secretly. Drinks—but definitely on the sly. Everything is neat and tidy: The house is neat and tidy, she's neat and tidy, she has a neat and tidy job working for a neat and tidy man in a position of authority. She needs to know her place, and she's happy to stay in it.

"How am I doing so far?" he asked.

"You're a fucking freak, man," Hamilton said.

"Women like Sharon Farman get beaten to death by their bully asshole husbands every day of the week," Vince said. "But they aren't the women that drive men out of their homes to kill other women."

"Janet Crane is," Mendez said.

"She sure as hell could drive me to homicide," Vince said. "What do you know about Peter Crane tonight that you didn't know this afternoon?"

"I spoke to a cop in Ventura about Dr. Crane's lady friend," Hicks said. "She's known for her special talents."

"S and M?" Mendez guessed.

"Yep."

"But I don't think See-No-Evil would be paying for rough sex," he said.

Vince arched a brow. "Why not?"

"Because it wouldn't excite him anymore. Maybe playing pretend was fine for a while, but now he's had a taste of the real thing. He doesn't want fake fear when he can have the real deal. It's not enough to pretend to strangle a woman now that he's choked the life out of a couple."

"Good theory. Very good," Vince said, pleased with his protégé. "Let's go back to something Crane said this afternoon when you were interviewing him."

Mendez went to the TV/VCR and put in the tape of the Crane interview. Vince grabbed the remote and skipped through most of it.

Crane: ". . . a married man."

Mendez: "He should have thought about that before he unzipped his pants."

Crane: "I'm really not comfortable talking about this."

Mendez: "You said Steve is a complicated guy. In what way? He's your friend, man. Tell me about him."

Crane: "I just meant that Steve is very driven. He's passionate about the work he does for the center. Steve comes from a tough background—single mom, not much money, desperate times—"

"You need to know more about that," Vince

said, hitting the Pause button. "Desperate times and a single mom could add up to something."

"His motivation for working for the rights of disadvantaged women," Hamilton said.

"Or his unhealthy attraction to disadvantaged women," Vince said. "For every good man drawn to the priesthood, there's a pedophile two confessionals down. Dig into Morgan's background—and Crane's."

# 75

Typical for a beautiful autumn Saturday night, the plaza and the streets branching off it were full of people dining, socializing, listening to music. Anne let her mind wander as she walked to her car in one of the public lots. She allowed herself the girlish luxury of wondering about the man she was attracted to. Where was he? What was he doing? Was he thinking about her?

She chided herself for being foolish. The man she was attracted to was hunting a serial killer, not sitting around daydreaming about her.

But maybe later.

She thought back to the afternoon when they had had a few moments together alone.

"How are you feeling about last night?" he asked.

She felt the blush that swept across her cheeks.

"It's a little late to be shy," he said, chuckling. "Regrets?"

"No," she said without hesitation. "I haven't quite figured that out, but no."

"Good."

She still hadn't quite figured it out. But maybe there was nothing *to* figure out. Maybe she was just a grown woman enjoying the attention of a man. Maybe she didn't need a reason or an agenda. And if she was supposed to be wondering where it would go . . . she wasn't.

She pulled out of the parking lot and headed down Sycamore.

He had said he would probably be working late, but if it wasn't too late when he hung it up, could he stop by?

Yes. Especially after the day she had had, yes. She was so tired. Tired in her soul from the things she had seen this past week. No one would ever have accused her of being Pollyanna, but she had certainly started out the week with a much sunnier opinion of the world than she had five days later. She felt like her optimism had been dragged down a gravel road behind a truck.

It would have felt very good to slip into Vince's embrace and let him tell her it would all be fine, that he would take care of her. Definitely politically incorrect for a young, single, career-minded woman to think, but there it was. She had been strong a long time. Someone else could be strong on her behalf every once in a while.

She turned onto Via Colinas and noticed the

car behind her turn as well. She turned on Rojas. It turned again.

Her heart picked up a beat. She was no longer downtown. She was on quiet residential streets. People were inside their homes, watching television—just as they would be on her block when she pulled into her driveway and had to walk to her door alone.

She could drive straight to the sheriff's office, she thought, uneasy.

As soon as the thought crossed her mind, red and blue lights came on behind her.

Groaning, she pulled over. She had probably forgotten to signal at one of those turns. That was what she got for letting her mind wander—her second traffic citation in a week.

She rolled her window down and reached for her purse.

"License, registration, and proof of insurance."

The voice came from behind a ball of blinding white light and sent an instant burst of fear through her.

Frank Farman.


Tommy felt very satisfied with himself as he and his dad cut through the dental office to their car parked in back. He felt very grown up having had a dinner meeting, like his mother was always having.

"That was fun, huh, Sport?" his dad asked.

"Yep."

"And you understand what Miss Navarre was saying about asking you those questions, right? She didn't mean anything bad by it."

Tommy nodded his head, but reserved comment. He understood that Miss Navarre hadn't meant anything bad, but he was still mad at Detective Mendez and the FBI man for what they had said to his mom the night before. They sounded like they meant every word of what they said, and what they said was that they thought his father might be a killer. It was their job to be suspicious, but it still made Tommy mad. This was probably one of those things he would automatically understand when he got older—or that's what grown-ups would tell him, at least.

"That was very nice of you to give Miss Navarre a gift," his father said. "What was it?"

"A necklace."

His father glanced over at him in the glow of the dashboard lights. "Where did you get a necklace? You never left the house today."

Tommy made a face as he contemplated his confession. "Mom threw it away. She had one of her fits this morning and she threw it away. But it was pretty, and I figured she kind of owed Miss Navarre on account of she yelled at her in public last night, so it made sense to me to give the necklace to Miss Navarre. So I did."

His father stared ahead at the road. "Your mother threw away a necklace?"

"She's always throwing stuff away. She shouldn't have nice things if she doesn't take better care of them," Tommy said.

Now he was feeling a little guilty about it, though. He knew he shouldn't get mad at his mother for things she did when she was upset. She couldn't help herself when she got that way. He was supposed to feel badly for her, not give her stuff away.

"Did I do something bad?" he asked.

"No, son. You meant well," his father said.

"It's the thought that counts," Tommy said. That was another thing adults always said that never quite made sense to him. But it sounded good.

Anne handed her papers and license out the window to Frank Farman.

"What are the charges, Deputy?"

"I ask the questions here," he said. "But then that's always your problem, isn't it, Miss Navarre? You never know when to keep your mouth shut."

"I'm pretty sure that's not against the law."

"Get out of the car," Farman ordered.

"No." Her response was automatic.

Farman yanked open the Volkswagen's door. "Get out of the car. Your careless driving and belligerent attitude are leading me to believe you might be intoxicated. You can get out of the vehicle or I can remove you from the vehicle and place you under arrest."

Then he would put her in the back of his squad

car and . . . what? She would never be seen again? The scene was fresh in her mind: Dennis saying, "He killed her," and Anne turning to see Frank Farman's face in the window.

Shaking inside, she got out of the car. Farman shined his flashlight in her eyes.

"You called Child Protective Services on me," he said. "You filed a report."

"It doesn't mean much now," Anne said, "in view of what happened today."

"That goes in my record," he said. "You embarrassed me and put something in my record that could affect my chances at promotion."

Anne didn't know what to say. *Are you delusional?* seemed a poor choice. His wife was missing. His son had attempted murder. He was worried about a notation on his record impacting his career prospects.

"You embarrassed me," he said. "Now I embarrass you. Stand with your arms straight out at your sides. How will a DUI charge go over at school, Miss Navarre?"

"I'm not intoxicated."

"Touch the tip of your nose with your left finger."

As she did, he reached out and shoved her sideways so hard she stumbled.

"That doesn't look good," Farman said. "Putting one foot directly in front the other, I want you to walk in a straight line away from me."

"You've had your fun, Deputy," Anne said,

attempting to maintain some kind of control over the situation. "You won't get a positive breathalyzer test from me. If you set out to frighten me, you've succeeded."

He kept the light in her eyes so she couldn't see, but there was nothing wrong with her hearing. She heard a gun being cocked.

"Don't worry about that breathalyzer," he said. "I've been drinking enough for both of us. You'll have a positive reading. Now walk. Back toward my car."

The shaking wasn't just on the inside now. She was genuinely scared. There was no one on the street. They were in the middle of the block— where the corner streetlights didn't quite reach.

He was holding a gun on her.

"Walk!"

She put one foot in front of the other. As she went to take the second step, Farman tripped her from behind and she fell to the pavement, scraping her hands as she tried to break her fall.

A car turned the corner from Via Colinas and the headlights splashed over her. Anne looked up at it, putting every bit of the fear she was feeling into her expression.

*Please stop.*

"It's Miss Navarre!" Tommy called out.

His father pulled to the curb in front of her Volkswagen.

"Tommy, stay in the car."

"But Dad!"

"Stay in the car!"

Anne scraped herself up off the pavement.

Farman turned away. "Sir, stay in your vehicle."

"What's going on here?"

Peter Crane. Relief ran through Anne like water.

"You're interfering in a traffic stop," Farman said. "This woman is intoxicated."

"No, she isn't. My son and I just had dinner with her. I can vouch for her. She drank a soda." He looked past Farman. "Are you all right, Miss Navarre?"

"No," Anne said. "I'm not."

"I have a phone in my car. I can call 9-1-1."

If Farman had been angry before, the fury rolled off him now in waves. Anne could feel it vibrate in the air around him. She thought he might explode with it, but he abruptly walked back to his cruiser, got in it, and drove away.

"Oh my God," Anne said, leaning against her car for support as her knees went weak.

"What the hell was that about?" Crane asked. "Is he out of his mind?"

"I think there might be a chance of that, yes," Anne said, breathless. Her heart was racing.

"What can I do for you?"

"I think you just did it," Anne said.

*I think you just might have saved my life.*

• • •

They escorted Miss Navarre home, which Tommy found both highly exciting and very important. He didn't understand exactly what had happened. From inside the car, he couldn't hear what everyone was saying. And his dad wouldn't explain it to him, but Tommy could tell he was upset about it, which meant it must have had something to do with Mr. Farman. But Miss Navarre was very grateful, and she must have thanked them ten times.

"You guys are my heroes," she said before she went inside her house.

Tommy could have floated on air.

He chattered on the rest of the way home, saying what a great team he and his dad made. What a cool night it had been—having had almost a date, and then being a hero. Wait until he told Wendy. She wasn't the only one with a story to tell now. He was a hero.

His mom's car was in the driveway when they pulled in, but even that couldn't spoil Tommy's mood. Of course he wouldn't be able to tell her what all had happened. He and his dad had gone out for pizza, that was all. The rest was their secret.

What a great night.

# 76

He had to have followed her, Anne thought as she went into the house. She sat down at the dining room table—the nearest chair. She was still shaking.

Frank Farman had to have been following her. The odds of him randomly stopping her, of all people, were too long. He had to have followed her out of the parking lot downtown. And in order for him to follow her out of that parking lot, he had to have known she would be there. He had to have followed her from home hours before.

He shouldn't have even been on the street. She couldn't imagine Dixon hadn't taken him off duty after everything that had happened.

"You forgot the ice cream," her father announced.

Anne looked up at him as he came in from down the hall, wheeling his slender oxygen tank out in front of him as if it were a dapper accessory to his ensemble of burgundy pajamas and black silk robe.

"I put it on the list, but you didn't get it," he complained. "Butter pecan. I wrote it right at the top."

"Are you kidding me?" Anne said. "I had one student try to murder another student today, and you're complaining that I forgot the ice cream?"

"I don't see what one thing has to do with the other."

"No. You wouldn't."

"A deputy stopped by here looking for you after you left for your dinner," he said disapprovingly. "I didn't raise you to be a criminal."

"You didn't raise me at all."

"He wanted to know where you had gone."

"So you told him."

"Of course. And he thanked me profusely for my annual contributions to the sheriff's fund," he added smugly.

"That's great. You might be interested to know that deputy is suspected of killing his wife last night."

"That's nonsense."

"Why am I arguing with you? You haven't even bothered to ask me why I look the way I do," Anne said, taking in her scraped and dirty hands, the dirt and a tear at the knee of her black slacks. She got up and looked at herself in the mirror over the buffet. She was as white as a sheet.

She could see her father get a face behind her.

"Because you take after your mother," he said, completely missing the point. "I'm going to bed. Without my ice cream."

Anne went into the kitchen and poured herself a glass of cabernet to steady her nerves. At least the one mystery was solved: Frank Farman had known where to find her because her own father had set him on her.

She dug Vince's pager number out of her purse and dialed it. He called her back immediately.

"How's my favorite fifth-grade teacher?"

"I'm okay."

"What's wrong?"

"I went to dinner tonight with Peter Crane and Tommy."

"How did that go?"

"It went well. Tommy and I are squared away," she said. "But on my way home something really scary happened with Frank Farman."

"Yes," he said, the tone of his voice suddenly different, cold, businesslike. Something wasn't right.

"Yes? What do you mean, yes?"

"Yes," he said again. "Frank is here right now at the sheriff's office with a gun to Cal Dixon's head."

# 77

Farman had Dixon in a chokehold, the nose of his .38 pressed to the sheriff's temple.

It had happened so quickly, so easily. No one had seen it coming—but they should have, Vince thought.

Frank Farman defined himself by his career, by his uniform. More than a decade in law enforcement with a sterling record, he could have worked in any area he chose. He could have made detective. He could have worked narcotics. As straight an arrow as he was, he was tailor-made for the Bureau or even Secret Service. But Frank Farman chose to remain in a uniform because he *was* the uniform.

Vince had known plenty of Frank Farmans over the years, going back to his days in the Marine Corps. Rigid. By the book. Humorless. It wasn't difficult for guys like that to grow a chip on their shoulder. It was almost inevitable that they became hyperfocused on every tiny aspect of the job, right down to the nuances of speech of their coworkers and superiors.

If the job was everything, then everything in their lives was about the job. And if the job was threatened, the sense of self was threatened, and guys like Frank Farman ended up in watchtowers with sniper rifles, or holding a gun to someone's head.

In a matter of a few days, Frank Farman's carefully structured world had begun to fall apart, and that buck stopped—in Farman's mind—with his old friend, Cal Dixon.

They must have arrived one right after the other, coming in the side door down the hall from the war room—Dixon first, Farman behind him. Dixon, just returning from what had to have been a taxing few hours at the hospital with Jane Thomas and Karly Vickers's mother, wouldn't have been paying attention. He was tired, preoccupied. He wouldn't have even glanced over his shoulder as he walked into the building, but Farman had to have been just a few steps behind him.

As Dixon opened the door to the conference

room, Farman was on him—arm around his throat, gun to his head—pushing him into the room and getting a wall to his back.

That was how they stood now.

Vince had just called Anne back when it happened. Never taking his eyes off Farman, he disconnected the call, put the receiver down, and punched 911 on the keypad, just in case no one out in the hall had seen what happened.

The operator came on the line. "Nine-one-one. What is your emergency please?"

"Frank," Vince said loudly. "This is a conference room. You don't come to the sheriff's office and bring a gun in a conference room. Why don't you put the weapon down? We can talk."

Farman looked right through him.

"Everybody up against that wall," he said, indicating the wall with the only door in or out. He wanted to be able to see through the glass into the hall.

Vince stayed where he was—opposite the door. Hamilton and Hicks followed his lead and stayed where they were, spreading Farman's attention over more of the room than he wanted to watch.

"Up against that wall or I blow his fucking head off!"

"Looks like that's the plan, anyway, Frank," Vince said. "You want to take the sheriff out."

He purposely didn't use Cal Dixon's name. He didn't use the word "friend." Even though Farman and Dixon had been friends for years. In Farman's eyes Dixon had betrayed him. No sense fanning that fire.

"We've all of us got guns, Frank," Vince said. "You can't shoot all of us at once. You plug the sheriff and you're done, we drop you right where you stand. Is that what you came here for? Suicide by cop? The coward's way out?"

"I'm no coward," Farman said.

"Shoot the sheriff and you're worse than a coward. You're a coward and a killer. All these years in the uniform, Frank. All these years building your rep. You want to blow it all away because you're pissed off?"

Farman didn't seem to know what to say. This wasn't going the way it had in his head when he'd been driving over, fantasizing about going out in a blaze of glory, Vince imagined.

His eyes were glassy and a little unfocused. He'd probably been drinking—probably a lot—just as he had been the night before—the night his wife went missing.

For a man who needed to be in control, losing control was a hell of a scary thing that called for a lot of alcohol to numb the fear and the pain.

"Talk to us, Frank," Vince said, moving a little to his left. Half a step, no more. "You've got something to say or you wouldn't have come here."

Dixon's face was almost purple, either from lack of oxygen or an impending stroke. It wouldn't have been the worst thing if he passed out, Vince thought. Dixon might have been thinking the same thing, but his judgment would be complicated by the fact that he and Farman went back. He wouldn't want to see Farman shot. He would want him disarmed.

"Come on, Frank," Hicks said. "Put the gun down. You've had a little too much to drink. Nobody's going to hold that against you."

Hicks shifted a little to his left.

Farman shuffled his feet, moving to his left. He still had a clear enough view of the door if he turned his head a little.

Mendez had to be in the coffee room, watching this drama unfold on the monitor, Vince thought. He had gone to use the restroom not half a minute before this mess started.

"What is it you want to tell us, Frank?" Vince asked.

Farman said nothing, but Vince could see him chewing on the words in his head. He just had to get him to spit them out. If he was talking, he wasn't shooting.

"You don't know me," he said at last, his voice as tight as a drum, vibrating with the tension within him. "My record was spotless."

"I know that, Frank," Vince said, shifting his weight from one foot to the other, moving another two inches to the left. "I looked you up. I checked you out. Your service record is impeccable.

You've always been a righteous stand-up guy. So why are you doing this?"

"It doesn't count for anything," he said. "Sixteen years. It all comes apart because I wrote some whore a traffic ticket, and the man I go back with all those years turns on me without blinking an eye."

"I know from where you're looking at it that wasn't a fair shake, Frank," Vince said. "But you're not helping yourself here. Put the gun down."

"It's too late."

"No, it's not. You've been under a lot of stress, Frank," Vince said. "Stress at work, stress at home. Everybody gets that. Put the gun down. We'll work it out. You'll take some time off, get a little help with that stress. Sixteen years with a spotless record. This night is just a blip on the screen, Frank."

Farman shook his head. "You don't know . . . It's too late."

"Your son is right down the hall, Frank. He's eleven years old. He's in trouble. He needs you, Frank. He needs his dad. You can put the gun down now. We can straighten this out so you can be around for him."

"I tried to raise him right," Farman said. "Same as my old man raised me. I don't know what's wrong with him."

"He's got some problems, Frank," Vince said,

shifting over another step. "It happens. Who knows why? You're the one who can still help him. A boy needs his dad."

The color came up in Farman's face again. He adjusted his hold on Dixon's throat, flexed his fingers on the grip of his weapon.

"Yeah? Well that bitch called Child Protective Services on me," he said. "Now I've got that on me."

A bad feeling ran through Vince's stomach as Anne's words played through his head: . . . *on my way home something really scary happened with Frank Farman.*

"It doesn't matter, Frank," he said. "That's just a misunderstanding. You've done your best. You've been a fine example to your son, Frank. Everybody here knows that. So, come on. Put the gun down and we'll sit and work this out. Your arm has to be getting tired by now."

"No," Farman said, but he was sweating like a horse, and his gun hand was trembling.

Vince hoped for Dixon's sake it had a heavy trigger.

# 78

Mendez had only stepped out of the conference room to make a pit stop. Too much Mountain Dew. He was living on caffeine. When he came back out of the men's room, the world had turned on a dime.

He watched now on the monitor in the break room, thankful the county had spared no expense in outfitting the building with state-of-the-art security. Cameras in every room but the john.

Farman had his service weapon jammed to Dixon's temple. Vince was trying to talk him down. Frank wasn't having it.

Mendez thought back to the conversation they had just been having about the possibility of Frank Farman being See-No-Evil. Vince didn't go for it, but Mendez thought it could be.

If the killer was a man in a trust position of authority, who personified that more than a man in a uniform? Moreover, he could easily incorporate himself into the investigation. He could even maneuver himself into the position of would-be hero as they pursued suspects.

"Mendez." Trammell stuck his head into the room. "We've got a big problem."

"Yeah. I'm watching it."

"No. Out front. Come on."

He looked up at the monitor, thinking he shouldn't leave. What could be more urgent?

"Really," Trammell said. "Come on. Leone can keep him talking. You've got to see this."

They jogged down the hall and out the front doors of the building, stepping into a scene out of *Close Encounters of the Third Kind*.

The grounds were being lit from above by the white glare of chopper-born spotlights. Parked smack on the lawn was a county cruiser, doors and trunk open. Deputies held a perimeter beyond the car, keeping cameras and people at bay.

"Frank's car?" Mendez shouted to be heard above the beating of the helicopter blades.

"Yeah." Trammell led him around to the back of the car and the open trunk. "And Frank's wife."

Sharon Farman lay dead in the trunk. Beaten, strangled, cut. Eyes and mouth glued shut.

# 79

Dennis lay on the cot that had been brought into the room. The detectives had brought him a TV to watch and some pizza and soda, but he didn't want to watch TV, and he wasn't hungry. Some ugly fat cowgirl deputy was supposed to be watching him, but she was sitting at the table reading a book, and she hardly ever looked at him.

All Dennis really wanted was to go home. Miss Navarre had said he wouldn't be going home. But what did she know? She didn't work for the sheriff. His dad worked for the sheriff. His dad would get him out.

But he had only seen his dad through the glass in the door. His dad hadn't come in to talk to him or to yell at him or anything. He had only looked in the window the one time, and he hadn't come back.

Maybe he never would.

Not for the first time, Dennis wondered what it

would be like to be a part of real family like the ones on TV. Like Wendy Morgan's and Tommy Crane's.

He had always hated Tommy Crane. Tommy Crane had everything. Tommy Crane was smart. Tommy Crane was talented. Tommy Crane had cool parents who gave him everything he wanted.

He had always hated Tommy Crane, but as he lay on his cot in a room in the sheriff's office with no one caring about him and no one coming to see if he was all right, Dennis thought it would be pretty darn good to be Tommy Crane tonight.

Tommy's bedtime ritual went the way it had every other night in the past week. His mother—still in a terrible mood—made him take his allergy medicine. He had then run into his bathroom and thrown it back up.

He was mad at her now. Even though he had vowed she wouldn't ruin his perfect evening with his father, she had. His mother always had to be the center of attention, and she managed that any way she could. Usually by yelling.

Tommy was tired of it. Why couldn't his mother be somebody else? Or why couldn't it be just him and his dad? Sometimes he secretly wished they would get divorced, but then he always got afraid that he would have to stay with his mother instead of his dad.

They were arguing now. Tommy crept down the

hall as far as he dared and tried to listen. He couldn't make out most of what they were saying on account of they had gone into their bedroom at the far end of the hall and shut the door.

Every once in a while a word stood out. His name. Why would you . . . ? How could you . . . ? Anne Navarre . . .

Tommy felt sick in his stomach in a way that had nothing to do with his allergy medicine. He didn't want to be the problem. Tears filled up his eyes, and he hurried back down the hall to his own room.

He didn't have to listen, anyway. He knew what would happen. His dad would get fed up with fighting, and he would leave and not come back for hours.

Only this time he wouldn't be going alone.

# 80

Anne paced around the kitchen, wondering what to do. What could she do? Nothing. She had called 911 as soon as Vince had disconnected from her line, and she had been told they were aware of the situation at the sheriff's office.

The Situation. Frank Farman was in the sheriff's office with a gun to Sheriff Dixon's head.

Anne shivered at the thought of how close she had come to disaster herself at the hands of Farman. If Tommy and his father hadn't come by . . .

She wondered now just how disturbed Frank Farman really was. Had he killed his wife? Had he killed *only* his wife?

It would have been so easy for him to pick his victims. Every woman would stop for a police car. Every woman would trust the man in the uniform who got out of that car. All he had to do was pull them over on a lonely stretch of road . . .

The breach of trust was unconscionable. And when she thought of what had been done to those women . . . No nightmare could have been more terrifying.

Shivering at the little jolts of adrenaline still zapping through her, she walked the entire house, checking windows, checking doors. Wishing Vince was there. Funny how quickly that was becoming a habitual thought.

She went into the living room and turned the television on just for the company of voices, and was presented with a bird's-eye view of the sheriff's office. The banner across the bottom of the screen read: SIEGE AT THE SHERIFF'S OFFICE: SHOWDOWN IN OAK KNOLL.

The building was surrounded by press and media helicopters sweeping the ground with spotlights.

Anne grabbed the remote and turned up the volume, catching the handsome LA reporter midsentence.

". . . suspected in the alleged beating and strangulation death of his wife, whose body was allegedly discovered less than an hour ago in the trunk of this police car located on the lawn behind me— presumably Deputy Farman's department vehicle."

*Oh my God.*

"In an even more bizarre twist, the deputy's eleven-year-old son is said to be in the building. He was arrested earlier today in connection with a stabbing in a nearby park.

"Speculation is, of course, rampant that the deputy may in fact be the notorious See-No-Evil killer who has been stalking this idyllic college town—"

Anne flipped from channel to channel to channel, every one of them showing the same scene from a different angle. None of them showing the drama going on inside the building, where lives were hanging in the balance.

# 81

"What can we do for you, Frank?" Vince asked.

They had been at it for thirty-five minutes. Him trying to pull answers out of Frank Farman, slowly trying to get him to turn his back to the door. Farman, sweating and shaking now from the strain of holding on to the sheriff and keeping the gun up to his head.

Vince was fighting his own war of attrition, his own energy reserves draining to the last drop. He was starting to feel shaky too, but if he could just keep Farman occupied for a little while longer something would happen. The deputy would give up, or the cavalry would burst in.

The trick was to keep him talking.

"You need to sit down? You need something to drink? What?" Vince asked, planting those needs in Farman's head over and over.

Farman blinked hard as sweat ran down his brow and dripped into his eyes.

"Give me something, here, Frank."

"I've given this department everything I have," Farman said, his voice cracking under the strain of his emotions.

"Then let's try to salvage some of that," Vince suggested. "You've done a lot of good, Frank. Credit where it's due. Let's don't fuck that up now."

He risked taking a full step toward Farman, angling away from the door.

"Don't come closer," Farman said.

"I just want to help you out here, Frank," Vince said, lowering his voice so Farman would have to concentrate a little harder to hear him. "Let's end this in a good way."

Farman shook his head. "It's too late. It's done. You don't know."

"What don't I know, Frank?" Vince asked. "Tell me. I'll help you any way I can."

"It's too late," he said again, his eyes filling. "She's gone."

"I know your wife left. We can find her, Frank. We can bring her here. You can talk."

Farman shook his head. "It's too late."

*Oh, shit,* Vince thought. *She's dead.* The risk of the situation going totally wrong multiplied by a hundred times. If he had killed his wife, there really was no going back for him. He would go to prison. Prison would not be an option for Frank Farman. He would choose death.

Vince took a deep breath and let it out. "I understand," he said quietly. "I get it, Frank."

"I didn't mean to," Farman whispered, a terrible pain carving deep into the lines of his face.

"Let's not make it worse," Vince said, taking another half step toward him. "Let the man go."

He kept his eyes on Farman, not flicking so much as a nanosecond's glance at the door easing open behind him.

Mendez slipped into the room, holding his breath. Three quick strides and he was behind Frank Farman, gun to the back of his head, just as Farman said, "I can't go to prison."

"Drop the gun, Frank," he said. "Right now. It's over."

Three things happened simultaneously: Cal Dixon dropped, dead weight, straight down to the floor; Vince Leone shouted *NO;* and Frank Farman put the barrel of his .38 in his mouth and pulled the trigger.

The bullet traveled on an upward trajectory

through the roof of his mouth, through his mid-brain, and exited out the back of his skull, two inches right of center, slicing a shallow groove along the outermost edge of Mendez's cheek and traveling on to bury itself in the wall.

Farman dropped where he stood like a sack of bones, falling across Cal Dixon's legs, the entire back of his head shattered like an egg.

# 82

According to the handsome reporter from LA, THE SIEGE AT THE SHERIFF'S OFFICE was coming to some kind of conclusion. Shots had been fired. The sheriff's department tactical squad had stormed the building.

Anne was shaking. The conclusion wasn't guaranteed to be everyone's happy ending. She wouldn't relax until she knew Frank Farman had been subdued, one way or another, and that everyone else was safe. That Vince was safe.

Needing something to busy her hands, she brought her purse into the living room and dumped the contents on the ottoman. She actually managed to smile as Tommy's gift tumbled out. This was what she needed—a sweet surprise.

The box was about the size and shape a ring might come in. Tommy had obviously wrapped it himself. Anne opened it as carefully as if it might contain a Fabergé egg.

Inside the box was a small puddle of fine gold chain. A necklace, she thought, a little bemused. Where did a ten-year-old boy get the money to buy his teacher a necklace? And what would she do if the gift was too extravagant? It would break his heart if she gave it back.

She emptied the box into her hand and carefully sorted out the ends of the chain, lifting it up and letting it unfurl like gold thread.

A simple gold figure dangled from the chain.

A figure of a woman standing with her arms raised in victory.

The necklace Karly Vickers had been wearing in her photo on the MISSING poster.

Anne's blood ran cold.

Her heart was beating so fast she felt faint. Her hands were trembling so the small golden figure danced this way and that, catching the lamplight.

Where could Tommy have possibly gotten this? Could there be any reasonable explanation that he would have access to a piece of jewelry given only to the women who made it through the Thomas Center program and graduated to independent living?

Her brain stalled as she tried to make sense of it. Had he found it in the woods? Would Lisa Warwick have had one too? It could have fallen in the dirt and leaves. Tommy could have picked it up during that time he and Wendy had been sitting waiting outside the yellow crime-scene tape—the time between finding the body and when she had gotten there.

That didn't ring true, but her brain wanted to believe it anyway. Funny how the mind would willingly twist itself into a pretzel trying to make sense of something using just the incomplete information it had, filling in its own blanks.

If Frank Farman was the killer, as the news-people were speculating, maybe Dennis had the necklace, and Tommy somehow had gotten it from Dennis.

Right. Like Dennis would give Tommy anything. Dennis would have beat up Tommy to get the necklace from him. There was no version of that story that worked in the reverse.

Wendy's father did a lot of work for the center. Maybe somehow Wendy had come by the necklace and Tommy got the necklace from Wendy.

Peter Crane donated his services to the center.

But only women who graduated the program got the gold necklace. Not even Jane Thomas herself wore a gold one.

Of course there would be a perfectly reasonable explanation for it, she thought. There was no reason to find it troubling . . . and yet she did.

She gathered the necklace into one hand and walked around with it in her fist, as if she thought it might speak to her somehow.

She would have to ask Tommy. Or maybe she

would bring it up to his father. There would be an answer.

Sooner rather than later, she thought, as the doorbell rang, and she opened the door to Peter Crane.

# 83

"You're going to have a scar," Vince said.

"Just one?" Mendez asked.

"The ladies will find that one sexy," he said, pointing to the angry red line that creased the detective's cheek. "The ones they can't see . . ."

He shrugged and sat down on the stone bench beside Mendez, and leaned his forearms on his thighs.

They sat outside, neither of them noticing the damp chill of the night air. It smelled like lavender and rosemary with a hint of the ocean that stretched beyond the small mountains to the west. It didn't smell like gunpowder or death.

The media had given up for the night, Dixon shutting them down and sending them on their way. What had happened inside the sheriff's office might have made for compelling news, but it was also a family tragedy, and enough was enough for one night.

The paramedics had come and gone. Mendez had refused the ride to the hospital. Once he had showered the blood and brain and bone fragments off, a little cut on the cheek didn't seem like anything to lose time over. He could have just as easily been as dead as Frank Farman.

"You want to share some of that pharmacy you're carrying around on you?" he asked.

Vince dug the pill bottle out of his jacket pocket and shook a few into his hand.

"I recommend the long white one," he said. "Unless you're thinking about having a seizure. Then I'd go for the pink one."

Mendez arched a brow. "A seizure?"

"The bullet went in right here," Vince said, pointing just beneath his right cheekbone where an odd smooth shiny patch of new skin smaller than a dime marked the spot. People rarely noticed the scar for what it was. The mustache he had grown since Mendez had last seen him was a far more noticeable feature.

"Bullet?"

"Do I need to call the paramedics back here?" Vince asked. "You're repeating me."

"What bullet?"

"If only I'd seen it coming," he said wistfully. "I could have turned my head a little, maybe got a nice razor line like you. Or maybe ended up with an eye patch. My ex-wife used to have a thing for pirates in the romance novels."

"What happened?"

"The *Reader's Digest* version: a junkie mugger with a cheap .22. That's the thing about those small caliber handguns—what goes into the vic doesn't always come out."

"You're walking around with a head full of lead?" Mendez said, incredulous.

"Explains a lot, doesn't it?"

"Actually, yeah."

"I'm officially on a medical leave."

"Why didn't you say something?"

"Uh . . . because I don't want anyone to know," Vince said. "Call me paranoid, but I think people treat a guy different when they know he's got a bullet in his head."

"You should be dead."

"Yeah. But I'm not," he said with a shadow of the big white grin. "Life's a funny old dog. Don't take it for granted, kid."

They were quiet for moment. A couple of county cruisers rolled past them into the back parking lot. Just another night at the SO now. The show was over.

"You really are going to quit, aren't you?"

Vince nodded. "If I didn't know it when I came out here, I know it now. I know it tonight.

"You don't want to end up like old Frank, kid; just a hanger for a uniform," he said. "Nothing means anything to you except the job. It's who you are. It's what you are. Been there, done that, time to go.

"Love what you do. Don't get me wrong. Have passion for it. But don't make it your only mistress."

"What will you do?"

"I want to do some teaching, some consulting, a little recruiting for old time's sake," he said. "But I really want the wife and the life. And at the end of the day, I want a soft place to put my bullet-riddled head that isn't a cheap pillow at a Holiday Inn. Time for a young hotshot like yourself to move in and for me to move on."

"You think I could make it to Behavioral Sciences?"

"You'd have to put in some field time, but yeah. You've got a good head for it, Tony. I'd like to see you think about it, anyway."

"I will."

"You poaching my best detective, Vince?" Cal Dixon said, wandering over to take the last spot on the bench. Like Mendez, he had showered and changed clothes in the locker room, trading the uniform with Frank Farman's blood on it for jeans and a sweater.

Vince spread his hands. "What can I say? I'm a son of a bitch. I want him to be all he can be."

"I'll let it slide," Dixon said. "You saved my ass tonight."

"You did your part. I'm just a loudmouth. The nuns used to kick my ass for running my mouth like that," Vince said. He let a beat pass, then changed his tone. "I'm sorry about Frank."

Dixon shook his head. "You think you know a guy . . ."

"You did," Vince said. "Once. People change. Life changes them."

"I just couldn't see him doing the things that were done to those women."

"Farman didn't kill those women," Vince said.

The men on either side of him sat up straight in shock, and said, "What?"

"Farman killed his wife. He wasn't See-No-Evil."

"But it all fits," Mendez argued.

"Almost. But not quite."

"But Vince, I saw what he did to his wife. She looked just like the others—"

"And why wouldn't she?" he asked. "Frank knew the details of those cases."

"You think he just pulled a copycat?" Dixon asked.

"My story of Frank Farman goes like this," Vince said. "Last night Frank got drunk, he got mean, he beat his wife. Not for the first time, but this time it went wrong, and she died. But Frank's a smart guy when he sobers up in the light of day. He knows he's got a lot to lose. He figures he can make his wife's death look like the other murders. Hang it on a real bad guy. It was an accident, anyhow, and he'll never do another bad thing in his life, so why should he go to prison?

"He *can't* go to prison, he's Frank Farman, Chief Deputy. Four more years working up to his twenty, and he's got a boatload of commendations.

He should be sheriff one day, damn it. He's worked his ass off for it.

"So he does a copycat job after the fact—glues her eyes and mouth shut, cuts her up. She's dead already. It's not like he's hurting her.

"He's keeping his cool at this point. He's got to do what he's got to do. It's business now. He figures he'll plant her someplace once it gets dark. Only Frank's day goes from bad to worse, to worse still.

"His kid tries to kill someone, then fingers him for killing his wife. He never counted on that. The people he respects most—yourself, Sheriff—are already looking at him sideways on account of him writing up the Vickers girl, and the business with the finger. Above anything else that's happened to Frank, he can't take that: tarnish on his image. He's all about the image.

"So now he's starting to fray around the edges. He's not a killer by nature, so that's weighing on him. He can't stand people thinking he's a bad cop, he's a bad father. He goes home. He starts drinking. Then Child Protective Services pays a visit because Anne Navarre called them yesterday and reported him for possible abuse. More tarnish on the armor.

"Life's all bad now for Frank. The wheels are coming off the tracks and he can't stop the train. In his mind he's done everything right—except for accidentally killing the missus—and he wants someone to take the blame."

543

"Me," Dixon said.

"You," Vince said. "You should have trusted him. You should have taken him at his word. You took him off the task force. That's when things started going wrong. Must be your fault. And here we are."

Dixon looked at him. "You have all of that going on in your head?"

"All that and a bullet," Mendez said.

"Frank wasn't the bogeyman," Vince said. "He was a guy that was wound too tight and he blew apart. Plain and simple. And I'll bet I can prove it," he said, pushing to his feet. "Where did you send Mrs. Farman's body?"

The bodies had been taken to Orrison Funeral Home: both Farmans, Mr. and Mrs. Vince figured it was a safe bet the funeral home had never had a more macabre tableau laid out in their embalming room.

Sharon Farman's body bag was opened, and Vince steeled himself against the violence that had been done to her both before and after her death.

"I only want you to look at the cutting wounds," Vince said. "Look at the placement of the wounds, the length, the depth, the way the edges look."

He had brought along his Polaroids from the Lisa Warwick autopsy. Also his drawing of the placement of Lisa Warwick's wounds, and the sketch he had made earlier that evening of Karly

Vickers's identical wounds. Each mark was precisely placed, precisely sized.

Now he made a sketch of Sharon Farman's wounds on the simple human outline on another one of his forms. When he had finished, he laid out everything on a clean stainless steel embalming table, placing the drawings side by side by side.

None of them spoke as they studied the sketches: two exact matches, one sloppy forgery. The cutting wounds on Sharon Farman varied in length and depth. The placement didn't match the other victims. The wounds appeared random rather than deliberate.

"Frank Farman didn't kill those women," Vince said. "These cuts made on Warwick and Vickers mean something specific to the perpetrator. He makes them where and how he makes them for a reason. Sharon Farman is just hacked up."

Mendez continued to stare at the sketches, seeing something more than what Vince had seen after staring at them for hours on end. He had looked for some kind of message in the placement of the wounds, in the length of the wounds, in the depth of the wounds. They meant something to their killer, but he still wasn't sure what.

Mendez bummed a pen off his boss and connected the wounds one to the next, to the next. First on the drawing of Lisa Warwick, then on Karly Vickers.

It took some imagination, but the pattern was

there: long legs, long neck, long head . . . and two wings.

"It's a bird," Dixon said.

The rush of realization went through Vince, but he let Mendez say it.

"It's a crane."

Peter Crane.

# 84

"Dr. Crane," Anne said, surprised to see him, but not that surprised. She had just been thinking about him. She had spent the evening with him. It wasn't so strange he would show up at her door, she rationalized.

He smiled sheepishly. "Anne, I'm so sorry to bother you."

"No, no, not a problem."

Her mother had raised her to welcome guests, to be courteous. Of course she stepped back from the door, and allowed him to come in. Why wouldn't she? He had been her hero earlier in the evening.

"Can I offer you something to drink?" Hostess with the most-est. That had been her mother's role.

"No, thank you," he said. "I don't want to interrupt your evening more than I already have. What a lovely home you have. Is it original?"

Charming, disarming. Half the women in town would have killed to have him in their foyers.

"Nineteen thirty-three," she said. "Renovated, of course."

"But very true to the architecture," he said, looking around, taking in the Craftsman detail . . . and seeing that she was alone.

"What can I do for you, Dr. Crane?"

Again the self-deprecating smile. Very Tom Selleck without the mustache. "This is a little awkward, but it's about the gift Tommy gave you."

"Oh?" The necklace she had tucked in her pants pocket before she opened the door. The necklace only graduates of the Thomas Center program owned.

Peter Crane had been the last person to see Karly Vickers before she disappeared.

*"You can't possibly think he's involved," she said to Vince. "He's the nicest man."*

"Have you, by any chance, opened it?"

Something was not quite right. Anne couldn't have put her finger on it. She couldn't have described the feeling in a way that wouldn't have sounded silly.

Without exactly knowing why, she opened her mouth and lied. "No, not yet. I haven't. Is there a problem?"

He stepped a little farther into the house, very casually taking it all in.

"I'm afraid I have to ask for it back," he said, perfectly apologetic, and yet goose bumps chased down her arms. "Tommy . . . misunderstood . . ."

"No, really, you don't have to explain," Anne said, her heart tripping over itself. "I left the box in the kitchen. I'll just go get it."

"I'm so sorry," he said, his gaze sliding to the right, toward the living room, where the contents of her purse lay scattered on the big leather ottoman in the middle of the room . . .

"Not a problem."

. . . with the small box and scraps of wrapping paper strewn over the pile . . .

"I'll just go get it," Anne said.

Her heart was beating like a drum in her chest as she turned and walked toward the kitchen. She would go through the swinging door and just keep on going. Her car keys were on the kitchen counter by the phone. She would pick them up and be out the back door. Her car was parked in the driveway.

Even with the alarms sounding in her head, there was still a part of her that told her she was overreacting, that she was just spooked by everything that had happened that evening . . .

She remembered what Vince had said to her about trusting those instincts.

Her step quickened just slightly as she pushed open the heavy, swinging door.

One word exploded in her brain: RUN.

Even as she bolted, he was charging through the door, slamming it back against the wall as he closed the distance between them.

Anne tried to grab for her car keys, her hand just brushing them, sending them skittering down the counter and onto the floor.

Peter Crane swatted at her with one hand, trying to catch hold of her shoulder. Anne dodged away, already reaching for the back door, for the deadbolt. She had locked it to keep intruders out, not to trap herself in.

He caught a handful of her hair and yanked her back toward him. Anne swung backward with an elbow, connecting with some ribs, earning a guttural sound from deep in his belly. She jabbed him again, got loose, grabbed the tea kettle off the stove, turned and hit him with it upside the head as hard as she could.

Crane's head snapped to the left, blood spraying from his nose onto the white cabinetry.

Anne lunged for the back door, turned the lock, pulled it open, tried to throw herself through it. Instead the tremendous force of his body hit her from behind and she went down onto the porch floor, face-first, her arms trapped at her sides as he tackled her.

The air left her lungs in a painful gust. Stars burst before her eyes. But she kept her legs moving, kicking, trying to push herself out from under him. Squirming, twisting, she gained an inch, got one arm free, grabbed for whatever she could.

Her fingers closed on a small concrete relic, a painted green frog a little bigger than her fist. Her other arm came free. She pulled herself out from under him, twisted over.

In that split second she saw his face, she knew what it was. Even in the dim yellow light of the back porch she recognized the thing that wasn't quite right. His eyes—as flat and cold as coins. His face was no longer handsome. It was the face of a monster.

She slammed him in the jaw with the frog.

He punched her full in the mouth, and her consciousness dimmed.

He held her down with a knee on her chest, his left hand pressing down on her throat, choking her. He fished for something with his right hand in his jacket pocket and came out with a small tube.

The glue.

Anne doubled her efforts, thrashing, scratching, snapping her head from side to side to keep from letting him get it into her eyes. She slapped the tube of glue from his hand and heard it land away from them on the porch floor.

His knee slipped from her chest. Her knee came up and connected with his groin. His body contracted in on itself, and Anne rolled out from under him.

She half ran, half fell down the porch steps, hit the lawn on all fours and kept scrambling. If she could get around the corner of the house—If she could make it to the neighbor's—If someone would drive by—

"Fucking bitch!"

The words were harsh and hot on the back of her neck as Crane caught her and slammed her into the side of the house. She tried to scream, and couldn't, the sound catching dry and raw in her throat. He punched her in the stomach and she doubled over.

Somewhere in the dim reaches in the back of her mind, she was aware they were right below her father's bedroom window. If she could just make a sound—If he could hear her enough to wake up—

But she couldn't and he didn't.

And then it was too late.

# 85

Tommy pulled the blanket off his head, sat up, and looked around with no idea where he was. It had taken no more than ten minutes to get there, but he didn't know what direction they had headed once they left his block.

He had traded his pajamas for sweatpants and a sweatshirt. And he wore socks and his purple snowboarding hat from their winter vacation in Aspen because it was cold. And while his parents were still arguing, he took a blanket and crept downstairs and out of the house. He crawled into the backseat of his father's car and made a nest for himself on the floor, and covered himself up.

It hadn't been long before his father had gotten into the car and started driving.

Once the car stopped, Tommy waited and counted to one hundred after his dad got out of the car before he even thought about sitting up.

The car was parked on a side street in an older neighborhood with a lot of trees. It was very quiet and very dark.

He hadn't thought about getting afraid. He hadn't thought about what he would do when his dad got out of the car. Somehow he hadn't thought of anything beyond tagging along. Tommy didn't want to be left behind again to deal with his mother in the aftermath of another fight. He and his dad were partners, buddies, heroes together. They had saved Miss Navarre. Who knew what else they might accomplish?

If only his dad would come back to the car.

Suddenly a dark figure emerged from behind a wall of oleander that seemed to glow silver in the moonlight. Fear shot through Tommy as the figure advanced toward the car. A tall, menacing, shadow figure, carrying something . . . a bundle of something . . .

Tommy's heart was in his throat. He crouched low, pulling the dark blanket over his head, only his eyes exposed as he peered out at the apparition coming toward him. He could hear his pulse in his ears as the Shadow Man drew closer.

He wished his dad would come back. What if the Shadow Man tried to steal the car? With him in it?!

The doors were locked, he reminded himself.

But what if Shadow Man had attacked his dad and got the keys? Tommy would have to save the day. But he was just a kid, and kids weren't meant to be heroes all by themselves.

The black lace curtain of unconsciousness began to recede from Anne's vision. He must have choked her. She thought she could still feel his hand around her windpipe even though he was carrying her.

As consciousness rushed back into her, adrenaline followed like a torrent of water from a burst dam. Her body jumped in his arms as if she had been shocked back to life, and automatically, Anne started to fight with what she could. He had somehow bound her hands to her sides, but her legs still worked and she started kicking.

Like a stunned fish coming to on the shore, she flopped and twisted, and Crane, taken by surprise, couldn't hold her. Anne plunged from his hold, unable to break her fall, landing hard on one shoulder. Tucking herself into a ball as she hit the ground, she tried to roll up onto her knees. And from her knees, she tried to gain her feet.

Crane drove his knee into the middle of her back, and she went face-first hard into the back passenger door of his car. Her head bounced off the window and the black lace reappeared at the edges of her eyesight. Eyes stared back at her from the other side of the glass—wide, terrified eyes.

*Tommy.*

The recognition was swift and brief. The look of shock on the boy's face was absolute and terrible.

Then Crane grabbed her up by one hand in her hair and one on the belt he had tightened around her, and he dumped her into the trunk of his car and closed the lid as if she were nothing more important than a bag of golf clubs.

Tommy felt like a bomb had gone off in his chest. He couldn't breathe, he couldn't move. He didn't know what to do. His stomach hurt. He thought he might be sick.

Shadow Man had Miss Navarre! He put her in the trunk!

Then there was the monster's bloody face staring in at him—eyes dark and hard, mouth open, showing its fangs. They stared at each other for what seemed like an hour.

"Tommy!"

The Shadow Man knew his name! He pulled the car door open and reached in with talon-tipped hands.

"Tommy!"

"NO!!!" Tommy screamed at the top of his lungs.

Arms and legs scrambling, he shot backward like a crab to the other side of the car, grabbed the handle, and fell out the door. His feet hit the street and he ran.

He ran for his life. He ran like he was in a nightmare—his legs flying but not seeming to take him anywhere. And that fast, Shadow Man had hold of him, scooping him up off his feet like a bird of prey snatching up a rabbit and carrying it away.

"NOOO!!!" Tommy shouted, and he kicked and he hit.

Shadow Man ran back to his dad's car, threw him into the backseat, slammed the door, and jumped behind the wheel. The door locks snapped down. He was trapped.

# 86

Vince turned down Anne's street, hoping she hadn't already turned out the lights and gone to bed. He didn't want to scare her, waking her up, but he wanted to see her. Hell, after this night, he needed to see her, just to have his eyes rest on something beautiful. He'd had his fill of death and dark souls.

If he could have, he would have put off telling her about Peter Crane. It was going to be hard on her to think about Tommy and how hurt the boy would be to lose his father, how shattered he would be to learn his father was a monster. And it would be harder still to think that he would now be left entirely to the care of Janet Crane.

They still had to build their case. They had no forensic evidence at this point. No evidence at all. They had a dead-on profile and a couple of connect-the-dots drawings of stick-figure birds. They had a living victim who could neither see nor hear. They had speculation and conjecture.

Unless Peter Crane made a mistake, they had jack shit. If they lived in an hour-long TV drama, they could have just gone and arrested him based on nothing but their hunches, and none of the women he had killed would really be dead, and none of the lives he had touched would really be ruined. But that wasn't how a real investigation worked. In real life the hurt counted.

Anne had gone to dinner with Crane and his son. The idea that she had been that close to him made Vince's stomach clench like a fist.

Light still glowed in the windows of the Navarre living room as Vince pulled into the driveway behind Anne's Volkswagen. He wondered if she had watched the coverage of what had gone down at the sheriff's office. He wondered if the media had gotten any of it right.

He went to the front door and knocked lightly at first. Her father was probably sleeping.

No one stirred.

He knocked a little harder, then a little harder as his instincts began to growl.

He tried the knob, and the door opened without protest.

"Anne?" he called. "Anne? It's Vince."

In the living room, the television babbled to itself. Anne's purse lay on the sofa, its contents spilled out on a big leather ottoman. His pulse picked up a beat. He pulled a clean handkerchief from a pocket and gingerly handled her wallet. DL and credit cards. Eighty dollars in cash and a photo of who Vince guessed was her at about five posed with a woman who was unmistakably her mother.

"Anne?" he called again.

He didn't like that open front door. She wouldn't have been that careless. They had talked about it.

He checked the old man's room down the hall —no lights and intermittent snoring. He went upstairs to check out empty bedrooms. Every second that passed, those instincts growled louder and louder.

In the kitchen, her car keys were on the floor, and so was the heavy old teakettle. A fine mist of blood splatter had dried on painted white cabinets.

"No," he said, denying the scenario even as it automatically played through his head.

She knocked her keys to the floor as she tried to get to the now-open back door. She grabbed the kettle on her way past the stove and used it as a weapon. And, good girl, she whacked him hard enough to make him bleed.

The scene continued on the back porch, where furniture had been shoved out of place during a struggle. More blood on a concrete frog the size of a croquet ball. Whose blood?

*Oh Jesus God, no.*

He was shaking now. Sweating like a horse. His

brain began to throb. His stomach twisted like a rope.

Then his eye caught on something small, something that would have seemed insignificant, no bigger than an inch, a little piece of trash on the floor . . .

A tube of superglue.

# 87

"STOP! STOP! STOP!!!" Tommy screamed from the backseat.

He stood on the seat, pitching forward, holding on to the headrest with one hand, pounding his other fist against the shoulder and head of Shadow Man behind the wheel of his father's car.

The man shouted at him. "SIT DOWN!"

"STOP THE CAR!" Tommy shrieked like a girl at the top of his lungs. He swung his fist again and hit Shadow Man's ear so hard it felt like all his fingers shattered.

Shadow Man turned the wheel hard to the right and hit the brakes. Tommy was thrown clear across the backseat and banged his head against the window so hard he saw stars, and to his horror, he started to cry.

"SHUT UP! SHUT UP!"

The monster loomed over the seat back, his face twisted with rage.

Tommy buried his face in the blanket he had brought with him and sobbed, choking on a terror bigger than anything he had ever known.

"I want my dad!" he cried over and over. "I want my dad!"

Anne struggled against the belt that bound her arms to her sides. Crane had pulled it so tight around her, her hands had gone numb. Her back and ribs hurt like they were on fire, and she felt like she might never get another full breath.

The car had come to an abrupt stop, and she expected the trunk to fly open and Peter Crane to loom over her. Instead she heard him shout at Tommy, and Tommy crying, "I want my dad!"

Anne's heart broke for him. He had to be terrified at what was happening, at what he had seen. He must have stowed away in the car, thinking he would have some grand adventure with his dad. His dad was a great guy. His dad was a hero.

His dad was a monster. So much so that Tommy couldn't bring himself to recognize the man he loved in the man behind the wheel of the car.

What would happen to him? Anne wondered now. He had seen his father abduct his teacher— who would shortly be killed. How could Peter Crane deal with him, short of killing him too?

It was Anne's turn to start to cry.

# 88

They stormed the Crane home like commandos—Vince, Mendez, Hicks, and Dixon, backed up by a full SWAT unit. There was no chance of Peter Crane having taken Anne there, but the show of force was calculated to strike shock and fear into Janet Crane and rock her back on her heels before she knew what was happening.

Dixon took the fore as Peter Crane's wife opened the front door.

"Mrs. Crane, we need to speak with your husband," he said without preamble. "Can you please get him for us?"

Janet Crane had clearly been asleep. Though she was in a smart red velour tracksuit, her makeup was smudged on the right side, making her look a little drunk. She blinked at Dixon as she tried to gather her wits about her.

"I'm sorry, Sheriff," she said. "What is this about?"

"We need to speak to Peter," Dixon repeated.

"What about?"

"Is he home?"

"No, he isn't." She squinted to look past him at the SWAT commander standing in her driveway. "I want to know what this is about. Has something happened? Is Peter in some kind of trouble?"

"We have reason to believe he abducted a woman tonight, ma'am," Mendez said.

"That's insane!"

"Where is he?" Dixon asked.

Vince hung back, not trusting himself to speak. Renowned for his patience in interrogations, now he would have backed Janet Crane up against a wall and wrung the truth out of her with his bare hands.

She looked around nervously, as if she were hoping her husband might pop up out of a shrub. "I—I don't know."

Dixon's brow furrowed. "What do you mean, you don't know? It's the middle of the night. Where's your husband?"

"He went out," she said.

"*Out* is not a place, Janet," Dixon said impatiently. "We can step inside and discuss this further, or you can come down to headquarters with us and we can do it there. It's your choice."

She seemed genuinely rattled, stepping back into the front hall of her lovely home, allowing them access. The four of them moved almost as a unit into the house and took positions in a loose semicircle around her.

"Peter is sometimes restless at night," she said. "He likes to go for drives."

"In the middle of the night," Dixon said.

"Are these drives related in any way to his fictitious Friday night card games, Mrs. Crane?" Vince asked. "Say, in your imagination?"

"I don't know what you want from me!" she snapped. "I've told you everything I know."

"I don't think so, ma'am," Mendez said. "As a licensed real estate agent you have access to a master lock-box key, don't you?"

"Yes."

"And that key will open any lock box on any listed piece of property, allowing you access to the keys to those properties. Is that correct?"

"Yes, but—"

"Do you keep your key here?" Hicks asked.

"Not as a rule, no," she said, her attention bouncing from one of them to another to another.

"But . . . ?" Dixon said.

"But I had to show some property late in the day today, and—"

The sheriff held up a hand to cut her off. "Janet. A woman has been abducted. Her life is in jeopardy. We don't want to hear about your day. Do you have the key? Can you produce the key and show it to us? Now?"

She went to a drawer in an antique painted cabinet that stood near the front door, looking like she expected to reach in and come out with the key, but that didn't happen. She dug through the drawer, frowning.

"Do you have it or not?" Dixon prodded.

"I don't understand," she said. "It should be here. I must have left it in my purse."

"Jesus Christ," Vince growled. "Slap the cuffs on her and bring her as an accessory."

"You can't arrest me! I haven't done anything!"

"No, you haven't," Vince said, stepping toward her. "You know the big thing you haven't done? You haven't once asked us who the abducted woman is. Don't you find that a little strange, Detective Mendez?"

"Unless she already knows the name," he said.

"Exactly."

"I don't know anything about it!" she said. "And I don't believe you can think Peter would know anything about it, either!"

"Peter, who's taking an imaginary drive in the dead of night with your lock-box key in his pocket?" Vince asked, the volume of his voice increasing with every word. "Maybe he's having an imaginary tea party with Anne Navarre. What do you think, Janet?"

She had to be thinking she wished he would drop dead before her eyes, but she was so flustered, she seemed not to be able to respond at all.

"Where's the boy?" Vince asked the room at large. "Maybe he knows where his father goes when he can't stand to be in the house with this woman anymore."

Janet gasped her outrage and drew breath to fire something back at him.

"Where's your son, Janet?" Dixon asked.

"He's in bed!"

Mendez took a couple of steps toward the staircase and called out, "Hey, Tommy!"

"Don't shout in my home!" Janet Crane shouted

at him. She pushed past him and started up the stairs. "I won't have you frighten my son."

"Hey, Tommy!" Mendez called again.

Peter Crane's wife disappeared into the second story of her home. Vince jammed his hands at his waist and paced. Every minute that ticked past . . .

He knew exactly what Peter Crane had done to his victims. He died inside again and again as he thought of Karly Vickers lying blind, deaf, and mutilated in a hospital bed.

"Tommy?" Janet Crane's voice called out. "Tommy? Tommy, answer me!"

Mendez started up the stairs. Janet ran down to the landing, paper white and breathing hard.

"He's gone! My son is gone! Oh my God! My son is missing!"

# 89

He wanted control. He needed a plan. None of this had been a plan. All of it was going wrong.

He would never have chosen the teacher as a victim. She would fight. She had. Now his nose was broken and his mouth was bleeding. He wouldn't be able to hide that.

He hadn't been able to subdue her in his usual way. The deviation from routine would lead to mistakes. It already had. He needed to get the necklace, first and foremost, but because she had fought him and it had taken so much more effort to control her, he had forgotten about the damn thing.

Where was it? In her house? Who would find it? He couldn't know that she hadn't told someone about it already. But that wouldn't have mattered if he had recovered it. Now what would he do? He couldn't go back there.

*Fuck, fuck, fuck.*

He had been raised to always have a plan, to keep an orderly mind. These principles had been drilled into him, beaten into him, day after day after day. He always had a plan, and he always took his time. And he never made a mistake.

Everything about this clusterfuck was a mistake: the teacher *and* the boy.

The boy.

What the hell could he do about the boy?

Everything had been under control. Every component of his life had been in its assigned compartment. Nothing overlapped.

What the hell would he do about the boy?

The car was going slowly now. He would stop soon, Anne suspected. Time would run out. She wondered if Vince would have stopped by the house, or if he would have been too exhausted after the ordeal at the sheriff's office. The difference would be either people looking for her or no one missing her.

Where would they look? How would they find her?

Half-buried in the ground?

She thought about dinner, about the Peter Crane who smiled and laughed with his son. So charming, so easy to be with. She thought of him stopping to come to her rescue when she thought Frank Farman might hurt her. How could he do that, then turn around and do this? How could that man be this monster?

The car slowed again and turned from a smooth road to a rougher one. He would stop soon. He would try to kill her. He had all the control.

She needed a plan.

# 90

"I can't believe you're asking me these questions, making these allegations when my son is missing!" Janet Crane shouted.

"The alert has gone out to all personnel—county and state," Cal Dixon assured her. "And to the media. Everyone will be looking for Peter's car. Where would Peter go?"

"Why do you think Peter took Tommy? Why would he take Tommy? That doesn't make any sense! Peter is a GOOD MAN!"

Mendez shook his head as he watched the monitor. "Could she really be that ignorant?"

Vince watched her, studied her. "People are as ignorant as they want to be. Do you think that woman wants to know that her husband is a monster? Do you think she wants to own that? She'll go to her grave saying he's a good man if we don't prove otherwise beyond all doubt."

He walked out of the room with a file folder under his arm, went across the hall, and knocked on the door. Dixon came out.

"Let me come in for minute."

"You think that's a good idea?" Dixon asked. "Can you keep your cool?"

"I can do what I need to do," Vince said quietly. "I'm in and out. You stay with her."

"Okay."

Vince walked into the room and placed his file folder on the table. Janet Crane glared at him. She was on her feet, arms crossed.

"Please have a seat, Mrs. Crane," he said, his tone quiet, civil, formal, respectful.

She hesitated.

"Please," he repeated in the same quiet tone.

Janet Crane sat. Perched might have been a better word—her back straight, her arms still crossed.

"I apologize for my outburst earlier," he said, taking a seat himself. "I've been belligerent and disrespectful to you, and I apologize for that. I let my emotions get the better of me. I'm sure you can appreciate that now, as you have to deal with the emotions of not knowing where your son is."

She lifted her chin like a queen and looked him in the eye. "I am *choking* on my emotions right now."

Vince nodded, looking down. "I know. Over my years in the Bureau, I've sat with many parents of missing children. It's a terrible thing to know someone you care about is out of your sight, out of your influence.

"I'm quite fond of Miss Navarre," he admitted. "I'm very upset that she's missing—and that your son, Tommy, is missing. I believe that they are both probably with your husband, and that they are both in grave danger."

"Peter would never hurt Tommy," she said, lifting a forefinger for emphasis. "Never."

"Not the Peter you know," Vince said. "The Peter you know is a fine, upstanding family man. A really nice guy. I've met him, spoken with him. Heck of a nice guy."

"Yes."

He nodded earnestly, agreeing with her. "Yes. But that's not who we're talking about now, Mrs. Crane. We're not talking about your husband. The man we're talking about—you don't know him. You've never met him. Your son doesn't know him."

She said nothing. The lack of response in and of itself spoke volumes.

"The man we're talking about did this," Vince said.

From the file folder he removed a full-body photograph of Lisa Warwick taken at autopsy, which he placed on the table in front of Janet Crane.

She didn't look away, but every drop of color drained from her face, and her eyes seemed to double in size, the white showing all the way around. Her whole body began to jerk and shake.

"The man who did this," Vince said in the same calm, measured tone. "*Not* your husband. The man who did this has your son. If you have any idea at all where that man might have gone, please tell Sheriff Dixon. Thank you, and please excuse me, Mrs. Crane."

Vince walked out of the room with the same calm. He walked down the hall to the men's room and went in. He just made it into a stall before his legs buckled under him and he vomited until he nearly blacked out.

The man who did those terrible things to Lisa Warwick, and to Julie Paulson, and to Karly Vickers, and to Christ knew how many others— *that* man had absolute control of the woman he wanted to spend the rest of his life with.

# 91

The boy had finally stopped crying. The loud sobs he had started with had subsided to a constant, almost whispered crying that seemed to go on and on. Finally, silence. Peaceful silence.

He would kill the boy first. That was the kindest thing he could do. He would hold him, comfort him, and suffocate him with the blanket he was lying on.

It would be over quickly. The boy would struggle hardest for the second and third minutes of the suffocation—while his brain was being starved of oxygen and panic set in—but he would quickly lose consciousness, and that would be all. It would be over.

In another part of his mind, in another self, he would be devastated. But there was no other choice to be made.

This meant his own life would now change forever, and he was quite angry about that. He would lose everything he had worked so hard to build. If only everything had simply gone on according to plan. Law enforcement had nothing on him with regards to the other women. Nothing. He knew that because he had made certain of it. Even though he signed his work, they had no concrete forensic evidence linking him to any crime.

A slice of moon cast a smoky glow over the country landscape of tree-studded rolling hills. He turned off the dirt road and into the field, gaining access to the property through the same open gate he had come through before. No one would be watching it. No one would think he would use it again.

Now that the search for the last woman was over, the field had been cleared of the tents that had offered shade and shelter for the volunteers and backgrounds for the TV newspeople. They would all be back here in a day or two, but no one was watching Gordon Sells's field of junkers tonight.

He pulled the Jaguar in at the end of the back row. He would leave it here with the bodies in it, then hotwire something that could get him to Mexico.

Tommy had stopped crying. The car sat idling, exhaust fumes leaching up into the trunk.

Anne was dizzy and nauseous on fumes and fear and from struggling against her bonds as the car rose and fell over a road she couldn't see.

She had managed by twisting and squirming to finally get her hands free of the belt Crane had bound her with. Feeling around inside the trunk, she had found a couple of potential weapons. She had to think about how and when to try to use them. She would probably have only one chance. If she tried and failed . . .

Why wasn't he doing something? Why hadn't he turned the car off?

Maybe they were in a closed building and this was his plan: to gas them.

Or maybe she wasn't his priority.

*Tommy.*

Instantly Anne began to kick and scream and thrash. If he would just open the damn trunk . . .

Tommy pretended to be asleep. He had had lots of practice at that, fooling his parents on a regular basis. Now he would have to fool Shadow Man, who had opened the door and stood staring at him. Tommy could feel the monster's eyes on him. If he had dared to look, they probably glowed red in the dark night.

He stayed perfectly still as Shadow Man crouched down in the open door and touched the back of his head, stroked the back of his head, then put a hand on his back—like his father sometimes did when he came to check on him in the middle of the night.

Tears rose up again in Tommy's throat.

*I want my dad. I want my dad. I want my dad.*

He stared at the boy for a moment, then reached out and touched his hair. The moonlight on his face made him look like a sleeping angel.

He rubbed the boy's back and prepared himself for what he was about to do, pulling a cold steel curtain across his mind, relegating the job to its proper compartment.

Then the car began to rock and the teacher started screaming.

As the trunk opened, Anne attacked, coming up in Crane's face with a spray can of something that smelled like oil, shooting in the dark and hoping to blind him.

He cried out—startled?—hurt? She didn't know and couldn't wait, scrambling out of the trunk in the second he jumped back.

She had to run. She needed cover.

Her ribs hurt. She couldn't get a breath.

Rows of cars, one after the next.

If she could duck out of his sight—If she could get under one of the cars—If she could get more than three steps ahead of him—

He lunged for her, hit her hard with a fist between the shoulder blades. Anne went down, hit the ground, rolled, holding tight to her last chance.

He kicked her as hard as he could.

Anne tucked into a ball like a small animal, trying to protect herself. She got her knees underneath her and ducked her head.

Tommy watched in horror from beside the car as Shadow Man attacked Miss Navarre, hitting her, kicking her, tearing at her like a wild beast from a nightmare.

Tommy had never been so scared. He had never imagined anything as horrible as this. He felt so small and so alone. He was just a little boy and the Shadow Man was a demon.

They needed a hero, him and Miss Navarre. But there was no hero. He had to be the hero. He had to save the day. That was what his father had taught him.

He willed together as much courage as he could find and started running.

"STOP IT!! STOP HURTING HER!! STOP

IT!" he shouted at the top of his lungs until his throat burned raw.

He ran as hard as his legs would go, and he hurled himself at Shadow Man like a small missile, fists swinging, feet kicking.

It was the second's distraction Anne needed.

Crane turned to intercept Tommy's attack, and she sprang to her feet, turned, and swung with all her might.

The tire iron connected with the side of his head and Anne imagined she felt bone give way beneath its force. Crane staggered sideways, his knees folding under him, his hands grabbing hold of the side of his face.

"TOMMY, RUN!" Anne shouted. "RUN!!! GET IN THE CAR! GET IN THE CAR!"

Tire iron still clutched in one fist, she grabbed at the boy, catching him by the back of his jacket, pulling him around.

"RUN!! RUN!!"

He caught hold of her free hand, and she ran for all she was worth, dragging him with her.

"GET IN THE CAR! GET IN THE CAR!"

Tommy jumped in through the open driver's-side door and landed on the passenger's seat.

Anne was right behind him, pulling the door closed after her. She could see Crane in her peripheral vision, lurching toward them, one arm outstretched, the other hand clamped to his face.

The seat was back too far, set for a man. She could hardly reach the pedals, had to hold tight to the steering wheel to keep from falling back.

"HURRY!!!" Tommy squealed, bouncing like a ball in his seat. "IT'S COMING!!"

Peter Crane flung himself against the passenger's door, his left eye hanging out of the shattered socket as he let go of his face to try to pull the handle.

Anne threw the car in gear and hit the gas. The Jaguar's tires spun on the damp grass and the car fishtailed away from Crane, leaving him falling.

They flew toward the closed front gate, then crashed through the gate, and then they were on the road and skidding sideways as Anne wrestled the wheel.

She drove as if Crane was flying behind them, a demon from hell bent on snatching them back into the darkness. She didn't know exactly where they were. She pointed the car toward the glow of light that had to be town and didn't slow down and didn't look back.

# 92

Neither of them spoke as Anne drove. She glanced over at Tommy several times, wondering when the enormity of what he had gone through would hit him. Was it now? Was he seeing his father in his mind's eye, or the monster he had saved her from?

Would he ever have to realize what his father might have done to him? Would his mind ever be able to make sense of any of it?

How could it? Why would it? He was a little boy who loved his dad like he was a god. What would be the point of him understanding it now or ever?

Anne didn't think about how she would handle it. She thought only about getting to the sheriff's office on the last little drop of adrenaline trickling through her veins. She was beginning to feel her physical injuries in a serious way. All other injury would have to wait its turn.

She pulled the car into the parking lot—not up to the doors of the building. Once they went inside, everything would change. She wanted this one moment alone with Tommy.

She got out of the car and went around to the other side to take Tommy's hand—the same way she had the day he and the other kids had found the body, and she had taken him home to face his mother.

She knelt down and looked at his face, his eyes, trying to read him, feeling that in the snap of a moment his soul had aged a thousand years. Her heart ached for him and for herself as if God had taken it from her chest and wrung it out like a sponge.

"You are so precious," she whispered, tears filling every part of her. "And this is going to be so hard. I wish I could change it for you, Tommy."

"I'll be all right," he said, as if to reassure her.

Anne nodded, knowing that he wouldn't be. He wouldn't be all right. And there was nothing she could do about it.

She touched his cheek like touching an angel. "You're my hero, you know," she said, tears falling.

Anne gathered him to her and held him tight, and he held her back. Then they both dried their eyes, and she held his hand, and they went up the sidewalk together.

And when they walked through the doors, everything changed.

People swarmed them, meaning well, wanting explanations, needing statements, demanding answers. With everybody added to the crowd, Anne watched Tommy drift away from her. His mother emerged from somewhere and flung herself at him, hysterical and grasping.

His eyes met Anne's for just a fleeting second, and she knew exactly what he was feeling—like he had been dropped into space as the safety net was pulled out from under him. He had no one. And no one had him.

Anne turned to Vince. Taking the gold necklace from the pocket of her torn, dirty pants, she pressed it into his hand, then pressed herself into his arms and turned herself over to him. As he held her tight and told her everything would be all right, she just pressed her ear to his chest and listened to his heart beat. For those few moments, everything else was just noise.

Closing her eyes, she slipped away from consciousness. The last thing she remembered in her mind's eye: Tommy standing alone in a little red boat, his hand to his heart as he drifted out of view until all that remained was the faintest memory of his sad little smile.

# 93

Anne came to to the sound of hushed voices in the hall outside her hospital room.

". . . broken ribs . . . collapsed lung . . ."

". . . oh my God . . . we're lucky she's not d-e-a-d . . ."

"I can spell."

Her voice was rusty and dry and didn't carry very far, but it carried far enough.

"Hey, look who's back," Vince said with a soft smile as he came to her bedside.

"Oh, Anne Marie!" Franny exclaimed with a pained expression. "You look like a raccoon!"

Anne raised the head of the bed with the remote control, catching a glimpse of herself in the small mirror on the wall. Two black eyes. A fat lip. Stitches in her chin. Raccoons would have been offended by the comparison.

"Hey," Vince objected. "You should see the other guy. They had to airlift him to LA. Our girl got a couple of good licks in. She knocked his eye out with a tire iron!" he said proudly.

Franny was horrified. "Oh my God!"

"Gave him a skull fracture, broke his nose . . ."

"Who *are* you?" Franny asked her, as if perhaps she had been possessed by some much-tougher entity than the one he thought he knew.

"I'm alive," she said simply.

"Oh, sweetheart," he said, melting. "I don't even know what to say."

"I'll be sure to mark this day on my calendar," Anne said dryly.

"I want to hug you, but I'm afraid you'll hurt me. I was going to say that the other way around, but you beat a man's head in with a tire iron, so . . ."

Anne tried to smile. She hurt everywhere. Her ribs hurt, her head hurt, her lungs hurt. She felt like she'd been run over by a truck.

"My dentist," Franny said as it dawned on him. "A serial killer put his hands in my mouth!"

Anne looked at Vince. "Has he confessed?"

He shook his head. "He got a lawyer. We can't touch him."

"But he did this to Anne," Franny said with his trademark outrage. "I don't care if he hires F. Lee Bill-Me-Out-the-Ass. He won't get off for this!"

"No," Vince said. "He's a slam dunk for this, and he knows it. I think he'll try to cut a deal."

"Fuck that!" Franny said. "Fry his ass!"

Vince patted him on the shoulder. "I like how you think, my friend. If that was an option . . ."

"But the murders?" Anne said. "And Karly Vickers?"

"Right now, there's just not enough physical evidence. In fact, there's almost no physical evidence. He didn't make a mistake—until he went after you," he said. "How did you get the necklace?"

Anne sighed at the sad irony of it. "Tommy gave it to me. He must have found it in their house. He thought he was doing something special, something sweet."

His sweet gesture had set off the chain of events that led to his father being revealed as a monster. The Greeks couldn't have come up with a better tragedy.

"Have you talked to Tommy?" she asked.

She knew the answer by the tension in his face.

"The mother won't let us near him."

He read her distress just as easily and closed his hand gently around hers. "There's nothing you can do, honey. Let it go."

A deep sense of sadness settled in Anne's heart, almost as if she had lost a loved one. In a way, she supposed she had. Somehow she knew right then that she wouldn't see Tommy Crane again. She didn't say it. No one would have believed her, but she knew it in her heart. He was gone from her life.

"I brought you a get-well present to cheer you

up," Franny said, setting a colorful gift bag on the bedside tray.

Anne peeked into the bag, suspicious. She reached in with the hand not burdened by an IV catheter and plucked out a scrap of black silk and lace.

"Some people give flowers or candy. My friend gives lingerie."

"Nothing says 'Get well' like a negligee," Franny said.

"Always makes me feel better," Vince confessed. "See?"

Anne would have rolled her eyes if they hadn't hurt so much.

Franny leaned down and found a square inch of cheek to kiss without causing her pain. "I'm going to let you rest," he said, then gave Vince a big comic wink.

"He's something," Vince said, chuckling, as Franny made his exit.

Anne managed to arch a brow at the negligee. "Yeah, the two of you."

"Seriously, now," he said. "How are you feeling?"

She felt no need to try to be brave or analytical with him. The tears came high in her eyes as the emotions flooded through her, leaving her trembling. "I've never been so afraid in my life."

Vince eased a hip onto the bed so he could put his arms around her.

"You should have seen me," he murmured. "When I knew that bastard had you . . ."

"Will you just hold me for a while?" Anne asked him in a small voice.

"I'll hold you all night long," he murmured, stroking her hair.

"I don't think they'll let you stay past nine."

"Let them try to get me out of here," he said. "God hasn't made a nurse mean enough to get me away from you. And that's saying something."

He kissed her forehead, and she felt herself let go some of the tension still trembling through her.

"I mean it, Anne," he said quietly. "I'm not going anywhere. I might be a big dumb lummox from Chicago, but I know the real deal when I see it. I love you. I want to spend my life with you. Is that all right with you? Or is there a restraining order in my future?"

Anne smiled and shook her head. He was right. After looking death in the face, all of life's other choices became so much simpler and cleaner.

Vince leaned down and kissed her lips, and she had never felt more safe or loved in her life.

# 94

In the days that followed, properties Peter Crane might have accessed using his wife's lock-box key were searched, but no madman's lair was discovered. Wherever Crane had tortured and killed his victims remained a mystery—along with any physical evidence that might have tied him to the crimes.

Karly Vickers had begun to recover from her ordeal. She had been taken off the ventilator and was breathing on her own, but communication with her was difficult. While she could speak a few words at a time in a hoarse whisper, she could neither see nor hear. She had not indicated that she knew the identity of her attacker.

Doctors had expressed hope of repairing some of the damage to her ears and possibly giving her back at least partial hearing. While that was good news, it was a long shot, and would be a long time coming.

Vince doubted the young woman would have much to tell them at any rate. He didn't believe for a minute Peter Crane had made the mistake of leaving a victim alive. Karly Vickers was his masterpiece, his living tribute to his own criminal cunning and brilliance. She was Peter Crane saying, *Look how much smarter I am than the cops. I give them a victim back and they still don't know who I am.*

Crane might have given her back, but he would have damn well made sure she wouldn't be able to tell them anything.

It was chilling to think how long Crane might have gone on with his killing career. And just as chilling to imagine how long it had gone on to that point. His crimes were too sophisticated, his fantasies too finely honed for the three victims they knew of to have been his first.

The Bureau was thoroughly involved at that point, Vince being officially assigned to pursue the case and investigate Peter Crane's past. It would be his last case as an agent. And while he had had an illustrious career, he was focused on what would come: his life with Anne.

Dixon had given him a desk in the war room. He sat now reviewing videotape, playing the interview forward, rewinding, replaying.

Mendez came in with lunch.

"Jane Thomas had Karly Vickers taken out on the hospital lawn in a wheelchair this morning so she could pet her dog. That's going to be the first seeing-eye pit bull in history," he said, putting the bags down on the table. He nodded at the television. "Why are you looking at that?"

"Come sit down."

It was Dixon's interview of Janet Crane the night her husband had abducted Anne. Vince watched, fascinated, as Peter Crane's wife led Cal Dixon around in circles.

She had collapsed in hysterical tears after Vince had left the room that night, supposedly driven to panic by the idea of her son in the hands of a madman. Dixon had offered her comfort, coffee, to call a doctor. She had refused all, preferring to carry on intermittently.

Dixon had continued with the interview. They needed answers from her. Where did Peter like to go? Was there a particular place he might feel safe to hide? Were there vacant properties she knew of that he could get into using her key? Places that were hidden, out of the way, forgotten?

Around and around they went. Dixon got nothing. Janet Crane got attention.

It probably wasn't even conscious on her part. That was just how she operated and had since childhood, Vince suspected.

She couldn't believe this was happening to her.

*To her*. Not to her son, not to Anne, not to any of the other lives her husband had wrecked and ruined.

"What a bitch," Mendez said.

"What a case study," Vince corrected him. "She's a textbook narcissist. Everything in her world revolves around her. The rest of us are just actors in her play."

He paused the tape, rewound it again, found the bit he wanted Mendez to watch: the point in the interview when he had laid out Lisa Warwick's autopsy photo in front of Janet Crane.

Mendez said nothing.

Vince rewound and replayed.

He turned to his protégé and said, "She doesn't look away. She doesn't look away, and she doesn't become hysterical for a full two minutes."

"She's in shock," Mendez offered.

"She's enjoying it."

Mendez looked at him like he was crazy. "No way."

Vince rewound the tape and played it again, and again. He wound it back to an earlier point in the interview.

"... *your son, Tommy, is missing,*" *he said.* "*I believe that they are both probably with your husband, and that they are both in grave danger.*"

"*Peter would never hurt Tommy,*" *she said, lifting a forefinger for emphasis.* "*Never.*"

" 'Peter would never hurt Tommy.' She doesn't say Peter would never hurt anybody. She doesn't say he wouldn't hurt Anne," Mendez said, frowning. "And when we went to their house that night and told her her husband had abducted a woman, she never asked who."

"Either she knew, or she didn't care," Vince said. "Or both.

"Janet Crane volunteers at the Thomas Center. She knows the staff wears the silver necklace. She knows only the graduates wear the gold necklace. The boy gave the necklace to Anne. He had to have found it in their house."

"If Janet Crane knew that necklace was there . . . ," Mendez started.

"She had to have known where it came from," Vince said.

"Jesus," Mendez muttered, staring at the video monitor, watching Janet Crane play Cal Dixon like a concert violin. "I spoke to her this morning. I'm trying to get her to bring Tommy in to speak with us."

"She'll never let it happen," Vince said.

"She told me she was taking him today to see a psychiatrist in Beverly Hills. She should see if she can get a two-for-one discount.

"Do you really think she knew all along?" he asked.

"I don't know," Vince said, shutting off the monitor. "And even if I said yes, what I think and what I can prove are two very different things."

# 95

Days passed Tommy in a kind of a blur, his mind turning reality just slightly out of focus. He felt numb, and that seemed like a good thing. He didn't go to school. He didn't go anywhere. He didn't leave his mother's side. She needed him now.

The day they left Oak Knoll, his mother told Detective Mendez she was taking him to a child psychiatrist in Los Angeles. But when they got to Highway 101, she turned the car north instead of south, and just kept driving.

They traveled all that night and all the next day, leaving behind everything and everyone Tommy ever knew. He hadn't seen it coming, but he wasn't surprised either. Nothing his mother did surprised him.

She couldn't be married to a notorious killer. Nor could Tommy be the son of one. And never in a million years would she have allowed him to testify in court to what he had seen that terrible night he and Miss Navarre had been taken away.

What would he have told them, anyway? That a Shadow Man had come and taken away the one person who mattered most to him—his father.

When darkness fell that first day on the road, Tommy sat looking out the back window at the stars, imagining each of them was someone he knew in Oak Knoll, growing farther and farther away until they were only the tiniest points of light. The last two he counted before he fell asleep were Wendy and Miss Navarre.

Now they stood on the deck of a ferryboat floating away from their newest city as the setting sun splashed gold across the faces of the sky-scrapers.

His mother had cut her hair and dyed it blonde, and looked nothing like his mother had his whole life. It was as if an actress in a movie were talking to him, pretending to be his mother. He wished that were so, then felt guilty for thinking it.

She had dyed his hair too, so when he looked in the mirror, a stranger looked back at him.

The Crane family had ceased to exist.

They had new names now to go with their new life.

His mother went to the back railing of the ferry and took a small metal box from her purse. The last tie to the past, she said. She stood there for a moment, looking at the water, her eyes far away from where they were. Finally, she opened the lid of the box revealing the tangle of jewelry inside. In one smooth motion she threw it into the sound, the chains and bracelets fluttering like gold and silver ribbons as they fell to disappear into the deep blue.

"We're free," she whispered.

And Tommy looked up at the purple twilight sky and watched the smallest star go dark.

# ABOUT THE AUTHOR

Tami Hoag's novels have appeared on national bestseller lists regularly since the publication of her first book in 1988. Her work has been translated into more than twenty languages worldwide. She lives in Los Angeles and Palm Beach County, Florida.

## Center Point Publishing
600 Brooks Road ● PO Box 1
Thorndike ME 04986-0001 USA

(207) 568-3717

**US & Canada:
1 800 929-9108**
www.centerpointlargeprint.com